A lawyer with an appetite for risk.
A gorgeous socialite
accused of murder.
It's the case of a lifetime—
if only she were innocent.

P9-BZR-904

# STEPHEN HORN

# IN HER DEFENSE

**HarperTorch**
*An Imprint of HarperCollinsPublishers*

This is a work of fiction. Names, characters, places, and incidents are products of the author's imagination or are used fictitiously and are not to be construed as real. Any resemblance to actual events, locales, organizations, or persons, living or dead, is entirely coincidental.

HARPERTORCH
*An Imprint of* HarperCollins*Publishers*
10 East 53rd Street
New York, New York 10022-5299

Copyright © 2000 by Stephen Horn
ISBN: 0-06-109875-2

First HarperTorch paperback printing: April 2001
First HarperCollins hardcover printing: May 2000

HarperCollins ®, HarperTorch™, and ❦ ™ are trademarks of Harper-Collins Publishers Inc.

Printed in the United States of America

Visit HarperTorch on the World Wide Web at
www.harpercollins.com

10  9  8  7  6  5  4  3  2  1

**FOR KERRY**

**AND**

**FOR MY PARENTS**
*They always enjoyed a mystery*

# Acknowledgments

My wife, Kerry, traveled every step of the journey that was this book. She provided the encouragement, enabled me to make the time, and guided the effort with affirming "uh-huhs" when I was on track, and "ughs" when I strayed. She made it possible, as she has made possible the best parts of my life, beginning with Caitlin and Ben.

Pat Joinnides and Rubee Scrivani courageously agreed to be readers for a first-time novelist. As usual, they called 'em as they saw 'em. No one could have dearer friends.

Doris Mortman generously introduced me to the Peter Lampack Agency. Loren Soeiro read my manuscript and offered suggestions, then with Peter and Sandra Blanton, marketed the finished product. I am most grateful for their counsel and their labors on my behalf.

Now that I know what editors do, I understand how fortunate I am to be in the hands of Adrian Zackheim and Carolyn Marino at HarperCollins. They have been dedicated to making the most of the material they were given, and along with Marjorie Braman, were encouraging and forthright as they prepared me for the experience of going public.

# 1

I was thinking about destiny when Harry Gregg appeared in the doorway. It could have been a coincidence.

"Excuse me, I'm looking for an honest lawyer."

"Have you looked in Baltimore?"

"You'll do." Harry eased into the chair, set down his coffee, and laced his fingers across his vest. He was taking his usual moment to survey my desk when his gaze fell on the front page of the *Post*. "Been reading about the Ashley Bronson thing?" he asked. "Some story, huh?"

"You sound like that news anchor I heard this morning: 'Stay tuned for more on the Ashley Bronson case.'"

"So?"

"So, when Kennedy was killed, they didn't call it the 'Lee Harvey Oswald case.'"

He blinked. "If I may paraphrase a former senator," he said, grinning, "Raymond Garvey was no Jack Kennedy."

"He was a former Secretary of Commerce, a leader of trade delegations, and served on a dozen boards. The man's not even cold and he's a footnote in the story of his own murder."

Harry snorted, then leaned over and stabbed the *Post* with his forefinger. "He didn't look like *that*," he said, "and she's better known."

I looked at the photograph. He had a point: *nobody* looked like that, even in handcuffs. She'd been the darling of the *Post*'s "Style" section for years: parties, travels, romances real and rumored. A lot of people dreamed about her life, or just being part of it. But no one dreamed about the Secretary of Commerce.

"She's got the perfect name, too," I conceded. "A marquee name for a real-life melodrama. Do you think there could be a link between your name and your destiny?"

He shrugged. "I suppose."

"Think about it, Harry. Jonas Salk couldn't throw a spiral and there's no Johnny Unitas vaccine." He stared at me, creases forming across his forehead. "You don't know who Johnny Unitas was, do you?"

He spied the puck that doubled as a coaster. "A hockey player?"

"Never mind. What's up?" It was too early in the week for his big brother act, usually featured on Friday afternoons when he ambled into my office, propped his loafers on my government surplus desk, and launched into his continuing seminar on life, liberty, and the pursuit of wealth. After my wife left me for American Express I endured those sessions as penance, but eventually came to think of them as just part of the rent.

"Frank," he said, "you're not making any money."

"I've got the Giants next weekend plus three."

He laughed. "The partners here care about you, fella. Three years ago we leased you this office and threw in the facilities and our best wishes. The rent was modest. It wasn't an economic proposition for us, just an opportunity to help a deserving guy get . . . get going."

"I appreciate that, Harry."

"We know you do." He set down his mug, taking a moment to align the handle with the edge of the desk. "Here's how we see it. The people here like you and respect your skills. From time to time, we've had occasion to send you some business and we've been glad to do it."

I didn't like the tense of his verbs.

"The firm is growing," he continued. "We need an experienced litigator to back up Marty and you've demonstrated the skills we're looking for. Besides,"—he winked—"you're already here. We can save the headhunter's fee." We smiled at each other and he became earnest. "The fit makes sense, Frank. All things considered, we can't offer you a partnership right now. We're thinking of an 'of counsel' position for a couple of years and then we'll all take stock."

"Of counsel, then take stock," I repeated.

"Right. Look, I know Marty's got a way about him but we think it can work." He picked up his mug again and peered at me over the rim.

Marty did indeed have a way about him: the way of the asshole. A few years ago I might've mentioned it, but I was maturing—that or just getting nervous about how I'd end up. "I'm flattered, Harry," I said, "and I'm grateful for everything. But I'm going to have to think about it to be sure it's the right fit—for all concerned." A mature response: I would weigh this option against the others—as soon as I figured out what they might be.

Harry took off his glasses and began to clean them with the end of his tie. "Frank, a couple of things," he said deliberately. "We need to do something soon. And to be completely candid,"—he examined his lenses—"some of the partners have grown a bit uncomfortable with your clients passing through the offices."

Two months before, after a series of thefts, the office manager called security when she saw a suspicious character in a black leather jacket, green pants, and sneakers pass by her desk. I was strolling in from lunch when I heard the confrontation in progress. One voice, something like the sound of squealing brakes, warned, "*Don't touch me, motherfucker!* I am here to see my *lawyer*!" Figuring he had trapped his prey, the security guard asked him who his lawyer was. The suspect surveyed the landscape over the guard's shoulder and shouted, "Him!" his long finger bisecting my chest. The crowd turned on me. "Save the conference room," I quipped, "we'll use my office." No one laughed.

Harry himself had taken to shadowing my clients in the hallways.

I was still groping for a response to the warning when my secretary appeared. "The clerk's office called," she announced. "You've got a case." My bread and butter: a court appointment.

Harry rose and tugged on his vest. "Business calls," he rumbled. "Why don't you get back to me next week? I'll say that you have our offer under consideration."

"Sounds fine. And please express my thanks for the vote of confidence. I'm going to give it a lot of thought." He gave me a thumbs-up as he left.

I packed my briefcase, buffed my shoes, and inspected myself in the mirror. You'd never know I wasn't making any money.

\* \* \*

Once upon a time, the Superior Court of the District of Columbia was a temple of justice, constructed in the nineteenth century in the Greek-revival style, with Ionic columns and recessed window arches, all clad in Indiana limestone. When the inevitable overflow occurred litigants went across the street to a palace, the "Pension Building," a mammoth post–Civil War creation inspired by Michelangelo's Palazzo Farnese, with arcaded passages and even more impressive Corinthian columns, seventy-five feet high. But as the law devolved from a profession to a business, it was only natural that temples and palaces gave way to office buildings.

The new courthouse, described in one guide as a "vast, off-putting heap," was boxy functionality wrapped around an atrium, proving that less isn't always more. There were modern conveniences, but mahogany pews, carved railings, murals, and twenty-foot, inlaid ceilings were things of the past. Functionality ruled on the assembly line of modern criminal justice, where more is definitely less.

I made my way to the stairs and descended to a basement cellblock that made the rest of the place look opulent: no wood, leather, or fibers to absorb prisoners' odors or mark their passing; no scratched chairs, graffiti-covered walls, or mattress stains. Just block and steel and the cool smell of cement. I posed in front of the camera until the door yielded with a click, entered the anteroom, and made directly for the women's cells. The deputy marshal acknowledged my status as a regular by not looking up.

A cellblock regular. Not something you aspire to in law school, nothing you plan; something that happens. The third anniversary of my first court-appointed case was a few weeks away—a milestone—but I had been at it only a few months when I made a promise to myself one evening on a bar stool. There was a lot of promising in those days but this one I kept. That day I had been walking to the courthouse from the Metro station when I spied Seymour Hirschfeld, the dean of the court-appointed bar. Unlike many of his brethren, Seymour had more arrows in his quiver than just courthouse smarts. He really knew the law, and the amalgam of scholarship and courtroom flair had yielded the occasional paying client and some personal-injury cases with actual injuries.

But Seymour never really broke free of the cellblocks and the bulk of his practice was still at the immutable hourly rate authorized by law for aiding the poor, shriveled by twenty years of inflation. For him and his colleagues on the professional dole, necessities became luxuries, and luxuries weren't in the budget. The subscriptions to keep up his precious library went first, followed by the library, his secretary, and finally, his office. Seymour became one of the professional homeless, courting clients in the hallways and peddling legal services like so much fruit. The cafeteria became his conference room, his briefcase a filing cabinet, and his pockets in- and out-boxes. To make a living, he overbooked like an airline, but his passengers demanded frills like zealous representation and every day was a gruel of conflicting court dates, conflicting demands, and just conflict.

So, Seymour the peddler had been shuffling in front of me, embroiled in an argument that gained intensity and volume as we neared the courthouse. Back and forth it went, capturing the attention of passersby, and for good reason: Seymour was alone. Whether he fell to one deep thrust or a thousand nicks, he was done, bled dry. That night I promised myself I would never become another Seymour. I had an office, a library, and part of a secretary—and I could keep them all if I just said "yes" to Harry.

"Rasheeda Crispin?"

"Yes." Her voice was soft but the hard surfaces carried it from the back of the cell where she stood, clutching herself in a bulky sweater with shoulders that hung nearly to her elbows. She approached the cell door and stopped a few feet away, giving a physical dimension to the gulf between us. I stared at her through the bars, another cocaine case; her eyes went to the lock and stayed there. She was less than thin, with cheekbones pressing through her skin, small scars on her hands and ankles, and bruises on her shins. The form in my hand said that she was twenty years old but her life had crested long ago; nothing good was in store.

"Miss Crispin, my name is Frank O'Connell. I've been appointed to be your lawyer." She nodded. "There's going to be a hearing in a few minutes and you'll be going into a courtroom. I'll be in there, waiting." Over time, I'd learned to give a very simple explanation of the process, at least until I knew whether my client was more experienced than I was. "The purpose of the hearing is to set your bail," I told her. "No one is going to ask you any questions about the charges. Do you understand that?"

Her eyes remained on the lock. "Will I get out?" she asked.

"I think so." I pulled out a bail form. "I have some questions for you. You live at Two-one-two-one Brownlee Terrace?"

"Uh-hum."

"How long have you lived in the District?"

"Always."

"Do you live with anyone?"

"My daughter and my aunt. She's coming to court. She's got a wig store I work at."

"Have you ever been arrested before?"

Her eyes shifted to my moving pen. "They said I took somethin' from a store."

"Did you show up for court when you were supposed to?"

She nodded and I moved on to other things: convictions, family connections, prior residences, and more—anything related to the likelihood that she would become a fugitive if released. In fact, very few of the District's felons ever ran, even those clearly headed for long prison terms. It never ceased to amaze me: they'd show up, be sentenced, and "stepped back"—taken into custody. I'd seen the insides of some prisons; they'd have to find me first.

We were nearing the end of my checklist when I became aware of something on the periphery of my vision. I looked to my left and saw a pair of legs. Their owner was lying on her side, the upper half of her body concealed by the wall, and a pair of women's shoes were on the floor. It had to be her. As her name became a thought it echoed off the walls.

"Miss Bronson? Ashley Bronson?" Coming toward me, searching each cell, was Mark Stuart Preston of Preston, Scott & Wilde, with two associates in tow. Preston was one of D.C.'s most important lawyers, a player whenever titans clashed, but as far as I knew he never touched the criminal stuff. He certainly looked out of place in a cellblock, like one of those offbeat advertisements in *GQ*.

The click of women's heels on concrete turned me back to the cell door. Ashley Bronson was looking at me through the bars. We were twelve inches apart but I could have hardly described her a moment later: my stomach contracted and the sensation made it hard to focus. I could say for sure that her eyes were a gray green that Jaguar used to call "tungsten." I know that because I followed one a mile to find out.

I recovered just enough to point in Preston's direction when he appeared alongside me. "Ashley, Mark Preston," he announced. He touched the bars and they seemed to annoy him. "I've been asked by Tom Hardaway to assist you. I'm here to do what I can." The modest words were belied by the self-important tone. She only nodded but her eyes were on him now instead of me, where they belonged. Preston and I were brushing shoulders and he moved an inch forward and slightly in front. Apparently, my departure was expected. One of his associates was staring at Ashley; the other fixed me with a look that said I was standing in his spot.

I turned back to my client. "Miss Crispin, have you been interviewed by the Pretrial Services Agency?" I startled her. She nodded but kept glancing at her cellmate.

"Excuse me," said Preston, "we have an arraignment at ten o'clock and will require a few moments alone with our client." Those were the words. The tone was, "We'll be four for dinner."

I might have been tactful but I'd just been that with Harry and twice in one morning was still heavy lifting. I turned on him and lowered my voice as if I didn't want to embarrass him in front of the help. "Unless your client has already been indicted," I said, "and I doubt that she has, you have an initial presentment, not an arraignment. An arraignment is when the client enters a plea of guilty or not guilty. The purpose of your hearing is only to set bail. In the cellblock, for bail matters, clients are interviewed side by side, but if you'd prefer to wait I have a few more questions for my client and I'll be through."

The associates blanched. Preston stared for a moment like he was filing my face for future reference. "Go ahead and finish," he replied evenly. "We'll wait."

"Suit yourself." I turned my attention back to Rasheeda, whose gaze was riveted on the floor. I asked her a few more questions, then gave my form a once-over while an awkward silence prevailed. Ashley Bronson's face remained impassive but her lawyer's cheek had developed a distinct twitch. Finally, I slipped the completed form into my briefcase and removed a blank one that I proffered toward Preston. "Here's a bail form with a series of questions to go over with your client," I told him. "The judge is used to the format and that helps." One of the associates stepped forward but I shot him a look and he froze. Preston took it quickly, mumbling his thanks. I could feel the tungsten eyes on my back as I left.

\* \* \*

Even if you hadn't read the paper you'd know something was up when you entered the courtroom. The regulars were supplemented by the press, which filled a good portion of the seats and squeezed cops, defendants, and lawyers into closer quarters than any group preferred. I managed a seat on the aisle in the front row, the province of counsel with court business. A few of the reporters made eye contact, then sent over a delegate. "Are you here on the Bronson case?" he asked quietly. I gave a small shake of my head, which he amplified to his cohorts.

At ten A.M., the Honorable Wilfred J. Robbins made his entrance. At sixty-three, he was close to retirement and he'd witnessed a transformation during his career on the bench, although he might prefer the word "deterioration," for the quality of everything had declined—even the crimes. After too many years of too much crap the focus of his energies was reducing the choking caseload.

The clerk handed up a file. While the judge read, just-arriving lawyers navigated the aisles, searching faces and whispering names of clients they'd never met or had met and since forgotten. Cops read newspapers and did their paper-work. Other lawyers hovered around the clerk's desk to note their position on the docket and whether there was time for another courtroom appearance before that one. The regulars showed more regard for the clerk than for Robbins. Judges were the concern of defendants; in a system where juggling clientele was the preeminent skill, the goodwill of the clerks was key.

The judge nodded at the clerk, who turned toward the spectators and announced, "Number Cr One-four-one-one, *United States versus Luther Evans.*"

"The government is ready," replied the Assistant United States Attorney, but no rejoinder was heard from the defense. Robbins looked at the clerk, who was already scanning the docket with a phone in one ear and a lawyer whispering in the other. It took only a moment to solve the mystery of the missing counsel, who was handling a sentencing in another courtroom. The case was continued, as was the next one when the defendant didn't show, and the one after that when the AUSA couldn't locate his file. A typical day in Superior Court.

We plowed on. Fifteen minutes later Preston and his lieutenants came down the center aisle and took their places with other firm employees that had saved an aisle seat for the boss. The reporters took turns crouching alongside, scribbling his utterances while the sketch artist's attention switched back and forth between her tablet and his profile.

Many defendants were in custody, which meant delays while prisoners were brought up and returned from the cellblock. A deputy marshal was summoned by Robbins to the bench and for the remainder of the docket call the prisoners were brought in two at a time. I figured the odds and it didn't surprise me when Ashley Bronson and Rasheeda Crispin finally entered together and stood by while the marshals led out the preceding pair. The reporters and sketch artists recorded the irony of the situation, heavy enough to impress the entire assembly. Behind me, a lawyer whispered, *"The Defiant Ones*—Tony Curtis and Sidney Poitier."* The marshals led them to the defense table and Preston and I took our places, placing me between the two women. Ashley glanced at me as I took my seat but Preston started to whisper and she turned to give him her full attention.

"Number Cr One-four-two-seven, *United States versus Rasheeda Crispin."*

"Ready, Your Honor," said the AUSA.

"Francis O'Connell for the defendant, Your Honor," I announced.

"I'll hear from the government on the matter of bail," said Robbins.

The AUSA scanned his file jacket. "Your Honor," he said, "the defendant is charged with possession of cocaine with intent and she has a prior record. We believe a ten-thousand-dollar cash bond is appropriate." That meant posting one thousand dollars in cash, pretty reasonable but still beyond the means of Rasheeda Crispin.

Robbins looked at me and I rose. "Your Honor, the government's position essentially acknowledges little risk of flight in this case and it would be hard to reach any other conclusion. My client is a lifelong resident of the District and her extended family lives in the metropolitan area, including her child, whom she supports. She has had prior involvement in the criminal justice system but she has never failed to appear as ordered. I would also like to note that this is another 'proximity' case, Judge. Miss Crispin was one of seven people in the apartment at the time of the search. The drugs were not found in her possession and she is neither the owner nor lessee of the premises."

I had watched Robbins address that issue in similar cases. "Mere proximity" to the drugs, he had ruled, was insufficient to prove the crime of possession. Technically, guilt or innocence is not the issue in a bail hearing, but it's difficult for a judge to ignore the probability that a case will never go forward when making a bail decision. He acknowledged my point with a nod, so I closed. "My client cannot post the requested bond, Your Honor. We ask for O.R. or that she be placed in the custody of her aunt, who is a resident and proprietor of a business in the District. She's present in the courtroom."

The AUSA started to rise again but Robbins waved him down: the nonissue of whether Rasheeda Crispin was going to flee the jurisdiction had consumed its allotted time. "Ask the aunt to come forward," he said. She did, and in short order Rasheeda was on her way back to the holding cell for out-processing and release. I stalled a few moments, hoping for an opening to say something—anything—to Ashley, but she was listening to Preston, who was pointing to the form I had given him earlier. When I became obvious I got up and headed for the door. Pairs of lawyers and clients were collaborating on their scripts while loved ones sat by looking anxious or bored, but the attention of all the spectators coalesced when the clerk called *United States v. Ashley Bronson* and Preston's sonorous baritone filled the courtroom. I looked back as I pushed through the door. The associate who had wanted my spot was now flanking Ashley with his boss. I couldn't blame him: sometimes, mere proximity is the best you can do.

# 2

The intercom purred. "Frank, it's Mr. Brennan," said the receptionist. I shut the door before I picked up the phone.

"Hello, Pop. I can't imagine why you're calling."

"Doing my duty, lad, in the service of Herself."

"Tell her it won't happen again."

"I've done that, lad."

"Tell her I was drunk."

"Perhaps a more positive message."

"I'm positive I was drunk."

"Hah! You've become the driest Irishman I know. You know what they say, don't you? 'Drink is the curse of the land. It makes you fight with your neighbor. It makes you shoot at your landlord. And it makes you miss him.'" He laughed and the sound of his tenor tinkling through the earpiece pulled me along as it never failed to do. I loved the sound of his laugh and his talk. Forty years in America hadn't dulled his brogue, owing to determination and regular polishing in a pub that catered to new immigrants from the Olde Sod.

"So, I heard you ran into Mark Stuart Stuffed Shirt," he said.

"I helped him out a little in the cellblock last week and we got real close. We'll probably be lunching at the club, so do I stop by your table or what?"

"There will always be a place at my table for you, lad, you know that."

"I know, Pop. I just wish you didn't have to get in the middle of this."

"She says it's the police next time, Francis."

"That should be good. 'Yes, officer, I'm peeping through those windows over there. No, not a woman, my little boy growing up inside. I'll come quietly.'"

"Francis, lad—"

"You know what, Pop? He was sitting in that chair in the study with his thumb in his mouth, staring off into space."

"I told her about that thumb, lad. I said—"

"And I was wondering, you know, what's going through his mind? What is he thinking about? Is it something I could help him with? And I'm imagining all the things that a six-year-old could wonder about or worry about, all the stuff I never talked about with my dad. How do planes fly? What happens when you go to heaven? Then I wondered if he ever just sits and thinks about what's happened, and I just want to run in the house and squeeze him. . . ."

"You can see him whenever you want, you know that."

"Yeah, we go out. Where do you take a kid that age, Pop? How many times can you go to the park or the zoo or the same museum? How many movies can you go to? We go someplace for the twentieth time and wind up at McDonald's, our booth. And it's always *to* somewhere. I take him out and I bring him home."

"Keep him at your place. Play some games, sit and talk."

"I took him to the apartment. He walked around—it took all of a minute to see where Daddy lives. There's no room for him and no place for his toys and things. He asked me where I slept so I opened the bed, tried to make like it was special, you know? Look, it's a couch *and* a bed! You should have seen the look on his face, Pop. He was so confused. I suggested a movie and he literally ran for the door. I'll never take him back there again."

The phone exploded. "*Jesus Christ!* And who did this? Whose fault is this? You had a home! A family! We had a *partnership*, for God's sake! Everything was good, Francis. It was right, what she wanted—what *anyone* would want! But it wasn't right for you, was it? You had to find your own way! Well, now you've done it. She's alone with the boy and you're staring through the *fucking windows*!" The sound ceased; he must have been covering the mouthpiece.

I felt the tingling in my face. Until that moment he had never shown any anger over what I'd done, not a word since that day years ago when I walked into his office to tell him my plan. I remember that he'd just listened until I was through, and then only asked if I was sure. I lied. He closed his eyes and swiveled toward the window, and was still there when I said good night, with a bottle on the desk and a melancholy about him that shook my resolve. Was it my leaving that had pained him, or his judgment of my prospects?

I waited until I could hear him breathing. "Look, Pop, tell her I'm sorry. I won't do it again. I mean it."

He wasn't listening. "You blame her, don't you? For not going along? You think she's disloyal or spoiled or some shit like that because she wants a home and some security in her life."

"That's not true." It was once, but no more. The realization that I might have been wrong—was probably wrong—loomed over me each night as I lay in my folding bed, and it seemed that I hung over an abyss, clinging to shreds of confidence in the choices I had made. Sometimes, after I took the boy home I was in free fall, terrified of my dreary little room, sensing that I was perilously close to losing something that once gone, could never be recovered. I'd come to dread the nighttime because I couldn't go home and the bars were no longer an option, so I'd taken to walking the streets until I was weary, trying to ration just enough energy for the trip home and collapse, with none left for dreaming.

I was in trouble and I knew it. I'd come to rely on little tasks and routines, like closing the sofa bed each morning and washing the dishes as soon as I ate—not to mark my progress but as hedges against a backslide into oblivion. I joined the neighborhood Y and spent an hour each evening on the machines before heading out on my walks. Physically, I looked like the guy in my old platoon photographs; emotionally, I was crippled.

The brogue broke through, this time with a conciliatory tone that wrapped around me like a lifeline. For all the pain I had caused he had never cut me loose. He specialized in human frailty, smoothing wrinkles and mending tears in the social fabric wrought by the venality, foibles, or sheer stupidity of some client or politico. For years I'd watched him ministering in his office, at fund-raisers, in pubs and family gatherings—chin in hand, head inclined toward some penitent, hearing confession and dispensing something more comforting than penance and far more useful: a promised good word or a favor exchanged, the deliverance of a fix. "Francis, lad," he said softly, "people get used to things, a way of living, and they don't want to do without. Is that wrong? I gave her the advantages, maybe more than was good sense, but you knew who she was when you married, and it was you who changed the rules, lad, not her."

That wasn't completely true. I really didn't know her, any more than she knew me, but we thought that made it more romantic. She used to love to tell our story: *I'm watching the Redskins game and this guy spills a beer on me. Then he leans over and starts to wipe it off. So I say, "I usually make 'em wait till the first date to rub those." And he says, "I got some in your lap, too. Hold still, we're about to get engaged." We were married in the spring.*

Whatever I knew or didn't, I couldn't complain about Pop's generosity toward his daughter. He was still supporting her, long after he'd committed her to my care, and now he was supporting our son, too. My paltry checks couldn't cover the groceries, let alone the mortgage and the rest of their expenses. The fact was they didn't need my money at all but she took it anyway, and crazy as it seems, I don't think she did it to punish me. The first time she caught me watching the house we stared at one another until I finally drove off, and when I picked up the boy a few days later, nothing was said. It was our secret, one of those little ties that bind, and in a way my checks were another. She didn't want to cut it, and for all the difference the money could make to me, I didn't either.

"Pop, I've got to go. Tell her what I said. Please."

"I'll tell her, lad, be sure of that." He clicked off.

* * *

I have a therapist. Another milestone.

"How are you, Frank?"

"Fine."

"Where should we start?"

"I've got a question."

"Go ahead."

"Are you Noah Applebaum because you're a doctor, or are you a doctor because you're Noah Applebaum?"

"Interesting question."

"I'm working on a theory."

"I see. Definitely the latter."

"Really? Why?"

"Well, there is a higher correlation between Jews and the professions than between the professions and Jews."

"Meaning?"

"Well, it's a matter of cause and effect. I would guess that the proportion of Jews who are doctors is greater than the proportion of doctors who are Jews. So, if the fates produce a Jewish doctor, religion was more likely the determining factor than the profession."

"So, it was your destiny as an Applebaum to be a doctor?"

"No, it was my destiny as a Jew to be a doctor. It was my destiny as an Applebaum to be a therapist."

"Why's that?"

"You'd have to meet my mother."

"Oh." The sound of the clock ticking filled the room while I considered this application of my theory. "So where does that leave an O'Connell?" I asked. He shrugged. The fate of an O'Connell was the reason we were there. "I want to start coming every other week," I said.

"Weekly would be better."

"I can't afford it. I'll come every two weeks and you can give me homework."

"Come every week. We'll work it out."

"I didn't know you did pro bono work, Noah."

"C'mon, Frank. You represent people who can't afford you. It's part of what we do as professionals." I had to admit there was a certain symmetry to his point. My clients were indigent so I couldn't afford to pay my own way, either. At least I didn't have to wait long to learn my fate: O'Connell the mendicant. Perhaps when my therapist could no longer pay his bills he would find a grocer who needed legal services. We could build our own barter economy.

I said, "If my theory pans out I'll name it after your mother."

"Deal." He filled a couple of water glasses while I looked around. Signs of family life were abundant: a picture of his wife and two daughters on the credenza, a larger one of each of the kids adorning a bookshelf, a paperweight that looked like an arts and crafts project, a crayoned card, a "World's Greatest Dad" mug. Noah, the doting parent.

"Do you read to your kids at bedtime, Noah?"

"Every night. Would you like to talk about your son?"

"I don't think so."

"Okay. Been walking?"

"Every night."

"Looks like you're getting in shape."

"If things don't get better I might win the Mr. Universe title and pay you with the prize money."

"Have you been dreaming?"

"Everyone dreams every night; I read that."

He waited while I worked up to it. I wouldn't call it dreaming. Dreams are supposed to be fantasy and blurry images of real events, but the movies playing in my head were crystal-clear, faithful reproductions; it was the events themselves that were surreal. More than twenty years later it turned out that my subconscious was a kind of video recorder, capturing a panorama of horror replete with colors, sounds, and details that were mercifully unremembered in the aftermath when the impact was still resonating through my psyche. The prevailing theory was that the stress of the past few years had managed to press my playback button and it was stuck in the "on" position. "I've been dreaming," I told him.

His pencil moved across the pad. "What kind of week has it been?"

"Up and down."

"Tell me about the up."

"The firm offered me an 'of counsel' position and a chance to talk partnership in a couple of years."

"What did you tell them?"

"I said I'd think about it. What should I do?"

"I don't know. Tell me about the down."

"My former father-in-law has weighed in. It seems my interpretation of his silence all these years as some kind of grudging approval was mistaken."

Noah blinked. When he spoke it was mostly to himself. "His support was important to you." The words banged around my insides like a pinball, striking nerves and glands; I could feel the acid gurgling in my stomach. It was the truth I had avoided since our conversation and now my mind was on full automatic, each involuntary thought linking to the next, leading inexorably to the conclusion that my situation was now well beyond my ability to rationalize. I wasn't some solitary, heroic figure in some existentialist fantasy; I was just a guy who'd made a bad choice and was living the consequences. I was past forty. There weren't going to be any do-overs. And tonight's walk would be a long one.

"You know what bothers me most, Noah? That when all is said and done it was about ego. I screwed up several lives to become a member of the self-made men's club. Swap Horatio Alger stories in my golden years, hang around some piano bar singing, 'My Way.'"

"Is that what you think this is about?"

"Don't you?" He didn't answer right away. I had never considered an alternative. I felt torn, at once hoping and fearing that I had some deeper purpose more noble or contemptible than self-gratification, hidden even from me. But what could be worse? "Don't you?" I repeated.

He put his notebook aside and cleared his throat. "Look at your life. What you've done, the choices you've made. Do you see some pattern there?"

"Pattern? I've never thought about it."

"I suppose you wouldn't."

"Look, Noah, I've enjoyed about as much of this as I can stand. If you've got some cosmic theory about what makes Frank run, let's forget the prescribed timetable for leading the patient to some catharsis. I've had enough of analyzing my every thought and deed so just tell me what it is."

"You like the risk."

"People take risks every day."

"Sure, stuff like should we buy that house? Do I take that new job? Do I make that investment? Making choices based on some formal or even gut level assessment of risk versus reward. It isn't the calculated risks that attract you, Frank. You don't care about the odds, you just need to push in all the chips."

"And why would that be, Noah?"

He frowned. "I'll tell you what I think. A few years ago everything was settled for you, personally and professionally. In a manner of speaking, all that remained was to put in

your time. I don't mean that in a disparaging sense but the
fact is that most of us reach a point when the major moves
are behind us: we get a family, a career, a mortgage, and we
come to realize that we're not going to climb Everest or be
secret agents or do any of the stuff of childhood fantasy or,
for that matter, collegiate dreams. Life becomes largely a
matter of staying the course—not that it's easy. God knows,
most of the people who I see are trying to do just that. You
remember what Thoreau said? 'The mass of men lead lives
of quiet desperation.' But you, Frank, you got a taste of the
other life. One day you're in the jungle: heart thumping,
glands secreting, terror, exhilaration, victory and defeat—
living on the big scale, the ultimate competition. And you
liked it. Then you turn around and it's Saturday in the suburbs and you're standing in some hardware store, comparing
paint chips for the foyer, you and millions of other guys. The
difference is you broke out of that store; you had to."

I thought about that while the clock ticked away the rest
of our session, playing back what I thought and felt in the
months leading up to my decision to turn my life inside out.
"I've got another question," I said. "Last one."

"Shoot."

"How do I get back in?"

*   *   *

My Ford compact whined up the hill to the residence of
Moira Brennan O'Connell. The first time I saw that house
was the month before our wedding, and that night my fi-
ancée and I had a discussion about finances, the first of
many. Having grown up in a series of Bronx apartments I
understood the American dream of home ownership. But I
had this notion that I should pay for my own shelter and the
down payment was seventy-five thousand dollars, leaving
me seventy-one thousand short. I figured our love nest was a
few years away but Moira had other ideas; so did her father,

and he didn't get to be who he was without being persuasive. He needed my full commitment to sustain the practice, he said. It was important that I "get the family matters settled" so I could focus on the task at hand. Then there was the entertaining of important clients and contacts, he said, an essential part of a Washington practice like his—now, ours. As hostess, Moira would fulfill the role her dear departed mother had performed so well.

In the end, I rationalized it. Part of it was the old man's blarney, part was an excusable desire to provide for my wife in the style to which she was accustomed; I like to think reason played a small role, too. In any event, my father-in-law established his own Marshall Plan for his daughter and me. Half of Washington owed Edward Brennan, the other half wanted to curry favor; both decided that his daughter's wedding offered opportunity. The gifts were delivered while we were on our honeymoon, and when I carried Moira across the threshold I nearly dropped her. It was a scene worthy of a game show contestant's wildest dreams. China and silver for twenty-four, Baccarat crystal, French copper pots, sterling silver candlesticks, Porthault linens, lithographs and a sculpture, a restaurant-size cappuccino machine, and appliances whose function I couldn't even imagine. When he saw the bounty my father-in-law laughed and quoted one of those Irish proverbs of which he was so fond: "Take gifts with a sigh, lad," he said, "most men give to be paid." Then he threw in a car.

Pulling into the driveway of my new home used to fill me with a sense of well-being. Just married, we had the trappings of middle-age affluence, and the first time my son toddled out to meet me I almost cried with pleasure. Then a few more years went by and one day I wasn't happy anymore. The reality gnawed at me: my life had been handed to me on a silver platter, literally. And I used to laugh at guys like that.

I knew I loved my wife; I also knew things had to change. We didn't get to try a piecemeal approach. I said that I was thinking of leaving Pop. I announced it to the ceiling in the middle of another miserable night. Moira was stunned, and implying I hadn't decided only made it worse. She tried to argue me out of it, and as I blathered on, trying to explain what I didn't understand myself, her expression went from bewilderment to fear, and from fear to anger. By the time I reached the part about selling the house the unthinkable had become a stark possibility. Where to? she demanded. What could we afford? And what would it mean for Brendan and school? I didn't have any answers.

After an agonizing week she offered a compromise: quit the firm but keep the house; let Pop tide us over until I got established. I told her I couldn't do it. It would be like showing up at the pay window after you quit the job.

So, there we were: she wouldn't leave and I couldn't stay.

We were slow to come to grips with separation, and if there's such a thing as doing it well, we didn't. I took a small studio to keep expenses down. We still saw each other on the weekends and even slept together a few times. It was like regressing to the dating stage, taking another run from the starting line to get it right, and even my father-in-law seemed only mildly perturbed: "A bump on life's road, lad," he said. But the weeks stretched into months, and when Moira realized that it wasn't just some midlife hiccup her tolerance for my comings and goings began to wane and the process of detachment began in earnest. The house became a metaphor for our breakup. First, the furniture simply moved about, and then the surroundings began to change. New paint, new decor, new life.

I rang the bell. I used to wait until my son would peek through the mail slot, then stick my finger inside so he could clutch it and laugh. The memory of that little ritual still returned each night as I stood in front of my steel door at the end of the hallway.

Moira answered the door in the last stage of dressing for her evening out, wearing makeup, stockings, and a robe. "Hi," I said.

"Hi. I'm on the phone." She headed directly for the kitchen so I wandered into the study. We'd once had a fight of sorts about what to call that room. I suggested "den" and she rolled her eyes. "The room is twenty-five by eighteen," she explained. "It has a twelve-foot ceiling, ornate moldings, plank oak floors, French doors, custom bookshelves, and a marble fireplace. I'm afraid it's a library." She produced the original drawings that came with the house. "Your Honor," she said with mock solemnity, "I would like to offer exhibit A into evidence." The label was there but I argued that "library" was pretentious. She took my face between her hands and laughed. "If it will soothe your working-class soul we'll call it a study." That night we opened one of our presents, a sterling silver wine stand, and broke in the plank oak floors good and proper, right in front of the marble fireplace. Afterward, we lay tangled up in a blanket and toasted our clever compromise. It should all have been that easy.

"Hi, Dad!" My son was standing in the doorway wearing corduroy overalls and a turtleneck, holding a glass of juice with a seal on it to prevent big spills.

"Hi, bud! How's my big guy?" I walked toward him and crouched, spreading my arms.

"Good," he said, stepping forward into my grasp and wrapping his arms around my neck. Those moments were the best that I had and I lived from one to the next. He took his cheek from mine and began to play with my tie. "Dad?" he said.

"Yes, bud."

"You like the Giants, right?"

"Yup."

"You like the Giants because you lived in New York when you were a kid."

"That's right."

"But now you live in Washington."

"Uh-huh."

"Dad, can I root for another team, not the Washingtons?"

"Not the Redskins?"

"Yeah. The Washington Redskins. Do I have to root for them?"

"No, buddy, you can root for whatever team you want. People like to root for the team that lives in the same place they do, but you don't have to. Is there another team that you like?"

"Dad?"

"Yes, honey?"

"Are the Forty-niners a good team?"

"Sure. Do you want to root for the Forty-niners?"

He shook his head like this was something he had been considering but had rejected. "I want to root for the *Redskins*," he said emphatically. "They're my favorite team, Dad."

"Then that's what you should do, bud. Stick with 'em win or lose."

Moira came in ready for her date. For a long time I'd managed to avoid the fact that my beautiful ex-wife would reject spinsterhood, and standing there in her cocktail dress she was doing a good job of reminding me. "You look great," I said.

"Thank you," she replied. We were always very civil in front of our son. One thing I didn't have to worry about was a deliberate poisoning of my relationship with him; she was too good a person to go in for that crap.

"We're going to go. I'll have him back by seven-thirty. What's the sitter's name?"

"Why don't you two stay here?"

"Here?"

"Why not? You'll have more time together. There's meatloaf in the refrigerator and you guys can watch TV or play with his toys. He can stay up till eight and I'll be home by eleven."

"Sure. That sounds great." Apparently, Pop had spoken to her after our conversation.

"Unless you have somewhere to be?" she added.

Somewhere to be? Except for an evening with my son there wasn't anywhere I had to be after six P.M. in years. There were just places not to be, like my apartment or any bar. "No," I said, "I've got nothing planned."

"Then we're set. His toys are on the shelves in his room. He really likes the Candyland game—he always wins." The doorbell rang. She swept our son up in an embrace. "Have fun with Daddy and go to sleep when he says, okay? I'll be sure to kiss you when I get home." She smiled at me and headed for the door without another word. There was an exchange of "hi's" and she was gone.

So, I spent the evening in Candyland getting my ass whipped. Afterward, Brendan gave me a tour of his room, which I hadn't seen in months because Moira always had him ready and waiting to minimize the protocol. There were a few new toys, including a remote-controlled car given to him by somebody named Rob, whom he talked about with great enthusiasm. My clumsy attempts to turn the conversation to other, weightier matters went nowhere. It seemed that six-year-olds are not stimulated by questions like, "Is there anything on your mind you'd like to talk about?" or any other openers favored by therapists. At eight o'clock we said our prayers and I tucked him in, then watched from a chair until he was asleep. I stared straight ahead as I passed the master bedroom in case there was further evidence of Rob lying about.

The next hour was spent in the study listening to the radio and reading the newspaper. I used to enjoy spending the evening that way but stopped when I got the apartment. Relaxation could lead to contemplation, and contemplation to all sorts of things best avoided. When I finished the papers I began looking around for something else to read and noticed that the family photo albums were gone. There was a Brennan family tradition of creating an album for each year. Moira became the curator when we married and we'd been well on the way to filling a shelf of our own when things fell apart.

After rummaging around I finally found our pictorial history stuffed in some grocery bags in the bottom of a cabinet, and the next two hours were a reprise of some of the happiest moments of my life: our honeymoon; the announcement of Brennan & O'Connell; parties, holidays, and vacations; Moira's pregnancy, Brendan's birth, and about every hour of his first two years. I lingered over my favorite photograph— Pop's, too—taken at his summer place in Nantucket: Pop, Moira, Brendan, and me, holding hands on a beach. The three adults had their backs to the camera but Brendan had spotted the photographer and was half turned, mugging for the photo. Reflecting on Noah's thesis, I searched for clues to my growing discontent: forced smiles, averted eyes, something in the body language. I didn't find any.

The sound of a key in the door jarred me from my reverie. As I scrambled to stuff the albums back into the bags I could hear murmuring in the foyer, followed by a moment of silence before the door closed again. I quietly shut the cabinet and tiptoed to the window to catch a glimpse of a man climbing into a big Mercedes. Trust Moira not to make the same mistake twice. I scuttled back to my chair just in time to jump up again when she walked in.

"How'd it go?" she asked. There was no smeared lipstick, no buttons undone.

"He cheats at Candyland."

She nodded. "Too many lawyers in the family. Did you get enough to eat?"

"It was great. He ate all his dinner before we played and went to bed right on time. I've been in here reading the news." I gestured toward the papers for corroboration but they just lay there.

"Good." She sank into the opposite chair. I didn't know if that was an invitation so I continued to stand.

"How was your evening?"

"It was nice," she said, removing her shoes. "I've been seeing this guy and we get along pretty well." She looked at me and added quickly, "He's very good to Brendan, Frank. He respects the fact that you're his father, but he genuinely likes him and goes out of his way to show it."

"Good," I said. There was an awkward pause while I tried to think of something to add before repeating, "Good."

"How are things with your practice?"

"Birch and Hayes wants me to become of counsel, then maybe a partner in a few years."

"Well, that's good isn't it?"

"I guess. It's that or leave." She looked puzzled. "My clients make them nervous."

"They've been good to you, Frank. Where were all your friends when you went out on your own?"

She had a point. Criminal lawyers need a referral network to survive. My father-in-law had admitted me to the biggest one in town, so I announced my new firm and waited for the phone to ring; it never did, and there was a certain irony to my predicament. Pop kept his distance to respect my independence, but the legal fraternity feared that embracing me was taking sides, especially after the separation, and no one wanted to take sides against Ed Brennan. Without the family connection and far away from the city where I'd made my reputation, I was cut off. I had leaped before I looked— nothing new—and fell a long way before hitting the safety net at Birch & Hayes.

"They have been good to me," I agreed, "but I don't think I can give them what they want."

"But what would you do if you left?"

"What I'm doing now. I'd just have to find a new arrangement or maybe practice out of my apartment."

"But how long can you go on like that?" she asked plaintively. "Isn't it time to . . ." She looked away.

"To what?"

"Never mind," she muttered.

"I'm not playing some game, Moira. I'm trying to succeed. I'm not a quitter."

She stared at me, then shook her head. "You have to be the only lawyer in Washington—in the whole damn world—who would look at that opportunity as quitting! Quitting what?"

"Look, there's no use arguing about this because I've already made up my mind." About ten seconds before.

"You're going to turn them down." She sighed. "I don't believe it." She got up and headed for the foyer. It was time for me to go.

# 3

When I entered the firm Monday morning I made straight for Harry's office. There wasn't any point in putting it off, and turning him down might be the last fun I'd have for a long time. Move over, Seymour, I thought, here goes nothing. Harry was on the phone but covered the mouthpiece when he saw me.

"Frank!" he cried. "I know you've got a lot on your plate so let's table our little talk till you're ready!" He started speaking into the phone again, still making big eyes at me, so I waved and wandered back to my office. A lot on my plate? Maybe he'd been talking to my therapist, which suited me fine. Noah could warn him that if they kick me out I might come back with a rifle.

I reached the doorway and froze, transfixed. Ashley Bronson was seated in front of my desk. She was lost in thought, turning the hockey puck over and over in smooth hands with pale nail polish and no jewelry, save for a tank watch you could trade for a car. There was a mug of tea steaming on the desk.

"It's a coaster," I said. She looked up. "For your tea."

"Of course," she replied. She set the mug on it and stood to face me, extending her hand. It's funny what goes through your mind at a moment like that. I knew her handshake would be just right, not too weak or too strong, but just right. I held on a second longer than etiquette prescribed, but if she noticed it didn't show. "I'm sorry, I don't have an appointment," she said, managing to look contrite. She didn't need to introduce herself, so she didn't.

"It's okay. Please sit down." I held a chair for her and moved around to my own. It was our second face-to-face meeting but this time her auburn hair was down to her shoulders and she hadn't just spent the night in jail. My throat felt a little constricted when I asked, "How are you?"

"In trouble," she replied.

"I know. Why are you here?"

"I've been told that I'm going to be indicted next week. For murder."

No surprise there, but she'd misunderstood the question. "I thought Mr. Preston was representing you."

"He said he didn't handle criminal cases but he gave me the names of some good lawyers who did." She didn't blink when she added, "He didn't include yours."

No surprise there, either. "But you're here."

"I had already decided I wanted you to defend me."

"You had? When?"

"In the jail," she replied. The jail: our brief, first meeting, without a word passed between us. I wondered whether we would go for the big wedding or just elope. "I trust my instincts on such matters"—she smiled—"but under the circumstances, I suppose I should ask if you're as good as the ones on his list."

"Yes."

She raised an eyebrow. "I haven't told you the names yet."

"Right."

The corners of her mouth turned upward. "I like a man with confidence," she said quietly.

I considered several openings that sounded like something Preston might say before opting for the direct approach. "Would you like to get started?"

"I'm ready."

"Miss Bronson, lawyers have different approaches to the first client interview in a criminal case. Some will never ask the client what he or she did, only what the police can prove. Others might outline the available defenses before asking any questions." I reached for a pad and pen.

She looked at me quizzically. "Don't they want to know the truth?"

"It's more complicated than that, and not as sinister as you might think. Things are rarely as presented by anyone involved. Into the mix you have to add misperception, faulty recollection, hallucination, hysteria, wishful thinking, and outright lies. But once the tale is told it takes on a life of its own. The client feels wed to it and it can cripple the defense, even if the story changes later on. Of course, sometimes the lawyer's motives can be less than noble, too."

"What does that mean?"

"The Code of Ethics prohibits a lawyer from allowing a client to lie under oath. For example, if my client claims he didn't steal the money, he can take the witness stand to say he's innocent, even though other evidence indicates he's not. But if my client *admits* to me that he stole the money, then I know he's guilty for an absolute fact, and I can't let him commit perjury. That means he won't be taking the stand in his own defense, even though he wants to testify."

"In other words, knowing the truth can limit a lawyer's options."

"That's right. So, if the lawyer doesn't want to lose an option he never asks the client for the whole truth."

She considered this a moment. "And what about you? What's your approach?"

"I like to hear the whole story without any input from me. It might mean you won't testify, but if I don't know what actually happened the right defense may never be developed, or worse, the prosecution could pull off a big surprise at trial. As your lawyer I would want to know everything."

"That seems to make the most sense," she agreed.

"Good."

"Shall I tell you what happened?"

"Go ahead."

"I killed him."

Professional training kicks in at moments like that. I heard myself say, "Go on," while my insides were still resonating from the jolt.

"I went to his home and let myself in through the side doors to the sitting room. I got his gun from the secretary, and when he entered the room, I shot him." She was going to continue but her lips compressed into a line and she averted her eyes. There was a hint of vulnerability there, and just enough tremor in the jaw to suggest that she wasn't as matter-of-fact about murder as she tried to appear. I could have said, "It's all right," but the grand jury was about to say otherwise, so I just drew circles on the pad and wondered whether there would be any daylight for us at all.

She noticed the photograph on the wall, a fifty-five-foot ketch named *Jezebel* heeled over in a mammoth pewter and white sea. I had crossed the Atlantic in that boat the year after I came home from the war. "You're a sailor?" she asked.

"Not lately."

"We have a boat in Annapolis. We used to have outings when my father was in good health." In one of the stories on her arrest there had been a mention of Henry Bronson's passing. The *Post* said that he had been a physicist as a young man, and in recent years a supporter of humanitarian causes through a family foundation created by *his* father, who made a fortune in timber. A lot of trees had been felled to support the lifestyle of Ashley Bronson, and now she was going to transfer some of the proceeds to me. I, in turn, would make some humanitarian gestures of my own and pay some of my debts.

"I understand that your father died recently. Had he been ill?"

"He'd had several strokes and was confined to a wheelchair. Mentally, he had good days and bad." She looked at me as if there was a point.

"I see," I said, although I didn't.

"My father committed suicide."

"Suicide? I'm sorry. . . . I don't recall reading that."

"It wasn't in the papers. He took an overdose of sleeping pills. The only people who know are his doctor and me. And now you."

"You said he had good and bad days. Couldn't it have been accidental?"

"That's what his doctor thinks. He was a devoted friend of my father's and spared the family name by not reporting it."

"But you think he's wrong."

"I know the truth." She opened her Coach bag and removed a leather-bound book about the size of a paperback. "My father kept a journal for as long as I can remember," she said. "This is the last volume and the final entry leaves no doubt about his intentions." Her voice took on an edge. "In a very real sense, Raymond Garvey murdered my father."

"*Murdered?* How?"

"By hounding him until he killed himself."

"Hounding him about what?"

"I don't know. The journal doesn't say but I'd never seen him so distressed. I warned Raymond to stay away. I told him he was making my father very ill, that he could kill him. But he wouldn't listen. He . . ." Her voice broke off and she just shook her head.

"Take a minute," I suggested.

She composed herself and then continued. "My father was a gentle soul, Mr. O'Connell. His life was books and music and art and . . . and his daughter. Less than three weeks ago I entered the library to tell him I was going to bed. He couldn't speak well then but he said my name and held my hand, knowing that he would never see me again. And when I think of the profound sadness he must have felt in our last moment . . ." Her eyes flashed and the edge returned to her voice. "What Raymond Garvey did was *worse* than murder. I killed him for it. I'm not sorry."

So, she got revenge. And now I knew the why, to go with the who and the how. My elation was starting to ebb. "It's time to ask some of those other questions," I said. "What can the government prove?"

"My fingerprints were on the gun. A detective said so."

"What did you say?"

"I didn't say anything."

"That's good. You shouldn't talk about this with anyone but me. You'd been in the house before?"

"Many times. Raymond Garvey was a friend of my father's and practically an uncle to me."

"How did you know where the gun was?"

"He showed it to me about four months ago. There had been some burglaries in the area and he got it for protection." There was an awkward moment while we let that pass.

"That could explain your fingerprints. You said you let yourself in. You used a key?"

"Yes."

"Where is it?"

"The police have it. They took it when they searched my house."

"Who else had one?"

"I don't know. Probably his housekeeper. I don't know about anyone else."

"How did you get to his house?"

"I walked. We live five blocks apart."

"Did anyone see you going or coming back?"

"I didn't see anyone going there. Coming back is a blur, but I don't think so."

So far, so good. "What were you wearing when you fired the gun?"

"A raincoat."

"Where is it now?"

"They took it and a lot of my other clothes during the search. I don't know what they did with them."

"They're testing them for gunshot residue. Was it raining when you left his house?"

"There was a thunderstorm."

"No one has said anything to you about your clothing?"

"No."

With the rain it was entirely possible that her clothes were clean. I pointed at the book still in her lap. "Your father's journal, who else knows about it?"

"Maybe Martha, our cook. She's the only one of the staff who actually lives in the house. Why does it matter?"

"It might be evidence of your motive for murder—if they can prove you read the last entry."

"Of course it is," she whispered. "I didn't think. . . ." She clutched the volume to her chest. "What do I do with it?" she asked.

The classic question in every law school ethics exam: *The client shows you the bloody knife and asks, "What should I do with it?"*

"Well, first, I'd like to see for myself," I replied. "Let me have it until tomorrow."

She placed it on the desk. "What happens now?" she asked. She was tired and the vulnerability was beginning to bleed through.

"That's all for today. You go home and try to get some rest, and don't talk to anyone about the case. I'll contact the U.S. Attorney's office and let them know that I'm representing you and any further contact should be through me. I'll also try to get a head start on the discovery of their evidence, but that will probably have to await the arraignment." She nodded and seemed to straighten a little in her chair. "I suppose I know this," I continued, "but I just want to be sure. Who knows what happened besides you and me?" And the prosecutor, I'd bet.

"No one. I've never discussed it with Mr. Preston or anyone else. She looked right at me and said, "You're the only one."

The only one. And she knew from the moment we met. Under the circumstances, I felt I had license, so I stared back, wondering about the soul mirrored by those magnificent eyes. Then I did the math.

When she got out, we might still have kids.

I dialed the U.S. Attorney's Office and listened to myself say, "This is Frank O'Connell, calling on behalf of Ashley Bronson." The sensation was not unlike the entrance at your wedding reception, when the bandleader says, "Ladies and gentlemen, please welcome for the first time . . ." They put me on hold so I passed the time thinking about my entrance with Moira. A sea of champagne glasses parted to reveal Pop, beckoning us toward the place of honor. He was beaming, surrounded by the biggest names in the city. Our life together stretched before us: a home, a station wagon full of kids, Brennan & O'Connell—her old man and I were going to knock 'em dead. As I acknowledged the applause I remembered thinking, *Pinnochio, you're a real boy now.*

Another voice came on the line. "Mr. Rogavin's office." Kyle Rogavin. The big artillery. The standing joke was that he'd put so many guys through Lewisburg, they had their own cellblock and a newsletter.

"May I speak to Mr. Rogavin, please? This is Frank O'-Connell. I represent Ashley Bronson."

"One moment, Mr. O'Connell. I'll see if he's available." The assistants I usually crossed swords with in drug cases were rarely in for phone calls from the defense bar and almost never returned them. As Ashley Bronson's lawyer I would have plenty to worry about, but getting my calls returned wasn't going to be one of them.

"Kyle Rogavin."

"Frank O'Connell. I'm calling on the Ashley Bronson matter."

"What happened to Preston?"

"Preston?"

"I understood she was represented by Mark Preston."

"Oh. I believe he handled her initial presentment. I'm her lawyer now."

There was a long pause before he asked, "Have we met?"

"I don't think so but I have a lot of cases with your office."

"Really? What kind of cases?"

"Drugs, mostly."

"Drugs," he repeated. "I see. Retained or appointed?"

"Appointed. Listen, if it'll help you decide whether to speak to me I'll fax over my résumé."

There was a pause while he wondered how Ashley Bronson had ended up with a defender of indigent drug abusers. When he found out he could tell me.

"What can I do for you, Mr. O'Connell?"

"I'd like to meet."

"Are we going to discuss a plea?"

"Why would we do that?"

"Well, let me see. Maybe Miss Bronson would like to avoid indictment. Maybe she thinks that seven to ten years in prison is better than twenty."

"Probably, but prison is for guilty people."

"I've got a desktop full of evidence that puts her in that category."

"Then you won't mind giving me a peek—just so I can explain it to her when we do the math thing." He sounded awfully confident but that didn't mean they had her sewn up. I wondered what clues she left behind that she didn't tell me about—or even know about.

There was silence while Rogavin weighed my request. Prosecutors hated freebies, but showing some cards was the best way to coax a plea. His response might indicate how anxious his office was for a deal, and by extension, the possibility of a crack in the wall she was up against. "Okay," he said. "Come on by and we'll talk."

"Thanks. How about tomorrow?"

"Two-thirty." He hung up. Didn't even say good-bye.

\* \* \*

Assistant U.S. Attorneys are notorious about keeping defense lawyers waiting, but I had this notion that my new stature would have some impact so I showed up right on time. I figured Rogavin would keep me out there for ten or fifteen minutes, just to show me who was boss. Sure enough, at two-forty-five his secretary came into the reception area. "Mr. O'Connell?" she inquired. I began to reach for my briefcase. "Mr. Rogavin is in a meeting," she said. "He'll be with you as soon as possible." I sat down again and began to work up some steam. By three-thirty the gauge on my interior boiler was well into the red zone. I considered leaving but the embarrassment of having to explain to Ashley that I'd been snubbed kept me in the chair.

I was ushered into Rogavin's office at three-forty-five; it was empty. I took the chair in front of the desk and wondered idly about the penalty for maiming an Assistant United States Attorney. The room was larger than the others I had visited, more akin to the chamber of a senior partner than an AUSA, and the desk must have been Rogavin's own because it was a massive mahogany knee-hole type with a braided, gold leaf border and a leather insert. The typical assistant's desk looked like a landfill, but this one was empty save for an accordion envelope with U.S. V. BRONSON stenciled on it. It was a good five inches thick. My own file was just a three-page memo of the client interview. The government had a head start.

Behind the desk was a matching credenza with an avant-garde clock and a photograph of a tennis team. To my left was a table with documents sorted into neat stacks and a five-drawer cabinet with combination lock. To my right was his ego wall, featuring not one, but two Yale diplomas, a

B.A. and a law degree, both cum laude. They were surrounded by special commendations attesting to his service to the nation, and certificates of various bars privileged to have him as a member.

The most interesting decoration was a set of three courtroom sketches of the occupant in action, each apparently done by a different artist at a different, important trial. To my left, Rogavin addressing the court; to my right, Rogavin examining a witness; and directly ahead, Rogavin persuading a jury. I was getting the full treatment, with lots of quiet time to contemplate the fact that I was up against a big-time prosecutor whose attention was devoted to the case against Ashley Bronson.

At five minutes of four the door opened and in sailed the pride of the federal fleet, tacking toward his desk as if he had all the time in the world, taking a moment to straighten a certificate and check his mail before sinking into his high-backed leather chair and sticking out his legs, which reached almost to my side of the desk. His gaze fell to the folder as if he was stealing just one more moment to think great thoughts about our case. Rogavin was about thirty-five, tall and slender, with a receding hairline, a long thin nose, and alert brown eyes that assessed you through thin gold frames. The suit was Brooks Brothers, set off with a striped shirt and polka-dot bow tie. The wingtips just inches from mine were the slim version, polished and expensive. We'd just met but I knew him: one of those Ivy Leaguers who considered themselves renaissance men because they could tune an MG and name all the Lake Poets. He raised his eyes and gave me a patronizing little smile. "Mr. O'Connell, I presume?" No apology for keeping me waiting.

The needle on my interior boiler was pegged; the seals were failing and steam was starting to escape. I looked at the ceiling and began to slowly nod my head. "I get it. Your appointment with this O'Connell guy was two-thirty and it would be unreasonable to expect him to wait *this* long. On the other hand, you don't have a four o'clock and people don't usually break into your office during business hours. So you presume. You presume correctly. I'm Frank O'Connell."

The grin disappeared. He sat up and removed several folders from the Bronson envelope. Examining the contents of the first one, he said, "You're moving up in the world, Mr. O'Connell."

"Yeah, I used to be a prosecutor."

He fixed me with a stare calculated to turn court-appointed types into jelly until his irritation gave way to curiosity. "You were a prosecutor?"

"Yeah." I held up my palm. "Just a local district attorney's office, not a job like yours."

"Really?" he said. He put down the folder and leaned forward, chin in hand, studying me like something he found in the carburetor of the MG. "Where?"

"New York. Manhattan, actually."

He kept a poker face while he took a gold pen from his breast pocket and began to roll it between his palms. "What did you do in the Manhattan D.A.'s office, Mr. O'Connell?"

"This and that." I shrugged. "I didn't try many murder cases, mind you, maybe thirty, thirty-five tops. I was getting them regularly but they moved me into Special Prosecutions, which was mostly racketeering and white-collar stuff, the high-profile cases. But I'm boring you. I know that pales in comparison to all this." I motioned toward the plaques on the wall.

"I see." He smiled. "Well, that's pretty impressive." He leaned back in his chair and propped the wingtips on the corner of the desk. "So Miss Bronson got herself an experienced trial lawyer. That's good. I like the competition. You like competition, Mr. O'Connell?"

"Me? Nah. It upsets my stomach. I like a sure thing, the kind of case where I know I'm better than the other guy." My eyes drifted over his head to the sketch. "Neat picture. Is that you?" I had gone pretty far, even by my own low stan-dards, but he needed to learn you don't pick on people whose lives were coming apart.

Rogavin thought I had gone pretty far, too. He became brusque. "Let me begin by telling you that her fingerprints were on the murder weapon."

"Really? Were they the only ones?"

"Actually, no. There were others."

"Whose?"

"You'll find out, but none are suspects, just acquaintances to whom he showed the gun. Each has an airtight alibi."

"Well, I understand she knew Garvey pretty well. Maybe he showed her the gun, too."

"Perhaps, but that's only part of the story. Motive, means, and opportunity, right? She had a key to the house."

"Was that the only key besides Garvey's?" I knew the an-swer to that one and assumed he did, too.

"No," he acknowledged, "the housekeepers have a key, and so did his neighbor of twenty-two years. Again, all have alibis."

"Anything else?" So far, I wasn't impressed; no one would be.

"Your client had an argument with the deceased shortly before the murder. It was a loud one. They were overheard."

"What about?"

"She threatened to kill him if he didn't stay away."

"Stay away? From her?"

"Perhaps."

"Who overheard it?"

"Well, you'll figure it out anyway so I'll tell you: the Wards, Mr. Garvey's housekeeper and handyman. Ask your client about it. I'm sure she remembers."

"Was this argument the day he died?"

He shook his head. "Shortly before."

"So she lost her temper. That's not the same as a motive for murder."

"Well, it's one indicator. We're looking for others." He glanced at his watch. "As a matter of fact, I believe the police are searching your client's house right now." He fished a document out of the folder and pushed it across the desk. It was a search warrant.

I didn't pick it up. "I'll study it later. What are they looking for?"

"Any evidence regarding the relationship between Henry Bronson and Raymond Garvey."

I feigned a puzzled look. "What does that have to do with this case?"

He tapped the document. "It's all in the affidavit in support of the warrant. Mr. Garvey was a frequent caller at the Bronson household, in person and by phone. His primary relationship was with the father, who was in bad health. Your client warned Garvey to stay away and threatened to kill him if he didn't. Then poor Mr. Bronson dies and Mr. Garvey *does* get killed. Well, you can see the logic."

"Sounds like a stretch to me. Is that it?"

Rogavin grimaced. "Let me see," he muttered, "is that it?" He looked up at the ceiling and began ticking off the points on his fingers. "Mmmm. Motive . . . means . . . opportunity . . . Of course!" He snapped his fingers and grinned. "I *knew* I was forgetting something. It seems that the case has improved somewhat since your client's arrest. We can place her near the scene at the time of the murder."

I kept my voice matter-of-fact. "I see. Who's the witness?"

"Now, now." He smirked. "Just a peek, remember? You'll get it in due time."

"Is there anything you will tell me about him now?"

He shook his head. "I think I've been pretty forthcoming, considering where we are in the case. I will say that I've interviewed the witness and find the witness to be *very* convincing. The witness had a good opportunity to see her and was unequivocal." He was careful to omit any reference to sex, although I tried to smoke one out. My client was going to have to give a little more thought to her departure from the scene of the crime.

Once more into the breech. "Can you at least tell me where the witness was when the identification was made, and where my client supposedly was?"

"No."

"You're going to have to give that up in discovery."

"Then I will."

"Anything else you can tell me now?"

"That's it." Rogavin closed the folder and slipped it and the others back into the accordion envelope; then he leaned back in the chair and began tapping the pen against his palm. "Here's the deal. Miss Bronson pleads to murder two, no premeditation. My office stands mute at sentencing while you plead for leniency. With good behavior she should be out in less than ten years."

Now it was my turn to shake my head. "You haven't got a case. She knew the decedent and was in the house hundreds of times. Let's say he shows her the gun: 'Look what I bought, dear, for protection.' He hands it to her and you get fingerprints. That leaves you with an argument and your witness. The argument wasn't the same day, so she had plenty of time to cool off. Everyone has said words like that without killing anybody. As for the witness, even without the details I know it has to be a questionable I.D. because the murder occurred on the proverbial dark and stormy night. Besides, this witness can't be too good because my client didn't do it. Murder two? I couldn't justify a manslaughter plea on that evidence. If my client didn't want to chance a trial, you'd have to tempt us with a hell of a lot better offer than that."

Rogavin acted as if he hadn't even heard me. "So tell me: how did you go from the elite unit in the Manhattan D.A.'s office to your current practice?"

I stood up. "Well, I'd love to stay and chat but I have another appointment and I always try to be punctual. By the way, if we have another meeting I'd appreciate it if you were punctual, too."

"Of course." He smiled. "Anything for a former crime fighter." I went to the door. "One more thing," he called.

"What is it?"

"The offer's good until she's indicted. Then she's on her own."

# 4

I called my client at the end of the day. The phone was answered by a housekeeper who asked me to hold while she located "Miss Ashley." I reviewed my notes and thought about how long it would take to locate me in my apartment, where I could be as much as fifteen feet away at any given time.

A moment later she was on. "Hello, Frank."

"Hello, Ashley. I just got back from meeting a guy named Kyle Rogavin at the U.S. Attorney's Office. He tells me that they searched your house again."

"They were here for over an hour but they only took a few pictures and a couple of invitations. They left a list of what they took."

"I'll go over it later. I need to see you before my meeting with an investigator tomorrow at eleven. Are you free in the morning?"

"Can I offer an alternative? I was going to make myself some dinner. If you have no plans you could join me and we could talk afterward."

The invitation was for seven-thirty. I spent twenty minutes at my word processor typing the memo of my meeting with Rogavin, sticking to the essentials and omitting the snappy byplay. I used the remainder of the time to work on my to-do list, which I divided into "fact investigation" for my investigator and "research and writing" for an associate, leaving me free time to think great thoughts of my own. At seven-twenty I left Dupont Circle for the short drive to Georgetown. The Bronson house was on N Street, the most fashionable street in the area, and it wasn't a drag on the neighborhood. It was a three-story Federal brick mansion with a two-story frame side porch that overlooked a garden. The property was an acre or more, with a detached garage, a Georgetown rarity. I parked the car and as I bounded up the steps, the door opened and there stood the Lady of the Manor, barefoot and wielding a wooden spoon in her gun hand. She was wearing dark slacks, a white blouse with sleeves rolled to her elbows, and no makeup. She was magnificent.

"Is it that shocking?" She laughed. "Yes, I actually cook. I'll let you be the judge of how well."

"It wasn't that," I mumbled, but she pretended not to hear. She was probably used to guys gaping in her doorway, but none of them was her lawyer and she hadn't just placed her life in their hands. I gave myself a mental kick in the ass and resolved to do better as she led the way down the hall to a kitchen that was about what you'd expect in a house that size, just right for a half-court basketball game. Everything was industrial size. There were two ovens, a Vulcan stove, a side-by-side Sub-Zero refrigerator and freezer about seven feet high, and three sinks. Copper pots hung from hooks that circled overhead. The food preparation area was bounded on one side by a counter and stools that went across half its width. On the far side was a pine country table with eight chairs, probably for staff and midnight snacks. She told me to pull up a stool and help myself to the wine, propped in an ice bucket on the counter. "Thanks," I said. "Can I pour one for you?"

"Not yet." She was busy now, pounding on some veal with gusto. There was a large pot with boiling water and two pans standing ready on the burners. "Dinner is veal piccata with a little pasta and asparagus on the side. I hope you didn't have something like it last night."

"Not unless it's a TV dinner."

"I figured you for one of those bachelors who could cook."

"I used to cook a lot. I was pretty good at it."

"Why'd you stop?"

"I got divorced. I live alone and there's not much incentive."

She smiled. "I have a cook so I only do it when I'm in the mood; that makes all the difference." Toiling in her kitchen, her tongue protruding slightly through her teeth, she didn't look anything like a murderess. *I ask you, ladies and gentlemen, could a killer make a veal piccata like this?*

"This seems a funny question," I said, "but I didn't ask when you were in the office. What do you do?"

"As an occupation?"

"Yes. It could be important."

"The newspapers say that I go to parties and have romances."

"Sounds like a good job."

"It's steady work," she replied, laughing. "And when I have time off, I paint. I've had several shows here and in New York." She looked up from her labor and added, "Some of my customers aren't even friends."

"I'd love to see your work when we have the chance." I wasn't being polite; I was enchanted. I wanted to know everything about her.

"Thank you. I'd love for you to see it." She began to sauté the veal. "And when I'm not painting, partying, romancing, or cooking"—she bowed slightly—"I'm the editor of a small circulation monthly about the art world. So, all in all, I manage to stay out of trouble." She didn't look up when she added, "I guess I can't say that anymore, can I?" After a few moments she handed me the wine bottle and asked me to pour her a glass. I took it around the counter. "Turnabout is fair play," she said. "I don't know anything about you."

"You knew you wanted me to defend you."

"I acted on instinct." She took a sip of wine. "Tell me about yourself so I can see what a good choice I made."

What could we discuss? My personal life? Career path? "Let's not talk about me tonight," I said. "We'll save me for another time."

"I'm intruding." She frowned. "I asked for your help, then I cross-examine you like an applicant. I'm sorry, Frank, that was rude."

"Don't apologize," I said quickly, trying to preserve the mood. "In your place I'd want to know about me, too."

"You would?"

"Sure." I smiled at her. I was in no-man's land, putting up a good front. "What do you want to know?"

"Well, start with the professional side and we'll go from there."

"I was an Assistant District Attorney in New York for almost ten years. I started out handling misdemeanors and simple felonies like burglary and car theft, and then I moved up to the bigger stuff."

"Like murder?" she asked.

"Like murder."

"Did you prosecute a lot of murderers?"

"Yes."

"Did you convict most of them?"

"All of them."

"All of them . . . You were good at it."

"Yes."

"What about the prosecutor in my case, this Kyle Rogavin?"

"He's very good."

"Very good," she repeated quietly, staring at the stove. She noticed the veal and turned it over. "And after the murderers, what?"

"They promoted me to the Special Prosecutions Unit. I

handled the white-collar crimes: stock swindles, bid-rigging, public corruption. I won a couple of big cases and they made me chief of the unit just before I came down here."

"What brought you to Washington?"

"I got married and joined my father-in-law's firm. I was there for several years."

"And then you left."

"I got divorced." Reversing the sequence always made it easier.

"But you still handle big cases?"

"Just yours."

We passed an awkward moment with the wine. "Let's move on to the more interesting stuff," she said. "Are you from New York originally?"

"The Bronx."

"Tell me about your home."

"I lived in apartment houses, first with relatives, then in some foster homes."

"Oh. You lost your parents?"

"No."

"Should we skip childhood?"

"Okay."

"Start from high school."

"I left at sixteen and went into the Army."

"Didn't like school?" She turned over the veal again and placed the asparagus in a colander over boiling water.

"The Vietnam War was going on. I wanted to see what it was all about."

"I wasn't in high school yet," she said, "so I really didn't know anybody who went except for our gardener's son. When he got back he said that he hated it, everybody hated it." She glanced at me. "Did you hate it?"

"No."

She raised an eyebrow. "Did you *like* it?"

I shrugged.

Now, she was interested: her cross-examination was

bearing fruit. She came over to the counter, moving so close that there didn't seem to be a way to avoid those eyes. "What did you like about it? I'd really like to know."

Two years before, Noah had asked me that same question. I didn't have an answer so he eventually worked out the theory he related the week before. I wasn't sure then if he was right, but now, face-to-face with this remarkable woman on the brink of another war, I knew. So I told her: "The contest."

She stared at me for a moment, then finished her wine and went back to the stove. There were no more questions; perhaps she found out what she needed to know. As for me, my resolve didn't last very long: I watched her as she padded back and forth, wondering what life with Ashley Bronson would really be like.

Dinner was ready in a few moments. We sat side by side as I ate and she talked, both of us needing to fill a void. She told me more about painting and the magazine, eventually getting around to her upbringing, and the telling made her happy and animated. Her life was not unlike Moira's, filled with all the childhood experiences that wealth and indulgent parents could provide. The most pronounced difference was between their fathers. My former father-in-law probably had a lot in common with the Bronson who started it all: a nononsense immigrant who parlayed his wits and balls into a fortune. But Henry Bronson had made a world for himself in his books, unburdened by the necessity of earning a living. Ashley loved him dearly, though, as much as Moira loved Pop—more, if murdering Garvey was any yardstick—and became subdued when describing his last years in his library, working at his desk.

Sitting together in that kitchen, dwelling on something less stressful than her case or my problems, induced a state of contentment I hadn't felt in years. Her voice was soothing, deeper than you'd expect, with the diction of good schools harnessed to the family intellect, yet it still managed to convey warmth. It was her: a fusion of grace and competence that said she could take care of herself—and you, too, if you deserved it.

As we cleared the dishes I thought about the turns my own life was taking—not really turns but jagged tacks between euphoria and despair. The reality was that Moira Brennan O'Connell was still very much in my life, but now there was another man in *her* life. What did I feel when they stood in the doorway? What would she feel if she could see me now?

"How do you like your coffee?" she asked, proffering the pot.

"Black." It was time to move on to the more pressing subject of murder and its detection. I worked up to it while she poured. "Ashley, Rogavin says there was a witness who saw you in the area of Garvey's house."

She put down the pot and exhaled. "I suppose that's it then," she said quietly, more to herself than me.

"No, it's not. It's just the beginning. Think again about returning that night. Maybe you passed someone walking or getting out of a parked car."

She closed her eyes for a moment, replaying the scene in her mind. "Nothing," she said finally. "I don't remember anyone."

"What time did it happen?" That sounded better than "What time did you kill him?"

"I think it was between ten-fifteen and ten-thirty. I know that it was about ten o'clock when I left here, and I was back by ten-thirty."

"Well, it's almost ten now. Do you feel up to a walk?"

"Where to?"

"To Garvey's house and back. We'll see who's around at this time of night. It could refresh your recollection or give us a lead, but whether it does or not, I need to get familiar with the route."

"I understand," she said quietly. "Returning to the scene

of the crime—that's what murderers do, isn't it?"

"I wouldn't ask if it wasn't important."

"I know." We finished our coffee and I went to fetch my coat. In a moment she appeared in a belted black reefer coat and a wool beret, with a white cashmere scarf that concealed her face except for her nose and those eyes; it only enhanced the effect.

"Let's try to blend in," I said when we reached the sidewalk, "just two people out for an evening stroll." She linked her arm through mine and we headed east on N Street toward Thirtieth. The walk to Garvey's was six blocks and the witness could have been anyone who lived or walked along the route. I figured that Ashley would have been startled by someone passing, so he or she was probably stationary. The houses of N Street were set far back, making it unlikely that the witness had been inside, but the row houses on the other streets abutted the sidewalks and there were several whose interior lights illuminated us as we passed. Any house might have had its lights on and shades up that night, but people are creatures of habit and this exercise was about the laws of probability.

As we strolled along I dictated into a small tape recorder, noting the sources of light that could have revealed her face to Rogavin's witness. There were plenty of potential sites. Including streetlights I counted twenty-two places where her face might be illuminated enough to make identification possible. And looking at Ashley as a car passed confirmed that even a motorist was a possibility, albeit a slim one.

I could feel her trembling through the coat as we entered Garvey's block on the south side of Q Street. The house was in a row of Victorian mansions on the north side, one-half of a double villa in the Italianate style, according to my escort, with two stories and a "French attic." I didn't want to attract the notice of any neighbors so we stayed across the street, just getting close enough to make out the front and west side of the house.

"That's where I went in," she said, pointing toward the

French doors that opened onto the garden.

"You came out the same way?" She nodded. "And you walked home using the same route?"

"Yes. Let's leave now. *Please.*"

A moment later we were on our way back, still arm in arm, two lovers strolling along in silence. She was lost in thought and I was in a drift of my own, pretending that we weren't pretending. We were only a block from her house when I surfaced from my reverie to broach an unpleasant subject. "I've got something else to tell you about my meeting this afternoon," I said. "We've been offered a deal."

She stopped. "What kind of deal?"

"A plea to murder in the second degree, meaning no premeditation. The government will stand quiet at sentencing and we argue for leniency. Your sentence could be less than ten years."

"What if I say no?"

"Then we go to trial."

"A trial." She pondered that for a moment. "And if I'm convicted?"

"You could get twenty years. He said that the offer is only good until you're indicted. That could be a bluff but I can't be sure."

Ashley started walking again and I followed, watching her out of the corner of my eye. She put her arm back in mine and leaned close. "What do we do now?" she asked.

"The hard part about plea bargaining is that it's like poker. Sometimes you have to make choices without seeing the other guy's cards. They have the fingerprints; we might counter that. They also claim that the Wards heard you arguing with Garvey not long before he died. What about it?"

"It's true. That's the warning I told you about. I told him to stay away or he'd regret it."

"What did he say?"

"He said it was none of my business. That was pretty much it."

"What did you mean, he'd regret it?"

"I don't really know. That's what you say at a time like that, isn't it?"

"I suppose. An argument and fingerprints is nothing to sneeze at but it's hardly an airtight case."

"Then there's the witness," she said.

"Then there's the witness," I agreed. "It was dark"—I took in the surroundings with a sweep of my arm—"and the lighting doesn't appear to be great, but we don't know anything about distance or the witness's ability to observe, or even if he or she was familiar with you."

We reached her front door. "Do you think it could be someone I know?" she asked.

"Maybe. Do you know anyone who lives on the route we just walked?"

"I know most of my neighbors."

"What about people who live near Garvey's house?"

"I don't think so but sometimes people just recognize me."

I couldn't imagine why. "Ashley, the decision is yours. My job is to lay out the options and advise. If you plead, you'll go to prison for as much as ten years—that's it, you're going. If you go to trial you've got a fighting chance to remain free, but at greater risk."

"It's not much of a choice, is it?"

"We live in a society of rules. You broke a big one."

"Then I belong in prison."

"No, you don't."

She smiled. "Dispensation for me, is that it? Was dinner *that* good?"

"It's not dispensation."

"Then what, Frank?" Her eyes were bright. She had stood in the doorway with a lot of guys trying to reach for just the right words.

"Ashley, you haven't had to confront the horrors people are capable of, at least not directly. I've seen them, and not just on the other side of the world, either. I've prosecuted and defended psychos and all kinds of bastards who truly belong where they can't get their hands on anyone else. And then there's you. You've had a privileged life but you didn't do any harm, and you even brought some beauty into this world. I understand about that. Then you lost your father and you took revenge. Well, I'm sorry, but the world isn't going to be a safer or better place with you behind bars, not hardly. And if you're troubled by the possibility of escaping punishment, don't be, because you won't. You'll still have to live with it every night. I understand about that, too. I'm still trying to live with some of the things I did, and after all these years and a lot of professional help I haven't succeeded. And if I wasn't here right now walking with you, I'd be off by myself, wandering the streets until I was exhausted enough to sleep."

It had all come out in a rush, without thinking. "You wanted to know about me," I muttered. "Now you know."

"Now I know," she said quietly. "Tell me what to do."

"I don't want you to plead guilty."

"Then I won't." She opened the door and turned back to me. "Will you be out walking tonight?"

"No. Tonight, I'll be fine."

She nodded and put her hand against my cheek. "So will I."

It was either the aftershock of an epiphany or the wine, but I had this notion that if I just took her in my arms we would hold onto each other and the whole thing would go away, this mess we'd made of our lives, and we'd go on. If it were only that easy. The longest long shot ever to come through the door, that's all.

I drove home to the apartment more or less on automatic pilot, my head filled with the images of a woman: sitting in my office, clinging to my arm, preparing my dinner. Staring at me through steel bars.

*You like competition, Mr. O'Connell?*

Fuck you, Rogavin. You and your mind games. You can't have her.

She's mine.

# 5

Walter Feinberg, Detective First Grade, retired, had been assigned to the Special Prosecutions unit in New York. I was single then and he used to take me to cop bars to meet his pals and police groupies. "I'll get ya laid," he said, "and you'll cover me when I get my ass in a crack." After his wife died he moved from Queens to Falls Church, Virginia, to be near his daughter and grandchildren. It hadn't worked out.

"The Monday before Passover she calls," he explained. "She says, 'You got any plans, Dad?' Yeah, I got big plans. The Hot Shoppes is runnin' a seder special for fourteen ninety-five plus beverage. I been down here three months, I know nobody, and I'm living in somethin' called 'Bailey's Freakin' Crossroads.' I got plans? And I know she had to fight that Volvo-dick she married to let me sit at the table with his Volvo-dick friends."

"Volvo-dick" was Walter's term of endearment for liberals.

"So," he said, "it's Passover, right? I swallow my pride and go, and I keep my mouth shut and eat my dinner. Every time I look up Volvo-dick is watchin' me like I crapped in the punch bowl." Within three months Walter had a private investigator's license. I asked him how he was going to do any sleuthing in Washington, he didn't even know the streets. "Bein' a detective ain't about knowin' the streets," he explained, "that's TV shit. It's about knowin' people, and they're the same all over. I got a Ph.D. in people from the Police Department of the City of New York. That and a street map and I'm in business."

It was true. That shopworn face of his was a magnet that attracted the confidence of others as he sat there nodding, sympathizing, never judging; always respecting your dignity, even if you *were* a Volvo-dick. But his special gift was a sixth sense, the product of observation, intellect, and twenty-five years of experience. When Walter Feinberg told you that someone or something wasn't as advertised, you could bank on it. In our New York days prosecutors and other cops would ask him to sit in on interviews, even if he knew nothing about the case. "Walter," they would say, "listen to this and tell me if this guy's bullshittin'."

Rogavin had a head start but I had Walter Feinberg.

"Is she as good lookin' as the pictures?" The diviner of truth, a vision in polyester slacks, plaid sports jacket and clashing tie, was leering at me from the other side of my desk.

"The pictures don't come close."

"Jeez," he muttered, rubbing his jaw. "So, how'd she end up with you?"

"You, too?" It was getting annoying.

He raised his hands. "Hey, don't get me wrong—I'm so happy I could shit. I ain't had any real payin' work from you since you split with the old man, but you ain't exactly the mouthpiece to the stars around here."

I feigned a hurt look. "Wait a minute. I've sent you work. And the court approved a fee each time."

"Right. A coupla' more cases at those bullshit rates, I could be as broke as you." He beckoned with his forefinger. "C'mon, give."

I put my feet up on the desk. "She saw me in the cellblocks and . . . well, you know my effect on women."

"Yeah." He sniffed. "I keep readin' about that social life of yours in *Washingtonian*." He began picking at the permanent crease in his pants. "So . . . she whacked this guy, right?"

"That's what the government thinks."

He worked his toothpick from side to side. "That's . . . what . . . the . . . government . . . thinks," he repeated, eyeing me. "And what do *we* think?" He had my number. He probably already figured that I had dinner with her. If pressed, he'd say, "Some veal dish."

"I had a meeting with the prosecutor yesterday."

"Which one?"

"Kyle Rogavin."

He shook his head. "Not good for our side. That guy snacks on the defense bar around here."

"And I'm chopped liver?"

"No, not when you're on your game." He bent over to wipe an imaginary speck from one of his brogans. "Look, you're not poppin' her are you? I mean, it ain't my business but we got a case here an' all. . . ."

"I haven't and I won't, thank you. Can we get down to business or is there something else you want to ask me?"

"Go ahead."

"Rogavin says that he's got a witness who saw the client in the area of Garvey's."

"What the hell does that mean, *in the area*?"

"I don't know but the farther away, the better."

"And?"

"And I want you to canvass the route from Garvey's house to hers to see if you can find him—or her. Here's a map." I gave him a good map of the Georgetown area with circles around the Bronson and Garvey homes.

He studied it. "There's a coupla' ways from his house to hers, even if you go direct. This could take a while."

I took the map back and marked the route Ashley and I had walked. "Try this one," I said.

He looked at the map and then back at me. "You mean try this one first, or this one *only*?"

"Only." He nodded, relieved to see that I wasn't going to be coy about her guilt. "I walked the route last night," I said, and pushed a copy of my dictated notes across the desk.

Walter reviewed them. "Ain't a bad start but it ain't con-
clusive. She could've been made anywhere."

"That's why I need you to knock on every door. And
while you're at it, if you were to find a witness or two who
saw someone—*anyone*—that didn't look like Ashley Bronson lurking near Garvey's house around ten-fifteen on the
night in question, that would be a good thing."

His eyes rested on my face. "Would it?"

"She had a reason, Walter."

"There's always a reason."

"Just find me something, okay?"

"No promises." He got up and placed his palms flat on the
desk. His big head and shoulders loomed over me. "How
long we known each other?"

"A long time."

"You keep it in your pants." He left.

Harry was beaming in my doorway a moment later.
"Frank, I've got someone for you to meet." He ushered in a
kid in suspenders and bow tie who couldn't have been more
than twenty-five. I'd seen him before, laboring in the firm's
library. "This is Andy Gardner," he gushed, "one of our
brightest associates. I told him that you might be looking for
some help and needless to say, he's raring to go."

Andy smiled nervously. "I've never worked on any
criminal cases," he confessed, "but I aced criminal law at
school."

"Andy went to *Columbia*," added Harry, sotto voce.
"They turn out some pretty fair lawyers up there, Frank."

"I'm from New York, Harry."

"Of course," he stammered. "I knew that. That's why you
guys will make a great team." He was truly hopeless. He
stayed close to his wife at parties so she'd whisper the
names of people he'd met a dozen times before. But if you
were a potential client he'd remember your shoe size if you

happened to mention it within earshot. "Andy's ready to go as of this morning," he said.

"Your timing's impeccable, Andy," I said. "I could use some help right now."

"Wonderful!" cried Harry. "He's all yours." He gave us a thumbs-up gesture as he left.

I motioned the latest member of Team Bronson to a chair and reached for my to-do list. "So, Andy, what have you been doing around here up to now?"

"Research and writing memos, mostly corporate stuff. Nothing like what you're doing. I really appreciate this opportunity, Mr. O'Connell."

"Frank."

"Frank. I've read all the newspaper stories about the case and I did a computer search for other stories about her. There's stuff going back almost eighteen years and it's . . . uh . . . interesting."

"Well, you'll have your chance to get to know her." The excitement was dancing in his eyes. Yesterday he was trudging through the desert of corporate mergers, now he was embarked on an assault on Everest and only wanted to be told which way was up. "Our client will be indicted next week, probably Monday."

"Is there any chance the grand jury won't indict?"

"None. We'll get a phone call about the arraignment date. Then we'll go to court, get a copy of the indictment, and enter our plea of 'not guilty.' The court will set a deadline for filing any motions but it won't be far off and we need to get a head start. The prosecution will automatically give us most of the stuff we need, like the results of any scientific tests and the autopsy, but what's critical is the statement of a supposed eyewitness. Usually, we wouldn't get it till just before trial, but in this case that's too late. We need to know where that witness was and what he saw as soon as possible, so you're going to prepare a motion to persuade the court to let us have the statement now."

He looked up. "Got it."

"Okay. Next, speak to Cory Barnes, our paralegal. We need all of the newspaper articles on Raymond Garvey as far back as we can go. Did you save the stuff on our client?"

"They're in a file."

"Good. Note anything that the prosecution might use. I know that's pretty broad but when in doubt, include it."

"I get it. Stuff they'll use to cross-examine her."

"Well . . . anything that could be detrimental. And here's something else for Cory: the police keep reports of crimes called 'Incident Reports.' I want her to research the reports for Garvey's neighborhood for the last six months."

"What are we looking for?"

"Burglaries, robberies, assaults, rapes, and murders. Anything serious that involves an actual or potential confrontation inside a home."

"A pattern that Garvey's shooting could fit."

"That's right. That's it for now, plenty to get you started." Andy jumped up and marched out without ever asking whether she did it, making him either naive or very circumspect for a newly minted lawyer. Of course I had avoided the subject, too. First Walter, then Andy: I was having a tough time telling people the truth about Ashley Bronson, probably because I needed reminding myself. It was a good time to turn to the task I'd been saving for me. I unlocked the credenza and removed the leather-bound volume. The last entry was written in a labored hand.

## HENRY BRONSON'S JOURNAL

*October 25. There is no future. I look forward and see only the reflection of before. A most unfair thing—that the consequences of youthful idealism should endure as those of deliberation and experience.*

*I thought I had lived long enough to receive the absolution of events, only to be thwarted by my own van-*

ity. Like Frankenstein, I am terrorized by my own creation. My dear friend has become my tormentor. He
leaves me only one way.

My darling girl, I am so sorry. Do not condemn me
for what I have done or will do. You are my greatest
creation. Through you I have savored the life that was
denied me by circumstance and personality. I will
watch over you forever.

# 6

Rogavin called just before noon on Monday to deliver the news. "Your client has been indicted," he said.

"I'm shocked."

"The charge is first-degree murder. The arraignment is set for Thursday at ten A.M. Judge Warner. I presume an arrest warrant won't be necessary."

He was a big one for presumptions. "I'll wear my good suit," I replied. "Anything else?"

"I've seen her. You should've taken the deal." He hung up.

I called Ashley and told her to brace for reruns of the arrest footage and more comments from people she'd regarded as friends. She had already changed her telephone number and Walter had arranged security to fend off the press and other uninvited guests. I suggested that she might not want to go out for a week or so, and to plan accordingly.

Andy brought me a final draft of our motion that afternoon. It was good work and I decided to leave the research and writing to him and devote my attention to the rest of the list. One item was Ashley's fingerprints on the gun, another was her argument with Garvey. Dealing with both meant interviewing Edward and Charlotte Ward, Garvey's handyman and housekeeper. I was thinking about them when Walter showed up with news.

"I found someone."

I bolted upright. *"The witness?"*

He shrugged, then opened his notebook and began reading without preamble. "Mr. William Bradmoor, One-five-nine-four Twenty-eighth Street—that's around the corner from Garvey, a half-block south. On the big night he leaves the house to get his car, which is parked on Q Street, one block east of Garvey's. He walks up to the intersection of Twenty-eighth and Q and is about to cross when he hears footsteps behind him—that's in Garvey's block. He turns around and sees a woman half-walking, half-running in the street, coming toward him."

"That's from the direction of Garvey's."

"Right. He can't see her face but she's wearing a hat and a raincoat."

"How does he know it's a woman?"

"General size and shape, the way she moved and the sound of her shoes on the pavement. He's sure about it. Anyway, she jumps into a sedan parked on the north side of the street—about fifty, sixty feet from Bradmoor—starts it up and pulls away from the curb. He doesn't think much of it—it's rainin', she's runnin'—so he starts across the street. Then he hears the screech of brakes and turns around to see the car farther down the block. All he can really make out is its shape and the taillights but he hears the car doors slam—"

"Door or doors?"

"Two doors, and he thinks they was on the passenger's side 'cause he could kinda' see the driver's side. Anyway, she hits the gas and they go flyin' out of there like a bat outta hell. He watches the taillights until they reach the next intersection and turn left. That's it."

"Wow! What time was this?"

"Around ten-forty-five, definitely after ten-thirty."

"All right!" I cried. "This is great!"

"Maybe."

"C'mon! If this is Rogavin's witness we're home free! The guy never saw the woman's face. She could've been anyone!"

"What makes you think this is the witness?"

"Did Bradmoor speak to the police?"

"Yeah. They came to his house when they were canvassing the neighborhood."

"Then he could be the guy!"

"Not much of a witness, and how would Rogavin explain the passenger doors?"

"Maybe he was just yanking my chain." Walter looked dubious. "Okay," I conceded, "it's probably not his witness but it's still good news: *another woman near the scene of the crime*!"

"We need to get that freakin' witness's statement from the government."

"Andy's written a good motion and with a little luck, the judge will come through."

"Swell," he grumbled, "we're relyin' on a judge."

"Hey, cheer up! We're on a roll so why don't we drop that piece for the time being and move on? We've got to deal with Ashley's fingerprints on the gun and her argument with Garvey. That means you've got to find the Wards and make them talk."

"No problem," he replied. "Anything I can do on the way over? Run faster than a speedin' bullet? Leap a tall buildin' in a single freakin' bound?"

"It'll be a piece of cake. They've known her since she was in high school. She says they were always very fond of her."

"No shit? And me thinkin' they might be a little pissed."

"Maybe they don't think she did it."

"Yeah." He sniffed. "Why would they think that?"

"Are you going to tell me what the problem is?"

He exhaled, puffing out his cheeks. "What if Bradmoor saw the client?"

"Can't be. Ashley left Garvey's on foot, alone and walking west. And fifteen minutes earlier, at least."

"That's what she says."

"And I believe her."

"Is this the big head talkin' or the little head?"

"Go find the Wards, will you?"

\* \* \*

So, the great eyewitness hunt was suspended and the next two days were devoted to other tasks—with mixed success. Despite the fact that Garvey saw fit to arm himself the incident reports for his neighborhood indicated that most of the crime was just mischief, usually occurring during the wee hours of the weekend when frustrated bar patrons searched for cars parked on Georgetown's look-alike streets. The victims were mostly garbage cans, plantings, and the occasional windshield; serious offenses were infrequent and largely limited to daytime burglaries while homeowners toiled in downtown offices. The occasional convergence of housebreaker and owner was purely inadvertent and rarely violent, and we found nothing to suggest that Garvey might have been just one more victim of a burglar that had staked a claim in the neighborhood. Not a good start.

It didn't get better right away. The Wards were not where they were supposed to be, not at Garvey's house or their own residence in rural Virginia. We discussed the possibility that the government had them stashed somewhere and decided that it was too far-fetched, but I was worried. Walter was at full boil; he declared flatly that he would find them. Ordinarily, when he decided that he was going to find someone the earth wasn't a big enough hiding place. Ordinarily.

Thursday we went down to the courthouse to enter the plea. I didn't want the image of Ashley's limousine broadcast repeatedly into area homes so we took a sedan driven by Dan White, a former MPD detective who had joined the team, and Walter and Andy came along as human bulldozers to get us into and out of the courthouse. Andy's scrubbed face radiated excitement. Walter groused the whole way about the impending encounter with reporters and judges. Both were on his shit list, just below Volvodicks.

We'd anticipated a circus but weren't prepared for the sight of two hundred reporters, photographers, and cameramen on the sidewalk. "The Ashley Bronson case"—that's what they called it—was definitely a national story. We deployed around her as she was bombarded from both sides.

"Miss Bronson, did you kill Raymond Garvey?"

"What was your relationship with Raymond Garvey?"

"Are you going to trial?"

"Miss Bronson, is it true that your fingerprints were on the murder weapon?"

When we reached the door I turned to the cameras to make a statement. A gag order was a real possibility and I wanted to get in a few words from our side for that night's newscasts. "Miss Bronson will be entering a plea of not guilty to the charges," I announced. "She would like to thank her friends and acquaintances for all their support and asks that the public not draw any conclusions until the end of the trial. She is innocent. We expect that after it has heard all the evidence, the jury will agree. Thank you." We ducked inside as the cacophony started anew.

There was another media contingent waiting in the courtroom, and when the group from outside filtered in, the seats were filled. We were the only case on the docket so Andy and I took our places at the defense table. Walter sat in the first row and read his newspaper. A few moments later Rogavin entered with another assistant and took the government's traditional table closest to the jury box. There were several sketch artists drawing Ashley, the center of it all and the best face in the room.

At a few minutes after ten there was a knock on the other side of the door and we all rose as Judge Warner entered. He nodded at the clerk who called case No. Cr 1423, *United States v. Ashley Bronson.* "Counsel will please enter their appearances," said the clerk.

"Kyle Rogavin for the United States, Your Honor."

"Francis O'Connell for Ashley Bronson."

The clerk handed the file up to Warner, who announced, "This is the arraignment of the defendant. Mr. O'Connell, does your client desire a reading of the indictment?"

"No, Your Honor, we'll waive."

"All right. Is your client prepared to enter a plea?"

"Yes, Your Honor."

Warner looked toward her. "Miss Bronson, will you please rise?" She stood up. I moved a little closer so our shoulders were touching as we waited. I've had clients shaking so bad at moments like that you could almost feel them through the floor. But she stood completely still, looking directly at Warner. It could have been acting; I think it was pedigree. "To the charge of murder in the first degree," Warner intoned, "how do you plead?"

"Not guilty," she replied. There was that voice again. It managed to express conviction, poise, and the barest hint of defiance in just a two-word phrase. I could probably design a trial strategy around her physical assets alone—get a jury of men, put her on the stand, and have her look 'em in the eye and talk. Christ, she could read the phone book and we'd get a deadlock. It was too bad I knew she was guilty. I'd have to reconsider my approach to the client interview.

"Very well," said Warner. "The clerk will enter a plea of not guilty. Mr. Rogavin, how long will it take to present the government's case?"

Rogavin stood up. "Approximately two or three days, Your Honor."

"Mr. O'Connell?"

"I can't be sure until we've had some discovery, Your Honor, but I'd estimate the same."

"All right. The government will provide required discovery within the next two days. Any problems, Mr. Rogavin?"

"No, Your Honor."

"Any motions will be filed by next Wednesday morning; responses by Friday, close of business. That means, gentlemen, that they have to be brief, so come right to the point."

There was one thing uppermost in my mind. "Your Honor, when will the Court require the government to turn over witness statements? We'd like to have them as soon as possible."

Rogavin rose. "Your Honor, we're not required to turn over a witness's prior statement until the witness has testified."

Warner shook his head at the prosecutor. "If we applied the law literally, we'd have to stop the trial after every witness has testified to allow the defense to read the statement and prepare a cross-examination. You know better, Mr. Rogavin. I know you know better."

Rogavin didn't concede the point. "Your Honor, this is a murder case in which there is a lot of media interest." He gestured toward the spectators that filled the courtroom. "One of the purposes of the law is to protect the privacy of witnesses and ensure that there is no interference or intimidation. At the very least their statements ought not to be turned over until a week before trial."

That got me up quick. "Your Honor, this isn't an organized-crime case. To even suggest the possibility of witness intimidation is silly. And between the police and the U.S. Attorney's Office there are probably more than a hundred people who know the identities of the witnesses. Adding my small defense team to that group is hardly a threat to anyone's privacy. We have a motion that seeks all witness statements now, and ask that you consider it as soon as possible."

Warner made up his mind. "I'll consider your motion today and make a ruling. All right. Let's talk about scheduling." The clerk laid the calendar before Warner and they discussed it between themselves while the rest of us waited. "Counsel, what about February fourth?"

Rogavin bounced up again. "Judge, we would like a trial date in the beginning of January."

"Mr. O'Connell?"

"Your Honor, that's five weeks away and it includes the holiday season, when it's hard to reach people and get things done. Given the seriousness of the charges and the potential penalties we ought to have more time to prepare."

"Judge," Rogavin said, "the defendant has been accused of murder and is free on bond. We are talking about a case that is not complex and can be tried in five days. Five weeks is enough time to get ready, holidays included."

Warner looked at his calendar. "I'm going to set this down for December thirtieth. That will give us a couple of days to pick the jury, a day off for the holiday, and then we'll get started on Thursday with presentation of evidence. Mr. O'Connell, you ought to be able to get ready. If there are compelling reasons why not I'll be glad to hear them at the appropriate time, and that doesn't mean at the last minute."

"Yes, Your Honor." Warner wrote on the file jacket and said, "The bond will remain as set by Judge Robbins. I'll see counsel in chambers immediately after we adjourn." He nodded toward the bailiff and we all stood on command as he left the bench. Rogavin and I followed one of Warner's clerks to a conference table where the judge was waiting.

He didn't waste any time getting to the point. "Given

the public interest I'm not surprised to see that Mr. Rogavin will be presenting the government's case. Mr. O'-Connell, your previous matters in my court have been less sensational. You've done a good job in that type of case but this is a different situation entirely." Warner peered at me while just outside his line of vision the corners of Rogavin's mouth turned upward. "Anyway," he continued, "I just want you to understand that I have certain ground rules in these high-profile cases. I know what they can do for a lawyer's career. I had a few of my own when I was in practice and that's all fine and dandy. But I do not hold with grandstanding, inside the courtroom or out." He reached for the water pitcher, poured a glass, and looked inquisitively at both of us before he set it down. Kicking ass was thirsty work. "I didn't impose a gag order out there today but if I see or hear anything to indicate that this case is being tried in the media, there will be sanctions and they will be severe. Dammit! I am sick and tired of self-aggrandizing and sleazy behavior by members of the bar." He wagged a warning finger at us both. "I want this case conducted in an exemplary and ethical manner. Do either of you have any questions?"

"No sir," I said.

"None, Your Honor," echoed Rogavin.

"All right, that's all. You'll be contacted with a date for the hearing on the motions. Thank you, gentlemen."

No one spoke on the way back from the courthouse. Walter, Andy, and I got out at the office, leaving Ashley to continue on to Georgetown with Dan. It was hard to gauge the effect of her first public appearance as a defendant. When I told her that I would call later she didn't look at me when she nodded.

Andy went back to his research while Walter and I went for a walk. "We ain't got a lot of time," he said.

"We've got to start finding some witnesses, and I mean soon."

"I'm workin' on it."

I exhaled. "Five weeks. Five goddamn weeks—with holidays." I looked toward Georgetown, the scene of the crime, the place where she lived. "She handled it pretty well, didn't she?"

"She's somethin', I'll give you that."

"Does she look like a murderer to you?"

He fished out a fresh toothpick. "Tell me what a murderer looks like. I was a cop for twenty-five years, fifteen in homicide, and I still don't know." He looked across Dupont Circle. "You're followin' my advice about her, right?"

"Yeah."

He winked and clapped me on the back. "Don't worry, counselor. Now that you're in the big time I got a chance for some real paydays, so I'm gonna pull your chestnuts outta the fire, just like old times." He looked at his watch, a retirement gift from the detectives of his old precinct. "I gotta go find the Wards," he grumbled. "Everybody in this case must be hidin' in the same hole." Ignoring red lights and dodging traffic he made his way across the circle, only stopping to exchange pleasantries with a cab driver who blew his horn. You can take the man out of New York, but you can't take the New York out of the man.

The fax from the judge's chambers arrived shortly after lunch. It was the front page of Andy's painstakingly crafted motion, with "denied" scribbled vertically in the margin and a notation at the bottom: "All witness statements to be produced to the defense by December 23." Seven days before trial: Christmas week. Warner hadn't left us any time to investigate, which meant that we probably wouldn't know our chances until trial when the eyewitness took the stand, when there was no going back.

Worrying consumed the rest of the afternoon. As far as we knew Ashley's accuser could be anyone from Yasser

Arafat to the Mother Superior, but if it was Arafat it wouldn't matter because he'd show up in a habit and rosary beads or Rogavin's reputation wasn't deserved. It was seven o'clock when I finally called our client.

"I'm watching us on television," she said.

"Did the cameras make me look heavy?"

"No, you look very handsome. All the girls will be calling."

"Ashley, we heard from Warner: no witness statements until a week before trial."

"Oh."

"Don't worry, though. Walter is going to find this eyewitness and we'll be fine."

"He's a character, just what I imagined a New York detective would be like."

"And he's the best. He's going to come through for us."

"I'm sorry I can't remember seeing anyone. I know I haven't been any help."

"Don't worry about it. You did great today, did you know that?"

"Yes, I remembered to say 'not' before 'guilty.'"

Time to change the subject. "I read your father's journal, Ashley, the last entry."

"Oh . . . Not much of a good-bye, is it?"

"I didn't understand it, but he loved his daughter, that much was clear."

"Yes . . . he did. I miss him very much. It's a hard time to be alone."

"I'm a poor substitute but call on me anytime."

She laughed softly. "A full-service firm, is that it? On the job night and day."

"It's not business, Ashley."

That just popped out. For a moment neither of us said anything while I thought about my vow.

"Thank you," she said quietly. "I needed that."

Not as much as I needed to say it. "Why don't you turn off the news and get some rest? I'll call you tomorrow."

"Okay. Good night, Frank."

"Good night."

# 7

On Friday Andy went over to the U.S. Attorney's Office and brought back the materials that Rogavin was producing voluntarily: the fingerprint comparisons, the autopsy on Garvey, and the report of the crime scene search of his home. Cory had sorted all the available newspaper references to Ashley and Raymond Garvey in two piles. Garvey may have had a head start but her pile was bigger. It stood to reason that photographers would gravitate toward her at every event she attended and she had attended plenty: openings, charity balls, fund-raisers, and receptions by the dozen. The clippings were in chronological order and the first reported her sixteenth birthday party, given on the back lawn of the Georgetown house. The guests were a cross section of the Washington arts and science communities with a few politicos thrown in, including Secretary Raymond Garvey. The irony was too rich: he'd share her first public mention and her last.

The rest of the pile told the story of a life of privilege and accomplishment: horseback riding in hunt country and sailboat racing to Newport; graduation from the National Cathedral School and on to Wellesley; three years studying painting in France. At twenty-seven she had her first one-woman show and her work was selling for five figures before she was thirty. There was a wonderful photograph of her at her desk at *Atlantic Fine Arts*, in jeans and button-down shirt with a pencil between her teeth.

No surprise: there had been no shortage of suitors. There

were mentions and photographs of dozens, variously referred to as "boyfriend," "beau," "current beau," "love interest," and my personal favorite, "companion." There was even an announcement of engagement, to the son of an industrialist from Lyons during her Parisian interlude. I read them all and dawdled over the photographs, trying to decipher the body language and expressions. Who were the ones she really cared about? Some of them looked like rich jerks, others seemed to be regular guys; it was the men of genuine accomplishment that troubled me most. There were several recognizable names next to hers on the guest lists of seven—*seven*—White House dinners. Not bad for thirty-four.

The file was up to date. The last photograph was of us exiting the courthouse. It was the only one in which she wasn't smiling. Up until this episode her life had been perfect. Better than perfect. This was her nightmare and I had a leading role. If we won, if she was set free, she would be terribly grateful—for a while. But eventually she'd have to put the whole experience behind her, everything and everyone. Seeing me would always remind her of the time in her life when she didn't smile.

Whatever. The important thing, I reminded myself, was that there was nothing of any use to Rogavin. No dishonesty, no immorality, no public displays of temper, no awards for pistol prowess. Another plus, or at least no minus, for the defense. The big plus was delivered by Walter, who showed up Saturday afternoon looking pretty satisfied with himself. He plunked himself down on my couch and crossed his legs, revealing yellow wool socks and an ankle holster.

"I found 'em," he said

"Where?"

"Florida. Daytona Beach."

"How?"

"We got mutual acquaintances." That could mean a lot of things: a contact at a bank, the telephone company, the mailman, or stuff I didn't even want to imagine.

"So, they agreed to talk to you?"

He grinned. "Who's the most charmin' guy you know?"

"Definitely you. So?"

"Good and bad."

"I was hoping for all good."

"Yeah, and I was hopin' to find Sophia Loren in the bathtub when I got home." He settled on the sofa and took out his notebook, flipping the pages with one hand while he fished a toothpick out of his shirt pocket with the other. "I think we can deal with the prints," he said. "The old lady says that he showed her the gun; so does the husband. He also showed it to two visitors. They say he seemed pretty proud of it."

"Did any of them get to touch it?"

"Mr. Ward did and so did the visitors. I got their names."

"I take it that the Wards didn't see him show it to our client."

"Hey, there's luck and there's freakin' miracles. This ain't bad, though."

"Okay. Give me the bad."

"The argument was about a week and a half before she did the deed. They both heard it, or part of it. First, all they could hear was arguing behind closed doors in the parlor." He looked up from his notes. "I remember that from old movies. What the hell's the difference between a living room and a parlor?"

"Money."

"Oh. Well, they couldn't make out what they were arguin' about until our client threw open the door and stormed out. They heard the last thing she said real good."

"Don't keep me in suspense."

"They quoted it to me so I'll quote it to you." He read from his notes: "'Stay away. If something happens, I'll kill you. I will.'"

"That was less than two weeks before?"

"That's what they say."

"And they told all this to the cops?"

"They're good citizens."

I did the figuring. "Her father died on October twenty-sixth. Garvey was killed on November first. That means that the argument occurred only a few days before her father died. I was hoping it was farther back; the farther the better." The argument was a clear link between the two deaths. If the government found another one it would be trouble.

"Yeah," Walter agreed. He went back to his notes. "Garvey's stars musta' been crossed or somethin' 'cause the fight with the client wasn't his only bout before he died."

I came out of my trance. "What?"

"The fight with the client wasn't his only bout."

"I'm listening."

"They was walkin' home from the supermarket. They do the weekly shopping on Wednesdays and—you know somethin'? They use one of them pull carts just like people do in New York. I ain't seen one of them things since I got down here. Nobody walks in this freakin' city. If they ain't in the BMW they're joggin' around in them hundred-dollar sneakers."

"Are you going to make me beat it out of you?"

"All right, all right. Anyway, they're about two houses away from home and the front door flies open. This guy comes out, whirls around, and says somethin' to Garvey, who's standin' in the doorway. Then he turns around and spots this fancy pumpkin that Mr. Ward carved for Halloween. He takes one step and kicks a goddamn field goal. I mean there's pumpkin all over the place. Pissed off Mr. Ward real good. Then the guy hurries down the street, climbs into—get this—a freakin' Rolls-Royce with the steerin' wheel on the right side, and drives off real fast."

"When was this?"

"The day before Halloween. Mr. Ward had to buy another pumpkin to carve right away."

"That's two days before she shot Raymond. Who was he?"

"They don't know. He was a distinguished-looking guy with a mustache and gray hair. Never saw him before, and the boss didn't say nothin' about it, either."

"Now tell me they saw him lurking around the night of the murder."

"Nope. That's it. They never saw him again."

"Do you think there's a connection to Garvey hounding her father?"

"Did you ever know a cop who believed in coincidence?"

The man, whoever he was, could have been another link between the two deaths. It made me queasy. "Do the cops know about Mr. Rolls-Royce?"

"Never came up. The Wards didn't think it mattered."

"So they don't think there's a connection?"

"If they do they didn't say so, and I sure as shit wasn't gonna prompt 'em."

"Let's hope it stays that way." The contest to come was taking shape; we were starting to fill in some blanks. "If he showed the gun to other people there's a good chance he showed it to her, right? We'll get that out of the Wards on cross-exam and then we'll call the people who held the gun on our side of the case. That will give us at least three or four opportunities to create some doubt on the fingerprint issue."

Walter nodded. "Sounds good to me."

"All right. So, she had an argument with the deceased but it was more than a week before the murder—plenty of time to cool down. That means the motive evidence isn't a walkover, but it's not overwhelming, either. If we can get a draw with the eyewitness we've got a reasonable shot at creating some doubt. Things could be worse."

"Yeah," he agreed. "It's all in the way you look at it."

\* \* \*

One of the things Walter had preached when I was starting out was that you always visited the scene of the crime—always. The prosecution had a head start, having done its inspection within hours of the offense, but we had its report and we had the only person in the world who could describe what actually happened. I arranged our opportunity for the following Monday and a cop from the local precinct met us with a set of keys for the regular locks and the special one installed by the police.

Garvey's house had its charms. It was the westerly of the two mirror-image villas connected by a common wall. The arched front door opened to a marble-tiled foyer and a long hallway that extended to the back of the house. All the rooms were on the west side of the hall, opposite the common wall. The front room was the parlor where she and Garvey had argued. Farther back was the front staircase and just beyond it, the first of two hallway entrances to the sitting room where he died. It was a comfortable room furnished in a traditional masculine style, all leather and wood and paintings of ships, with an antique sea chest in the center that served as a coffee table. On one side was a rolltop desk and a swivel chair; on the other, a small fireplace with a wing chair and ottoman. Directly opposite were French doors leading to the garden and a flagstone patio with a wrought iron table and chairs. Ashley had entered there. Immediately to the right of the doors was the secretary where Raymond had kept the gun.

Walter surveyed the room then walked over to the desk and began peering into pigeon holes and drawers. "What are you looking for?" I asked.

"I don't know," he replied.

Ask a silly question. I turned around and saw Ashley standing by the wing chair, staring at the rug. As I walked over, the chalk lines came into view: Raymond Garvey's next-to-last resting place. I led her away to the sofa and went back for a closer look. Walter had examined the coroner's report and said that Garvey was dead before he fell. The outline showed that he had landed on his back, his legs in a figure "4" and his arms opened wide to embrace his fate. I had seen a lot of dead men but there was something peculiarly unsettling about reducing a man, body and soul, to a line on a rug. Ashes to ashes, dust to chalk dust: the alchemy of homicide.

Walter quit the search for whatever and sat down with Ashley on the sofa, going over in detail what she had generally described to me in our first meeting.

"Was there any lights on when you approached the house?" he asked.

"No. The house was dark."

"But you knew he was home?"

"I thought he was out. I called the house and there was no answer."

She hadn't told me that. I went over and sat on the other side of her as Walter continued, nodding and gently probing as he had done thousands of times before. "Why did you call?" he asked.

She stared at the floor a moment and said, "I'm not really sure. I was thinking about my father and what had happened. The phone was there and the next thing I knew, I was dialing his number."

"And there was no answer."

"No."

"So you decided . . ." Walter paused, leading her on.

"To go to his house. I showed Frank the way I came." She looked at me and I nodded agreement.

"Ashley, what were you thinking when you left your house?" I asked.

"Thinking?" She took a deep breath before she replied. "I wasn't really thinking so much as feeling. I was angry and I wanted to confront him—right then, as soon as I could. Can you understand that?"

Walter spoke before I could sympathize. "The house was dark and you had a key."

"Yes. I came in through there." She pointed at the French

doors leading to the garden, then turned to me and added, "I told this to you."

"You did," I assured her. It made me nervous when a witness began to grasp at straws for corroboration.

"We just need to get the full picture," soothed Walter. "You never know what can be important to a defense."

"That's right," I agreed.

She looked at me and I could see the reflection of my smile in those tungsten mirrors. "Of course," she said.

"The house was dark," Walter began again, "and you didn't think he was home."

"That's right."

"And you came in through there because—?"

She stared at the doors, then said, "I didn't want to use the front door. I didn't want to be seen."

"Go on."

"I got the gun out of the secretary." She stopped again.

"You were going to wait for him," said Walter, helpfully.

"Yes, but . . ." Her eyes began to tear up.

"It's okay, Ashley," I said quietly. "But what?"

"I'm not sure what I was thinking. I've thought about it a thousand times since that night and"—she shook her head— "I'm still not sure what I intended at that moment. I know it sounds terribly contrived but I really think I meant to frighten him, to make him . . ."

"What?"

"To make him beg for forgiveness!" she cried, and then buried her face in her hands. I started to reach for her but the expression on Walter's face said he would have broken my arm so I just passed her my handkerchief and left to do a little reconstruction of my own. I went back into the hall and turned left toward the rear of the house, past a formal dining room and a butler's pantry and through a door that led to the kitchen and a back staircase to the upstairs floors. I figured that if the house was dark, Garvey must have been upstairs. Ashley thought no one was home and she wasn't concerned about making noise. Garvey died near the second entrance to the study so he must have come down the back staircase, and if he didn't turn on any lights he may have been sneaking down for his gun, unaware that it was already in use. I went back into the hallway, following the route he had taken to his fate.

"Hold it. Stand there." Walter was near the French doors, extending a palm toward me. I stopped right next to the chalk outline and he beckoned her from the sofa. "Show me," he said, as he opened the doors. She went outside and he closed them behind her. She stood there for a moment looking at us through the glass, then opened the doors, stepped inside, and closed them again. They didn't squeak.

With Walter nodding encouragement she took two steps to the secretary, opened a drawer, and reached in for the imaginary gun. "Go ahead," he said. Ashley stepped toward the center of the room with her right arm extended downward as if carrying the weapon, then stopped. She was staring at me. "What's happening now?" he asked.

"There's a lot of thunder and lightning," she replied woodenly. "There's just enough light to make out the darker silhouettes of the furniture."

"Okay," he said. "The room is dark. Now what?"

Her eyes were locked on mine, her voice flat and the words deliberate. "There was a flash of lightning—just an instant—and he's there, then he's a darker form like the furniture but moving into the room. He starts to turn toward me and . . . I'm so scared."

"Go on," Walter urged softly, leaning close. "He's right there." She raised her right arm, her forefinger aimed at my face, and there it was: the last image Raymond Garvey ever saw, a silhouette against a window. She was in a trance; her eyes were opaque, unfocused, but she could see him standing in front of her. Her forefinger began to close on the trigger. I could feel the sweat under my arms.

The telephone rang.

Everyone flinched. Ashley staggered but Walter grabbed her and held her upright. The phone rang again. It was sitting in the rolltop, echoing off the wood enclosure and throughout the empty house, sounding incredibly loud. After three rings there was a loud click. "Hello," said the voice, "this is Raymond Garvey. I'm afraid I can't come to the telephone right now." Ashley was starting to sink; Walter was half-carrying her to the sofa. "Please leave your message at the tone and I'll call you as soon as I can."

I started over to help when someone called my name. "Frank? Walter? It's Andy. Anybody there?" I rushed to the desk and grabbed the receiver.

"Andy? What is it?"

"Frank! I didn't know if the phone was still hooked up. Rogavin's office called. They're turning over the eyewitness's statement! We can pick it up right now!"

"Jesus! Did Warner change his mind?"

"No, they're giving it voluntarily!" cried Andy. "I'm going over before they change *their* minds!"

Ashley was back on the couch, leaning against Walter. "Rogavin is turning over the eyewitness statement," I told them.

Walter raised his eyebrows. "What the hell? . . . Three days ago he fought to keep us from gettin' it!"

"He's had a change of heart—I'll find out why later. Andy's going over there right now."

Walter smiled broadly; there was detective work to be done. "Let's wait over at her place," he said, nodding at our client, who was about the shade of the chalk on the rug. "It'll be dark in a few hours and we can do some re-creation." Ashley probably had had all the re-creation she could handle for one day but she nodded silently in agreement. I told Andy to meet us there.

"Let's finish this up," I said. I went over and crouched in front of her. "A few more questions and we're done, okay?"

"I'm sorry," she gasped. "I just didn't expect . . . that."

"It's okay. Tell us what happened after you fired the gun."

She closed her eyes for a moment. "I dropped it and went out the door. I went across the patio to the hedge and along the hedge to the sidewalk. Then I waited for a minute or two."

"Why?" asked Walter.

"I waited to see if anyone was coming, then I walked home."

"And it was still raining?"

She was looking more tired by the minute. "Yes."

I looked at Walter. "Satisfied?"

"Just a couple of things, Miss," he said. "You said it was raining. What did you use to cover your head?" I had never asked her; that's why he was the detective.

"A hat."

"Where is it?"

"The police took it with my raincoat."

"Did you ever fire a gun before that night?"

"Never."

"How many shots did you fire that night, Miss?"

She looked surprised by that one. "Just one. And please call me Ashley."

"Sure," he said. There was about as much chance of that as Garvey returning a phone call. He glanced at me and shrugged. "Well, let's see how things look after we get the witness's location."

Thirty minutes later Ashley was back in her bedroom, recuperating from her encounter with Raymond's answering machine while we waited in the kitchen for Andy. Walter was having coffee and a buttered roll while he read his newspaper. The newspaper was his bible. He read it—studied it—every day. Years ago I had asked him about it. "I didn't get past high school," he explained, "and I didn't learn much there, either, so the newspaper is my college. If you read it, everything in it, you learn a hell of a lot about what matters in this life, especially to a detective. Besides, a lot of it is interestin' by itself."

I was too preoccupied to look at the newspaper and I had no appetite, so I stared at the copper pots and alternately worried about the last hour and the next one. Finally, I couldn't take it anymore. "Why don't you just get it off your chest?" I snapped.

"What?" he replied, not looking up.

"Don't bullshit me."

"I'm readin' the paper here."

"You're thinking," I said accusingly.

He turned a page. "What am I thinking?"

"You're wondering about her story. She says she wanted to confront him but she goes over while he's supposed to be out, uses the side door not to be seen, and gets out the gun. So, why doesn't she just admit she went to kill him, right? Well, what's so hard to understand? She's upset, crazy with hate. She wants him dead, sure, but that's not what she's about. She goes in, she grabs the gun. If he doesn't surprise the shit out of her, she waves the thing in his face until he pleads for mercy and nobody dies."

"Okay," he said, still reading.

"Okay?"

"People do crazy things."

"That's right," I agreed. "Crazy." A few minutes passed while the only sound was turning pages. "I'm still waiting," I said, fuming.

He sighed and folded the paper. "A man's in his house alone and it's dark. What's he wearin'?"

"This is a riddle? Okay—bermuda shorts." He frowned at me. "A tuxedo?"

"Listen, when you're in that dump of yours and the lights are out, what're *you* wearin'?"

"If you read *Washingtonian* you'd know I sleep in the buff."

"Right—you're sleepin'. The pictures show Garvey was dressed."

I thought about that. "Well, a house can still look dark

when there's a light on somewhere, or maybe he nodded off reading the paper. He's upstairs and hears something, comes down the back staircase to the study, and bang."

"Okay, bang. How far apart would you say they was when she shot him?"

"I was next to the chalk. If she was standing where she indicated, I'd say about twenty feet."

"A thirty-eight at twenty feet, in a dark room, and she never fired a gun before. If you could get ten scared women to shoot at a guy under them conditions, how many dead guys would you have?"

"She hit him in the head. It happens."

The doorbell rang. Martha's footsteps echoed in the hall-way and a moment later Andy entered, his face registering nothing. "I've got it," he announced. He placed a briefcase on the table then started fishing in his pocket. Ashley appeared a few seconds later, and though he had seen her before, Andy couldn't help staring.

"What are you doing?" I asked.

"Huh?"

"What're you looking for?" I gestured toward his pocket.

"Oh. I need the key to open it," he explained. I didn't know anyone who locked his briefcase. I didn't know any-one who actually kept those little keys. He finally got the thing open and placed a manila envelope on the table. The label said, STATEMENT OF MILES KELLOGG.

"Does that name mean anything to anybody?" I asked.

"Not unless he makes cereal," Andy answered. "I called Cory and told her to run a computer check on his name, though. She's going to call if she gets a hit."

The envelope was still sealed. "You didn't open it?" I asked.

"It's addressed to you," he replied, surprised. I slit the en-velope open and emptied the contents on the table. The statement was a three-page Metropolitan Police Department report of an interview with Mr. Miles Kellogg of 3087 Avon

Street, N.W., Washington, D.C. Suddenly, it was clear why Walter hadn't found him: Kellogg's house was blocks from Garvey's and Ashley's and not on the route between them. There was a folded diagram attached to the statement. I spread it open on the table and everyone leaned forward for a better look.

I don't think I felt anything for a moment, sort of like a fighter taking a knockout punch: first you're stunned, then comes the pain, then you fall. There was a drawing of a street, a sidewalk, and a house, with a few details thrown in. Near the sidewalk was a circle with an AB inside it. Near the curb, about twenty feet away, was another circle with a K. Rogavin had said he could place her "near" the scene; he just didn't say how near. The address printed on the house was Garvey's and the circled "AB" was right where she had waited before stepping onto the sidewalk. I hadn't noticed a light when Ashley and I walked by that first night, but I'd seen one just an hour earlier, an old-fashioned lamppost abutting Garvey's walkway.

It was Walter who spoke first. "Christ," he muttered.

"Ashley, was that lamp lit that night?" I asked.

She didn't look up from the diagram. "It must have been. It always was."

"And you didn't notice anyone where the "K" is on the diagram?"

"I've told you, no," she replied. "I just wanted to get away. He might have been there and I just didn't see him." I took the staple out of the report and spread it on the table. The paper stuck to the moisture on my hands.

Interview with Mr. Miles Kellogg
by Dets. Powers and Mathis

The witness was contacted at his home at 3087 Avon Street, N.W., Washington, D.C. He is a w/m, approximately 60–65 years old. He lives alone at the above

address. He states that he is a widower and is retired
from government service. The undersigned advised
the witness that MPD had been informed he had information about the Raymond Garvey homicide. The
witness confirmed that he had called the third district
the previous night, and had no objection to being
interviewed.

The witness stated that on the evening of November 1 he went alone to a movie at the Biograph Theater
on M Street in Georgetown. The movie's name was
*Strangers on a Train*. He said he often goes to this theater because it shows old classic movies. He attended
the 8:15 P.M. showing, which ended approximately
10:00 P.M. When he got outside it was raining. The
witness stated that he began walking toward home. He
was wearing a trench coat, hat, galoshes, and carrying
an umbrella.

The witness stated that when he left the vicinity of
M Street there were very few people on the street and
little traffic. The walk home usually takes about
twenty minutes. He went north on 28th Street, and at
about 10:15 he was crossing Q Street in the middle of
the block from the south side to the north, heading toward 29th Street. He said he could not hear very much
because of the sound of the rain on his umbrella. As he
reached the north side of the street he saw movement
to his left which surprised him. He states that there
was a w/f standing on the grass near the sidewalk
about fifteen to twenty feet away. He returned to the
spot yesterday and confirms the address of the house
as 2871 Q Street, N.W. (This is the address of the deceased.)

The lamp on the front lawn was on. He states that
he could see the w/f's face clearly. The witness described her as 30–35 years old, wearing a raincoat and
hat. The w/f was standing still and did not appear to

see the witness, who was standing between parked cars. The witness said that he did not move because he did not want to frighten the w/f and because he was curious. The w/f appeared to be familiar to the witness and he was sure he had seen her before, but he could not then recall who she was.

The witness said that the w/f seemed to be waiting for something. After a minute, she proceeded west on Q Street walking rapidly. The witness states he continued on to his home and arrived there at approximately 10:30. The witness did not suspect that anything was wrong.

The following morning the witness departed his home alone at approximately 6:00 A.M. and drove his p.o.v. to his vacation home near Berkeley Springs, West Virginia. He arrived there approximately 9:00 A.M. The house has no television and he does not listen to the radio. The witness does not receive any newspapers at that address and did not learn of the Garvey homicide while there.

The witness returned to his home yesterday, Tuesday, November 5, at approximately 10:30 P.M. At approximately 11:00 P.M. he was in the kitchen making a sandwich. The television was tuned to the Channel 9 news but he could not hear the sound. The witness was passing the entrance to the living room when he looked at the television and saw a picture of a w/f on the screen. He immediately recognized her as the person he had seen on the night in question. The witness says there was nothing shown on the screen that gave the w/f's name or referred to Garvey or the homicide. He hurried into the room and learned that the person was Ashley Bronson, and that she had been arrested by MPD detectives in connection with the Garvey case. The witness does not recall seeing her in person before. The witness then got his newspapers, which had been collected by a neighbor while he was away. The neighbor is Randall Kitchens, 3092 Avon Place, N.W. After reading the stories about the case, the witness then walked to the deceased's home to confirm that it was the place where he saw the w/f.

The witness returned home and called the MPD at 12:15 A.M. this morning and this interview was arranged. The witness appears to be in good health with no obvious condition that would prevent him from making an identification.

The telephone rang; it was Cory for me. "Frank," she said urgently, "I just got off the computer. Miles Kellogg had several mentions in the papers a few years ago during the Iran-Contra investigation. He testified for the government in a couple of the cases."

"In what capacity?"

"Well, he was supposedly a witness for the prosecution but he really helped the defense more."

"Cut to the chase."

"Kellogg was a CIA agent. He was at headquarters when Congress was conducting hearings on support for the Contras and got involved in answering Congressional inquiries. Before the headquarters job he was in the field, and described his assignments in court using a code to protect national security. He was in 'country A' working on 'program C' and stuff like that. He retired about a year before he testified."

My heart sank. Everyone was looking at me and I didn't keep them in suspense. "Kellogg's government service was with the CIA. He's a former field agent." Andy grimaced; Walter's toothpick went up, then down. Ashley's eyes were on me and for the first time I could see resignation. "Anything else?" I asked Cory.

"That's it for now," she said. "I'm still checking."

It was quiet when I hung up the phone. Andy was watching me closely, trying to gauge my reaction to the news. "What happens now?" he asked.

"Well, we'll deal with it," I said, trying to sound matter-of-fact. "First, we've got to get another look at the scene."

"We'll need the lamp on," Andy said. "I'll call Rogavin's office and see if they'll send a cop back with the keys."

"That's not necessary," I told him. I looked at Walter. "The lamp was on when we left, remember? The cop must have turned it on by mistake."

Walter nodded his understanding. "When do you want to go over?"

"After the neighbors get home from work and settle in. Maybe you should go over first and call us when the coast is clear."

"Want company?" Andy asked him.

Andy couldn't be around when Walter went back to Garvey's. "You've got work to do at the office," I told him. "I want you to arrange to get copies of the tapes of the newscasts from the night that Ashley was questioned."

"But there's probably no one around this late," he protested. "I can do it first thing in the morning."

"Try anyway!" I snapped. Andy recoiled; Ashley touched my arm. I took a deep breath and tried to regain my composure while everyone else looked at the floor. "Andy," I said quietly, "the station will cooperate if you hold out the possibility of a little tit for tat. Tell them we'll be grateful for any assistance. And try to get a copy of the photo they used that night."

Andy nodded. "I'll get all the stations, just in case he changed channels."

"Good thinking. Start getting everything on Kellogg. There's been several books published about Iran-Contra that might have more background on him. The Government Printing Office probably has an official version of the hearings, too. And get the names of the *Post* and *New York Times* reporters who were covering the story. We may have to talk to them at some point."

"Okay," Andy said quietly, "is that it?"

"Tell Cory to keep Kellogg's name to herself. If it gets in the papers Warner will want to hang someone and it won't be Rogavin."

"C'mon, counselor," Walter said, clapping him on the shoulder, "I'll give you a lift to the office." They went off to their respective chores. Martha retired to her quarters, leaving Ashley and me alone in the kitchen.

"Walter won't get in trouble, will he?" she asked. She didn't miss much.

"We can't call the cops to turn the light on. Having one of them around tonight might give Rogavin an idea."

"What kind of idea?"

"A demonstration for the jury: bringing them to the scene to look at you under the lamplight. It isn't done often but judges will sometimes permit the unusual or dramatic. If Warner ordered one and the jurors thought they'd recognize you, we'd be sunk." I folded the witness statement and stuck it back inside the envelope. "Why don't you go upstairs and rest a bit?" I suggested. "I'll come get you when Walter calls."

We drove past Garvey's house at eight-fifteen. The lamp was on, looking only slightly brighter than your average lighthouse. Walter was sitting in his car down the street, and when we pulled in on the opposite side he got out and walked past the house while we waited. The street was quiet and curtains were drawn across the windows of the neighboring houses. He signaled and we got out. Ashley had on a wide-brimmed hat and a trench coat similar to what she wore that night.

"We're not going to stay long," I told her as we walked toward the house. "I'll stop where Kellogg stood and you go right to the spot where you waited at the hedge. Stand as you stood that night. Every few seconds look over at me. If someone comes out of a house or is walking up the street, just start walking in the opposite direction." She nodded. "Your collar is down. Did you have it up that night?"

"I don't remember."

"Let's try it both ways."

Walter approached from the other direction. I stopped and she walked past Walter and up to the hedge, where she stepped onto the lawn and turned around. The lamp was low and the hat made very little shadow when the light fell on her face.

Subjectivity is a bitch. I didn't want to recognize her so I was inclined to imagine difficulty. On the other hand, I could tell it was her. Did I know because I could recognize her, or did I recognize her because I knew? The more I looked, the worse it got. Could I pick her out of a lineup? I tried to imagine another woman standing next to her, someone beautiful about her size and age, so I imagined Moira.

Go ahead, pick.

Walter was standing beside me and staring hard. "What do you think?" I asked.

"Maybe, maybe not." I signaled to her and she put up her collar. "That's a help," he said. "That makes it harder." We tried it a few more times, with slight alterations. She had to be anxious as hell but she didn't show it as she put the collar up and down and turned this way and that. Finally, he said, "There's no point anymore. We've been starin' at her for five minutes."

I motioned to Ashley and we walked quickly back to the car and got in. She didn't say anything as we drove away but I could feel her eyes on me all the way back to the house. "I'm not sure," I said finally. "It's hard to be objective." I parked in the driveway and we were climbing the steps when Walter pulled to the curb and waved. I told her I'd be along, then went to his car and climbed into the passenger's seat. "What's on your mind?" I asked.

"Alibis," he replied.

"*Alibis?* That's not really our defense but right now I'm open to anything."

He stuck a toothpick in the corner of his mouth and said, "Do you remember that guy on Central Park West who did his wife with a claw hammer?"

"Yeah. What was his name?"

"Arthur Tilden."

"Right. Tilden. Do you like him for Garvey's murder? It might be a tough sell because he's been in Attica for twelve years."

He ignored me. "Remember where he said he was when the wife got killed?"

"No."

"Yeah, you do. It was a real pain in the ass."

"I'm cold, I'm tired, and I'm a little stressed. Get to the point."

"He said he was at the movies." He looked at me like a light should be going on in my head but it was still dark, which irritated me even more.

"I get it," I said. "We point the finger at Kellogg. I like that better because he's not in Attica."

He tapped my chest to make his point. "Listen. A guy goes to dinner or shopping or for a nightcap and you can check it out. There's got to be a waiter or a bartender or a salesgirl and a receipt, not to mention your customers and your shoppers. But a guy goes to a movie, who's to say otherwise?"

"What are you getting at?"

"A guy lives in Georgetown with a TV and a radio and newspapers and neighbors. Somebody gets murdered a few blocks away, he's gonna know, and if he knows somethin' he's gonna come forward or have a damn good reason why he didn't. Can you think of one?"

"He's out of town and cut off from communication?"

"Yeah. Can you think of another?"

I worked at it. "Aside from a coma that's about it."

"Right. A story like Kellogg's, all you can check out is his movements and why he didn't come forward, and he's got both of 'em covered real good."

"So?"

"So, maybe he really wasn't there."

"Not there? That's interesting. That's very interesting. Now, I've got a riddle for *you*. How many people know exactly what the client did after she made a hole in Raymond—I mean, besides her, you and me?"

"Kellogg."

"Bingo. And you and I didn't tell anyone else. Do you think she did?"

"No."

"That would seem to take care of the idea that he wasn't there. By the way, Bradmoor has become useless. Nobody's going to be interested in his story once the CIA agent gets through—it's no contest. As for the delayed report to the police, there's a Mr. Kitchens who says that he collected the newspapers while Kellogg was gone."

"Yeah."

"So?"

"It's too neat."

"Jesus! We're five weeks from trial, don't go squirrelly on me! A woman confesses to murder; the accusing witness tells the same story. What the hell do you want?"

"It's too neat," he insisted.

"Then go out and make a mess!"

\* \* \*

I followed Martha to a cozy sitting room with opposing chintz love seats on either side of a small marble fireplace. Ashley was on one of them, staring at the fire. I sat down and watched her out of the corner of my eye. She didn't acknowledge my presence until she leaned over and rested her head on my shoulder. I could smell her hair. "Do you know where my favorite place is?" she asked quietly.

"Where?"

"The garden outside this house. In the spring, when the dogwoods and azaleas bloom, you can sit on the bench and feel like you're in the middle of a box of crayons."

"That sounds wonderful."

"I was thinking: when the garden blooms again the trial will be over."

"That's right. And you'll be here to see it."

She seemed unconvinced. "You looked worried in the kitchen tonight." She turned to look at me. "You look worried right now."

"That's what lawyers do—worry about cases."

"Do you worry about all your cases?"

"Some more than others."

She tilted her head back. Her face was only inches from mine. "And this one?" she said softly.

I felt my stomach contracting again and remembered Walter's warning. One step down that path and there'd be no turning back. "There's something I want to ask you," I said.

"Anything." She smiled, her eyes luminous.

"You said that you just intended to frighten Garvey."

She blinked, then her smile faded. "That's right," she said tonelessly.

"In the office you told me that you're not sorry about killing him. So . . . I was just wondering about that."

She looked at me for a long moment before she replied. "I'm not . . . and I am. Can you understand?"

"I think so."

"I'm tired," she said, sitting up.

"Ashley." I reached for her hand and she leaned back again, putting her other hand on mine. I immediately regretted it; I knew how stupid I was going to sound even before I opened my mouth. "We're going to find a way out of this," I told her. "I promise."

"I know." She smiled again but the light in her eyes was gone.

Driving home I tried to convince myself that I'd done the right thing: she was vulnerable; by tomorrow she'd realize the mistake we could have made. But who started it? I'll be there day and night, I said. It won't be business, I said. Her middle-aged savior, flirting like a college sophomore.

As foolish as I felt, the professional concerns soon overwhelmed the personal. The case against Ashley Bronson had taken a bad turn. *In summation, ladies and gentlemen, the defendant was seen by a reliable witness leaving the home of the victim, a moment after the fatal shot was fired from a gun with her fingerprints, and shortly after she threatened to kill him.*

Like Walter said: it was all in the way you looked at it.

# 8

We were determined to find out all we could about Miles Kellogg, eyewitness: background, education, career, and retirement; income, assets, and liabilities; friends, relatives, associates, and enemies; places he visited, frequented, and shopped; his passions, habits, hobbies, and vices; and whether he owned any pets. Did he lie under oath during the Iran-Contra hearings? Did he ever cross paths with Garvey? Did they know him at the box office at the Biograph?

It was a big job so Walter decided to add another investigator, Harry Lerner, a former detective sergeant who had mentored him in the Bronx. I wasn't stoic about the choice.

"Why *him*?" I whined.

"Why not?" He sniffed. "We needed another dick. Besides, the case is gettin' funny and you never know."

Precisely. In his salad days he was "Harry the Horse," and as Walter could tell you, "a legend from one end of Fordham Road to the other." Deservedly so. One of the toughest things a cop ever had to do was arrest a man surrounded by his friends in a barroom. The combination of alcohol, testosterone, and peer pressure could turn an ordinary guy into King Kong, and a crowd into a mob. More than one cop had been beaten senseless—or worse—in a "working man's bar." But Harry's reputation preceded him. He'd saunter in, throw a pair of handcuffs on the bar, and tell the collar that he had two minutes to finish his drink and come out—wearing the cuffs. As he would leave he would simply say, "I'll be waitin' in the car. Don't make me come back in to get ya."

Every tavern in the Bronx knew about the time Harry had to come back in. He was carrying a shotgun. The grand jury eventually declined to indict but the Citizens' Complaint Review Board wanted his badge real bad. Fortunately for Harry, everyone involved was white. Without racial overtones there was no constituency to keep the thing on full boil, and when it finally cooled down it became a department matter. He took a three-month suspension and came back a legend.

"I get two hunnert a day, plus the expenses," he announced in an accent that made Walter's sound positively Shakespearean. "And"—he grinned—"I wanna meet the filly."

Funny case or no, the addition of Harry to the team made me nervous. "I draw the line at our little burglary the other night," I told Walter. "Keep a leash on him."

With our expanded team concentrating on Kellogg I tried to keep my mind on other tasks, but worry sapped my concentration and I was feeling anything but bullish on Wednesday morning when I got a call from my favorite prosecutor. "I presume you got my little present," he said.

"I got it. You fought disclosure so why the change of heart?"

"Tomorrow's Thanksgiving. Be thankful."

"Sure. I'll think of you when I carve the turkey."

"Good, you haven't lost your sense of humor. Bring it to our meeting."

"What are we going to meet about?"

"I think the case has . . . *evolved* since our first encounter. It might be useful to exchange views."

I'd bet the view was a lot better from his side. "Okay, when?"

"How about Friday? Say, nine o'clock?" The voice was almost cordial.

"Nine o'clock. Uh . . . you won't be late, will you?" He hung up; cordiality has its limits.

I spent most of Thanksgiving in my apartment, then went to a diner with four customers and a television showing motorcycles flying over big piles of dirt. Afterward, I wandered over to the office to sit at my desk and fret about the eyewitness. Was he legitimate? The forces of logic were arrayed against the Feinberg instincts, but either way Kellogg was a dagger in the heart of the defense. Anxiety finally impelled me to motion so I left the office to keep the streets safe for night-shifters and insomniacs. I toured the Capitol grounds at midnight, the Lincoln Memorial at first light, and greeted the sunrise on Key Bridge. I still hadn't had any sleep when I showed up at Rogavin's office.

He smiled from across his desk. "You're looking a little peaked. Getting enough rest, I trust?"

"I've been partying a lot. I do that when I'm feeling invincible."

The *U.S. v. Bronson* file lay between us. The case *had* evolved: it was now three accordion envelopes, the fruits of the labor of all the police officers, scientists, and junior prosecutors working to send Ashley to prison. "I do hope you found a little time to study Mr. Kellogg's statement," he said.

"I read it."

"Good. I wanted to see if your position had changed."

"Why would it change?"

He affected a bemused expression: the professor coping with a dim-witted student. "Because you now know"—he held up one finger—"we have a *very* credible witness who saw your client"—two fingers—"at *close* range"—three fingers—"standing on the deceased's property at the time of the murder."

I shrugged. "No, I don't. What I know is you've got someone who *says* she was there. But she wasn't, so that raises some questions."

He sighed. "Such as?"

I held up one finger. "He sees someone by lamplight twenty feet away"—two fingers—"on a dark, rainy night"—

three fingers—"and picks her out *from a TV screen across a room*"—four fingers—"four days later? Maybe he's credible, but then again, maybe his last sighting was Elvis at the Kmart."

"He's a former CIA agent."

"Is that supposed to be a plus or a minus? Anyway, there's got be something wrong because she didn't do it. She's got no motive."

He pulled at his lip. "I told you: she blamed Garvey for her father's death."

"Yeah, that's your *theory.* Her father's death was a real blow but she didn't blame anyone because there was no one to blame."

"Maybe not. But if there's a connection, we'll find it."

"Let me know when you do."

"By then it will be too late."

"I thought it was already too late. Your plea offer was good until indictment."

"Let's say the sale has been extended."

"Really? First, you turn over Kellogg's statement, now this. What's going on?"

"It's not very complicated. Our United States Attorney is a political appointee and this is a small town with a long memory. Princess has a lot of important friends who haven't abandoned her—yet. As I said, be thankful."

"So, what's the offer?"

"Same deal. The government stands mute while Miss Bronson tells her tale of woe—virtuous woman driven to extraordinary lengths, blah, blah, blah. That crap plays well these days." He made a lazy turn in his chair and leaned back until his tasseled loafers perched on the desk. "Anyway, said friends write lots of letters and buttonhole the good judge at Christmas parties. Who knows? She could get very lucky. Time of the season and all that."

"Very generous. We'll get back to you."

"Please do. Nothing lasts forever."

*  *  *

Things didn't get better when Walter showed up the following Monday.

"So," I asked, "what about Kellogg?"

"Solid citizen."

"That's not what I wanted to hear."

"Widower. No kids. Sister in Saint Louis. Registered independent. Pays all his bills on time, no big debts. Decent stock portfolio but not out of line for a career government servant. Subscribes to the *New York Times*, *The Economist*, and *National Geographic*—no *Playboy* or *Hustler*. Eats out two, three nights a week; two glasses of wine. Tips fifteen percent."

"Fifteen? We'll crucify him."

"Plays bridge Wednesday nights with the neighbors. Collects classical records that he buys from a specialty shop in New York that caters to . . . audiophillies."

"Audiophiles."

"Whatever. Buys his suits from Brooks Brothers and casuals from L.L. Bean. Doesn't spend much with either one. Shops for food at the Safeway on Wisconsin Avenue, healthy heart diet. No golf, tennis, or jogging, but in decent shape. Wears glasses for reading. Has a prescription for high cholesterol.

"I know this is gonna get better."

"Spends a lot of weekends hiking trails around a cabin in West Virginia he bought in nineteen seventy-one for thirty-one thousand. He got gas in an Exxon station in Berkeley Springs on Saturday, November second, and made a telephone call from the cabin at eleven thirty-five that morning to the neighbor, Mr. Kitchens. There was also a call from there to the sister on Monday. The cabin has a stereo with a radio but no television. There's no newspaper delivery except for a weekly county rag and it had nothin' on Garvey."

"What about the Biograph?"

"It was showin' *Strangers on a Train* on the night of November first. There was a show at eight-fifteen that let out at ten. The manager says our guy is a regular but can't say one way or another about whether he was there that night. The kid in the box office is lucky to recognize his own mother."

"Go ahead with the good stuff. Don't hold back."

"The route he took past Garvey's ain't the most direct way from the Biograph to his place. It's about two blocks longer and a zigzag course through the neighborhood."

"So? He walks through the neighborhood all the time. He gets bored going the same way."

"It was rainin'."

"He had his raincoat, umbrella, and galoshes."

"It was chilly and rainin'."

"He's the hardy type, a hiker."

"Are you bustin' my balls here?"

"I'm playing devil's advocate."

"Play this," he growled, pointing at his crotch. "Okay, here: first thing he does when he gets to the cabin is call the neighbor, probably to ask him to pick up the newspapers. So, why didn't he leave him a note or ask before he left?"

"He's spontaneous. No wife or kids so he just decided to go."

"This guy never did anything spontaneous in his whole life."

"Maybe, maybe not. Where does it lead?"

He frowned. "Right now, nowhere."

I looked up at the ceiling and exhaled. "Why not concentrate on getting stuff I can impeach him with and stop wasting time checking out his movements before and after the murder? I thought we agreed that he must have seen her—his description of what she did is dead on."

"*You* agreed," he shot back. "*I* didn't agree to nothin'." Before I could reply he held up a palm and said, "Savin' the best for last. He's a member at a video store on Wisconsin

Avenue. Guess what movie he checks out the day after he gets back from the cabin?"

"*Strangers on a Train?*"

"Ta-da!"

"No shit? He's just seen it in a theater on Friday and he rents it on Wednesday. Why?"

"Maybe he didn't see it. Maybe he just wants to be prepared in case he's asked about it."

"Stop it, will you?" I said. "You're giving me a goddamn headache. Look, maybe he didn't go to the movies that night. Maybe he was coming from his mistress's house when he saw the client, so he invented the whole Biograph thing to avoid embarrassment. He saw the client but he lied about where he was coming from—big deal."

"Yeah? Then why does he go off to the mountains?"

"Why? Maybe he has a home there and likes to hike, which is what *you just told me* a minute ago. Who the hell cares why he went off to the mountains? *He was at the cabin!*"

Walter shook his head. "It gives him a perfect cover for not calling the cops till Tuesday. It's too neat."

"Great. We're back to 'too neat.' Can I take a moment here to give you some legal insight into our case? We are exactly twenty-eight days from trial, and right now my cross-examination of the prosecution's chief witness consists entirely of, 'Wasn't it *dark*, Mr. CIA agent? Wasn't it *rainy*, Mr. CIA agent?' Just how far do you think that's going to go?"

"Not far," he muttered.

"You see? You should have gone to law school because without any legal training whatsoever, you have divined the fact that we are *totally fucked*!"

"Maybe we'll get a break," he grumbled. He stood up and buttoned his sport coat, a green plaid number. "You know, you never told me the why."

I sighed. "Revenge. Garvey was responsible for her father's death."

He glared at me. "Wait a minute! The papers said the old man was dead. They didn't say nothin' about how."

"The cover story is complications of a stroke, but it was an overdose of sleeping pills. His doctor knows but thinks it was accidental. The truth is, he committed suicide."

"You're sayin' Garvey drove her old man to kill himself?"

"That's what she says."

"You believe her?" He looked dubious. At that moment it seemed important that he believe her, too.

"Her father's journal backs her up."

He exhaled and sat down heavily, looking wearier by the moment. "What journal?"

I got up and closed the door. "Her father kept a journal. I've got it—the last volume of it anyway."

"She gave it to you?"

"Yes."

"And it says that Garvey made him do it?"

"Just about."

"Christ! The cops get that, she's done. That's your premeditation right there. Murder one."

"I know."

"Why the hell didn't you tell me?"

"It may not be a good thing to know."

He rubbed his jaw. "You holdin' the evidence, is this one of them legal—whatchamacallit—cononums . . . contonon . . . ?"

"Conundrums."

"Yeah. Is it?"

"I suppose."

"What are you goin' to do with it?"

"I'm not sure. Right now, it's the least of my problems."

The rest of the day was a total loss. I spent it rooted to my chair, door closed and taking no calls. We were cornered, and looking back I wondered how I could have been surprised. Rogavin had laid the whole thing out for me that first day but I wasn't listening because I was too busy matching wits and protecting my girl from the government bully.

My new, famous girl. Her news clippings were still bundled on my desk, mementos of a privileged child grown into an extraordinary woman pursued by accomplished men. And at the most critical point in her life, she chose me. Now she was facing twenty years because her lawyer was a little lonely. My eyes wandered to the photograph of *Jezebel* and I had a moment of inspiration: provision a boat and smuggle her out, down the Chesapeake Bay, out to sea, and gone. And I thought I was out of ideas. The reality pressed me deeper into the chair. When all this was over, *I* would escape. I'd use all the money she'd paid me to defend her, but she wouldn't be going anywhere, not while she was still young.

I drifted in and out of sleep. I doodled on a legal pad: a street, a sidewalk, a couple of circles. I dialed the telephone.

"Hello?"

"Hi."

"Hi."

"How's everything?"

"Everything's fine. How about you?"

"Good, good. I thought I'd come by tonight—if it was okay."

"What's wrong?"

"Nothing. I just didn't make it over on the weekend and . . . you know."

"Sure. He'll be excited. He's been asking about you."

"Great. That's great. . . ."

"Tell me what's wrong."

"Nothing. Really."

A pause. "Come at seven. I'll make dinner." When the going gets tough, the tough get going; the rest of us seek refuge. I stalled as long as possible and rang the bell at 6:45.

A moment later I was face-to-face with the former Mrs. O'-Connell. "You didn't get home this early when we were married," she said.

"Earlier than we arranged. I'm sorry."

"It's okay." We brushed cheeks and I had a flashback to the night we made it right there against the door; I didn't even get my coat off. Now we were brushing cheeks. My life was absurd: professionally and personally, I was living it backwards. She led me into the family room and called for Brendan. "Honey, Daddy's here."

Brendan was sprawled on the floor, playing with a board game, but he was up and running at the announcement. "Dad! I got Chinese checkers!" He leaped and I caught him in midflight.

"Hi, bud. How's my big guy?"

"Good. Do you know how to play, Dad?"

"I'm a little rusty. You'll have to show me."

"That's okay. I taught Mom how to play." He began to pull me down toward the game.

Moira whispered, "Think Candyland." I took off my jacket and tie while Brendan prepared the board by moving four colors of marbles into apparently random positions, although experience had taught me that one side was already in deep trouble.

"Okay, bud. How do you play?"

"You try to get your men over here and I try to get my men over there." He didn't explain how this was supposed to happen. I could hear Moira snickering in the kitchen when he told me he'd go first. I had even less success than in Candyland. I thought I had him once, only to be blindsided by an abrupt rules modification, and after a while he grew bored with the lack of serious opposition. "Dad?"

"Yes, bud."

"Do you like pie?"

"Pie? Sure. What kind?"

He thought about it for a moment, his little brow furrowed with the effort. Then he shouted, "Mom!"

From the kitchen: "What is it, honey?"

"What's the pie that I like?"

Silence. Then: "Mincemeat pie, honey."

Brendan smiled broadly. "Mincemeat, Dad. I had mincemeat pie."

"Sure. At Thanksgiving, right?"

"Uh-hum."

"Did Bridey bake a mincemeat pie?"

"Bridey?" His brow furrowed again.

"Did you have mincemeat pie at Grandpa's house?"

He rolled his eyes in exasperation. "No, Dad, at a restaurant."

"A restaurant?"

"With horses! They live right there, Dad! In a . . . the house that horses sleep in."

"A stable?"

"Yeah! A stable! They live at the restaurant!"

"Were there ducks in a pond?"

"Yeah!" He was delighted. "Me and Rob fed the ducks, Dad! Have you been there, too?"

All sound from the kitchen had stopped. The inn with stables and a duck pond was just east of the Shenandoah Park. It was where Moira and I had gone on special occasions, like the weekend the pregnancy test came up blue.

I looked up and she was watching. "Brendan," she said, "it's time for bed." The usual protests were quickly stifled and soon we all paraded upstairs, Moira leading and Brendan riding on my back. I helped him get into his pajamas and supervised the toothbrushing; she handled the debate on the merits of football jerseys as school attire. Then the three of us read a story about a boy who rescued a dragon. I didn't want it to end. When it was time for sleep I tucked him in.

"Dad?"

"What?"

"I like playing games with you."

"Thanks, buddy. Your dad loves you very much, you know that?"

"Yeah." We kissed and then he rolled over and latched onto his favorite space commando, the leader of the plastic army that was occupying the room. It was a wonderful world when all a guy had to worry about was saving the earth from mass destruction. I took an extra moment to take it all in while Moira watched from the door, then we went back downstairs.

Dinner was by candlelight. She had set a place for me at the head of the table, which, under the circumstances, I thought was pretty generous. "I needed this evening," I told her. "Thanks."

"You're welcome. Now tell me what's going on—and don't dodge."

"The case is going down the tubes."

She put down her fork. "What happened?"

"It's not any one thing—the evidence is just piling up."

"Is that surprising?"

I shook my head. "No, that's the hard part. For a while I had this feeling we could win. It wasn't justified, and now we've had a reality check."

"She's going to be convicted?"

"Yeah." I didn't have to tell her this was confidential. Moira was closemouthed about business and personal matters. I'd bet no one had ever heard the story of our breakup— not even Rob.

"What about a plea bargain?"

"We turned it down once. I don't think she'll change her mind."

"Well, don't beat yourself up over it, Frank. I understand she's a very smart woman, and she made her own choice."

"She's smart but she acted on my advice. She believed in me."

"And I'm sure it was the right advice at the time. Pop says that you're canny—that's the word he used—and that he never met a lawyer with better judgment."

"I don't think she got the benefit of it." There was an uncomfortable silence while she stared at me, sifting the contents of my secret compartment.

"She's very beautiful," she said quietly.

"Yes, she is."

"Is that what happened?"

"That was part of it."

She tried to hide it but I could see she was upset, which made me feel at once guilty and elated. "So what happens now?" she asked evenly.

"I have no idea."

"Well, I'm sure you'll think of something."

"Right, I'm canny." Her manner had changed. I didn't want to talk about the case anymore but all the things we used to discuss, the strategies and tactics of a family making its way in suburban life in the nineties, were pretty much foreclosed. What we had in common now was Brendan, the last link. I tried to recapture the mood. "Has he done his Christmas list yet?"

She covered her eyes. "It was done by Labor Day. Do you believe it?"

"He's organized."

"It's a mile long."

"He thinks big."

"He wants a two-thousand-dollar computer."

"He's crazy."

"That comes from your side."

"Can I see the list?"

"I've got it in the kitchen." She got up and returned a moment later with a piece of yellow construction paper with blue crayon writing.

"When did he learn how to write like that?"

"He didn't, but he found a girl in his class who can. Apparently, she's become his secretary."

"Does she sit on his lap?"

"Probably. I think the paint set is for her."

My son *did* think big: seventeen toys and games ranging from the traditional stuff to state-of-the-art electronics. One item, however, caught my eye. "Cross off the baseball glove," I told her. "I've got it covered."

"What about the Nintendo? It's a little expensive, I know, but I think he's really got his heart set on it and—"

I shook my head. "I don't want to give him something that will have him in front of the TV for hours on end."

"Frank—"

"Moira, it'll be a kid's mitt and . . . what?" She looked nervous.

"The baseball glove is already taken care of."

"Pop? He'll swap with me. Let him go for the bow—"

"Rob."

"Rob is getting Brendan a baseball glove?"

"Yes."

"*Rob* is getting my son his first baseball glove?"

"Brendan had already told him that he wanted a glove. I showed Rob the list and he picked it out. Pick something else."

"Tell Rob to pick something else."

"No."

"Then *I'll* tell him."

"No, you won't! For God's sake! What's the big deal? You both love him and you'll both give him presents!"

"Oh. Well, thank you for explaining it to me, Moira: Rob and I are just two guys who love Brendan. I don't know what came over me! I had this crazy idea I had some special rights."

"No, they come with the special obligations."

"Don't do that, Moira! Goddammit! I'm doing the best I can!"

"No, you're just doing it *alone*, which to you is more important. And it's a luxury you wouldn't have if my father wasn't paying our support."

"Maybe his support wouldn't be necessary if his daughter had given me hers."

"And maybe we'd all be sleeping in your folding bed. You had obligations and you walked away. Your father may have done it to you but he couldn't help himself."

I leaned toward her. "My father? Let me tell you about my father, Moira. He didn't give me a home but even he came through with a baseball glove. And I told every kid I knew: 'My father gave me this.' My *father*, Moira, not some stranger."

"*Stop it!* This isn't about baseball gloves at all! And Rob is no stranger."

"Right. He's one of the family, which is why you couldn't even take him to Pop's for Thanksgiving."

"Leave Pop out of this. He's never accepted the fact that we're divorced. It's *my* feelings that matter here."

"Yeah, and Rob and I are equals."

"No, Frank, you're not. You and I *were* married. Rob and I are *going* to be."

The room began a slow spin. "When?" I croaked.

"In June. He sold his company to an investment group and has an employment contract until then."

"When was this decided?"

"Just recently."

"Like about a minute ago?"

"Go to hell!"

"Look, I mean . . . the way you reacted when I said those things about Ashley Bronson. I don't know. . . . Jesus . . . I can't think right now."

She looked away. "There's more," she said softly.

A sense of dread overcame me. "What?"

"Rob's home is in San Francisco. When he goes back Brendan and I will be going with him."

*Are the Forty-niners a good team?*

There was a jolt, followed by that pins and needles sensation in my face. I put my palms flat on the table to steady myself as the room moved and the nausea hit me. "I have to go," I gasped, struggling to my feet with the chair for support.

She stood up and grabbed my forearm. "We need to talk, Frank. Now!"

I held up a hand indicating "no more." I didn't want to talk and I didn't want to throw up all over the dining room, either. I mumbled, "I've got to go," and started for the foyer but she stepped in front of me, walking backward and trying to block my path.

"I want you to *talk to me!*" she shrieked, looking more frightened than angry. I brushed past her but she grabbed my sleeve and got pulled along toward the door. "What was I supposed to do, Frank, wait for you to come home? I did— *three fucking years!* Was I supposed to play the single mom forever? Tell me what I was supposed to do! I'm listening, you . . . *you bastard!*"

I opened the door with my free hand and turned. She was in agony, looking nothing like the woman who had greeted me just a few hours before. We'd been kicking the shit out of each other for years but this was the topper, the new record. I muttered, "I've got to go," again and pulled free. She slammed the door behind me and I could hear her sobbing as I stumbled toward the car. I was too shook up to drive; I rested my head against the wheel for a moment before I turned the key and went down the driveway. As I pulled away I took one more look at the house. Brendan was standing at his window. He waved.

\* \* \*

*The Huey nosed down toward the landing zone that looked like a wound in the jungle vegetation. I stepped out onto the strut, into the current, my M–16 slung around my neck and a red smoke grenade in my free hand. I could see the face of the pilot of the Cobra gunship alongside. The Gatling gun swiveled automatically in synchronous motion with his helmet as he turned his head, looking for something to kill. As we neared the LZ, he fired one rocket, then another, then the*

*Gatling gun, and the LZ disappeared in the explosions. Behind me I could hear the clatter of rifle bolts slamming forward as the rest of the team got ready to jump out. The Cobra peeled off and we dove right into the smoke, blind until the jungle materialized just six feet below the struts. I jumped, ran a few yards, and dove behind an uprooted tree. The whomp-whomp of the rotors drowned out the crack of AK–47s, but the telltale green tracers were already crisscrossing the clearing. I pulled the pin on the smoke grenade and threw it over my head, and red smoke blended with the brown clouds churned up by the explosions and the rotor wash, signaling a "hot LZ" to the rest of the platoon in the sky above. The Huey should have been gone by now. I looked over my shoulder and saw the pilot slumped sideways. The aircraft commander was wrestling with the stick but the ship nosed up awkwardly, gasping for altitude and starting to spin. The tail rotor circled toward my legs, chewing up the vegetation as it came. I was pinned against the tree. I kept screaming but the helicopter wouldn't go away.*

\* \* \*

I woke up. My eyes didn't open right away but I was awake. The rapid thump of my pulse echoed in my ear pressed against the mattress. I moved my legs for reassurance, and as the fear receded I became aware of the pain in the back of my skull and the thickness in my throat. Aftereffects. I opened my eyes and turned my head a little at a time until I could see the wall, barely visible in the dull light from the window, then dragged my arm across the sheet until my watch came into view: six minutes past five, the dawn of a new day.

I didn't remember drinking. All I remembered was Moira's but I wasn't going to dwell on what happened there. Later on, when I felt better, I'd visit Noah and we'd plan my descent into terminal depression. As the moments passed the wall became harder to see, which concerned me until I remembered that dawn came a lot later than five A.M. in December, and then concern gave way to despair: it wasn't dawn, it was twilight, and I'd been passed out for an entire day. People were probably looking for me. I decided I was better off where I was.

Which became the next problem—where I was. The wall was at least twelve feet away, too far for an apartment that was only fifteen feet wide, and the furnishings I could see without moving my head weren't familiar. Analytical guy that I was, it didn't take very long to figure it out but to be sure I got out of bed and staggered to the window. There was no mistaking the view, there were so few properties in Georgetown with detached garages. I proceeded directly into the bathroom, stuck my head in the toilet, and took care of the nausea from the night before. My thoughtful hostess had left a bottle of aspirin on the sink; I took four and got into the shower, alternating between the hottest and coldest settings for a full ten minutes. By the time I toweled off the only illumination was from the security lights outside, but I managed to find my clothes, cleaned and pressed, hanging on a closet door. I got dressed, made the bed, and settled into an armchair by the window. The glow from the restaurants and bars on M Street was visible over the rooftops to the south.

Sitting in the dark, I'd finally arrived: the end of the odyssey that was supposed to be the prime of my life. It's a strangely liberating feeling to confront the worst that can happen. In the end, fear is really nothing but anticipation, and when it all goes to shit, when you're surrounded and the cavalry just isn't going to show, you can reach a point where you just don't care. Nothing that can happen, nothing anyone can do, holds any terror for you. Then fear goes away and things just are. I'd faced a moment like that half a lifetime ago and I'd survived; maybe I'd do it again.

I heard footsteps in the hallway, followed by a light

knock on the door. A shaft of light fell across the carpet and the lady of the house entered and sat down opposite me on the bed. "Walter's downstairs," she said quietly. "I thought we'd all have some dinner."

"I'm withdrawing as your lawyer tomorrow. I'll suggest some replacements and when you pick one there'll be a substitution filed with the court. You don't have to worry about the timing because your new lawyer will seek a postponement and the judge will grant it. I'll be returning your money tomorrow, too, but I suggest you keep Walter because he knows the case and you won't get anyone better." With that, I stood up.

"Frank?"

"What?"

"Does it get any easier?"

I turned around. "Does what get any easier?"

"Walking out."

"I don't know what you're talking about, but if you think about it you'll understand that I'm doing this for both of us."

"Is that what you told your wife?"

And I thought things couldn't get worse. "Have I been talking in my sleep?"

"You were drunk and I couldn't have stopped you if I'd tried. Anyway, that's over and now we've got to go on."

"You need a new lawyer."

"I'm not disillusioned, Frank. I asked Tom Hardaway some questions before I ever hired you. He told me about your . . . troubles."

"You know, that's funny. I seem to remember something about seeing me in jail and deciding I was the one. Is it my imagination or am I still drunk?"

"Frank . . ."

"Hey, never mind. You had a right to get the facts and you hired me anyway. Actually, I'm flattered. But tell me something: what was that crap all about? Was I supposed to work harder if I thought it was kismet or blind faith? And while you're at it you can tell me about that stuff in the sewing room the other night."

"I don't like you when you're like this."

"This is *me*. The stories you heard? They're true."

"I didn't care then and I don't care now."

"Then care about this: I've mishandled your case. I told you to turn down a plea bargain that you should have accepted. The evidence was stacked against you from the start and I didn't allow myself to see it because I was a lawyer in need of a case and because you're you and . . . whatever. That's it—that's what happened. I'll tell you something else: Rogavin and I don't get along. I insulted him and he wants to show what happens to commoners who mess with the king. With a new lawyer, somebody he respects, you may get a better deal."

Ashley got up from the bed and headed for the door. "I didn't turn down the plea bargain just for you, Frank. I turned it down because I don't want to go to prison. Not twenty years, not ten. Whatever reasons you may have had for giving the advice, it still makes sense."

"Ashley . . ."

She reached the door and turned. "I don't want to hear any more. I believed in you. I still do. What I really need now is for you to believe in yourself. Now, I'm going downstairs to have dinner with my investigator. Are you coming or not?"

So there we were. It had really been a remarkable twenty-four hours. Knowing me as they did, the two women in my life had made their choices; now it was my turn. My worst fears had been realized, the confession had been made, and all the guilt was behind me. All I had to do now was decide what I wanted and that wasn't hard: whatever was left. "I'd like dinner," I said.

Martha was tending a soup pot when we entered. Her usual benign smile was not in evidence, a sign that my protracted visit had upset the equilibrium of the Bronson household.

Mindful that she might have removed my pants the night before, I avoided eye contact as I passed through the cooking area to the table where Walter was seated with a bottle of Ashley's imported beer and his own *New York Post*. He didn't look too happy, either. I was supposed to stay away from the bars and I was supposed to stay away from the client. He had taken my passing out in her bedroom as a bad sign.

Martha set a tureen and a hot loaf of bread on the table, then brought a glass of wine for Ashley, a second beer for Walter, and mineral water for me. I was the only one who hadn't actually voiced a beverage choice but I figured that was deliberate, so I ate my soup and kept my mouth shut while they made small talk.

After dinner we went into the library for coffee. It was "the library" by any standards, a good sixty feet from end to end with rolling oak ladders to reach the topmost of the shelves, which were all crammed. The books were organized by subject matter and author. Henry Bronson's devotion to science was evidenced by old volumes about mathematics, physics, chemistry, electrical engineering and circuits, several relatively new works about computer science, and lots of materials that seemed to be about number theory. But his interests were far broader than science and math: there were tomes on horticulture, ecology, city planning, and astronomy; and there were histories, biographies, and the classics of fiction and nonfiction.

The room was furnished with comfortable sofas and chairs, book cradles and carousels, and tables with books, manuscripts, photographs, and mementos. At its center was a handsome octagonal table with a mariner's chart, an antique microscope, and more piles of books. I craned my neck to gape at the moldings and chandeliers while Walter wandered around, touching the leather bindings, admiring the paintings, and studying the photographs with his detective's eye. "Jeez," he said, "the last time I saw anything like this, there was stone lions out front."

Ashley brought in the coffee tray and set our places on a low glass table resting on more books. "What do you think?" she asked.

"It's cozy," I said.

She laughed. "Cozy, it ain't." She took in the surroundings with a sweep of her arm. "My father was a bibliophile. This is his English country house library, inspired by the one at Badminton House in Gloucestershire. He spent most of his time here after my mother died, working at that desk." She pointed toward one corner of the room at an ormolu desk larger than my apartment but proportionate to the surroundings.

We all settled in to watch the fire, Ashley on a love seat and Walter and I on the couch. No one was saying much so it seemed as good a time as any to get back in the game. "Any developments?" I asked Walter.

"None," he replied. "We don't know any more about Kellogg than we did a few days ago. I'm telling ya, this guy's life is buttoned up tight."

"What are we going to do?" asked Ashley.

Walter inclined his head toward me. "The counselor here is going to have an inspiration just as soon as the cobwebs clear."

Ashley smiled at him. "Are you sure? He doesn't look very inspired." They were having a grand old time discussing my fragile condition.

"Well," he said, "I know that sometimes he can be freakin' worthless—pardon the expression—but believe it or not, he can be pretty good in a pinch."

"I believe we're in a pinch," she said.

"Yeah," he agreed. He studied me, then turned back to her and winked. "I know that look. He's got an idea."

Ashley eyed me and asked, "Does the counselor have an idea?"

"The counselor has an idea," I replied.

"Don't hold back," said Walter. "Let 'er rip."

"Yeah," said Ashley. "Let 'er rip."

"We're going to investigate the murder of Raymond Garvey."

They looked at each other, then back at me. Ashley spoke first. "I think we already know how it turns out. It was the debutante in the sitting room with a gun."

"The jury doesn't know how it turns out," I said.

Walter was rubbing his jaw. "That's true."

She looked at him and back to me. "There are two kinds of defenses," I explained. "In one, you try to create reasonable doubt by shooting holes in the government's case. It's kind of like a tennis match but the prosecutor always serves while the defense stays back and hits returns from the baseline, hoping to force an error. That's what we've been doing, trying to find some weak points with Kellogg."

"And the other kind?" she asked.

"You return serve as before, but then you go to the net by raising the possibility that someone else committed the crime. Then the trial isn't just about whether the evidence is sufficient to convict Ashley Bronson, it's about who killed Raymond Garvey, which is a whole different exercise. As a practical matter the government not only has to prove you did it, it has to prove someone else didn't, and proving a negative can be very hard. The bottom line is that the jury *has* to have a reasonable doubt about your guilt if it even *suspects* that someone else might be the murderer."

She frowned. "But there is no other suspect."

"Yes, there is."

"Who?"

"Mr. Rolls-Royce," said Walter.

"He's our prime candidate," I agreed.

"Who's Mr. Rolls-Royce?" asked Ashley.

"A distinguished-looking gentleman with gray hair and a

mustache. The Wards saw him leave Garvey's house in a bit of a huff."

"That's all?"

"That's enough for now."

Ashley looked dubious. "How can we say he committed murder? That's like framing him, isn't it?"

"We're not going to frame anyone. All we're going to do is suggest another solution to the whodunnit. If there are two possibilities instead of one, then there should be reasonable doubt about your guilt."

"But the evidence points to me."

I shook my head. "Not all of it, just what the government has selected. We're going to present the *other* evidence, the facts relating to Raymond Garvey and his murder that point in another direction."

Walter was smiling again. "We'll need a motive," he said.

"We haven't got one yet," I replied, "but I know where to start looking." I went over and sat next to Ashley. "So you still believe in me?" I asked. She nodded. "Okay. I need the rest of your father's journal, all the volumes."

"Why?"

"Raymond was upset with your father and Mr. Rolls-Royce was upset with Raymond. It could've been a coincidence, but if it wasn't, the story might present an interesting alternative to the one Rogavin's going to tell."

"Where does the journal come in?"

"The last entry indicates that Raymond was tormenting your father about something he did when he was young. You told me that your father kept a journal for as long as you can remember so the key may be in there somewhere." I took her hand in mine. "Ashley, we need to figure out what those men were up to."

The distress was plain on her face and in her voice. "You want to find out why my father killed himself, is that it? Frank, I don't—"

"I wouldn't ask if it wasn't absolutely necessary."

"I don't know where it is."

"How many volumes are there?"

"I don't even know that. There could be a lot."

"What about a safe deposit box?"

"I've looked. There were the usual papers but no journal."

I couldn't accept that we'd been stymied before we even started. "Don't worry, we've got a detective on staff. Now it's *his* turn to get inspired." I turned to Walter. "We've got to have it," I told him.

The prospect of another search didn't seem to bother him at all. He sat back and reached for one of his toothpicks. "You remember when I was breakin' you in?" He grinned. "What's the first thing I taught you about bein' a detective?"

"I don't remember. Which coffee shops had free refills?"

He shook his head. "That was the second thing. The first was: never ignore the obvious."

"What's obvious about the missing journal?"

He cocked his head at me. "If you wanted to hide a bunch of books where would you put 'em?" As if to provide a clue, he let his eyes wander over my head to the shelves above.

Ashley sat bolt upright. "You think they're *here*?"

"It stands to reason," he replied.

There had to be thousands of books in that room. "Ashley," I said, "why don't you have Martha put on more coffee? I'll call Andy. We'll save the high shelves for him."

As soon as she walked out of the room, Walter warned, "You bring him into this, you're gonna have to tell him about that book you got stashed in your office."

"If he's part of the defense he's going to find out about it sooner or later."

"What about our conundrum?"

"You know what they say."

"What?"

"Where there's no alternative, there's no problem."

We found Henry's journal at dawn the following day, all twelve volumes, hidden on a shelf in a wooden box that was inset with a faux book front. To the casual eye, the journal of Henry Bronson was *The History of England.*

# 9

HENRY BRONSON'S JOURNAL

*August 12, 1952. Today I begin my journal. If I am faithful to the enterprise, I will have a complete record when all is said and done, although not of what was said, or done, for it is not my intention to record events. I would rather trust that to memory and grant myself the grace of time and subjectivity. Besides, there are practical limitations I am sworn to abide.*

*This will be a journal of reflections. Our world, under the governance of God and science, is a perpetual motion machine, possessed of the energy to do good work and bad. I have been given the opportunity to assist in the work of dreams. I can only pray it will come to good, but it may turn out badly for all concerned.*

For a detective who could deduce the location of a missing journal in a moment, identifying and locating the owner of a yellow Rolls-Royce with right-hand drive wasn't much of a challenge. The other suspect in the murder of Raymond Garvey had a name by midafternoon: "Sherman P. Burroughs," he announced.

"Sherman P. Burroughs," I repeated.

"Sherman *Pierce* Burroughs."

"Sherman *Pierce* Burroughs," I repeated.

"The freakin' third."

"The third . . . ?"

"The third Sherman Pierce Burroughs."

"Oh. What do we know about him?"

"He drives a yellow Rolls-Royce, Virginia registration."

"And?"

"He kicks the shit out of pumpkins."

"That's it?"

"For now."

"What about later?"

"Later we'll know which hand he wipes his ass with."

"Swell. How much later?"

"A week."

"We're running out of weeks. Let's talk in terms of days."

"Seven days."

"Very funny. We need every day we can get."

"We lost one yesterday."

"Let it go, Walter."

"No, *you* let it go. What the hell got into you? Christ, I never thought I'd see you drinkin' like that again and I'm goddamned tired of fishin' you out of them waterin' holes." He stood over my desk and aimed his thick forefinger right between my eyes. "Bein' around her is makin' you sappy. You stay away like I said."

"Moira's getting married. She and Brendan are moving to California."

"Moira's getting . . ." He raised his eyes to the ceiling, then backed to the couch and sat there running his fingers through his thinning hair and muttering to himself. When he looked up there was genuine pity in his eyes. "I'm sorry as hell, kid," he said. "What I can do?"

"You can shoot a guy named Rob."

"When's all this supposed to happen?"

"In June."

"June? June's a lifetime away." He sighed, then shook his head. "So, what are you going to do?"

"I'm not going to brood. I'm going to concentrate on the case till it's over, then I'm going to step in front of a bus."

He nodded as if that seemed like a good plan. "And if we win?"

"I'll celebrate. *Then* I'll step in front of a bus."

"I like them Irish wakes." And a hell of a wake it would be: me stretched out in the parlor, looking pretty good for a guy who'd been hit by a bus. My ex–father-in-law accepting the sympathies of a continuous stream of favor-seekers. Walter and some of New York's finest old bulls in a corner swapping stories. Maybe a sprinkling of my clients to add texture and racial balance. And flanking the casket, hankies in hand, Moira Brennan O'Connell and Ashley Bronson. Talk about going out in style.

"What are you going to do first?" I asked.

"Talk to people who know somethin' about rich guys who live in Virginia."

"All right. Let's see what kind of case we can make against Sherman Pierce Burroughs."

"The third," he added.

"Right. The freakin' third."

After Walter left I called Ashley. Martha answered the phone and said she would fetch Miss Bronson. Her tone indicated she had in fact seen me in my underwear.

"Hello, Frank."

"It's your mouthpiece, still on the job. I need to talk to you and I've been in the office all day. Feel like a walk?"

"I'd love one."

Fifteen minutes later I parked in her driveway and we were off, heading east to Rock Creek Park. "I don't get out much anymore," she said. "I can't go too far without attracting attention."

"That has nothing to do with the case."

"Thanks. These days, all compliments are gratefully accepted."

"You're alone too much. What about your friends?"

"They're supportive but they want to know the truth. I mean, they don't ask—they wouldn't—but our conversations are so uncomfortable. Everyone in Washington is talking about the Ashley Bronson case. We're talking about everything *but* the Ashley Bronson case. And what could I say, 'Girls, he had it coming'? So we talk all around it, then lapse into these awkward silences while they smile at me as if I've got some terminal disease. I won't be seeing them again till this is over."

"You need someone to talk to."

"I wish my father were here," she said softly. "If I could talk to him now—"

"That reminds me." I took an envelope from my breast pocket and removed the photograph inside. "Do you recognize this?"

It was a black-and-white photo of three men at a park bench. Two of them were seated, smiling and squinting into the sun behind the photographer. The third was standing behind them, looking off at an angle as if someone or something had caught his attention. Ashley looked at it and brightened. "That's my father sitting on the right! Where did you get this?"

"I'm just starting his journal. This was in the first volume, wedged into a slit inside the binding. Who are the other guys?"

She stared at it a moment before shaking her head. "I don't recognize either of them but it's a pretty old photograph."

"Take a look at this." I turned it over to reveal the penciled notation on the back: *L3—1953*. "Do you know what your father was doing in nineteen fifty-three?"

"I don't. He never talked much about what he did in those days. I know he stayed on at Princeton after he graduated, and he also did some research at the University of Chicago."

"Research into what?"

"I think he mentioned radar or sonar or something. I really don't remember."

"Well, there are some mountains in the background so this wasn't taken in Princeton or Chicago. Any idea what 'L-three' could mean?"

She examined the writing closely. "It's not 'L-three.' The three is above the L. See? It's a math expression: L-cubed."

"L-cubed?"

"L to the third power."

"Right, I took algebra. Are you sure about that? There are three men in the picture. I thought it might have something to do with that."

"I've seen plenty of my father's scientific notation. It looks like L-cubed."

"All right. So what does L-cubed mean to a scientist?"

"I don't think it means anything by itself. Is this what you wanted to talk to me about?"

"Actually, no. Does the name Sherman Pierce Burroughs mean anything to you?"

"Sherry Burroughs?"

"Sherry? I don't know. Is it Sherry the Third? Lives in Virginia and drives a yellow Rolls-Royce?"

She stopped short. "*Sherry Burroughs* is Mr. Rolls-Royce?"

"The one and only. How well do you know him?"

"Not well. But his family's very prominent. I believe they're FFV."

"FFV?"

"I'm sorry." She had to translate for the financially impaired. "First Families of Virginia—descendants from the original colonists."

"Oh."

"The Burroughses owned a lot of land in northern Virginia and were very big horse people."

"Were?"

"Maybe they still are, I don't know. Sherry used to be one of the organizers of the Gold Cup, the annual horse racing event out in Fauquier County. But I was there last spring and he wasn't on the organizing committee and they didn't have any horses running, either."

"What was his connection to Garvey?"

"I don't know. I didn't know that they knew each other."

"Is there anyone who might know?"

"I suppose there are some people I can ask." She sighed. "I don't know about this, Frank. Sherry's a nice man, and he's older, my father's generation."

"This is important and you have access to people who won't talk to me or Walter."

"But there's no way to ask without raising suspicion. Are we really doing the right thing?"

"Yes, we are."

Raising suspicion was the whole idea.

*　*　*

Andy had a troubled expression when he entered my office Friday morning. "Frank, I, uh . . . did some research."

"On what?"

"The journal . . . Your having the journal in your possession. I thought you'd want me to check it out."

"Really?" I might have asked him when he began creating his own assignments but that was hardly the issue at the moment. "What'd you find?"

"Well, there's not a lot of cases dealing with this kind of situation, but I think I've figured it out. Basically, when a lawyer gets between the police and the evidence it's considered tampering or obstruction of justice."

"How does that bear on our case?"

He blinked. "Well . . . you were holding the journal when they executed the search warrant at Ashley's house. They could call that obstruction."

"But when I got the journal Ashley had already been arrested and was about to be indicted. How could I know they were going to search the house?"

Andy made a face. "I don't think a defense lawyer can hold on to incriminating evidence *at any time*, but it really doesn't matter because you found out about the search and still kept the book."

"What were my options?"

"Return it, I guess."

"To the client? I got it from her."

He considered that for a moment and said, "That wouldn't do any good. You'd have to turn it over to the police."

"But that would put the police in a better position than if I had never accepted it in the first place. Let's face it, the journal isn't evidence of Ashley's motive unless they could prove that she'd read it. If the police find it sitting on a shelf it gets them nothing, but if they get it from me the jury could infer that I got it from her. I would be helping the police make a case against my own client."

Andy replied, "If they found the book sitting on a shelf and it had her fingerprints on it, that would prove she read it, too."

"Yeah, *if* they got good fingerprints, and they'd have to be on the last page to mean anything."

He dug his hands into his pockets. "I think your argument only proves that lawyers who hold on to evidence can make things worse for their clients."

"Andy, how could I be sure it was evidence unless I looked? And even if it was, don't I get a reasonable chance to examine it? Where is it written that the government has a greater right to evidence than the defense?"

"Nowhere."

"Right. And while I was doing my job the police conducted a search. Why should that put my client in a worse position?"

He wasn't convinced, but hesitated, torn between job diplomacy and his professional training. Finally, he said, "All I know is you have evidence that the police were searching for. That's an ethical problem to me."

"You might be right," I conceded. "Do you have a case that says so?" I held up a warning hand before he could speak. "I mean a case *directly* on point."

"No. Like I said, the cases are skimpy." He stared at me, waiting for a solution, or at least some comfort for his troubled conscience. But I'd been wrestling with the problem since the moment she laid the journal on my desk, and I still hadn't come up with an unassailable rationale for what I'd done.

"So," he said, exhaling, "what are we going to do?" Only one answer would satisfy him, that much was clear.

I wasn't in the mood to be dictated to. "I'll tell you what I'm *not* going to do. I'm not going to march my client into a prison cell for twenty years because some rookie thinks an ethics committee might approve."

He turned red with embarrassment. That wasn't what he'd expected. "Okay, Frank," he stammered. "I'll . . . I'll get back to what I was doing." He stayed put, uncertain of his route of retreat.

"Andy, I'm sorry but this isn't an exam, and if you end up a criminal lawyer you're going to find yourself in situations that don't lend themselves to neat textbook solutions. We have a living, breathing client here, and if we have to make a hard choice, we protect her, not our own asses."

"I understand."

"I know that you want to do whatever you can to help Ashley."

He straightened. "Absolutely," he replied. He was infatuated with her and I took full advantage of it, which made me about as much of a mentor as Harry.

"Good. Now, I've got something important for you to tackle next. Arrange a visit to the police property room.

We've got reports of everything they seized, photographed, or noted at Garvey's house, and I want you to examine every item and compare it to the reports. Be sure to compare pictures with descriptions. Look for any inaccuracies or inconsistencies because any screwup by them might be useful. We'll have our own experts go over the autopsy and fingerprint evidence, so don't worry about that, but if there is anything else that doesn't seem one hundred percent accurate, we want to know. Okay?"

He was pleased at the thought of getting out of the library and doing a little sleuthing. "Okay. Anything else?"

"Yeah. I want you to do a memo summarizing your research and your recommendation on the ethical issue. Lay it out just as you did today."

"Why?"

"I may want to revisit the subject. It will help me think it through." And if it ever came to light he'd be on record, a young associate who was overruled by his boss. There wouldn't be much appetite for him when they got through with me.

\* \* \*

Six days into Plan B we met to review progress. The kitchen at Ashley's had become headquarters for Team Bronson by default. The firm was out: when she came to my office everyone found an excuse to exchange a word, pat a shoulder, or just get a look. Restaurants and other public places were never options. It came down to somebody's home and hers had chairs for the whole team. Not coincidentally, it was dinnertime. Walter and I were at the table, removing our ties and fluffing our napkins while our client-hostess was at the stove, ladling marinara sauce—"a special recipe, known only to Wellesley graduates"—on meatballs and spaghetti. She was wearing jeans and a gray green sweater just a shade darker than those tungsten headlamps. When Walter was around I avoided looking into them as I would an eclipse; the feelings were that strong.

We were just beginning to eat when she made the announcement. Whatever her misgivings about making poor Sherry the Third part of our defense strategy, Ashley had come through. "Sherry and Raymond Garvey dined together at the Middleburg Inn in early October."

"Says who?"

"Cynthia Bates. She saw them sitting in a corner by themselves." I had to resist the urge to plant a kiss right on those gorgeous lips. A clandestine meeting of the deceased and the suspect: it was perfect.

Walter spoke up. "Who's Cynthia Bates?"

"Someone I barely know, a friend of Ann Seymour. The Seymours host a lot of parties and fund-raisers at their home in Great Falls. I've seen Cynthia there a few times."

"And you called Ann Seymour?"

"No. She's the sister-in-law of Barbara Stockman, who's one of the four people I called." She grimaced. "This is just what I was afraid of, Frank. I asked Barbara to keep it to herself but she said that there was just one person she wanted to ask, someone who would be discreet. It went on from there. There was never any way to keep this under control. It's too . . . whatever."

I nodded sympathetically. "And this Cynthia Bates knew Sherry and Garvey?"

"She knew Sherry, probably the same way I did. She didn't know it was Raymond until she saw the newspapers."

"Did she know anything else?"

"Only about Sherry himself, and it was the same thing that everyone else has been saying. The Burroughs family is in serious financial difficulty. Their horse farm has been for sale and they've been keeping a low profile for the past few years."

"What happened?"

"As I understand it the family owned a lot of land in Fairfax and Loudon Counties when development took off. But they made a series of bad investments in the eighties and never recovered from the last real-estate collapse."

"What is Sherry supposed to be doing now?"

"Nobody really seems to know."

"Do you think he was seeing Garvey about money?"

"I doubt it. Raymond inherited a house and a lot of family connections but he never had any real wealth. What he had was a reputation as someone with *access* to wealth, and he made a living bringing ideas and money together. He was always on the lookout for the next deal but I never knew him to be anyone's financial angel."

"Burroughs already had an angel," Walter said.

Ashley and I spoke as one: "Who?"

"Some outfit called Octagon. It bought the mortgage to the farm when the bank was about to foreclose. And it arranged a deal for the Burroughs family to roll its debts into one note with a stretch-out on the terms."

"How?" I asked.

"By guaranteeing the paper. Between the mortgage and the other debt Octagon went for seven and a half mil."

"Where do you get this stuff?" With all the attention our new strategy was about to draw, Walter's use of "mutual acquaintances" could land us in the cell next to Ashley's.

He shook his head. "Not to worry. Routine police work. The mortgage assignment was recorded. The stretch-out is no secret, either. I got it from a Virginia lawyer who throws me some business. He represented one of the creditors."

"Did he tell you who's behind Octagon and why they rescued Sherry?"

"Nope. The creditors dealt with some lawyer from New York, and he wasn't talkin'."

"You think Octagon is connected to this thing?"

Ashley broke in before Walter could answer. "Connected

to what? Frank, I'm having second thoughts about this. I don't want Sherry Burroughs on my conscience, or these Octagon people, either. I've got all I can deal with in that department. I want you to drop this strategy before any more damage is done."

"Ashley," I said quietly, "we're taking your best chance at acquittal—maybe your only chance."

"It isn't worth it," she declared.

"Yeah, you say that *now*," I scoffed, "but wait till they lock you in a cell smaller than your linen closet."

Ashley wasn't used to men taking that tone with her. "I've made up my mind," she said, raising her chin.

She caught me at the wrong time. I was under a lot of stress, and coming on the heels of Andy's challenge, her mutiny was the last straw. "*You've* made up your mind?" I snapped. "When it comes to your defense, *I* decide what's right, not you."

She glared at me. "Is this about me, Frank? I think it's about you and Rogavin. Or maybe just you!"

"Ashley, do you think Kyle Rogavin is thinking about anything but winning? That he's not prepared to do what's necessary? I'll bet the first time Kellogg identified you he wasn't half as sure as he's going to sound from that witness stand. The rules get bent and sometimes they get broke. The bigger the case, the bigger the rule. It doesn't matter that the players are lawyers. There are ultracompetitive types on both sides."

She was nodding as I finished. "People like you," she said angrily. "You said so that night here in the kitchen. It's the contest!"

"Right, people like me! And you were goddamned glad to hear it!"

She had better self-control than I. She put down her napkin and said quietly, "You two finish your dinner, I'm going upstairs. There's some dessert in the refrigerator and there's coffee. Martha will take care of the dishes." She got up, said good night to Walter, and left.

Neither of us spoke until we heard her footsteps on the stairs. "So, what about Octagon?" I asked.

He shrugged. "I'm workin' on it." He didn't elaborate but I'd bet it wasn't routine police work.

My brain was in overdrive. "It adds up, doesn't it? Octagon is keeping Sherry's head above water, and for that much money it wanted something in return, something big enough to justify the investment. So Sherry's real motivated and he's leaning hard on Garvey."

"Makes sense. But why does Garvey lean on the old man?"

"I don't know. Maybe he figures he's too old to keep chasing the next deal. This is the big one. This one's retirement. There could be a time factor, too, so Raymond is relentless."

"But the old man doesn't shut him off, so what's Garvey got on him? He didn't off himself because Raymond's a nag."

"Something that happened a long time ago," I said.

"And you think it's in the journal."

"I hope so. I'll keep looking. You work on Octagon."

"What about Miss?" He jerked a thumb toward the ceiling.

"You've got to admire her. Her life's at stake but she'd rather protect Sherry and some people she doesn't even know."

"Yeah." He drained the rest of his beer and stood up. "That's somethin', isn't it?"

"Well, don't worry about it. I'll talk to her." He rolled his eyes. "Lay off, will you? I'll handle it."

He smiled. "Just lookin' out for my meal ticket."

I waited awhile but Ashley didn't return. The smart thing would have been to let her cool off but I didn't want to break my stupidity streak, so I went upstairs and tapped on her door.

"Who is it?" she called.

"The dog."

"Please go away."

"I can't. My leash is under the bed."

A moment passed. "Come in." She was propped up in bed with pen in hand, staring darts over her reading glasses. I sat down on the edge of the bed.

"What's doing?" I asked.

"I'm writing a letter to Sherry," she declared, defiant.

"What are you going to say?"

"I'm going to apologize and tell him that I'll do everything possible to undo the damage."

I shook my head. "You can't write that letter."

"I'm going to do what I think is right."

"Look, the last time we had one of these little bedroom talks, *I* was the one who wanted out, remember? You told me you didn't want to go to prison, that you needed me to believe in myself. Well, you convinced me. Then *we* needed *me* to have an inspiration so I had one, and you went along knowing full well what was going to happen— don't bother to deny it. Well, now there's no going back. We're fighting for your life and we'll do whatever's necessary."

"What about Sherry, Frank? What about *his* life?"

I clenched my teeth. Under the circumstances I thought she was being just a little too judgmental. "Sherry probably had something to do with your father's death."

"And that justifies what we're doing?"

"It's a helluva lot less than you did to Garvey!"

I saw it coming but let it happen, a roundhouse slap that landed with a crack just below my ear. It surprised her, though: she looked from her hand to me with eyes wide, then turned away. It wasn't what I had in mind when I told

Walter I'd handle it, and it sure as hell wasn't what *he* had in mind when he doubted me, but I was well past the point of caring about anyone's sensibilities, even hers.

I stared at the wall while she recovered, looking but not really seeing, and a couple of minutes passed before I noticed the photographs. They were mostly street scenes of Paris. One was of a woman reading a book in an outdoor cafe while an appreciative waiter watched from the doorway. The woman behind me had fallen in love in France, and in a perfect world that's where *we* would have started. I would've sent over a glass of wine and she would've invited me to her table. Soon, we'd be lovers, cavorting about the city with me playing Bogart to her Bergman till fate took a hand. But we'd always have Paris.

That's what hurt most: no Paris. She walked into my life with the bad guys already in pursuit. All I could do was hold them off till the big airport scene.

One photograph was a black-and-white of Ashley and her father sitting in the garden. She was dressed in slacks and a turtleneck with her arm linked in his. Henry was wearing a three-piece suit with a shirt buttoned to the neck and no tie. One hand rested on a cane, the other held a cap. He was looking at his daughter and all the love and concern were right there to be seen. *I'll watch over you forever.*

The bed shifted as she moved behind me, wrapping her arms around my neck and resting her chin on my shoulder. We didn't speak, just swayed a little from side to side. "I'm sorry," she whispered.

"It's all right." I opened my eyes and nodded toward the photograph. "He loved you very much."

"Yes, he did."

"It's easy to do."

Her arms tightened around me and she touched her cheek to mine. "There was a story in the *Post* the other day about the trial of a banker. He'd been on bail but they took him into custody when the guilty verdict was announced."

"That can happen. If the jury finds you guilty, sometimes they revoke bail even before you're sentenced."

"Could it happen to me?"

"No, because we're going to win."

"I know. But if something went wrong it could happen to me, couldn't it?"

"Yeah." I turned my head, bringing our faces closer together. "You should have your affairs in order by the time we go to trial." I could feel her nod. That wasn't the first time I'd said that to a client, and I was glad that I couldn't see her face. *Get your affairs in order.* Suddenly, the idea of being snatched from your very existence is transformed from a concept, like death, to a looming presence. But first-timers, especially the white-collar guys, usually remained in denial until the moment of truth. I'd seen it happen before: the accused strides into the courtroom from some restaurant where he's been waiting it out. The jury says "guilty" and the poor bastard rocks back, then slips into suspended animation, oblivious to the more immediate issue that's animating everyone else. Suddenly, his lawyer is talking to him but he doesn't understand the words, like the record is being played at the wrong speed, and someone's got a grip on his elbow, and then he's in a small room emptying his pockets and being readied for his little ferry ride across the Styx. And then it finally starts to sink in that the restaurant meal he can still taste was his last for a long time, that he won't be going home, and that someone should really call the family.

"Do you know that you're the only man in my life?" she said softly.

"I wish it weren't by default."

Her cheek rubbed mine as we swayed some more. "If I'm convicted it will be a long time before there'll be another."

"I told you. We're going to win and you'll be free."

"But if we don't, by the time I'm released I won't look or feel the same, will I?"

"You'll still be you. As for looks, you might be only spectacular instead of totally off the charts."

"We're in love, aren't we?" she whispered.

"Speak for yourself. I'm in this for the money."

"You're in love with me."

"Who said? It was Walter, wasn't it?"

"The case is just how we met. Any other way, I would love you just the same."

My chest was pounding so hard she must have felt it. "You know what's on my desk?"

"What?"

"Newspaper clippings about you and lots of other guys."

"So?"

"So I was thinking that you should kiss me like you never kissed any of them. That's a crazy thing to ask, isn't it?"

"No." She eased me backward and moved on top of me. At first our lips were barely touching, then they gradually pressed together. I ran my hands over her bottom and up her back, squeezing her to me. To feel and taste after all that time just looking—I had to keep reminding myself that it was real.

She sat up astride me, grinning. "Do you want to turn the lights down?"

"No."

"Good. Sit up." She kept her eyes on mine as she unbuttoned my shirt, then ran her hands slowly over my arms and shoulders and the curvature of my chest. "Well," she murmured, "if we're in for a fight it feels like you're ready." She sat back and pulled her own sweater over her head. Her clothes never concealed the shape of her, but that didn't prepare me for the sight. I was barely breathing myself as she moved close so her nipples just touched my chest, brushing them against me as her lips brushed against mine. A moment of that and I thought my heart was going to leap out of my chest. Then she took my hands in hers and filled them with her breasts, her nipples hard between my fingers. I stroked them with my fingertips and palms, then leaned to kiss them. She began to groan, holding my head and pushing her breast deeper into my mouth.

Things began to accelerate. She pushed me down onto my back and quickly pulled off my clothes, leaving just my shirt. Then she took off her own jeans and reached for the band of her panties, but stopped. She leaned down and smiled. "Can you handle those?"

"I'm a licensed professional." We rolled over and I took off my shirt, then reached under her, hooking the band of her panties with both hands. I tugged them slowly, over her hips, all the way down those incredible legs, past her ankles, and off. Now, both naked, we took our time looking each other over. I was sitting on my heels between her legs, with her calves resting on my thighs. I lifted one of her legs and kissed the inside of her ankle, calf, and knee. Her eyes were half-closed; murmurs of pleasure came from deep in her throat. The sight of her in heat was the most erotic thing I'd ever seen. I wanted every part of her and all at once, but more than anything I wanted her face close to mine and her voice in my ear as before. I moved on top of her and we kissed again and again while she rubbed my calves with the balls of her feet.

I don't know why, but the images started flashing by: Pop, Rogavin, my father, Walter, Brendan—and Moira. I could hear her sobbing from inside the house. And everything that had been bottled up started pouring out: I was afraid and excited, angry and guilty, all flooding out of me and over her; she felt it, too.

"What?" she panted.

"Don't let go." I gasped, afraid she would.

She lifted my face so she could see me. "What is it?"

"Nothing. . . . Everything."

She put her fingers to my lips. "It's—"

"We'll get out. I promise. We'll get out."

She shut her eyes tight, and when she opened them they were focused on something far away. "Now, Frank . . . please!" she cried. She reached between my legs and guided me into her as her feet slid up to my buttocks. She gasped as I entered her, then pulled my face down and locked her lips onto mine, pushing her tongue into my mouth as I reached under her and squeezed her bottom. Her legs tightened around me and we were off, slowly, then building speed, then galloping, faster and faster, breaking free. I was lost. She put her lips to my ear, urging me on, but I couldn't understand the words. It was frantic, scary. Then she began to moan, a low, stirring sound that grew into a wail as her back arched, lifting me, and then I heard my own grunting as I emptied into her and we collapsed back onto the mattress.

We remained coiled for some time, clinging to each other and the sanctuary we had made until our breathing slowed and the room began to cool. Her hands moved soothingly up and down my back, over my shoulders, and through my hair. Then she turned my face to hers and touched her lips softly against mine.

"I did it," she murmured.

"I think I did it, too."

"I think you did." She smiled and then whispered, "I kissed you like I never kissed another man."

"Then I can't let you go."

"We'll stay like this forever?"

"Uh-huh."

"Mmmm. I wonder what Martha will say."

"Let her get her own man."

She started to laugh and grimaced. "Stop! I can't laugh with you crushing me."

"Should I get up?"

She shook her head and continued to run her fingers through my hair. "What about Walter?"

"I don't think he's Martha's type."

She punched me in the ribs. "I'm serious! If he finds out—"

That made me laugh out loud. "Right!"

"What's so funny?"

I shook my head. "He's going to know."

"How?"

"The first time the three of us are in a room together, he'll know."

"Swell." She frowned. "You think a lot of him, don't you?"

"He's the best at what he does."

She kissed me. "So are you."

"Now all I have to do is prove it to Rogavin."

She laughed. "I wasn't talking about lawyering. Let me up." We unraveled and she turned off the lamp and pulled the blanket over us. I put my arm around her and buried my face in her neck. She backed against me, her breasts resting on my forearm and her bottom pressing against my groin. "Did you break a big ethical rule tonight?" she asked.

I spoke into her neck. "A small one. I already broke all the big ones."

She sighed. "You're breaking them for me."

"Don't try to take the credit. I've never had much respect for the rules. We're just beginning to understand why."

"We?"

"Me and my therapist. We're trying to find whatever I'm looking for."

She turned and put her hand on my cheek. "Those clippings on your desk . . ." she whispered.

"Yeah?"

"Throw them away. I've found what *I'm* looking for."

Soon she was asleep, leaving me to face the consequences of what we'd done. Walter's reaction was the least of it; how it would affect the case remained to be seen. The only thing I knew for sure was that if she went to prison and we'd never been lovers, we'd always wonder. Now, it would be worse.

# 10

*August 31, 1952. California! Home of the stars! And around them, planets; and around the planets, moons like me, obscured in the shadows of our own limitations. To encounter true genius is a disquieting thing. We marvel at the capabilities of our species and lament that our own blessings are, at last, only vicarious.*

*What endeavor, then, has afforded such opportunity for communal joy and private anguish? I am late to the enterprise but I am part of it—owing less to my faculties than my stamina and stripped bare of all illusions, I am still part of it—and I am determined to make my contribution.*

There was a message on my desk urging me to return the call of Robert L. Burnside, Esq., of Delbarton & Brand, the city's oldest firm. With about fifty lawyers D & B wasn't big by Washington standards, but it had the bluest of the blue-chip practices as counsel of choice for the city's old money, the "cave dwellers." Like its clients the firm kept a low profile, eschewing the hurly-burly of downtown in favor of a row of townhouses on New Hampshire Avenue. The "re:" space of the message was blank, which I was going to chalk up to the inexperience of my newest secretary until she explained that Mr. Burnside declined to state his business and "didn't sound very nice, either." The lawyer's directory said that he was a fifty-four-year-old graduate of the University of Virginia law school and a specialist in tax law. It didn't say whether he was very nice but he managed to clear that up right away.

"This is Frank O'Connell returning your call."

"I want to meet you in my office—today."

"What about?"

"I represent Sherman P. Burroughs. Does that tell you anything?"

"Maybe. Which one?"

"Which one?"

"I understand there are three."

"The one you and your client are slandering. The one that will see you in disbarment proceedings. You can meet me here today or in court tomorrow."

"Your office would be fine. Eleven o'clock?"

"I'll be waiting."

No, not very nice at all.

\* \* \*

Aside from whatever it was that drove me out, I loved just about everything about practicing with Pop, and one of the things I loved most was our offices. Most of the city's lawyers were interned in glass and steel containers with a few architectural flourishes and windows that didn't open. But Brennan & O'Connell had a three-story brick townhouse on Jefferson Street, just around the corner from The Palm restaurant. There was a little garden in the back where we would eat lunch while Pop would regale me with stories spanning from his youth in County Clare to the latest political gossip. Some of my happiest moments were spent in that garden.

Delbarton & Brand lawyers enjoyed the same arrangement, only they had three connected townhouses, each four stories tall and twice as wide as Pop's. There were two limousines with license plates DB–1 and DB–2 parked in the circular driveway in front of the center building entrance. The place was as quiet as a library, and the only sign that it was a law firm was the portraits of Supreme Court justices encircling the foyer. The receptionist behind the Queen Anne desk escorted me into a small elevator and pressed the "3" button before sliding the gate closed behind me. A moment later it was opened again by Burnside's secretary. Apparently, many of D & B's clientele could no longer open doors or never learned how. She led me to Burnside, who was standing in his doorway as if he could hardly wait to get at me. He didn't offer to shake hands; he just turned his back and gestured toward one of the chairs as he marched toward his desk.

Physically, he was a slightly slimmer, slightly older version of Harry Gregg, but the similarities ended there. Burnside had the aura of a player of the no-quarter-asked-or-given school, and if he had a warm and fuzzy side he was careful not to leave any clues strewn about: no wedding ring, no family photos, no golf trophies, no "man of the year" certificates. The only decoration was an array of photographs of an unsmiling Burnside shaking hands with an assortment of white males that looked like the membership of Indianapolis Lions Club, circa 1955.

He opened a folder. "You're O'Connell," he rumbled, more an accusation than a statement.

"Himself."

He closed the folder and put it in a drawer. "Sherman Burroughs is a distinguished member of one of Virginia's oldest and most prominent families. He has retained this firm to look into the matter of a slander of his reputation, as well as the origin of some mysterious inquiries into his financial affairs. We believe that you are responsible for both."

"The inquiries about Mr. Burroughs were at my direction. I don't know anything about slander."

"Implying that Mr. Burroughs had a part in the death of Raymond Garvey is a vicious slander that is being compounded by the inquiry into his financial affairs. I add that there has been an invasion of his privacy as well."

I shrugged. "As I said, I know nothing about slander, and nothing about invasion of privacy, either. I'm representing a client accused of murder and I have a responsibility to investigate the case. Mr. Burroughs and Mr. Garvey were engaged in some dealings at the time of Mr. Garvey's death and I have reason to believe that matters might have become heated."

My casual tone was gasoline on the fire. "What in the hell are you talking about?" he snarled. "What kind of dealings?"

"I'm not free to discuss that right now, but you may be able to help your client anyway."

"Is that so?"

"Yes. If he would submit to an interview we might be able to clear up some issues without causing him any further embarrassment."

Burnside bolted upright in his chair. "You want me to consent to an interview of *my* client by *you*?"

"That's right. I want to ask him about his relationship with Mr. Garvey and maybe a few other things. Of course, you could be present. I don't mind."

"You don't mind." He clasped his hands on the desk. "I have a counterproposal. You stop inquiring into Mr. Burroughs's affairs, and then you send him a letter of apology—very sincere—begging his forgiveness and acknowledging that he had absolutely nothing to do with the death of Garvey. If all goes well *and* we're feeling generous, next year you might still be practicing law in this city. How does that sound?"

"Pretty rough."

"Good."

"How much time do I get to think it over?"

"About twenty seconds. You've used ten."

"Okay. No deal."

Burnside leaned back in his chair. "Then let me tell you what's going to happen to you. When you finish this case no one is going to hire you. No one. You are going to be asked to leave your current firm and no other firm is going to want you or even rent you space. I understand you make your living loitering around the jail, getting paid a minimum wage to represent poor people who have no choice but to use your services. Well, that, too, will end because you're going to be dropped from the list of distinguished counsel qualified for such work. In no time at all your life as you know it will be over. Perhaps you can pass the bar in some distant state but if we were to find out about it there would be nothing there for you, either. By the way, I understand that you used to drink to excess. I suggest you start again because the numbness may be a comfort. Now, how does *that* sound?"

"Not very good."

He was in charge now, clearly enjoying himself. "And what will you do when all that terrible misfortune befalls you?"

"I have no idea. I'm not the one to ask."

"You're not the one to ask." He sneered, shaking his head with disgust.

"You might try Noah Applebaum."

His jaw muscles began to twitch. "Is he another jailhouse lawyer?"

I shook my head. "My therapist. He's been treating me for several years."

"You're even more stupid than I imagined."

"No, not stupid, stressed. You've probably heard of it—posttraumatic stress syndrome. I had some bad experiences in Vietnam and I have these flashbacks when I'm under stress." I leaned forward and lowered my voice. "Once, in a place called the A Shau Valley, I strangled this VC sentry with a garrote made of piano wire and clothespins"—I pantomimed looping the wire around my victim's throat—"almost severed his damn head. Sometimes, when I'm really upset"—my fists jerked from side to side—"I can still feel him flapping and kicking like a fish on a line." I gave a hard, last yank, the coup de grâce; Burnside flinched. "Noah feels that I might hurt someone if I'm pushed too hard, so it's therapy once a week and stress management techniques in between." I relaxed and let the body drop; he stared at the spot where it lay. "He says I'm to avoid stressful or threatening situations but that's hard to do in our business." I shrugged at the futility of it all, then picked up a pad and pen from his desk. "Listen, I know it sounds like bullshit. Let me give you his number. I'll tell him that he's free to discuss my problems and what might happen if you ruin my life." I tossed the pad across the desk.

Burnside recoiled. His forehead was moist and he was breathing through his mouth, emitting little croaking noises. "I was just trying to . . . uh . . ." His voice failed but his hands picked up the thread and motioned apologetically.

It was time to take my leave. "Look, I'm sorry that Mr. Burroughs is upset but we all have our jobs to do, right? If you have to ruin my life because I'm doing mine, well, I'll try to deal with it but I just can't promise anything, you understand." I stood, stretching to my full height.

Burnside looked up. "Wha-what?"

I leaned over the desk; he flattened against his chair. "I said, 'Do we understand each other?'" He nodded vigorously. "Good. Then I think we're all going to come out of this okay." His secretary scurried for the elevator button when I emerged but I took the stairs.

In the law, there is this thing called "self-help," as when the car dealer repossesses the vehicle instead of suing a deadbeat. I'd just engaged in a little myself: a touch over the top, perhaps, but he had it coming. There was a bounce in my step as I sauntered back to the office.

\* \* \*

The aroma of crab gumbo was in the air when I arrived at our kitchen headquarters. Walter was ensconced with a beer and his paper, too engrossed in the crossword to acknowledge my arrival. Ashley was curled up in the chair opposite with a glass of wine. Our eyes met as I was removing my coat and she probed for regrets or second thoughts. *None, thank you, and you? Likewise.* So, wordlessly, we made our little pact: no looking back, and no looking forward, either. One day at a time. It might have been pragmatism; it was probably fear.

Martha almost smiled when she set my usual on the table. Apparently our mistress had set her straight on the new arrangement, which meant that there was only one party who hadn't gotten an announcement. Ashley took care of that little detail as soon as the three of us were alone.

"Walter," she purred, smiling. "Frank and I slept together last night."

"I'm shocked," he muttered, not looking up. "What's a six letter word for 'dark,' startin' with 'G'?"

"Gloomy," she replied. "Look, don't be angry. I didn't want to go to prison a virgin. It was a mercy fuck."

He grunted. She winked. I wiped mineral water off my chin.

Eventually, we moved on to the gumbo and business and her good humor vanished when I reported my summons from Burnside. "What did he say?" she asked.

"They're unhappy. They feel that Burroughs has been slandered."

"What are they going to do?"

"I don't think there's much they *can* do."

"What did he *say* they were going to do?"

"Well, he talked about taking action but I explained that we were simply investigating a case as we had a perfect right to do, and no court would fault us for asking questions about Garvey's activities before he died."

Ashley slowly swirled the wine around in her glass. "He didn't accept that, did he?"

"Well, I think he came to understand our position." I turned my attention to the gumbo a bit too quickly, but before she could follow up Walter fished out his notebook and began his report without preamble.

"Octagon Associates is a New York corporation with a business address care of a downtown law firm, Charlton and Revis. It's been registered since nineteen thirty-nine, but for an outfit that's been doin' business over fifty years it hasn't made much of an impression—no phone number, no D and B rating, no lawsuits, no credit report, no nothin'. There's an account at a downtown branch of Chase Manhattan Bank but they got it under a power of attorney held by the law firm."

"That's it?" I asked.

"That's it."

"Then what next?"

"We've gone about as far as we can legally go." The choice of adverb seemed to go right past Ashley, who was still ruminating about Burroughs and slander.

"Frank, you're still sure we're doing the right thing?" she asked.

"Absolutely. Listen, there's something to all of this, we're sure of it. Burroughs and Garvey were involved with Octagon and whatever they were up to had something to do with your father."

She wasn't convinced. "Raymond was responsible for my father's death but how can you be so sure about Sherry and Octagon? Aside from the time period there's nothing tying it all together. It's all circumstantial."

I looked at Walter. "Well," he said, "now that we're all one big happy family . . ." He took an envelope from his breast pocket and spread the contents on the table. "These are copies of Riggs Bank statements for Garvey's account," he explained. "There are two fifty-thousand-dollar deposits, in August and September, both cashier's checks drawn on the Chase Manhattan bank in New York, and the money came from Charlton and Revis. Garvey was actin' for Octagon because it was payin' the freight."

Ashley examined them. "How did you get these?"

"Detective work," he said. There are some things you don't share, even with family.

"How can you tell where the deposits came from? The statements don't say."

"Detective work," he repeated.

"Do you have more detective work planned?" I asked.

"Yeah. Harry's come up with a lead. Sherry fired some old biddy who was his housekeeper for years and she's supposed to be pretty steamed. She's working for some family over in Chevy Chase but she's a tough nut—won't talk to cops or detectives."

A witness from Burroughs's own household could be a godsend. "What's her name?"

He checked his notes. "Maureen Carmody."

"There's your problem right there. You need a smooth-talking Irishman for the job."

"Some of that blarney, huh? She's all yours."

\* \* \*

Walter left after coffee in the library and Martha had gone to bed; we were alone and Ashley was lost in thought. I was doing some thinking myself, mostly about how the evening was going to end. As enamored as I was, I had enough sense to realize that the more time we spent together the harder it would be to do my job.

She spoke first. "I want to ask you something. It's about my case."

"Go ahead."

"You haven't said anything about the journal."

"I've only read part of it and it's not the usual kind of journal. Your father didn't write about events so much as what he thought about them, so you can't really tell what's going on."

"So, you haven't found the reason why Raymond and Sherry were tormenting him?"

"No. I think that photograph I showed you might have been taken in California, possibly around Hollywood or Los Angeles somewhere. You don't have any idea what he might have been doing there in the fifties, do you?"

She shook her head. "He never talked about it and I never found any records."

"What about people? Is there anyone still around who he was close to at the time?"

"There's a man named Herbert Epstein who lives in a little town in Pennsylvania. He and my father were classmates at college and I think they kept in touch."

"When was the last time you saw him?"

"I don't recall ever meeting him. What I've just told you was in his letter of condolences."

"I may pay him a visit."

"Should I go along?"

"I'd love the company but I think I should do this alone."

She rested her head on my shoulder. "You've been pretty quiet tonight," she said.

"I suppose."

"Does it have anything to do with last night?"

"I've been thinking about this article I read in *Cosmopolitan*."

"Hmm. I didn't figure you for a *Cosmo* kind of guy."

"Well, you haven't plumbed my depths."

"The checkout line at the supermarket, right?"

"I have to stay in touch with the needs of the modern woman."

"Keep it up. You handled *my* needs real well."

I put my arm around her and lowered my voice. "Did you know that the interval between 'stay-overs' defines the course of a relationship as much as the decision to go to bed in the first place?"

"No, I didn't."

"Uh-huh. And good sense should rule, not libido."

"Do tell."

"*Cosmo* said it would probably fall to me to make the right choice."

"Of course," she murmured, running a finger along my ear. "Did it explain how you're supposed to do this?"

"There was a chart with categories for different kinds of relationships. It's a little complicated, actually."

"Did they have a category called 'Couples Operating under a Compressed Schedule Because One of Them Might Be Going to Prison for a Long Time'?"

"Uh, no."

"Then let's go to bed. I'll plumb your depths."

She had a way of simplifying things.

\* \* \*

A criminal trial is a morality play for a small audience, and a good lawyer aspires to be its producer, director, and star. But before the play there's the rehearsal, and before the rehearsal there's the script, written during the investigation. It can be the hardest part of the job and the most interesting: the lawyer as biased historian, chronicling some order that succumbed to a calamity of its own making, striving to understand how people thought, acted, and related to one another, their idiosyncrasies, habits, customs, and predilections, all to reconstruct and interpret the past in the manner most favorable to the client.

I considered my approach to Sherry's former housekeeper during the drive over to Chevy Chase. Usually, I'd yield to Walter as an interrogator but my instincts told me to handle this one myself. The first task when dealing with a witness is to get your foot in the door, so I managed to be suitably vague when I telephoned and she didn't press for particulars. But if she was anxious to discuss her former employment, she'd managed some concealment of her own.

"Kerry, is it?" Maureen Carmody arched an eyebrow as she poured the tea. So much for instinct: I'd been in the house for over an hour without asking a single question; she, however, was a match for Walter on his best day. We'd covered my professional history, the parishes I'd lived in back in New York, my marriage and divorce ("a pity"), and were now playing the Irish version of *Roots*.

"I think so."

"Killarney?"

"Um, I'm not sure."

"Mostly tourists, Killarney. We're from Sligo. Yeats country."

"I see."

"And your dear mother's side?" she cooed, handing me a cup. Her pallor was barely distinguishable from the porcelain.

"They're not Irish," I mumbled. She received my confession without comment but began to pay great attention to her tea. My mission was in jeopardy. It seemed I'd spent my whole life paying for the improvidence of Terry O'Connell.

"So, Mr. O'Connell," she said, sighing, "what is it all about, then?"

"It's about Raymond Garvey. I suppose you know that my client has been accused of killing him."

"The whole world knows, doesn't it? Why have you come to see me?"

"We believe that Sherman Burroughs knew Mr. Garvey, and it's important that I find out about their relationship."

"Why?"

"That's difficult to explain right now. As a lawyer there

are certain confidences I must respect. I'm sure you understand."

"Oh, of course. And as a former employee *I* have to respect certain confidences, don't I?"

"Of course."

"Not that I owe them anything, you understand." Her lips
compressed into a thin line; a bit of color seeped into her
cheeks. "Twenty-four years!" she spat. "Twenty-four years
of good service!" She paused, waiting; I nodded enthusiasti-
cally. "And what did I ask in return? Transport home? Not
once! A big raise? Hah!" She snorted. "Not likely in their
condition!" She put a hand on my knee. "Health insurance!"

"Health insurance?"

"Did they think I don't read the newspaper? Watch the
television? All those stories about people getting sick and
losing their life savings."

"Terrible," I agreed.

"Not my concern. I'm on the far side of fifty and never
took a sick day in my life! My mother is eighty-one and she
has six sisters and brothers between seventy-five and ninety-
two."

"That's wonderful."

"Thank God and the Blessed Mother. But does that mean
a body couldn't fall down a flight of stairs? Or get hit by a
car on the way to market?"

"Of course not."

"Of course not! We have to be prepared! Who doesn't
have health insurance today?"

Apparently, only a few domestics and lawyers. I frowned
at the unfairness of it all. "They discharged you because you
asked for health insurance?"

She looked indignant. "Discharged me? And find someone to slave for them like I did all those years? Not likely! I
quit! Gave my notice! If they wouldn't provide for my peace
of mind then I couldn't be of any use to them—that's what I
said. Two weeks later, here I was."

"And you've got insurance now?"

"I bought my own with a raise in pay. These are generous people, more caring people. The Burroughs—they're a cold lot, I'll say that."

"Well, I guess it's all worked out for the best."

"No one to blame but myself," she muttered, setting down the pot. She looked out the window on the rear yard and fell quiet. I needed her motivated so I sipped my tea while she silently rued her life of service.

Some time passed; she was doing a lot of ruing. For all I knew she began her indenture under Sherry the First, a lot farther back than I needed to go. Finally, I cleared my throat and she revived. "I wouldn't ask you to breach a confidence," I told her, "but if it's possible I need to find out some things about Mr. Burroughs's activities. My client would be very grateful. I'm sure these caring people you work for would be, too."

"I met her once."

"Miss Bronson?"

She nodded. "At a charity event at the Chandlers' home in McLean, one of those silly auction things. I was there to help with the service." She stopped to sip her tea, then shook her head at the remembrance. "Oh, she was something to see. Entered the room wearing this green dress and the conversation just stopped, didn't it? I thought to myself, 'Well now, what have we here?'" She leaned toward me and whispered, "Some of these wealthy people," she began, then thought better of it and shook her head. "But that one, she draws all the light in the room, if you get my meaning."

"I do."

"Well"—she sighed again—"you've come to the right place. It's an old broom that knows the dirty corners best."

"Did Mr. Burroughs know Raymond Garvey?"

"He did." Next to the courtroom, finding a witness was the best part of it.

"How?"

"He was a visitor to the house. I think he and Mr. Burroughs had some type of business together. They met a few times and Mr. Garvey called the house often enough."

"These meetings were all at the house?"

"The ones I know about."

"Do you know anything about a meeting they might have had at a restaurant out in Middleburg?"

"I wasn't his secretary, was I? He didn't tell me where he was going."

"Miss Carmody, this is very important. Do you have any idea what they were meeting about?"

She shook her head. "Not my business. Ask Mr. Burroughs."

"I'm afraid Mr. Burroughs doesn't want to talk—and Mr. Garvey can't."

"There was the third gentleman."

Thank God and the Blessed Mother. "Who?"

She smiled. "Mr. Brown and Mr. Clay."

"Two men?"

She shook her head emphatically. "One."

"I'm sorry. You said 'Mr. Brown *and* Mr. Clay.'"

"First he was Mr. Brown, *then* he was Mr. Clay. When Robert—the chauffeur—met him at the airport, he was told to hold a sign that said, 'Mr. Brown.' But one time he called the house all upset about something or other. I told him that Mr. Burroughs had gone out riding and he said, 'Tell him you heard from Mr. Clay.' And then he made me repeat, 'Mr. Clay.' It was the same man, though."

"How do you know it was the same man?"

"The voice, sir. Not one you'd forget: funny accent, European, but I couldn't say from where."

"How many times was he at the house?"

"Three or four, I think. More tea?"

"Yes, thank you. Was Mr. Garvey there each time Mr. Brown came to the house?"

"No. Mr. Burroughs met him a few times alone. Now, that's when *I* was there. If they met on my day off I wouldn't know about it."

"Well, can you tell me anything about him? Where did he come from?"

"No idea, sir. Robert always picked him up and let him off outside the terminal—Mr. Burroughs's instructions."

"What did he look like?"

"An older man, about sixty-five, I'd say. Thin but not frail, if you know what I mean. Stood very straight. A very hard-looking man."

"Hard?"

She nodded. "Never smiled. Had this gray-brown hair, very short. And very disturbing eyes."

"Why disturbing?"

"They didn't blink. God is my witness, the man was *always* staring. Gave me the shivers. And he had this scar on the back of his hand, an ugly thing."

"Which hand?"

"The left one. Ran right up under his watchband."

"When was the last time you saw or heard from him?"

"That telephone call."

"Miss Carmody, this could be important. Do you have any idea when that was?"

"Oh, I do indeed. It was a Sunday. The phone rang as I was on my way out the door and I almost ignored it. It was my day to serve as Eucharistic Minister and I was in quite a hurry."

"Of course."

"The church has changed so much in my lifetime." She sighed. "Do they let old maids serve communion at your church, Mr. O'Connell?"

"Uh, sometimes. So, you answered the phone and it was Mr. Brown, calling himself Mr. Clay?"

"It was."

"Is there any way you could recall what date that was?"

"It's on my calendar, isn't it?"

"Would you look it up? It could be important."

"It might help that girl?"

"Yes."

"Then I will." She went downstairs and returned a few moments later with a vinyl-covered spiral calendar bearing the name of a local insurance agency. "Here it is," she said, turning the pages to October. "My appointments." It was probably the only social calendar in Washington with less writing than mine. There were only two entries, and one was "off," penciled on a Wednesday. The other entry, though, was a red circle around a Sunday.

It was October twenty-seventh, the day after Henry's suicide. Mr. Brown-Clay had good reason to be upset: whatever they were after, Ashley's father had just taken it with him.

\* \* \*

A few hours later, I was in bed at Ashley's, where I'd been every night since our maiden voyage three nights before. When you're operating under a compressed schedule you can't dally, and after having taken care of the most important business we were dozing in each other's arms when she spoke.

"How did it go today? Did you find out anything more about Octagon?"

"A new member. Mr. Brown and Mr. Clay."

"Two new members?"

I shook my head, which given our positions, was also nuzzling her neck. "Just one," I murmured into the fold of her skin. "One man, two names."

"He sounds sinister."

"Looked it, too. Old, thin, and eyes that didn't blink." I felt her stiffen. "What is it?" I asked.

"Nothing," she said quietly.

"You sure?"

She turned to face me. "It's disturbing, that's all. This whole thing scares me." She moved close, putting her head on my chest. "I'm just glad you're here," she whispered.

# 11

*HENRY BRONSON'S JOURNAL*

*October 9, 1952. Often, matters are best considered in the abstract; consequences, certainly. Dwelling on realities, could we proceed?*

Fed by the rivulets of thousands of pols and staffers, lawyers and diplomats, lobbyists, publicists, socialites and servants, the river of gossip in Washington runs swift and deep. Inevitably, there is erosion and the occasional flood; reputations and careers get carried away, sometimes overnight. And the river is always changing course. One day, you're on the high ground admiring the view; the next, you're in the current, clinging to a rock.

On Monday, thirteen days after a trickle of telephone calls, the water rushed over the sandbags around the Burroughs estate. The story was page one, just below the fold: Ashley Bronson's defense team was investigating a connection between Raymond Garvey and Sherman P. Burroughs III, the patriarch of a socially prominent Virginia family that had experienced financial difficulties. According to unnamed sources, Garvey and Burroughs had business dealings and a fierce argument just days before the murder. Speaking for Burroughs, Robert Burnside "vigorously" denied any link between his client and Garvey's death. Ashley Bronson's defense counsel, Frank O'Connell, stated that he would have no comment about Mr. Burroughs's alleged relationship to the case.

For a lawyer handling his first high-profile defense, it wasn't bad. The story took longer than I'd figured to show up on the *Post*'s radar, but I felt compelled by Ashley's misgivings to let nature take its course without my help. The reporter had done the legwork to come up with the financial and social angles; I threw in the part about the business dealings and the argument.

We were riding a tiger. Everyone was interested in a twist to a sensational murder case. One TV station showed footage of Burroughs at the Gold Cup races, another did a remote broadcast from his front gate, and a third showed the patriarch alighting from his Rolls. By the time I reached the office messages from all over the country covered my desk: television, newspapers, magazines, and, of course, the tabloids. My primary objective, though, was reaching the local audience. Warner couldn't strike all the prospective jurors who had read stories about Sherry; some would get on our jury. But even if he somehow eliminated everyone who read a newspaper or watched TV news, we'd be left with the poorest, least educated citizens in the city, those most suspicious of CIA agents and rich guys with names like "Miles Kellogg" and "Sherman Pierce Burroughs." I'd settle for that.

Part of our new strategy was working fine but it wouldn't mean much without a decent story to go with it. We had to unravel Octagon and the secret in Henry's past.

I sorted through the messages until I found one that got my immediate attention, an urgent call from Maureen Carmody. She'd been contacted by a tabloid TV show and needed to speak with me *at once*. Jesus, those guys were good: they'd determined her existence and tracked her down in a matter of hours. I assumed I was in for a piece of the Irish temper but—*surprise!*—she was calling for advice: five thousand dollars had been offered for her tale of life inside the Burroughs household, and what did I think? More news, more interest—that was the upside. The downside was the American distaste for tattletales and informers. Witnesses who'd sold their stories were usually slaughtered on cross-examination. Rogavin would gut her, then toss her carcass on the defense table. But to her credit and my relief, Maureen wasn't keen on talking. The Irish took a backseat to no one in their distaste for informers, and a gentle reminder about the confidentiality issue was all it took to confirm her own inclinations. I hung up hoping we wouldn't have to revisit the issue when the price began to climb.

At two o'clock, I received a hand-delivered letter from Burnside enclosing a copy of a complaint lodged with the D.C. Bar. He closed by saying, "We regret this drastic step was necessary, but feel that the circumstances require that we commit this matter to the Ethics Committee for appropriate action." The implication was this was as far as he was going to go, and please don't strangle him in the parking lot. He didn't have to worry. There wasn't a significant defense lawyer in the country whose ethics hadn't been called into question at one time or another, usually by some "expert" who had no idea what it was like to step into the arena to fight for someone's life. But by the time the Bar got around to deciding whether I'd overstepped my bounds, the trial of Ashley Bronson would be history, and either way, its opinion wouldn't be high on my list of concerns.

I was providing "deep background" to *Newsweek* when another pile of messages were brought in. My secretary had taken to categorizing them and handed me two for special attention. One was from Pop; the other said, "your son."

I held it up. "My son?"

"I think so, Mr. O'Connell. A little boy."

"What did he say?"

"He wanted his father. I asked who that was and he hesitated—I think he was talking to someone else—then he said, 'Frank.' I told him you were on the phone and asked if he wanted to leave a message. He was so cute. He said, 'I miss you.' Just like that: 'I miss you,' like he was talking to you and . . . is something the matter?"

I waved her away, mumbling my thanks. It had been more than two weeks since the night he waved good-bye, with no visits and no calls. I couldn't deal with my family starting a new life so I avoided it by avoiding them. I took a deep breath and dialed; Moira answered the phone.

"It's me. I got his message."

"He said he missed you so I let him call."

"Thanks. I mean it."

She lowered her voice. "I told him that you were away on a case so just tell him that."

"Don't worry, I'll fool him. He's just a kid, right?" I exhaled. "Maybe he *is* better off with a new father."

"He's not getting one. That's never going to happen."

Knowing her, she meant it, but how would she feel in four or five years? "When can I see him?"

"What about tonight?"

"The sooner the better. I'll pick him up at six."

"No, we'll have dinner here."

"Listen, you don't—"

"Frank, let's just use the time, okay? For Brendan."

"Okay . . . For Brendan. Thank you."

Pop was next. His secretary said he was in conference but wanted to be interrupted if I called. I had a feeling about what was coming: he'd never been deterred by the small matter of the divorce, and he'd pull out all the stops to get his daughter and me back together if he knew about Rob and San Francisco.

He didn't waste any time. "Francis, we need to talk," he rumbled. The tone removed all doubt: he knew, and we—his daughter and I—we're in for the full treatment. I was summoned to his office the following day.

There was one more call to make before heading to Moira's. I dialed Ashley's new private number and she answered the phone herself. "Caught the news?" I asked.

"It's hard to miss."

"Not having second thoughts, are you?"

"No. And if you're seeking refuge from the storm I'm cooking again and this place is starting to smell pretty wonderful."

"Uh, I can't come over."

"Oh . . . That's okay. I—"

"I'm going to see Brendan. He called and left me a message and he sounded sad and said he missed me and I haven't seen him for a couple of weeks, so I figured—"

"Wait a minute, okay? Slow down."

"I'm sorry," I muttered. "Jesus, I feel like a guy breaking a prom date."

"We don't have a date, remember? We're taking this one day at a time."

"I lost my head. It's that damn *Cosmopolitan*."

"Frank, listen to me. I'll probably be awake till midnight. You're not expected—*not* expected, understand?—but if you change your mind later you can call me on this number. Either way, it's okay."

"All right." Noah would have called my condition "conflicted"; Walter would have chosen something more earthy.

*   *   *

Moira was determined to use the time. The three of us hadn't sat at the dining room table since I moved out, and Brendan was loving it. He never stopped talking, in part because his mother fed him a stream of leading questions to make sure I heard about school, indoor soccer, his decision to become a Navy frogman, and everything else that I could never seem to get out of him when we were alone. My boy was about to become a real person; I just never dreamed that it might happen without me. When I came downstairs after putting him to bed she was washing pots and rinsing dishes, so I fell in alongside to dry and load the dishwasher. It was our old routine, the time for discussing the big and small issues of family life. That was in the past, and anything that could precipitate another scene was taboo, so we discussed the case.

"I've been reading the paper," she said. "Should I feel sorry for Burroughs?"

"No."

"I don't understand. When you told me she was going to be convicted I assumed she was guilty."

"She is, but odds are Burroughs had a hand in what happened, at least indirectly."

"And you're going to give the jury a choice." She smiled. "Well, Pop said you were canny."

"Speaking of Pop, I've been summoned."

"Did he say what he wanted?"

"No, but it sounded like he meant business. Does he know about your plans?"

She shook her head. "I'm working up to telling him but he might suspect something." Pop's intuition was second only to that of a certain Jewish detective.

"This sounds pretty stupid, but is there anything I can do?"

She stared at the dishwater a moment before answering. "When the time comes," she said quietly, "just tell him you're okay with it."

"Sure." Just one more deception; they were beginning to pile up.

I stopped in a gas station on the way back downtown. I dialed Ashley's number, then hung up and drove straight to my apartment building. It was only nine-thirty and there was plenty of time for a walk.

# 12

*March 7, 1954. If I could only dwell on my own ac-
complishments, these days would be the best I will
ever know. I have exceeded my expectations of myself,
and the realization that I have, that I could, ought to
be my satisfaction. But the times require a broader
view. Reason compels it. If a family is threatened,
could any member be content?*

The firm hadn't changed. Pop had no partners, not since I
left, but there were three senior lawyers with first-rate credentials, a cadre of law clerks blessed with important relatives, and two full-time lobbyists who worked the Hill for
the firm's clients. Pop also had two assistants. Millie Fields
was a middle-aged woman from Minnesota who arrived in
1968 to toil in McCarthy's "flower power" campaign for the
Democratic nomination. She typed and filed while Gene
tilted at America's windmills, and now she toiled for Edward Brennan, windmill-protector par excellence. Pop had
tried to play the matchmaker for years but things never
seemed to work out, and she still returned each night alone
to a walk-up in Adams-Morgan.

The other assistant was Margaret McCauley, Pop's right
hand since Creation. "Maggie Mac" kept the calendars, sent
the gifts, forged his signature, and guarded the moat during
times of crisis. Depending on what or who needed fixing,

there could be a dozen people vying for the chair in front of Edward Brennan's desk. Maggie decided who got an audience and who didn't, and was privy to all the skulduggery plotted within the walls of Brennan Castle. She was also a cousin, blood ties being essential for the job. Pop always marveled at the never-ending parade of legislators, lobbyists, and executives carted off to the hoosegow on the say-so of trusted assistants. He'd just shake his head and say, "That's why the good Lord created family."

Maggie knocked on the oak sliding doors to Pop's office and then ushered me inside. I don't think I'd ever had a greater sense of well-being than the first years I'd spent in that office; entering again was like returning to the womb. The dark green walls were covered with a mix of paintings and photographs of Pop's favorite people and places. There were none of the standard photos of VIPs except for a small one on his desk, a black and white of him and a young John F. Kennedy sailing on Nantucket Sound. Dominating one wall was a panoramic photo of the interior of a Limerick pub, so real that every ruddy face told a story, and at one time or another I'd imagined a biography for each. There was a painting of Moira's mother over the fireplace, and that photograph of all of us on the beach at Nantucket hung between the windows that looked out onto Jefferson Street.

Pop pushed himself up from his chair by the fireplace. He had those good Irish longevity genes but the aging process was starting to accelerate and I felt a pang over the months that had passed since my last visit. We hugged for a moment longer than usual, just squeezing and patting each other's back before he lowered himself again and motioned me into my old chair across from his. We'd spent a lot of evenings in front of the fireplace like that. He would pour two whiskeys and we'd talk: business, politics, family matters, and the future. He said he wanted to live long enough to see Brendan in the firm.

Sometimes Moira would call and those were small, magical moments. I'd tell her that I was with Pop and I'd play the middleman, relaying their comments back and forth until he'd finally get on himself. He'd always ask, "Is he treating you good, my girl?" and her reply would made him laugh, until that one night, near the end, when she must have cried.

"So tell me," he began, "how does it feel to be a big shot?"

"If I wasn't worrying all the time I'd probably enjoy it."

"Ah, lad, worry is rust upon the blade."

"Another Irish proverb?"

"Henry Ward Beecher, but he must've stolen it from an Irishman because who knows more about worry than us?" He looked into his glass and frowned.

"Are *you* worried about something, Pop?"

He took a sip of his whiskey before answering. I was starting to get nervous: if this wasn't about Moira it had to be something almost on par. "Lad," he said, "you know I respect your judgment when it comes to courtroom doings, but this thing with Burroughs . . . Now, Francis, if I'm off base here just tell me to stow it before I start."

"Go on, I'm listening."

"Lad, the papers and television are having a field day and a lot of people are concerned—upset you might say—about what's happening."

"I had no idea you knew Sherman Burroughs, Pop."

"Barely. But I've been hearing from a lot of people who do." He took another swallow from his glass. "A lot of people," he repeated.

"And they asked you to have a family chat with the former son-in-law?"

"We'll leave family out of it. Let's just say a business discussion with a former partner. I'm told the man is pretty distraught."

"Action and care will in time wear down the strongest frame, but guilt and melancholy are poisons of quick dispatch."

"That doesn't sound like an Irish proverb, either."

"Thomas Paine. Pop, even if he didn't pull the trigger he's getting what he deserves."

"You mean he had a hand in it?"

"In a manner of speaking."

"I don't follow, Francis. Was he a conspirator?"

"No."

"Well, he didn't pull the trigger and he didn't conspire to have it done. That takes in all the territory, doesn't it?"

"No, it doesn't."

"It does as far as the rest of the world is concerned, and that's what people are thinking."

"I'm investigating the connection between Burroughs and Raymond Garvey. I can't help what people think."

"Maybe I've been at this game too long but I read the papers and thought I recognized the fine hand of Ashley Bronson's lawyer."

"C'mon, Pop. You know what I'm up to."

He looked into his empty glass. "Let an old man have one more question and I'll shut up. This is something you have to do?"

"This is something I have to do."

He exhaled. "Well, that's it then. I've had my say." He began to push himself up out of his seat. "A drink, lad?"

"Let me get it." I went to the sideboard and poured two whiskeys into Waterford tumblers. The announcement of the partnership of Brennan & O'Connell was next to the silver tray, encased in glass. I was completely surrounded by reminders of what I'd had, and starting to remember why I'd stayed away. We talked a little more about this and that, but the subject of Moira's new love interest never came up and we were laughing about Brendan's Christmas list when Pop excused himself to take an urgent call from a client.

I passed the time staring at the beach photo, imagining that the man with his back to the camera was Rob, and was at the bottom of my own glass when Pop returned. "This health care business," he complained, "there's a lot of pigs feeding at that trough." He clapped me on the knee and winked. "So, tell me about Miss Bronson. What's she like?"

"What's she like?" I hesitated. "Well . . . she's smart. She paints and edits a small magazine, and she seems to have the stuff to get through this pretty well."

"Seems to be in Moira's league for the looks."

"I suppose . . . In that league."

"Have you been to home, lad?" he asked quietly. He still regarded Moira's house as mine.

"Last night. We all had dinner together."

His face lit up. "You did! Well, that's good, isn't it?"

"Pop, it was dinner. Don't get carried away."

He raised his hands in surrender. "Can't a man hope? Would you deny him that, now?"

"Pop . . ." My voice faltered. If I had had the courage I would have told him right then and spared Moira the grief.

"All right." He sighed. "I'll mind my own business."

"I'm sorry, Pop. I'm really batting a thousand, aren't I?"

"It's all right, lad. We do what we must do."

"I've got to go back to the office. This Burroughs thing—it's not going to cause you any headaches is it?"

"I'll be fine." He looked at me with concern. "What about you?"

"Well, it's still better than kicking around the cellblocks, right?"

He smiled. "That it is." I helped him to his feet and we walked to the threshold and embraced. He held me a second longer as I turned to go. "Lad, one thing," he said. "If something is made of this situation I don't think there's much I could do. You should know that."

"Is something going to be made of it, Pop?"

He frowned. "I'd be surprised if there wasn't."

* * *

As usual, Pop's radar was infallible. The letter from the Ethics Committee was waiting when I got back to the office. The first paragraphs were what I'd anticipated: they had received Burnside's complaint and would be initiating an inquiry, blah, blah, blah. No problem, I thought, take your time. I skimmed to the last paragraph, stopped, and read it again, slowly: "As the issues raised by Mr. Burnside's letter involve a current criminal prosecution, it is the Committee's considered view that the matter ought to be referred forthwith to the presiding court for whatever action is deemed presently necessary. The Committee will commence its review immediately following the completion of the case."

It proved to be the first wave of a coordinated attack. An order from Warner's chambers arrived in the midafternoon announcing that the court would conduct its own review of the matter, to include an interview of all defense counsel. I was to meet with Warner on Friday. The order was sealed from public view: this was a matter between the defense and the court; even Rogavin was sitting it out, although he had received a copy.

I had underestimated Burroughs's pull, or Delbarton & Brand's, but I had ample reason to investigate the relationship between Sherry and Raymond Garvey and I didn't leak the investigation to the *Post*. Let 'em come, I figured, no problem.

It didn't take long to change my mind. Andy read the order as if it was his draft notice, the color draining from his face. "What does he need to talk to *me* about?" he whined.

I tried to sound reassuring. "He just wants to ask us questions about Sherman Burroughs—his connection to the case, what we did by way of inquiry, any press contacts, stuff like that. Maybe other things."

"What other things?"

"I don't know." I slid Warner's order back to my side of the desk. "It says that the court will look into '*any* possible breaches of the Code of Ethics.' There may be some general questions."

"Is he going to ask about the journal?"

"He doesn't know about the journal."

"But will he ask any questions that will require me to talk about it?"

"I thought we already covered that subject. There was nothing unethical about receiving the journal."

Andy's gaze remained fixed on the order as he spoke. "I'm . . . I'm not sure I agree. I think I feel the same way I did before." He exhaled and raised his eyes to mine. "What would Warner do if he found out about it?"

"I don't know. He could order me to turn it over to the police."

"Then Rogavin would have it?"

"No, because I wouldn't obey the order."

His eyes widened. "You wouldn't . . ."

"That's right, I'd appeal."

"Of course, an appeal!" he enthused, plainly relieved that I had something legitimate in mind. "You'd have to appeal and we'd know the right thing to do."

"And if it goes against us, Rogavin will use the journal and Ashley will be convicted of first degree murder."

"We don't have any choice."

"We can make up our own minds about the ethics question. If we decide there was no breach then there's no reason to bring up the journal in the first place."

"I've already thought about it—a lot."

"You've thought about it like it's some kind of law school exam. You need to think a little more like an advocate."

"I thought we're supposed to be objective about ethical judgments."

"Andy, I'm going to tell you this once, and regardless of what you decide, try to remember it: in the real-world practice of law there are *no* objective points of view. *Everyone* brings his own subjectivity to the process: prosecutors, defense lawyers, clients, witnesses, judges—especially judges. If you forsake your point of view in favor of some elusive neutrality, your client is in deep trouble."

He drew an arc on the rug with the toe of his shoe. "If you're right," he said deliberately, "then there are no ethical standards. It's moral relativism."

"Don't turn this into a dormitory debate. Lawyers have to make judgment calls and there's nothing wrong with giving our client the benefit of the doubt. What if the Court of Appeals goes against us by a two-to-one vote? Are you going to sleep well with Ashley in prison?"

"I will if justice is done," he declared.

"You only think you will. And I'll let you in on a little secret: there's no such thing as justice, in or out of court."

"Who says?"

"Clarence Darrow, a guy who knew a little about practicing law. Look, think it over. I'm hoping you come to see things differently, and I'm sure Ashley will be, too." That was as much pressure as I wanted to put on him right then.

"I'll think about it," he mumbled, rising from the chair. "But I don't think about defending Ashley like it's some kind of law school quiz. I just want to do the right thing." He waited for some conciliatory words but there was too much at stake and I was beyond playing fair.

I called Walter's pager and he was on the line two minutes later. "Where are you?" I asked.

"The Holy Land. Guess whose picture is on the front page of the *Times*?"

"All hell's breaking loose down here, too. Any progress?"

"Mr. Brown's description didn't register with the security and maintenance people at Charlton and Revis's buildin'. Neither did the name Octagon. I snagged the seat next to the firm's receptionist at lunch: same story. I'm gonna hang around to try the night shift. Meanwhile, I'm checking out the lobby and tomorrow I'm callin' on some friends to see if Octagon rings any bells."

"Sounds like a long shot."

"You want long shot? I got Harry and Dan looking for a connection between Octagon and Kellogg."

"Wouldn't *that* be the brass ring?"

"In your dreams, right? What are you gonna do?"

"I'm getting out of town. Sherry's fighting back and I'm under siege." I told him about the Ethics Committee and Warner's inquiry.

"You'll handle it," he said.

"It's more complicated than that. The judge wants to see Andy and our young associate is troubled."

"That little item in your credenza?"

"Don't say you warned me."

"I'd get out of town, too. Where you goin'?"

"Pennsylvania. I've got an appointment with an old friend of Henry Bronson's. With you working on Octagon and me on Henry's secret, maybe one of us will find the key. Meet back here tomorrow night?"

"Yeah, if you ain't arrested. Hey, the lobby's fillin' up with commuters. Gotta go."

# 13

*March 27, 1954. In science, there are no bad discoveries. All knowledge accrues to the common good. Not so, discoveries of the self. But great endeavor offers opportunities for self-discovery that might never have been contemplated, and if contemplated, might never have been sought: to know our own natures and not just the nature of things. And the greatest difficulty lies not in choosing between self-interest and the common good, but in knowing the difference. Alea jacta est.*

Herbert Epstein's house sat on the shoulder of a ridge paralleling the river on the west side of town, its roof visible from the gas station on the main street. I was thirty minutes early but I called from a public phone and he told me to come ahead, and was waiting on his front porch when I pulled into the driveway. At seventy-five he looked pretty spry dressed in khaki trousers, a plaid shirt, and work boots. Wisps of white hair and a neatly trimmed beard set off the ruddy complexion of a man who spent a lot of time outdoors. He offered a firm handshake and after a few pleasantries, led me inside to a kitchen in the rear of the house with a wood stove, pine furniture, and faded curtains.

"Take a seat," he instructed. "I was about to have lunch."

"I'm sorry, I should have waited before calling."

"No problem. It's only soup and I can open another can. What about it?"

"Thanks, I appreciate it, Mr. Epstein."

"Herbert. You're at my table."

"Fine. Make it Frank."

He opened a cupboard over the sink and tilted his head back to read the labels through his bifocals. "Chicken, vegetable, or barley. Your choice."

"Vegetable."

"One vegetable, one chicken," he muttered. "You're in for a treat. I've got homemade bread to go with it."

"You're a baker?"

"Me?" He snorted. "Shit, I can barely heat the soup. But the Lord provides. You know all those girls you chased in college and never caught? Well, you outlive their husbands and they all come 'round again. And this time they bring dinner."

"Something to look forward to."

"Know the best part?"

"What?"

"When you're an old man, an old woman doesn't look half-bad. You married?"

"Not anymore."

He poured the contents of the cans into two pots. "Better off without her, right?"

"No."

He glanced at me over his shoulder. "I'm sorry. You live alone too long and you say stupid things." He removed the bread from a coffee can and began slicing. "I was married thirty-six years. No one could replace her, though the widows around here keep tryin'."

"Well, you'll never starve."

He turned and winked. "Not as long as I hang on to my looks. I guess the roles are kind of reversed now, aren't they?"

"I guess so. Have you ever met Ashley, Herbert?"

"Saw her a couple of times. Once when she was an infant

and I think once or twice more when she was a toddler. I went to a few of Henry's parties—back when he had them."

The phone rang, and from his end of the conversation it sounded like another suitor. He winked at me when he asked if he could bring anything, and hung up grinning. "That's where I'll be having dinner tomorrow," he said, chortling. "The best stuffing you ever had. I may marry her for the recipe and go into business for myself."

"It'd be easier just to ask."

"You'd get the gold out of their teeth first. Those recipes are their stock in trade. Now, where were we?"

"Talking about Henry's parties. I understand you and he went to school together."

"Princeton, class of 'forty-four. We went our separate ways a couple of years after graduation; didn't see him again until our fifteenth reunion. After that, we'd exchange cards and an occasional phone call, and he invited me to his wedding. That was in 'sixty-three, just a couple of months before Kennedy was shot. From then on we stayed in touch and I went to several of their parties before Audrey died." He set the bread and soup on the table and sat down. "The last time I saw him was at her funeral. Poor Henry was devastated."

"What was his wife like?"

"Audrey," he said. "Audrey Taylor Bronson." He began to pick his words carefully. "She was . . . attractive, not a raving beauty, I suppose, but attractive in her own way." And by the look in his eyes, in his way, too. Too bad Walter wasn't there to fill in the blanks. "She was the perfect complement to Henry."

"How so?"

"She shared his interests, loved the arts. But Audrey liked parties and conversation, too, and there was plenty of entertaining after she moved in." He chuckled to himself. "You know, Henry was almost forty when they married, but I don't think he ever got five feet away from her when there were people in the house."

"Ashley told me that he was kind of shy."

"Shy?" He smiled. "Hell, he was awkward. A gentle, awkward soul. Loved his books. I think if he could have just stayed in his library he'd have been a happy man. Henry didn't have many friends."

"I understand Raymond Garvey was his friend."

Epstein pulled a face. "Garvey wasn't *anybody's* friend. If you had money or power he'd *act* like your friend, but if you didn't he'd look right through you. And he could work a room like a hooker at a convention."

"So, you knew him?"

"I saw him at Henry's parties. After Audrey died Henry was determined that his limitations not become his daughter's, so Raymond became his link to the outside world. I mean, Raymond knew *everyone*. Henry would have a dinner party and follow Raymond around his own house. It was sad, really, but Raymond got his networking all paid for and Henry kept the channels open for his little girl. Of course, all that changed when she grew up."

"Ashley became the hostess."

"Right. From what I've read, Ashley is everything Audrey was and more. You know what Henry told me once? He couldn't believe God had blessed him with a child like her. He said she was the person he was always admiring from a distance." Epstein shook his head in disgust. "How in the hell could they think she killed anyone? What crap!"

"Herbert, what did Henry do after graduation?"

Epstein paused with his spoon halfway to his mouth. "I think he went on to Chicago for more postgraduate work. I stayed at Princeton to work with Morley Bennett."

"Do you know what he did there?"

"At Chicago?" He shook his head. "I probably did then. Damned if I can remember now."

"Do you have any idea what he might have been doing in California? I understand that he got involved in some kind of project there in the early fifties, possibly in the Los Angeles area."

"Hmm. I think he did go to Los Angeles but I couldn't tell you what he did there."

"Does 'L-cubed' mean anything to you?"

"L-cubed?" He spent a moment concentrating on his bread, spreading butter evenly from the center to the edges before he spoke. "Well, 'L' is the notation for liter, which is a measure of volume, but liter-cubed doesn't make any sense." He bit into the bread and chewed thoughtfully. "You've got to understand: most of the work was done under contract to the government and you weren't supposed to talk about it with people who didn't need to know. A lot of scientists thought that was military horseshit, but I didn't, and knowing Henry, he didn't either."

"He *never* talked about it? Even years afterward?"

"Nope. Henry had left physics far behind by the time of the reunion. If I'd had any family money I would've gone with him."

"Why's that?"

He smiled. "Well, it turned out I was one of those fellows who peaked in his youth. That happens with scientists sometimes. You know, I was on the cover of *The Physicist* before I was thirty-five. It was the first and last time." He sighed. "The ideas just stopped coming. I'm not really sure why."

"What kind of work did you do?"

"Fluid dynamics. I published a paper that got a lot of attention and I was on top of the world." He chewed his bread thoughtfully. "I didn't know then that I'd peaked, of course. A few years later the grant money dried up and it seemed all the good faculty slots had been filled by refugees from Europe. I wound up with a teaching position at a little school near Harrisburg."

"Herbert, do you have any idea how I could find out what Henry did in California?"

He shrugged. "I don't know who he was working with at the time. Maybe I did once but it's been over forty years and"—he touched his head—"the cells die, you know. What about the government? If he was working on anything that was funded by Uncle Sam there'd be a record of some kind."

"Well, that's a bit impractical right now. If you should think of anything, will you call me?"

"Of course. Does this stuff help your case?"

"You never know. Background material can be useful."

"I thought you were going to ask me about that fella Burroughs," he said, and smiled at my reaction. "We *do* get television up here, you know! Anyway, I never heard of him until a couple of days ago."

I got up from the table. "Thanks for lunch and for the help. I've got to be going—plenty to do."

"Yeah, I remember when I had plenty to do. I'll walk you out."

I was buttoning my coat in the vestibule when he put a hand on my shoulder. "Hey!" he chirped. "Got one more minute? I want to show you something before you go." I followed him into a study with a bay window that offered a view of the valley and the Pennsylvania mountains beyond the town. He positioned me in front of a wall covered with photographs and certificates and pointed to one in the center. "There it is," he announced, "Herbert Epstein's fifteen minutes of fame." It was a close-up of a young, handsome Epstein, with a full head of curly black hair and the confident smile of a man with it all in front of him. He was leaning against a bookshelf and displaying a magazine with his own picture on the cover. "What do you think?" he asked, grinning. "Sort of a cross between Tyrone Power and Errol Flynn, right?"

I stared.

"Frank?"

"What? I'm sorry. . . . Errol Flynn. You bet."

The drive back was pretty much a blur. I had gone to Pennsylvania to unravel a mystery but returned more mystified than ever. Young Epstein didn't look like Tyrone Power or Errol Flynn, but he looked very much like a man I'd seen only recently.

In an old photograph.

\* \* \*

I'd promised to call Ashley when I reached the office. "I'm back," I told her.

"Did you see Herbert?"

"Yeah, I did. He doesn't know what your father did in Los Angeles. If he did, he's long since forgotten."

"Oh. Nothing interesting then?"

I wouldn't have said that but I did: "No, nothing," I replied. I said I'd give her the details later.

Walter showed up at seven, looking tired. Even by his standards he was pushing hard. There was too much cop in him to excuse Ashley for what she did, but you would have thought she'd found a soft spot—unless you already knew he didn't have one. What he had was a cop's loyalty and a misguided friend who'd crossed the line with a client.

"No Mr. Brown?" I asked.

"No."

"What about Kellogg? Tell me he's Sherry's half-brother."

"No connection to Octagon," he grumbled. "There was nothin' in his bank account, and your friend Maureen says she never laid eyes on him before. We even tried it the other way: made a sketch of Mr. Brown from her description and showed it around Kellogg's neighborhood."

"A total washout," I said.

"One thing: I bought breakfast for an old friend from the Fibbies, a counterintelligence guy."

"The FBI's on Rogavin's team! What're you doing?"

"Relax. He's retired a long time and I did him plenty of favors."

"You asked him about Octagon? What did he say?"

"Nothin'."

"Nothing . . . I don't understand."

"I mean *nothin'*. The guy just drank his coffee."

"And in cop talk"—I sighed—"that means . . ."

"Whatever Octagon is, it's somethin' that an old counter-intelligence guy knew about and still can't talk about—not even a crumb for an old pal."

"Okay. Now tell me what *that* means."

"A piece of the puzzle, that's all. How'd you make out with Herbert?"

"He says he has no idea what Henry was up to in the fifties."

He looked at me. "And?"

"He lied." I told him about the photograph.

"No shit? Do you think he's involved in this?"

"I don't think he's with Octagon, but if he was working with Henry there's a good chance he knows about the project and what they were after."

"Maybe Harry and I should go see him."

"Jesus, Walter, the guy's seventy-five! What if Harry gives him a goddamn heart attack?"

He considered this a moment. "All right. So, how're you gonna get it out of him?"

"I'm not sure, but we need more leverage before I go back because if I don't rattle him next time, we'll never get close again. By the way, don't say anything to our client about this. I want to find out what Henry was up to before we decide to fill her in."

"We're gonna figure this out," he declared.

"I don't know. We can't even figure Kellogg out. He knows what Ashley did when she left Garvey's but you've got this cockamamie idea that he's a phony. How could that be? And if he *is* a phony, what's his motive? Where's the connection to Octagon?"

"Maybe you're makin' it too complicated. He might have nothin' to do with Octagon. Maybe he's just standin' in for the real witness."

"Why?"

"I got no idea."

"If that's true we'll *never* find a motive."

"Probably not."

I slammed the table in frustration and a pen flew off the desk. "The whole fucking thing is a puzzle but we can't get one goddamn clue!"

He placed the pen back on the desk. "What about the old man's journal?"

"Another puzzle. I'd bet diaries surface in this town at least four times a year, each with more lurid detail than anyone would care to know. We get the exception. Ninety-nine percent of Henry's journal is just his own musings about life, the state of man, and his place in the universe. Here and there is another piece of the story, but it's all oblique reference with no details. He was involved in an important project in California and I think the 'creation' he mentioned in his last entry, the thing that terrorized him, was his contribution, but I'm guessing."

"Was Garvey blackmailin' him or not?"

"I think so, and he had something to work with: those 'consequences of youthful idealism' that Henry wrote about in his last entry. They probably had something to do with a decision he made in nineteen fifty-four that was related to the same project."

"This was some big choice?"

"Yeah. He wrote, 'The die is cast.'"

"What?"

"It's what Julius Caesar said when he crossed the Rubicon. 'Die' as in 'dice.'"

He squinted at me. "He was shootin' craps? What kind of stakes could matter fifty years later?"

"You know, you really have a way with words." But it was a good question, a sixty-four-dollar question.

"Don't finish or nothin', just leave me hangin'."

"That's it. That's all I know. The entries after that are just a mixed bag. If you know generally what happened, you can see it reflected in his writing. Life goes on, he eventually gets married, has a daughter, and man's place in the universe looks pretty good. Then his wife dies and there's a lot of musing about the meaning of it all."

"Nothing more about the big mystery?"

"One thing." I unlocked the credenza and took out one of the volumes, turning to an entry I had marked. "Listen to this."

*June 7, 1982. Enough time had passed that fear had receded, and in retrospect I managed to think myself virtuous, even brave. I woke this morning with the illusion, but I will lay tonight with the reality. My terror is palpable, numbing, far greater than I ever imagined. I thought my choice was informed, but I didn't know myself.*

"What do you think?" I asked.

"He got some bad news. The chickens came home to roost."

"If we knew the news maybe we'd know what this whole thing was about."

"Stands to reason," he said.

"So, what are you going to do next?"

"We're going to work a few new angles on Octagon. Burroughs's chauffeur took Brown to the airport on certain days. He says he can tell us when. We might get our hands on passenger manifests to New York around those times.

And then there's Charlton and Revis. Their bank account—"

I held up my hand. "Whoa. Stop right there, thank you."

He reached for his coat. "You know, you dreamed up this whole Burroughs angle and we started investigatin' on pure spec. But things are comin' together and there's probably a real story in there somewhere: an old man with a secret and an old outfit tryin' to pry it out of him. Who knows what shit Raymond was into? If the truth came out the jury might give her a medal."

"So, this is your way of saying I'm brilliant?"

"Yeah, you're a freakin' genius."

"Thank you."

"But you still ignore the obvious."

"What's obvious?"

"The mystery in the journal—the bad news that the old man got."

"What about it?"

He shook his head. "I break you in and I keep losin' you."

"Oh, I get it. You're Charlie Chan and I'm number one son." I turned and bowed. "Gosh, Pop, what obvious thing am I ignoring?"

"You want news, where do you go?"

"The newspaper."

"Ah so." He headed out the door.

I called after him. "What? You think it's in the *newspaper*?"

"It's where Honorable Ancestor would look," he said, and left.

\* \* \*

Thursday afternoon I got a call from my favorite prosecutor. "It's almost Christmas," he said. "You know what they say: it's better to give than to receive."

"You're dropping the case?"

"Yeah," he replied, chuckling. "It turns out Sherman Burroughs did it."

"What's the present?"

"I've already given you *your* present. Now, it's your turn to give—nothing major, I assure you. I'd just like to collect my gift before Warner bounces you from the case."

"I'm listening."

"Chain of custody on the bullet, from poor Mr. Garvey's head to the ballistics expert. The medical examiner gave the bullet to an FBI agent who played courier. The agent would testify that he took the bullet from the M.E. and hand-carried it to said ballistics expert. If we have to call him as a witness, we will, but he's been transferred to the San Diego field office and budget-conscious as we all are these days, we'd love to save the airfare and associated costs of bringing him back."

"How did an FBI agent get in the chain of custody? The case belonged to the MPD."

"True enough. But Garvey was a former member of the president's Cabinet and the Bureau wasn't taking any chances. So, the good agent was inquiring at the M.E.'s office and volunteered to play messenger. That's it. So, what about it?"

"I'll consider it. I may want to talk to the agent—just to make sure that he isn't dead or anything."

"Of course. Let me know and I'll set up a conference call. I'd appreciate it if we could wrap this up as soon as possible."

"I'll let you know by next week."

"You won't be disbarred by then, will you?" He snickered. "You know, getting ready for trial is tough enough without all these distractions. Why don't you just take our plea offer and call the dogs off of poor Mr. Burroughs, who, as we both know, didn't kill anyone? You can save your client a lot of pain—and ten more years."

"The offer's still on the table? You must be getting nervous."

"Hardly, but then again, all *I* have to think about is the trial. Now, if I were *you*, I'd be nervous."

The man had a point: I *was* me, and I was definitely nervous.

\* \* \*

I was ushered into Warner's chambers promptly at ten on Friday morning. Judges are usually less punctual than prosecutors but he probably couldn't wait to get at me. He was going through a stack of documents at the conference table where I'd left him, so I waited until he looked up and pointed to a place at the far end of the table. There, side by side, were copies of the Ethics Committee letter and the court's order. In criminal proceedings it was customary to furnish the accused with a copy of the charges.

Without a word spoken the point was made that I had not been summoned for a little chitchat, and if my reception was any indication of what was in store for Andy, he could be blathering about the journal before his backside hit the chair. Staring across the gulf at Warner, I reflected on how the decisions that get you into trouble are rarely made without that little warning light flashing somewhere deep within your bowels. The risk of sharing the journal with Andy was plain but I was flushed with the excitement of my clever new strategy, and in one careless moment I might have assured Ashley's conviction.

Another five minutes passed before Warner pushed the stack of papers to one side, then took off his glasses and began to rub his eyes. "Have you had an opportunity to read those documents?" he asked, still rubbing.

"Yes, Judge, I have."

"It's a serious charge."

"I suppose it is."

"Suppose? I wouldn't think there'd be much question about it."

"It's a serious charge."

He replaced his glasses and said, "I told you that I was concerned about how you were going to handle a case of this dimension. Didn't I warn you to conduct yourself in an entirely ethical manner?"

"You did."

"So?"

"There's been no unethical behavior, Judge."

"Not according to Mr. Burnside."

"He's mistaken."

He began to write on a legal pad. "I had several friends and colleagues in the Delbarton firm during my years in private practice, and I must say I always found them quite honorable and credible."

"They may have credibility, Judge, but they're not witnesses to anything. They're just advocating on behalf of a client who claims to be wronged. That's their job, but in this case, they're off base."

"But as lawyers," he countered, "aren't they required to exercise their own judgments about the facts before making serious allegations about someone's character—in this case yours?"

"Yes, they are."

"And, of course," he continued, weaving his web of logic, "you had a similar obligation to Mr. Burroughs, true?"

"I didn't make any allegations against Mr. Burroughs. I merely investigated some of his actions."

"I see. Haven't spoken to the press?"

"Only to respond to their calls. I didn't initiate any press contacts and I didn't leak the fact of my investigation, either."

"Well, *somehow* a great deal of speculation has been engendered about whether Mr. Burroughs is a murderer—or should I say, *the* murderer." He gazed at me, waiting.

"I'm sorry. What do you want to know?"

"For starters, how the *Washington Post* got this story

that you were investigating Sherman Burroughs."

"Your Honor, I can only assume that someone we contacted spoke to the papers or to someone else who then spoke to the papers. It's hard to say. These things get around."

"Indeed. Do you actually believe that Sherman Burroughs murdered Garvey?"

"I don't know that."

"I asked you whether you believe it."

"I'm not fencing with you, Judge, but what I believe has nothing to do with the ethics of my investigation."

"I think it has a great deal to do with it, Mr. O'Connell. A reputation is at stake here."

"Your Honor, I'm not trying to injure Mr. Burroughs's reputation. I'm just trying to fulfill my obligation to provide a zealous defense for my client, and that means presenting any evidence that might create a reasonable doubt about her guilt. I can't help it if that stirs up speculation."

"Whether what you're doing is within the bounds of ethical representation is for *me* to decide, at least for now. I want all the facts: the basis for investigating Mr. Burroughs, who you spoke to, and what you learned."

"I'd practically have to put on my defense right here."

"Go ahead, I've got time." He flipped to a new page on his pad.

Delbarton & Brand had credibility and I was a drug lawyer in over his head. I bit my tongue and reminded myself of my mission. "I have reason to believe that there was a relationship between Mr. Burroughs and the deceased, some type of business deal involving a third party and large amounts of money. I also have reason to believe that the arrangement had some . . . questionable aspects, and that there was a confrontation between Mr. Garvey and Mr. Burroughs shortly before the murder."

"That's all pretty vague. Go on."

I thought it was specific enough; it would have been coming from Delbarton & Brand. "I'm sorry, Judge, but I'm really not comfortable detailing my case under these circumstances."

"This is an *in camera* proceeding, Mr. O'Connell. The government isn't going to learn what you tell me until trial—*if* it's admitted into evidence."

"That's the problem, Judge. Under the circumstances, it's a short step from deciding what is an ethical investigation to what is relevant evidence. My concern is that your regard for Delbarton and Brand might ultimately influence your rulings at trial. Excuse me for saying so, but your objectivity is an issue here."

"We're not here to discuss *my* ethics, Mr. O'Connell."

"That wasn't my intention, Your Honor. I apologize."

Warner thought I was waving the white flag, and his face began to darken as the seconds passed in silence. "I don't care about intentions," he said deliberately. "If I don't get the details, Miss Bronson is going to be shopping for a new lawyer. I'm quite serious, Mr. O'Connell."

My plan to head this off was dead and buried. Now it was hardball. "She won't get one, Judge. She'll insist on being represented by me and you'll have to appoint a lawyer over her objection. It's going to turn into a debacle. I won't have any choice but to move to recuse you from the case. I mean no disrespect but I think your relationship with Delbarton and Brand is a problem."

"I advise you to tread lightly, counsel," he said tersely. "You are way over your head."

"I don't think so. I've got compelling evidence that Sherman Burroughs was up to something with Raymond Garvey that stunk to high heaven, and that they fought just before Garvey's death. All I did was follow up leads when it would have been malpractice to do otherwise and I'm not responsible if someone blabbed to the press. I've done nothing unethical and I shouldn't be here answering questions just because Mr. Burroughs has lawyers whom you respect."

Warner was beet red and fighting for control. "Are you

going to provide any more details about your investigation?"

"No, I'm not."

"All right," he said, nodding vigorously. "The record will so reflect." He wrote furiously on the legal pad for a full five minutes, much longer than our conversation had consumed. "A few comprehensive questions and we're through," he said finally. He flipped back a page on his legal pad and began to read. "Since you became counsel to the defendant, have you sought any ethical opinions from persons outside your firm regarding your conduct of the defense?"

Sought? Andy's research was on his own initiative. "No."

"Are you aware of any violations of the Canons of Ethics or the Disciplinary Rules committed by you or anyone assigned to the case since you became counsel of record?"

"No."

He was through. He turned the pad over and removed his glasses again. "There is one other defense counsel of record, right?"

"My associate. This is his first case."

"I want him in here on Monday at ten."

"He does research and writes memos, that's all."

"Monday. Ten A.M. You can go, but know that this matter isn't closed, not by a long shot."

Fifteen minutes later I was on a bench, replaying the meeting in my mind and trying to convince myself that there was nothing I could have done differently. Warner was of a mind to dismiss the relevancy of anything I offered about Burroughs and it would have been stupid to brief him on my case in advance: a judge can screw you in a million ways that would never be grounds for an appeal. The bottom line was that I had seventy-two hours to convince Andy that he could answer no to Warner's questions without burning in hell.

I trudged the mile back to the office, past decorated store windows and brigades of resolute shoppers on their lunch hour. I'd managed to suppress all awareness of the holiday season after the baseball glove episode, but threading my way along the sidewalks it occurred to me that I'd come full circle. I dreaded Christmas as a kid. My aunt and uncle were childless and essentially estranged; they shared an apartment because neither had the initiative to leave. My presence was a financial arrangement between my aunt and father begun when she was out of work and in need of her share of the rent. It was a little like boarding school, except I was the only boarder and the staff kicked the shit out of each other every night.

My board didn't include Christmas presents but my father usually managed a gift, always delivered while I was in school. I'd take it to my room and put in under my Christmas tree, a plastic three-footer that stood in the corner of a hall closet the rest of the year, decorated and waiting. Christmas morning would find me sitting on my bed with my bedroom door locked. For some reason it was important to have complete privacy when I opened my present, which I did with great care and ceremony. Afterward I would put the tree back in the closet and write him a card, usually a drawing of me holding my gift, which I would deliver to his mailbox that same morning. Every family has its holiday rituals, that was ours.

Things changed when I got married and indoctrinated into the Brennan family traditions, but I really got into the spirit of the season after Brendan was born. When I showed up with a bicycle, roller skates, and an Erector set big enough to re-create Chicago for his second Christmas, Moira suggested I might be overcompensating. After our divorce I tried to keep up appearances but it only made me feel as if I was trying to buy what I couldn't earn.

Andy was waiting when I returned; he began the interrogation as I hung up my coat. "What happened?"

I tried to act unconcerned. "He wanted to know about the investigation. I told him that we had ample reason to be asking questions about Burroughs and we didn't leak the matter to the press."

His eyes grew wide with hope. *"That's it?"*

"No, he wanted me to detail our evidence implicating Burroughs, but that isn't a good idea so I gave him a rough outline."

"And that satisfied him?"

"Probably not. We'll have to discuss how far you should go."

"Then he *does* want to see me?"

"Monday morning, ten o'clock."

"Shit," he muttered. "Was that it? He just wants to know about Burroughs?"

"He asked a few general questions, too. He wanted to know whether we had gotten any ethical opinions. I told him no. You can answer the same way."

"Ethical opinions," he repeated. He was starting to look queasy. There was no point in dancing around it.

"He also wanted to know whether I was aware of any breaches of ethics committed during the course of our representation."

He inhaled sharply. "And?"

"And I told him, no."

He gripped the arms of the chair like a man waiting for the switch to be thrown. "Dammit!" he cried.

"We've been all through this, Andy. Ashley's future is in your hands and you've got to give her the benefit of the doubt. Tell me that you'll think it over."

He stared at his feet a moment before replying. "I'll . . . I'll think about it," he said.

"All right," I said, trying to inject a note of optimism that I didn't feel. "Meanwhile, full steam ahead, right? We've got a trial coming up, the biggest criminal case this city has seen in several years! You better get a haircut for the cameras!" I was shameless. *Desperate* and shameless.

Walter checked in ten minutes later. "Bad news," I told him.

"Andrew won't be gettin' a pass?"

"Monday morning at ten."

"How wide is the net?"

"Wide enough. It's up to him now."

"I don't get it," he complained. "What the hell were you supposed to do when she brought that book to the office? Tell her to burn it? Hide it? Turn it over to the police?"

"No one really knows," I said. "That's why it's a conundrum. Why don't you lift my spirits and tell me how things are progressing?"

"Talk about your conundrums," he grumbled, "this case takes the cake: a guy who says he was someplace when maybe he wasn't, a guy who says he wasn't someplace when he really was, a guy with two names who ain't anywhere, and an organization that's been around but it's like it ain't. We're pullin' out all the stops but we're chasin' our tails."

"Listen, I don't want this thing to take all of us down. If they start an investigation on the conduct of this defense, there's no telling how far it will go. I want you guys to stop taking chances." There was only silence in response. "I mean it, Walter. It's time to draw the line."

"Sure," he said. "I'll let the other guys know. You two gonna be okay?"

He was going to ignore my warning. I knew it, and he knew I knew it. And there was nothing to be done about it. "We'll be okay," I said.

For the next hour I remained inert, trying to summon up the will to do something other than hold my breath until Monday. I was almost comatose when Cory Barnes knocked on the door. "Hey, Frank! No more to do?"

"Just taking a break."

"I meant for *me*," she said, laughing. "C'mon. Your stuff is a zillion times more interesting than anything else I get to do around here. Haven't you got anything for an eager paralegal?"

"As a matter of fact, I've got something right up your alley. You know your way around the Library of Congress?"

"Well enough to find my way to the information desk. What's up?"

"I want you to look up editions of the *New York Times* and the *Washington Post* for June seventh, nineteen eighty-two, and the preceding week."

Her eyebrows arched. "This is for Miss Bronson's case?"

"Yeah. Don't ask me to explain."

"Okay, no questions asked. So, what am I looking for?"

"Well . . ." What the hell *were* we looking for?

She looked at me quizzically. "I'm eager, but I'm not clairvoyant."

"I guess I'm not really sure but I can give you some categories. One would be anything sensational. You'll just have to use your judgment on that."

"Sensational. Check."

"Two would be anything having to do with science. Most likely physics or chemistry."

She was starting to look dubious. "Physics or chemistry," she repeated.

"Three would be anything to do with a crime."

She nodded. "Sensational. Science. Crime. Hmm. Something like, 'Students Caught Stealing Bunsen Burners,' is that it?"

"Perfect." I laughed. "Listen, I know that covers a lot of ground but I'll throw in a fourth, a catchall: anything that strikes you as something we might be interested in, given what you know about the case."

She made some notes. "Okay, I'm on it."

"I'm sorry I can't explain."

"No problem. It's still a lot more interesting than anything else around here. What's the deadline?"

"Yesterday."

She groaned. "Yesterday. Business as usual." The phone rang and she picked it up. "Mr. O'Connell's office . . . One moment, please." She covered the phone and said, "It's Moira O'Connell," then handed it over and waved good-bye.

"Hi."

"What are you doing right now?" she asked.

"Ricocheting between the rock and the hard place. What's up?"

"I just had lunch with a guy."

"Oh?"

"Cheap date. Always makes me buy, and I had to promise to show him the national Christmas tree to boot. How about making it a threesome?" Moira was pulling out all the stops in her quality-time-with-Dad effort, dealing head-on with the reality I couldn't face. A few moments later I was on the elevator, feeling a lot better than when I rode up less than an hour before.

I hadn't seen mother and son together outside the house in a long time. They were waiting across the street as I headed toward Connecticut Avenue, Brendan with his head tilted back as Moira tied his scarf. She spied me and said something to him and he turned and smiled. I trotted across the street and swept him up in a hug as she kissed me on the cheek and whispered, "We're glad you could make it."

"I'm glad you called."

Brendan was almost giddy with excitement. He hadn't been out with both of his parents since we separated. "Dad! Mom's taking me to see the Christmas tree!"

"Really! The big one near the White House?"

"The one that was on television!"

"Daddy's going to come with us," Moira told him. "How's *that* for a surprise?"

He looked at me, his eyes dancing. "Is this one of my Christmas presents, Dad?"

A Christmas present: both parents at once. "This is a special day for all of us, honey, and it doesn't even count as one of your presents." We headed down Connecticut Avenue toward Farragut Square with Brendan between us, hand in hand. There were moments in my life when I prayed to escape the present, just to the next day, or even the next hour. Now, all I wanted was for time to stand still. No trials, no marriages. No one goes to prison. Or to California.

We took our time getting there, sauntering down the avenue and window shopping along the way. We meandered around Brookstone while Brendan tried out all the gadgets. "I still haven't gotten him anything," I said. "What's prime on the list?"

"Get the baseball glove."

"I thought—"

"It's all right. And I talked to a salesman. Get him an eleven inch size, and if Ken Griffey's name happens to be on it he'll practically faint."

"Thanks, Moira."

"You were right. It's your prerogative."

"Thanks anyway. For everything."

We eventually made it to the Ellipse. Despite it being office hours there were at least two hundred people gawking at the forty-foot blue spruce. I bought hot chocolates for the three of us from a vending truck, and Moira and I found a bench while Brendan, the grandson of the consummate pol, chatted up the kids his age.

"Now, isn't this better than the office?" she asked.

"Much better. Believe it or not, this is my second park bench of the day."

"A park bench. So *that's* what's between the rock and the hard place. Want to talk about it?"

That was all the prompting I needed. I told her the whole story: Kellogg, the journal, Burroughs, Mr. Brown-Clay, Epstein—right up to my meeting with Andy that day. She asked a few questions but mostly listened as my tale of woe poured forth. When I finally finished, she asked, "What do you think he'll do?"

"Andy? I think he's going to tell."

"What will Warner do?"

"He's going to land on me like a ten-thousand-pound shit hammer."

She nodded her agreement. "Who else knows about your dilemma?"

"Right now, just you."

"You haven't told *her* yet?"

"No, I'm working up to it."

She sighed. "What are you going to do?"

"I really don't know. Short of having Andy kidnapped, there isn't much I *can* do."

Moira frowned and looked at her watch. "We're due at Pop's. He's taking us to one of those embassy parties. I think he's done all the Europeans so this one could be Japan or China."

I hailed a cab and ten minutes later we were in front of the townhouse on Jefferson Street saying our good-byes. Brendan ran up the steps to use the brass knocker. "Do you want to come in?" she asked.

"I'd like to, but you know Pop. If we go walking in there together . . . "

"You're right. Bad idea."

"Anyway, I've got things to do. People to inform and all that."

She put her hand on my arm. "The strategy is good, Frank. It's going to work." I watched until they disappeared inside and then gave the driver Ashley's address.

# 14

"What would happen then?"

She was sitting next to me at the kitchen table, drinking tea as I explained our dilemma. Nothing in her face or carriage conveyed distress. She could be disturbed, I'd seen it, but at their core people like Ashley Bronson were in repose. If jarred, they reverberate like anyone else, but they absorb the shock and soon return to their natural state. Then there were people like me—human tuning forks. Strike us hard, we break all the china. This was explained to me by Noah. I paid for it so I'm passing it on.

"Warner would conduct a hearing," I replied, "and after the legal maneuvering was over he could order me to surrender the journal to the government. Rogavin would want to show you had a motive to kill Garvey, and that means proving that you read your father's last entry. They'd try to make me testify that I got the book from you."

"How can you testify if you're my lawyer?"

"Warner would probably remove me from the case for obstructing justice. There wouldn't be any attorney-client privilege, either, not where there's a crime involved."

"So, they'd make you a witness against me." She said it without any emotion, just a statement of fact.

"I wouldn't testify."

"You can just refuse?" she asked.

I shrugged.

She shook her head and said, "You're going to sacrifice yourself for me, is that it?"

"No, testifying wouldn't save me, anyway."

She thought about that for a moment. "Frank, what if we made a deal right now—tonight?"

"You mean a plea bargain?"

"Why not? You could call Rogavin and accept the offer. Then—" I started to interrupt. "Hold on a minute!" she insisted, clutching my arm. "As things stand now, I'll probably be convicted, right?" I couldn't disagree. "Well," she continued, "with a plea bargain there's no case. Andy doesn't get interviewed, I get a lesser sentence, and the whole matter of the journal never comes up."

I shook my head emphatically. "Forget about it. I could never live with you in prison because I screwed up."

She glared at me. "But *I'm* supposed to live with *you* in prison, right? Why is that, Frank, because you're the boy?"

"Because I'm the lawyer and I made the mistake."

"You couldn't know how it would turn out. No one could."

"Maybe, but I took chances that I shouldn't have taken."

"Frank, please listen to me. If I go to prison, it would be because I killed a man. I'm prepared for that. But I'm not prepared to let it happen to you because you tried to save me."

"*Now* who's making the sacrifice?"

"This makes more sense."

"Sense? One of us goes to prison, the other lives with the guilt, and our only choice is who goes and who stays? Why don't we just flip a coin?"

"It's the safest course."

"That's true," I agreed. "It's the safest course."

She studied me. "But you're not going to take it," she said tonelessly. "I don't understand."

"My therapist says I like to take risks. The odds don't even matter." I smiled at her. "I'll bet you didn't know *that* when you hired me."

She gave me a wan smile in return. "It wouldn't have mattered."

I put my hand behind her lovely head and drew her face close to mine. "Feel like rolling the dice?" I said quietly.

She touched her hand to my cheek and nodded.

"My kind of woman. When you go, you go all the way."

We spent the rest of the afternoon and early evening in bed. We made love, dozed, then repeated the cycle. We were back to dozing when she spoke softly in my ear. "We've got to work through this problem," she said, running her fingers through my hair. "It's my boyfriend."

"Dump him," I muttered.

"He's got his uses but he doesn't take me anywhere. I don't think he wants to be seen with me."

"Perfectly understandable."

"But I want us to run away together."

I opened my eyes. "Where to?"

"If you don't have plans and you're feeling spontaneous, I have a ski cabin in Sun Valley. We could spend Christmas there."

"You on a bearskin rug in a ski cabin is the closest thing to heaven I could imagine."

"Good, then we could forget the skiing."

"I could forget the skiing, but not the trial. We've got a lot to do between now and then."

She lifted her head and looked at me. "Frank, this could be my last chance."

"It's my job to see that it isn't."

"I figured you'd say something like that."

"You don't have to be here. Why don't you go anyway?"

"Without you?"

"Why not? Go and have a good time. Just don't come home with a tan, that's all."

"Well . . . I thought we'd spend some time together, I mean, if you don't have other plans." I hesitated, trying to gather my thoughts, and she began to speak rapidly. "I'm sorry, I don't want to impose. I know you have a son and—"

I rolled over. "Hey, wait a minute! Hold on! I want to spend as much time with you as I can."

"I'm sorry I said anything."

"Don't be sorry. I just don't want you to give up the trip if that's what you really want. I, uh . . . Jesus! This is complicated, isn't it?"

"I've made it complicated. Never mind."

I could sense her disappointment. I rolled over and drew her against me. "I am going to see my son but I also want to be with you. Don't go to Sun Valley."

She pulled my arms tighter around her. "You convinced me. Anyway, I figured you wouldn't leave so I have a backup plan: dinner here on Christmas Eve. Formal."

"Formal? You mean black tie?"

"With cummerbund."

"Who's coming?"

She pressed her bottom against my groin. "Both of us, I hope, but me first."

"We have to observe the formalities. What else can I do?"

"We don't have a Christmas tree."

"They've all been sold."

"Not all. I took a walk over to Wisconsin Avenue and there are still a few on the lot."

"The dregs."

"It's the spirit that counts. Let's go get one."

"I'm at your service."

"Night and day," she said.

\* \* \*

I was in the office the next morning at nine. A fresh pot of coffee in the kitchen indicated I wasn't the first to arrive but that wasn't surprising: on any given weekend ten to twenty percent of the firm's lawyers were at their desks. Whoever made the coffee did it right and there was still some half-

and-half left in the refrigerator. I fixed a mug and walked back to my office, picking up a *Post* along the way.

With a sports section and a decent cup of coffee the world isn't such a terrible place on a Saturday morning—as long as you don't think too far ahead. I was just settling in when I noticed the message light on my phone: voice mail. I rarely got voice mail because, first, I didn't have much business, and second, I preferred to have a secretary take my messages, assuming that most people hated those recordings as much as I did.

Moira once suggested that I was born thirty years too late because I was enchanted by the forties: big bands, Lucky Strikes, film noir; a war with a purpose. White wine was Scotch, latte was coffee. Buildings had names and the cab drivers knew where they were. And there was no fax or e-mail, no paging or cell phones, and no voice mail. I ignored the glowing green dot for as long as I could but it wouldn't go away. Its beam went through my newspaper and reflected in my coffee. It began to emit a high-pitched whine: "hear me, hear me now." I became agitated, and when I couldn't stand it any longer I hit the button on the speakerphone and dialed my code. The recorded voice said that I had one message. It was from Cory Barnes: "I'm calling from the Library of Congress. I dropped a copy of a *Times* article in your in-box last night. It's probably not what you're looking for but it's as close as I could get. Call me. My cell-phone number is at the top."

It was a story about a KGB agent named Kovalev who had defected to the United States. Interesting, but the link to Henry Bronson wasn't obvious.

Cory picked up on the first ring. "Is that it?" she asked. "It's kind of about crime and kind of sensational."

"It's a long shot. Have you got anything more to prove a connection?"

"There's a science link of sorts. This guy is a legend, and

there's stuff about his career in the testimony of other defectors and a tell-all book written by a KGB officer after the collapse. He penetrated our atomic weapons program during World War Two and operated here for years before returning home to head the Kremlin's disinformation apparatus."

Atomic weapons. Passages from Henry's journal were running through my head. "What else?" I asked.

"Frank, this guy pulled off more dirty tricks than Nixon and the biggest one might have been his own defection! He supposedly had a change of heart and went home to Moscow a few months after he arrived, and he left the intelligence community in total disarray. There were charges and countercharges of bungling, although no one could be sure if the whole thing wasn't a ruse by the Kremlin from the get-go. Get this: he dies in nineteen eighty-eight and they give him a big state funeral, which *itself* may have been a hoax to prove that his defection was a hoax, and that nothing he gave the CIA was reliable. Is that confusing enough for you? Anyway, I've got another article here with his picture."

"Fax it to me as soon as we hang up. Then I want you to research something else."

"I've got a date tonight!"

"This shouldn't take long. I want to know the name of any site in California where atomic-weapons research was conducted in the early fifties. Can you handle that?"

"I'd love to know what this has to do with the case."

"Maybe nothing. Meanwhile, don't tell anyone else about this. When you find something out call me here. If I'm out I'm going to be carrying a cell phone."

I gave her the number and headed to the fax machine. A moment later I was staring at a photograph. A moment after that I was running for my car.

There wasn't much traffic on the interstate that morning. I had the road largely to myself, free to think and sort out all the pieces. Now that I knew what had frightened Henry so long ago, I was fairly sure what Raymond had for leverage, and why Epstein had lied; the trick would be getting him to admit it. He wasn't at home when I arrived and it occurred to me for the first time that he might be away for the holidays. I drove into town for more coffee, then back to the house to wait. It was a lot colder in the Pennsylvania hills than Washington; the car interior cooled quickly when I wasn't running the engine.

I was at the bottom of my coffee container when Cory called. "Okay," she said. "I've got some answers. If this fills the bill I can still make my date tonight."

"It's only two o'clock. This must be a big date."

"More important, this is the *third* date. You know what that means, don't you?"

"I get it. Go ahead."

"All right. So far I've found three places where atomic energy research was going on in California in the early fifties. The first is Cal Tech in Pasadena."

"That's right outside Los Angeles."

"Right. Robert Oppenheimer came from there, the father of the atomic bomb."

"That could be it. Where else?"

"The second is the University of California Radiation Laboratory at Berkeley. Ernest O. Lawrence was there. He was the inventor of the cyclotron and a major player in research and weapons development."

"Definite possibility. And last?"

"Last but not least: the big hush-hush place they built in Livermore for Edward Teller, the father of the hydrogen bomb: Lawrence Livermore National Laboratory—probably known as the Triple L to insiders," she said, laughing.

"No. L-cubed."

"Oh, I like that better—very scientific."

"That's all I need. Go get ready for the date. And good luck."

"*He's* the one who's getting lucky. Bye."

It was midafternoon when Epstein finally showed and he didn't seem delighted to see me, but he managed a smile when he grabbed my hand. "You're the last person I expected to see here today," he said. "You didn't drive up here to find a Christmas tree, did you?"

"No, Herbert, I came to see you. Can we talk?"

"Sure. C'mon inside. We'll freeze out here." He fumbled with his keys at the door, clearly nervous. "The cold affects me a lot more than it used to," he complained. "Maybe I should move to Florida like everyone else."

"That might be a good idea," I replied coolly. My demeanor unsettled him. We hung our coats in the foyer and he led the way to the study.

"Can I get you something? Coffee?"

"No, thanks. I've had plenty."

"Okay. No problem if you change your mind." He took one of the chairs by the bay window and I took the other. I stared at him but said nothing while he fidgeted. Finally, he asked, "Is there something you forgot last time?"

"No. Actually, I've come to give you some legal advice."

"Legal advice?" He frowned. "What kind of advice?"

"There's no statute of limitations on treason."

He blinked rapidly. "What?"

"That means you can be prosecuted for things you did a long time ago, even fifty years."

"I . . . I don't know what you're talking about! You come into my house and—"

*"Don't lie to me, Herbert!"* I shouted, slapping the arm of the chair. "You lied to me when I was here before and that makes me angry!"

He cowered in the chair. "Lied about what?" he whimpered.

"About Henry and California. You were there."

"Where?"

"Lawrence Livermore, with the stars of nuclear physics."

"I . . . I don't know anything about that," he stammered.

I reached into my jacket for the photograph and tossed it in his lap. The color drained from his face as he stared at it, and all at once he looked every bit his age. "Who do you recognize, Herbert?"

"That's me," he mumbled, "and that's Henry."

"And the man behind the bench?"

His hands began to tremble. "So long ago," he said.

I reached across and tapped the face. "C'mon, Herbert," I snarled, "you must remember *him*."

Epstein's lips moved but emitted no sound, as if the power of speech had faded with his complexion.

"I can't hear you, Herbert. Say his name."

"Kovalev," he whimpered.

He looked about to keel over. It was time to bluff. "Henry kept more than the picture, Herbert. He kept a journal. He admitted what he did—what you *both* did."

"Things I did . . ." For a moment he was still, then he covered his face and a pitiful sob escaped as his thin shoulders began to shake. "What's going to happen to me?" he cried.

"This thing may not go any further than me but I'll make no promises, except one: if you don't help me I'll turn you in. They probably won't electrocute you like the Rosenbergs, Herbert, but they'll keep you in a little cell until you're dead. No wonderful baked goods and no making whoopee with the widows."

"My God!"

"God can't help you. Are you going to answer my questions or not?" He wiped his eyes with the sleeve of his wool shirt and nodded. "Henry Bronson was passing information to the Russians. Yes?"

"Yes."

"And you were part of it."

"I—I had no choice."

"Tell me. All of it."

"All of it," he repeated softly. He was silent for a moment, then took a deep breath and began, his voice flat and his gaze fixed on the floor between us. "I grew up in the Depression. In my family, where I lived, it was fashionable to blame capitalism for society's ills. A lot of people thought the Soviet Union was the last, best hope for mankind." He looked up at me. "It was not unlike what your generation went through in the sixties. I'll bet you were out there burning flags and all that stuff, right?"

"Go on."

"They approached me when I was at Princeton. They were our allies, remember, fighting the Nazis, and I agreed to cooperate. I told them about the work we were doing at our lab but it was small potatoes stuff, nothing that they could really use. Sometimes they would ask me to attend a meeting and report on what happened, or to introduce people to other scientists that I knew."

"Did you introduce them to Henry?"

"I did, but we didn't have any real secrets. We were just students, for God's sake!"

"What happened next?"

"Henry transferred to another research position at the University of Chicago. We were just fresh faces without the experience and accomplishments to be recruited by Oppenheimer for Los Alamos. The physicists who built the bomb helped win the war and they were the elite. We thought we'd missed our chance."

"But Henry had ambition, didn't he?"

"Henry wanted to do something grand, we both did, and a split in the scientific community finally created opportunities. A lot of physicists had been opposed to atomic weapons development, but it was hard to be vocal when there was a war to be won and everyone was afraid the Nazis would get the bomb first."

"And that changed."

"The pictures of Hiroshima and Nagasaki changed a lot of minds. Oppenheimer became an opponent of further weapons development and he was very influential. Edward Teller wanted to develop what they called 'The Super,' which was the hydrogen bomb, and he quit Los Alamos in frustration. But when the Soviets detonated their own atomic bomb, the race was on."

"What happened next?"

"The government built Teller his own lab at Livermore to pursue The Super, and Henry landed a slot there in nineteen fifty-two. I didn't get one but Henry raved about the West, and when an opportunity arose at the University of California I jumped at it and we were practically neighbors. Of course, Livermore was a top-secret facility so I couldn't visit him there. We'd get together in Berkeley."

"Where does Kovalev come in?"

"He had been our contact at Princeton. He surfaced again in 'fifty-three and asked me to put him in contact with Henry. You have to understand. I was already committed. I couldn't refuse. We'd meet in Berkeley and Kovalev would preach to us about the need to share atomic secrets to prevent further wars—a widely held point of view, by the way." He paused, looking at me for some understanding.

"Finish the story, Herbert."

"Henry agreed to provide information, mostly documents that he left at drops around Berkeley. Sometimes I was the go-between. This went on for more than a year until watching the Soviets in action convinced him that nuclear parity was not really a good idea. He refused to cooperate anymore and Kovalev threatened to expose us. He was subtle but the threat was real. I thought we both were doomed."

"But he never made good on the threats?"

"No. We passed a nervous year and then we swore never to speak about it again. Things were quiet for almost thirty years, then the newspapers reported that Kovalev had defected and was being debriefed by the CIA."

"June seventh, nineteen eighty-two," I said. "Henry was terrified."

"We both were! We figured that we were headed for the gallows! I guess he never told them about us."

"What was Henry's contribution to the work at Livermore, Herbert? What was his creation?"

He stared at me a moment, like he was making up his mind. "Okay," he said finally. "As I said, the race was on. A lot of people were working on bigger, more powerful weapons. Others were concerned with a related issue, one just as pressing."

"Which was?"

"What good is a bomb if you can't deliver it? No one had intercontinental ballistic missiles then, and strategic bombers were just on the drawing board. All the important people were thinking big—literally—and Henry wound up assigned to a small project that didn't interest his colleagues: downsizing an atomic bomb to a scale that enabled conventional delivery."

"What does that mean?"

"Put it in a box and drive it to the destination. Park the car and walk away."

*"Christ! A car bomb?"*

"No, an *atomic* car bomb. In a very practical way, the ultimate first-strike weapon: no warning, just boom. Henry solved the hard part of the design."

"What was that?"

"The trigger mechanism. Do you know how those things work?"

"Tell me."

He found a pad and pencil and drew a diagram, relieved to be lecturing instead of confessing. "For the bomb to yield the maximum amount of energy the uranium or plutonium core has to be compressed to critical mass instantly and completely, otherwise you get fizzle instead of bang. So you need a trigger. Let me tell you, a lot of smart people worked on trigger design when they built the first bombs at Los Alamos during the war. In some ways it was the hardest part of the job. Eventually, they used two kinds. One was a sort of 'gun' that fired a uranium 'bullet' into a core; they used it on Hiroshima. The other was an 'implosion' device that they dropped on Nagasaki. Henry designed a small version of the gun device. It wasn't nearly as efficient as the one in the big bomb, but then again, that bomb weighed almost ten thousand pounds."

"How efficient was it?"

"Well, it couldn't destroy a whole city, but it was very capable of destroying a downtown area."

"Or, say, the Kremlin."

"Right. The genius of his design was in its simplicity. You could practically engineer the damn thing in your basement."

"Did the Russians know about Henry's design?"

"If they did, only that he had one. He never gave them the plans, I know that much."

"What happened to the plans?"

"What do you mean?" His eyes avoided mine.

"It's a simple question. What happened to the plans for Henry's trigger?"

"I don't know."

"You're lying to me, Herbert, I can tell. You saw them." I stood up and he cringed. "Go ahead, tell me I'm wrong."

"You're not wrong."

"Where are they?"

He shook his head. "I don't know." I glared at him and he raised his hands, pleading. "I'm not lying, I swear! He only showed them to me once—almost forty years ago!"

"So he kept them."

"It was his achievement." He sighed. "And let me tell you, if you had them today you could get rich."

My chest was thumping but my voice dripped with sarcasm. "Rich?" I scoffed, shaking my head. "Why would anyone pay for a fifty-year-old design?"

Epstein rose to the bait. "During the war," he lectured, "creating weapons-grade uranium or plutonium required harnessing a good part of our industrial capability. It was the biggest production effort of the war; the biggest in history. We literally constructed cities to do it, and virtually overnight. Well, you don't need to go to any extremes today. In the old Soviet Union you've got people who are broke and starving guarding weapons-grade material that's worth thousands of times its weight in gold. Now there's a black-market in plutonium in Eastern Europe, and from what I've been reading you've got intelligence agents posing as buyers all over Germany!"

"Go on."

"Well, having fissionable material isn't the same as having the bomb. You're missing a major component."

"The trigger."

"That's right."

"So Henry's trigger is worth money."

"It's perfect for a terrorist who only wants to blow up Wall Street or, say, the Pentagon."

"Herbert," I said casually, "who else did you tell about Henry's trigger?"

"*No one!*" he cried. "I told Henry and I'm telling you: I have never, *never*, said one word about the trigger or anything else. *Not one word!*" He was hyperventilating. I was afraid he was going to keel over before I finished.

"Why was it necessary to assure Henry?"

"He called me, very agitated, and asked, 'Did you breach our trust, Herbert?'" Epstein shook his head. "That's how Henry talked."

"And you told him you hadn't?"

"Like I'm telling you. C'mon, it'd be suicide."

"When was this, Herbert?"

He rubbed his forehead. "It's hard to keep track of time when you don't work," he muttered. "I think it was in August, early August."

"Tell me about Raymond Garvey. How did he figure in this?"

Epstein was either a good actor or genuinely puzzled by the question. "Garvey?" He frowned at me until it clicked. "Does *Garvey* know?" he squealed. "Oh no! No! No! No!"

"Relax! He's not going to be telling anyone, remember?"

He lowered his head into his hands. "Yes," he gasped. "Of course." His anxiety was soon displaced by curiosity and he looked up again. "The trigger has something to do with the murder?"

"I didn't say that."

"But you're here. You're asking."

"Herbert, don't jump to conclusions. The best thing you can do is forget I was ever here, understand?" I got up to go.

"Can I ask just one thing?" he pleaded.

"What?"

"Does Ashley know? Did she—?"

"Ashley knows nothing about this, Herbert. Nothing about you, and nothing about Henry. And it's going to stay that way. Do we understand each other?"

He flinched. "I won't say anything. I haven't . . . fifty years." His ruddy complexion was gone, maybe never to return. When he spoke his voice was barely audible. "What I did, what Henry did, will die with me."

That surely wasn't true. There were at least three other people who had known what Henry did at Livermore. Ashley killed one; another had vanished. The third was trying to get me disbarred.

The phone rang. He looked at it but didn't move. I went for my coat. "Better get it, Herbert," I said over my shoulder. "It could be your dinner."

* * *

"It was a shot in the dark. You got lucky. If you missed you woulda been on your way home with jack shit."

"Shot in the dark, my ass," I replied. "Two parts deductive reasoning, one part technique. Admit it. You're jealous."

"Yeah, whatever." Walter peered into the paper bag and fished out a package wrapped in white paper. He held it at arm's length and squinted at the black crayon marking.

"Why don't you just open it?"

"Hold your horses," he grumbled, turning the package upside down. "Okay. Onion bagel, nova, cream cheese, red onion, and tomato." He tossed it at me, then reached in for a container and read the scrawl on the top. "Yours," he said.

"Did they put sugar in it?"

He glared at me as he unwrapped the other package. "I went last Sunday. This was supposed to be your turn."

"I was in church praying for your soul."

He made an up-and-down gesture with his fist as he bit into his bagel and whitefish salad. "So," he said, chewing, "they were after the old man's invention?"

"The pieces fit. They knew all about his spying at Livermore and they must've been threatening to expose him if he didn't turn over the design. That's what he meant by being terrorized by his own creation. He was cornered, but he found a way out."

He sniffed. "Yeah, all the way out, which raises another question: how did they know? I don't figure him for sharin' his secrets with Raymond."

"The people trafficking in plutonium saw Henry's reports from Livermore. Maybe they found them in old files, or maybe they worked with Kovalev in the fifties. Who knows? With Henry's design they could offer one-stop shopping to anyone who wants to build a bomb."

"So they come after him."

"Yeah, and they chose Garvey as the contact. He was a natural: a middleman on the make and Henry's old friend."

"His commission on this deal woulda been big."

"I'm not sure where Burroughs fits in. My guess is that he was part of Octagon, too—he's old enough. He probably put them onto Raymond."

"And Mr. Brown-Clay?"

"Maureen said he had a funny accent, European. He's got to be the Russian link. And Octagon's been around since the thirties, too long to belong to one person or even a group. It could have been used by the Soviets for moving money or other spying activities."

He was staring into the bag again. "Where's the freakin' Sweet n' Low?" he muttered, then said, "How the hell are we gonna prove this fairy tale?"

"We're not even going to try."

His nose came out of the bag. *"We're not?"*

"Nope, for two reasons. First, our story is two separate pieces. One is Octagon: three guys—Burroughs, Garvey, and Mr. Brown-Clay—in some kind of conspiracy, complete with big payments, secret meetings, and one dead conspirator. We can prove that part. The other piece is Henry Bronson's tale of espionage, apparently ending with him being contacted last August by someone who knew what he did. There are only two ways to prove that part: Epstein's testimony and the journal. Herbert isn't about to take the stand to tell that story, and the journal only hints at it. Besides, we can't use the journal anyway."

Walter nodded. "It sinks her."

"Yep. Too bad we couldn't tell the whole thing. It's a story so big that Ashley isn't even a supporting character. Even with Kellogg's testimony the jury has to walk her unless Rogavin's got the shooting on videotape."

Walter shrugged. "No journal, no Epstein, no story."

"That's how it shapes up," I agreed. "The only other way you could prove what happened is if Burroughs decided to confess, and I don't think that's in the cards."

"You said there were two reasons. What's the second?"

"The story itself. If you tell it the whole world learns that

Henry Bronson spied for the Russians—starting with his daughter. She didn't want us looking into why her father killed himself, remember? Would you like to be the one to tell her?"

He made a face. "Okay, so tell me, now that you figured out this ancient mystery, what are we going to do when the gavel comes down, which by the way is next week?"

"We have to go with the first part, the one we can prove: Raymond Garvey was involved with some guys who met secretly, used code names, had lots of money, and trace their origin to a secret organization in New York with no history."

"And he got dead," he added.

"And he got dead. That's not bad, is it?"

"It's got no payoff. You don't know what they're up to or why Raymond lost his membership."

"It's still something," I replied. "If you combine it with a decent cross-exam of Kellogg, then throw in our explanation for the fingerprints on the gun, you've got the makings of a defense. We'll show the jury that the government's case has some weaknesses and then we'll offer another explanation for how Raymond got killed—incomplete maybe, but still possible."

Walter sipped his coffee thoughtfully. "So, how do you figure her chances?" I asked him.

"Hard to say. Maybe thirty, forty percent."

"You're probably right." I sighed.

"We still got a week. Whaddya want to do?"

I thought about it. "Do you think that Octagon's a dead end?"

"We got nothin' from the airlines or the bank account."

"Then the only left is to make a bigger dent in Kellogg."

Walter's beeper went off before he could answer, one of his team calling to report. I gave him my chair and went to the window. It was a typical December day in Washington, nothing unbearable temperature-wise but a gusting wind had pedestrians bundled up, heads bowed and clutching scarves. Ask anyone to identify someone he passed that day and it was a safe bet that he couldn't.

Walter finished his call and joined me at the window. "Don't look like New York, does it?"

"No, you'd need more of everything."

"I still miss it," he said.

"I do, too—sometimes. My life was a hell of a lot simpler, I'll tell you that."

"Any developments with Moira and the kid?"

"It's going to happen. The best thing about this case is that it's keeping me occupied, like having a migraine and hitting your thumb with a hammer."

He took that as his cue to change the subject. "I guess we gotta work on Kellogg," he agreed. "Rogavin's gonna have the jury thinkin' this guy's really somethin' special."

"A secret agent with eyes that see in the dark and a photographic memory."

"Double-oh-freakin'-seven."

Suddenly, it was right there, laid out in front of me. "Wait a minute! What if we prove he's not so special?"

"Swell. How?"

"We test him—right in the courtroom." I explained my plan.

He listened until I finished, then mulled it over as he finished his coffee. "What would happen if he passed the test?" he asked.

"We'd probably lose."

*"Probably?"*

"Okay, we'd lose. Look, I'm only suggesting this because we're desperate. If the case goes well for us, if we somehow hurt him on cross-exam without the test, then we won't risk it."

"When are you gonna decide go or no go?"

"I'll decide while I've got him on the stand. There's no way to know until then."

Walter frowned. "That's some freakin' decision to make on the fly—to put all our eggs in one basket."

"I don't like it, either, but I'm out of ideas. Now, can you do your part or not?"

"That's a pretty tall order in the time we got left," he muttered.

"Can you do it?"

"Maybe. I better get started."

"Keep this on a need-to-know basis. And don't say anything to Andy about your 'mutual acquaintances.' He's having a tough enough time with our little journal problem."

"I take it there's no word from the conscience of the community?"

"None."

He shook his head. "That ain't good. You want me to talk to him?"

"No. I've already pushed him pretty hard. You focus on Kellogg." He turned to go. "Just a minute," I said. "Boost my spirits and tell me again that I'm a genius."

"You're a genius," he said over his shoulder, "but it may not mean shit after tomorrow."

\* \* \*

Andy never showed up at the office, and he didn't call until five. I knew what that meant before he told me.

"I haven't changed my mind, Frank, but I'll do the best I can."

"What does that mean, exactly?"

"I'm not going to volunteer anything. I'm going to go in and emphasize that I'm a new associate who was detailed over to you to stay in the library and write memos. Maybe he'll never ask the right question."

"I see."

"I was thinking: what if we contact my old ethics professor from school? He's a practical guy, Frank. If he says you're right, then that's it. If he says it has to be disclosed, then you can change your answer before I go in to talk to Warner. That way I don't have to feel like I've betrayed the team."

"I'm sorry, Andy, I'm not going to do that."

"Why not?"

"Because I'm confident in my own judgments and I'm prepared to live with them. If you're not, you can practice law but you can't practice criminal law."

There was a momentary silence before he quietly replied, "Okay, I'll do the best I can. I'm sorry, Frank."

"Andy?"

"What?"

"Call me as soon as you leave his chambers."

\* \* \*

A watched pot never boils.

I had reminded myself of that little proverb a half-dozen times between ten-seventeen and ten-thirty. Walter had showed up at nine to share the vigil and was stretched out on the couch with his eyes closed. At eleven o'clock there was still no call from Andy. "It's been an hour," he announced. "How long were you in there?"

"Twenty, twenty-five minutes."

"Shit. They're probably tapin' his confession."

Andy shuffled in at eleven-forty-five and sat down heavily. He looked spent. "You were in there a long time," I said.

"I walked back from the courthouse," he replied wearily. We waited but he said nothing.

"How did it go?" I prompted.

"He asked me why we were investigating Burroughs. I told him the same thing you did. Then he asked me if I thought Burroughs killed Garvey."

"What did you say?"

"I told him that as far as I knew it was possible." He looked at me and shrugged. "Nobody ever told me different." That was true: I had never gotten around to it.

"Did he ask whether you were aware of any ethical breaches?"

"I wish we had called my ethics professor."

"I told you why I wouldn't."

"How confident are you really?" he asked me.

"Does it matter anymore?"

"It matters to me because now we're both clinging to the same limb. I hope nobody saws it off."

I glanced at Walter. "What did you tell him, Andy?"

"I said I wasn't aware of any."

Walter was grinning ear-to-ear. "What did Warner say to that?" I asked, stunned.

"Nothing, but he gave me a message for you before I left. He said, quote, 'Tell him that he'd damn well better be ready to try this case next Monday, and there will be no continuances for any reason,' unquote."

Walter gave him a playful squeeze. It took a moment for it to sink in: we were actually going to trial.

"You didn't get much sleep last night, did you?" I asked, smiling.

"None," he replied. "I was staring at the ceiling all night. I had no idea criminal law was this hard."

"If it helps, I used to stare at the ceiling, too."

"But you got over it, right?"

"Yup. Now I walk the streets."

"Great," he declared. "Something to look forward to."

"Does that mean this *isn't* your last criminal case?"

"It still beats the shit out of corporate work." He yawned and stretched, then wobbled toward the door. "I'm going to get a nap. I'll be ready to go again after lunch."

Walter winked at me and said, "We're in business."

I dialed Ashley and conveyed the good news. The joy in

her voice lifted my spirits even higher. It was all I could do to remember that we had won a battle, not the war. But we were definitely going to war, and I could only hope that we'd all be so happy when it was over.

# 15

With only Kellogg to stress over I managed to sleep a lot better on Monday night than I had all weekend. I walked into the office at nine-thirty and found a telephone message on my desk from Moira: "Said she tried to reach you last night." Last night I had been at Ashley's, where I had been every night for the past week. My first fear was that something was wrong; it was well-founded.

"It's me. I got your message."

"Which one? I left one on your machine last night."

"I was out."

There was an ominous moment of silence before she said, "Christmas is tomorrow."

"I was going to call today to make arrangements to come by."

"I called to ask you to come over tonight."

"Oh . . . I was wondering if tomorrow morning was good—it doesn't matter what time, whatever's convenient. I just wanted to be there when he opens the present." More silence. "It's the Ken Griffey model," I added lamely.

"Just when he opens the present. Sure."

"When would be a good time?"

"Around ten," she answered and hung up.

Things had taken a bad turn, and in my nervous condition I had made them worse. Caught cheating by my ex-wife: it didn't make any sense. My Christmas glow was already dissipating when I got the call from Rogavin. "I heard from Warner's chambers." He laughed. "Dodged one, did you?"

"I know you're happy for me."

"Oh, I am. I told you, I like the competition. Isn't it good to get all the distractions out of the way and get down to it?"

"It? Oh, you mean *the trial.* That's in—what?—six days? Jeez, I've been so caught up with the holidays. By the way, you're a medium, right?"

"You still have that sense of humor, that's good. Perhaps it will see you through the very dark time ahead. Now, about the chain of custody, what's it going to be? If poor Agent Windemere has to fly in from California he needs to know today. By the way, it'll screw up *his* holidays, if that matters."

"Tell him to stay home, my gift. I just wish I could find something for you."

"You could take the deal. This office might even be persuaded to go for manslaughter."

"*Manslaughter?* Taking the Christmas spirit a little far, aren't we?"

"It's not *my* idea, I assure you. The U.S. Attorney has been buttonholed by friends of the princess at every holiday party he's attended, so he feels obligated to find out if you've come to your senses. I told him that we're wasting our breath: you'd never walk away from an opportunity like this. It's a practice-builder, isn't it? Up from the cellblocks, the modern Prometheus."

"Boy, nothing gets past you, does it? You're right, it's a practice builder—*if* I win. Of course, I had to take a lot of things into account: the facts, the law, the quality of the opponent. Everything just said, 'go for it.'"

"You know," he said evenly, "I never make it personal but I think I'm going to make an exception for you."

"*Another* present! I've just got to get something for you. Listen, how about a nice courtroom drawing of you for your office? I know, some people might think it's tacky, but—"

"See you in court, asshole."

"And a Merry Christmas to you, too."

\* \* \*

With my personal and professional life in a broken-field run to oblivion, I was fortunate to have an appointment that very day with the man whose job it was to sort things out. I must have been keyed up because by the time I stopped for a breath, there were only a few minutes of our session left. "So, my life is in turmoil," I concluded.

Noah was staring at me with one eyebrow raised. "I like ending the year on an up-note," he deadpanned, shifting in his chair. "Things sound complicated."

"Complicated? No. Stressful, yes. Or scary. But not complicated. There are only a couple of ways it can turn out. One is a total disaster; the other, partial. It's all pretty simple, really."

"Is that how you see it?"

"I think so."

"If things—and I mean everything—could turn out exactly like you wanted, what would happen?"

"Besides Rogavin being carried out on a stretcher and me being proclaimed the new Darrow?"

"Besides that."

"You're referring to the personal stuff."

"Yes."

"Ashley, Moira, Brendan?"

"That's right."

"Okay . . . You want an answer right now?"

He just looked at me.

I sighed. "It's complicated."

\* \* \*

Walter called at five just to check in and let me know that Kellogg had some visitors from the U.S. Attorney's Office. "Rogavin is doing his witness prep," I said.

"Yeah, well, I'll tell you something: this guy is careful.

He went to the Biograph last night and took the route past Garvey's. It's as if he knows we might we watching and he's going the extra mile to make it look good."

"In this case, the extra two blocks."

"Yeah."

"You still think he's a phony, don't you?"

"Yeah."

"What about our test? Maybe tonight?"

"Who knows?"

"We pick a jury in five days!"

"We ain't had the right conditions," he replied. You understand the logistics in this deal? D-day wasn't this freakin' complicated! First, it ain't like he's walkin' the street all night. Second, there's no leaves on them trees. When it's clear the moon is like a giant goddamn streetlight. Third, my guys gotta keep changing cars and clothes so they don't attract attention. This ain't the ghetto, kid. Around here, they call the cops if the freakin' garbage man is late. And if we blow it, we've blown it for good."

"I've already blown it," I muttered. "Now I'm taking it out on you."

"Look, it's getting dark and conditions look pretty good tonight. Maybe we'll have some news by the time you get to bed."

"Tonight is Christmas Eve," I said, for no particular reason.

"Yeah. I'm gonna hang a stocking from my menorah."

"I hate to see you working when everyone else is enjoying the holiday."

"You wanna keep me company, I got no objections."

"I don't hate it that much. I'll be at Ashley's if you need to reach me."

"Right. I'll keep the number real handy."

"Merry Christmas. Happy Chanukah."

"Yeah. Same to you."

\* \* \*

According to the ticket stubs in my tuxedo pocket, the last official appearance of Mr. and Mrs. Francis O'Connell was at the Kennedy Center's Opera House exactly three years, one month, and four days before the Christmas formal at Ashley's. The tickets said it was *La Bohème* but it could have been the Marx Brothers for all I would have noticed. By then I had made up my mind to leave Pop and start over, and all my waking hours, twenty or so a day, were spent agonizing over the prospect of telling Moira. I had anticipated tears and resentment over the upheaval of our comfortably settled lives, but I never considered the possibility that she wouldn't be joining me on the road less traveled. In six months I was wondering how I ever believed she would; in twelve, I was grateful that she hadn't.

There was a taxi idling in front of Ashley's when I arrived. Martha opened the door with her coat on; a small suitcase stood near the door. She was going to spend the holiday at a cousin's in Maryland and was waiting for me to arrive before she left.

"Ah, Mr. Frank. Merry Christmas."

So, she'd finally settled on an appropriate address for me: "Mr. Frank." Suitor to Miss Ashley. Counsel to the House of Bronson. Defender of the realm.

"And Merry Christmas to you, Martha. I understand you're going visiting. Good for you."

"A cousin and her children and grandchildren. A house full of family at the holidays." Her regret showed as soon as the words left her lips. "I . . . I'm sorry, sir. I don't know if that was an appropriate thing—"

"No, no, that's okay," I interrupted, looking around as I removed my coat. "The house looks magnificent, Martha. You've done wonders." They had been busy. Saturday, there wasn't a trace of Christmas to be found, and now the place looked like a Hallmark card. The foyer was decorated with red and white poinsettias and there was garland draped on the banister all the way to the second floor. The doors to the drawing room were open and there was a fire in the hearth and a bottle of champagne in the stand by the couch. In the corner stood our tree, barely six feet tall and sparse, with a layer of Bronson heirloom ornaments to conceal its structural inadequacies. Perfect for the occasion.

"Miss Ashley wanted things to look just so," she said as she took my coat. "It used to be so busy here during the holidays. All the comings and goings—you can't imagine what it was like." The taxi driver signaled his impatience and I opened the door and gave an acknowledging wave. Martha hefted her suitcase and paused in the doorway. "Miss Ashley is upstairs dressing," she said, her voice shaking. "She looks so beautiful."

I took her free hand in mine. "Martha, I promise. Next Christmas things will be like they used to be. Ashley and I are going to enjoy ourselves tonight, so you do the same and try not to worry."

"I'll be at Christmas mass tonight and I'll pray for you both!" She choked back a sob and scurried down the walk.

The only sound in the house was the crackling of the fire. I leaned against the threshold and imagined it as Martha remembered, with violins and laughter and clinking glasses. The conviviality of the decor clashed with the looming silence, and suddenly this party for two seemed like a terrible idea, a recipe for holiday depression.

"Merry Christmas." Her voice drifted down from the landing.

Maureen Carmody had it exactly right: when I looked up the foyer receded into darkness; all the light seemed focused on the spot where she stood at the head of the staircase. She was wearing a fitted, black, floor-length silk dress that a slow turn revealed to be backless, and her hair was up in a French twist. Ashley's beauty was too extraordinary to get used to, but after six weeks I thought I'd finally experienced the full effect, all the variations of lighting, angles, and mood. I was wrong. Like the very best athletes and thoroughbreds, she could turn it up a notch or two for the big events, and I was one bundle of involuntary responses as she floated downward and stopped a few inches away. "What do you think?" she said.

My breathing was shallow and rapid. "I can't think."

"What do you feel?"

"I feel that if I don't hold you right now, I'll burst."

She moved close, pressing against me, wrapping her arms around my neck and brushing my ear with her lips the way I liked. "Holding is a good starting place. Where will we go from there?"

"We'll find our way. I brought my compass."

"I can feel it," she whispered. "Is that north?"

It's amazing what you can ignore when you put your mind to it. We drank champagne and danced in the drawing room. We dined by candlelight at one end of a table for twenty. We had coffee, sex, and dessert in the library, our trysting place of choice. And through it all we managed to blind ourselves to the elephant in the room. We forced it into a corner with a heat fueled by champagne and sex, and not a little fear.

But you can't keep it away forever. We were naked under a blanket when the grandfather clock in the drawing room struck midnight. "No more shopping days to Christmas," she murmured.

And just four more days to trial.

\* \* \*

The Mercedes was still in the driveway thirty minutes after my first pass through the block. I'd tried to kill some time but everything was closed and my frustration grew as I circled the neighborhood, feeling like a jerk. I had no desire to meet Rob. None. But I couldn't continue to drive around, either. I parked as far from the Mercedes as possible, then sat in the car and thought about how to play it, finally deciding to take my cue from Moira: if she acted guilty, I'd rub it in good; but if she pretended that everything was fine, so would I, even more so.

I rang the bell and practiced my smile until she opened the door. "You're here!" she said happily. She looked very much like Christmas, wearing black slacks, a green satin blouse, and a red ribbon in her hair.

"I'm sorry I'm late. Haven't held anything up, have I?"

"No. Rob is here."

I could see that. Is Rob *supposed* to be here? I gave her a second chance to excuse his presence. "Oh," I nodded toward the car, "I was wondering who was here on Christmas morning."

"Uh-huh." She nodded. I couldn't tell if she was distressed or tickled pink at the prospect of a *mano a mano* between her ex and her next. Leave it to her to strike a perfect middle, the one strategy I hadn't anticipated. "He and Brendan are playing with a video game that Rob bought him," she explained as she led me toward the family room. I could see the video game on the big TV screen before I saw Brendan and Rob sitting cross-legged on the floor. Brendan was still in his pajamas; Rob looked right at home himself in flannel slacks and a white turtleneck. They were manipulating their game controllers while figures bobbed and weaved around the obstacles that flowed across the screen. Brendan was transfixed and Rob was alternately smiling at my son and the screen.

"Rob?" Moira called. Her beau sprang to his feet and lunged toward me with his hand extended. He was two or three years younger than me, with wavy, light brown hair and the kind of wholesome, midwestern looks that some women find attractive. He had the build of a tennis player but what was most disconcerting was his height. At six-two,

I was used to looking down on most people, but he had at least an inch on me.

"Hello, Frank." He grinned. "Merry Christmas." He nodded toward Brendan, who was still too engrossed in the video game to notice my arrival. "Brendan and I were just vanquishing mutant hordes from deep space, a peace-on-earth, good-will-toward-men kind of thing." Behind me, Moira laughed appreciatively. Her new man was plainly self-assured, and according to her, a nice guy with no notable neuroses or communicable diseases. All things considered, Rob was shaping up as somebody a guy in my position could really hate, except for the fact that Brendan liked him, too. In my more lucid moments I realized that I didn't want my son raised by some jerk. "Brendan," he called, "your dad's here!"

Brendan put down the controller and came running. "Merry Christmas, buddy!" I cried, extending my arms.

"Merry Christmas, Dad!" He turned in my arms and pointed at the TV. "Rob brought what I wanted!"

"He did?"

"Yeah!" He was already focusing on the video game, which he had paused in midbattle.

"That's great. Could you stand to get just one more present?"

His eyes lit up. "What?"

I held out the box and he attacked the silver foil and red ribbon. "A baseball glove!" he shouted. He looked in the pocket at the lettering. "What does it say, Dad?"

"It says, Ken Griffey, Jr., buddy. It's the same kind of glove that he uses."

Brendan's eyes got big. "Is this *his* glove?"

"Well, not the one he wears in the game but it's the same kind, and he signed his name in there for you."

He worked his hand inside and pounded the pocket with his fist, smiling. "I'm going to play on a baseball team this summer, Dad. I'm going to play outfield like Ken Griffey."

"That's what he plays all right."

"Are you going to come to my games?"

Moira seemed to be looking at the TV. "I'm going to come to as many as I can, bud. And as soon as the weather warms up you and I are going to have a lot of catches to get ready for the season."

An awkward silence followed. There was nothing more to do with the baseball glove but Brendan continued to pound the pocket and steal glances at the beckoning video game. I thought that it was time for Rob to excuse himself but he continued to stand there, smiling and nodding his approval over my choice of gifts. Finally, Moira spoke up. "Brendan, why don't you show Dad what Grandpa gave you?" she said, then looked at me. "Something to drink or eat?"

"Coffee, thanks." She went off to the kitchen with Rob close behind. Apparently, he wasn't going anywhere. The frustration welled up in my chest and I could taste it in the back of my throat. I resented his presence, and I resented feeling resentment. All I wanted was to enjoy Christmas morning, a little time away from everything else. Was that a lot to ask?

Brendan was showing me his bounty. When it came to his only grandchild, Pop's ideas about Christmas were consistent with his approach to his daughter's wedding. I tried to focus on what he was saying but it didn't help that his attention kept returning to the video game, the gift Moira had suggested *I* buy for him. Not me: I knew better.

*"Dad!"*

"What?"

"I was talking and you didn't hear me."

"I'm sorry, honey. I was just thinking about something. What is it?"

"Do you want to play my video game with me?"

"The video game? Sure." We sat on the floor and began to play with Rob's gift. In no time Brendan was totally immersed and I was feeling isolated. When invading ships weren't exploding in stereo I could hear talk and occasional laughter from the kitchen, and when Moira brought the coffee I shot her a look just to let her know I wasn't having a good time. She seemed to get the message, which only proved that she knew exactly what she'd done, whatever that was.

We played the game for what seemed to be a decent interval while I watched the clock, dreading the disappointment on Brendan's face when I told him I was leaving. It turned out much worse than I feared: he put the game on pause and hugged me good-bye with one arm, never letting go of the controller. I squeezed him to me, feeling sad, guilty—and still resentful. By the time I took two steps the game was going again.

I found Moira and Rob sharing an amusing moment at the breakfast table. "I've got to go," I announced. "The trial is only a few days away."

"Already?" Moira asked. "Are you going to the office on Christmas?"

I took the opening and drove a truck through it. "No, I've got a meeting with the client. There's just a lot to do—you know how it is." I was hoping she'd use her imagination. I shook hands with Rob, who practically invited me to break his nose by refusing to look anything but completely at ease.

Moira followed me to the hall closet and stood by while I paid special attention to buttoning my coat. "I didn't expect you to be leaving so soon," she said evenly.

"Brendan is immersed in the game. He barely noticed."

"Couldn't you do something else?"

I put on my gloves, still not looking at her. "It's too cold to have a catch."

"If you remember," she bristled, "I suggested that you buy him the video game. You insisted on the glove."

I nodded. "Right you are."

"So, what is it?"

I looked at her. "Nothing. I've got to go."

She lowered her voice. "Rob was supposed to fly in from Chicago last night—a last-minute change in plans to accommodate you, by the way—but his flight was canceled so he came by this morning with his present. What was I supposed to do, tell him not to come?"

"So he gave Brendan his present, and then what?"

"And then he and I went into the kitchen to leave you two alone. That's why you're here, isn't it?"

"Did you tell him I was coming?"

"Why? As some kind of hint?"

"No, I wouldn't want you to go to any kind of trouble. I mean, his time with Brendan is so limited. They'll barely get to see one another in California."

She stared at me with her mouth open, then hissed, "Listen to yourself! You were just alone with Brendan and you could have stayed all day but you couldn't go an hour before your *dick* pointed the way to her house!"

I glared at her but she stood her ground. "You know that's crap, Moira."

"Really? Set me straight. Go ahead."

Neither one of us was going to acknowledge the truth. "Forget it." I exhaled. "It's Christmas. I'm going."

I opened the door and headed down the walk. A second later something whizzed past my head as the door slammed behind me. I walked over and picked it out of the pachysandra. It was a small package wrapped in gold foil with a red ribbon, with a little teddy bear-shaped card taped to it.

My present. Merry Christmas, Frank.

\* \* \*

I went to the apartment and lay on my bed until dark, then changed into warm clothes and comfortable shoes. I dropped the next day's suit and a toiletry kit at the office, ate dinner alone at a Chinese restaurant, and set out around seven. The temperature was already in the twenties. I re-traced the route of a few days ago to the national Christmas tree, then headed off toward Union Station where I bought a container of coffee before going down to the Mall. I had all night so I took my time. I crossed the Fourteenth Street Bridge, followed the bike path north to the Memorial Bridge, then re-crossed the river to the Kennedy Center. I was in Georgetown by eleven and found myself following Kellogg's route from the Biograph.

It was eleven-fifteen when I tightened the bulb in the lamp and moved to the spot marked K on Rogavin's dia-gram. There was no moon. I conjured up the scene in my mind's eye. Ashley was staring at me, wearing a green blouse with a red ribbon in her hair.

A strong hand clamped on my elbow. I spun, crouching and drawing back my fist to punch the groin. The figure took a quick step backward and the lamp illuminated his face. "Jesus Christ!" I yelped. "You nearly killed me. What are you doing here?"

"I'm workin'," Walter whispered. "What are *you* doin' here?"

"Working?"

"Our guy is at a party at the Four Seasons and we were waitin' on him when Harry spotted you walkin' through the neighborhood. What *are* you doing here?"

"Well . . ."

Just then, his pocket began to ring. He fished out a cellu-lar phone and flipped it open. "Yeah?" He listened for a mo-ment, then said, "Okay, monitor your radio." He put the phone back in his pocket and went to the lamp and un-screwed the bulb. "C'mon," he said, taking me by the arm. We walked eastward to a dark sedan barely visible in the shadows between streetlights. Its interior lights didn't go on when we opened the doors. He started the engine and said, "Say hello to your employer."

"Hello, Mr. O'Connell." I spun around, nearly suffering

another heart attack. The glow from the instrument panel revealed a smiling young woman sitting alone in the backseat. She was wearing a coat and a hat similar to the one Ashley had worn that night.

I said to Walter, "You're determined to kill me, right?"

"Relax. Say hello to Natalie. Natalie's a grad student at Johns Hopkins studying . . . what was it again?"

"Forensic psychology," she said. "I'm getting some on-the-job training."

"Hello, Natalie. How did we find you?"

"Through my dad. He's in a car a few blocks away."

Walter took a walkie-talkie out of his other pocket. "Three, this is one. Where is he?"

Harry's distinct New York accent came back. "North on Twenty-ninth, just crossed Olive."

"Two?" Walter called.

"I'm waitin' at O," said Dan White. "Stand by."

"He's not comin' down this street," said Walter. "He's farther west. We'll parallel him and see where he cuts over." He pulled out and drove west, not switching on the headlights until he reached the end of the block. He drove across Thirtieth to Thirty-first, then turned south down to N and made a U-turn. As we rolled slowly northward on Thirty-first Street, two blocks west of Kellogg, the only sound was a low hiss from the radio. I could feel my excitement growing, not unlike the sensation of a night patrol so many years before.

"One? Three."

Walter keyed his radio. "One."

"Passin' Dumbarton."

Walter drove across Dumbarton and slowed the car again. A moment later: "One? Two. West on O, north side."

"Okay," Walter replied. "Three, where are you?"

"Three. Thirtieth, just south of O."

Natalie had a small flashlight and a diagram on her lap. She said, "If he stays west at Thirtieth Street we've got

L–Seventeen on the north side between Thirtieth and Thirty-first."

Walter spoke into the radio. "First option is L–Seventeen if he stays west. Let me hear from you, Three."

Harry's voice came back. "Yeah. Stand by."

Walter killed the headlights and pulled into the curb at the southeast corner of Thirty-first and O. We waited, listening to the hiss of the walkie-talkie. The climate control in the car turned the blower motor on high and I could feel the warm air on my ankles until Walter shut it off. I looked eastward toward the invisible Kellogg now less than two blocks away. Without a moon visibility wasn't more than thirty feet outside the perimeters made by the streetlights.

Walter told Natalie, "Get ready for a radio check." I could hear her rustling in the backseat as he took out a recorder, extended the antenna, and turned it on. "Go ahead," he said over his shoulder.

"This is Four," she said quietly. "How do I sound?" The recorder's speaker amplified her voice.

"Okay," said Walter.

"One? Three. It's west, on the north side. Standard speed."

"This is One," said Walter. "It's L–Seventeen." He killed the engine and nodded at Natalie, who got out of the car, crossed to the north side of the street, then turned east and disappeared into the gloom. I took the diagram and the penlight. There was actually a pad of diagrams, one for each block in the area. L–17 was a streetlight about fifty yards away on the north side of the street. I could see it from the car. It lit an area of about forty feet in diameter, the ring where Natalie was supposed to encounter Kellogg. It had to be natural. She couldn't look as if she was waiting for him and she couldn't rush.

"How's she gonna time this?" I asked. Walter waved at me to be quiet.

The radio crackled. "This is Two. One hundred feet. Standard speed."

"Four. One hundred feet," I heard Natalie say. That answered my question. The diagram had been marked. One hundred feet was two houses from L–17. She had gone to her spot and waited until Kellogg was the same distance away from L–17 on the other side. Walter turned up the volume on the recorder's speaker. Her footsteps were audible as she covered the last hundred feet, standard speed.

Walter's eyes were riveted to the recorder. It seemed as if too much time had gone by when suddenly the needle jumped and Natalie's voice filled the interior of the car. "Excuse me. I'm sorry, but I'm looking for my car and I got turned around. What street is this?"

"You're on O Street," replied the man's voice, not friendly but not hostile either.

"Oh. I don't think this is where I parked."

The man's voice: "Well, where did you just come from?"

"A friend's house on Dumbarton Rock Court," she replied.

"That's just the next street up from here. How far away from there did you park?"

"I walked three or four blocks, I think. I couldn't find a spot anywhere closer."

"Do you remember anything about the area where you parked?"

"I remember that it was in the middle of a block. I thought I walked over to Thirtieth Street. I remember when I turned right to go up to P Street there was a large white house with an iron gate with an eagle on it."

"All right. I know where you were. That house is at Thirtieth and N Street. You need to go south one more block and then east. Just go to the end of the block, turn right, go down one block, and turn left. Your car is on N Street, between Twenty-ninth and Thirtieth. That's over there."

"Oh. Thank you so much. I might have been wandering around here until I froze. All the streets look alike."

"That's what everybody says."

"Do you know what time it is?"

"It's eleven-forty-five."

"Thanks. Bye."

"Good-bye."

The next few seconds was footsteps. Then: "This is Natalie White. It is eleven-forty-five P.M. on Wednesday, December twenty-fifth. I just had a conversation with a man whose photograph I have seen previously and who was identified to me as Miles Kellogg."

Walter spoke into the radio. "Three? Two? One."

"Two."

"Three."

"Take him home," said Walter.

Kellogg emerged at the northeast corner and turned north, followed a moment later by Dan, who walked to the west side of the street and turned north to parallel his quarry. Then a sedan went by heading northward with a piece of tape diagonally across one taillight. Walter drove our car east into the block and Natalie climbed in at the next corner.

"Nice going," I said.

"Thanks." She looked at Walter. "Okay, chief?"

"Not bad," he said. He looked at me. "So, what do you think?"

"I think we're ready for trial."

"Yeah," said Walter. "Let the games begin."

# 16

"Mr. Rogavin, your opening statement, please."

Rogavin rose and approached the lectern. His expression and movements radiated the confidence of a man in his element. He laid a single index card in front of him and took a moment to wipe his glasses with the end of his tie. That moment before you began was always the best part, the best part of law or theater or politics or any other calling that required oratorical skill: knowing what you would do and how you would do it; how you would talk and look and move, right down to the little gestures that always worked.

Watching intently, their blank notepads resting in their laps, was our jury, Ashley Bronson's "peers" only in the legal sense: a mix of races, generations, classes, and sexes; the product of three days' sifting by two lawyers at cross-purposes, intent on rooting out bias, and if we could get away with it, neutrality, eliminating all but the blindly sympathetic to our conflicting views.

On balance I'd felt that we'd gotten the better of the process. All the prospective jurors had heard about the case and they seemed to fall into two categories: those that knew that there was an Ashley Bronson charged with murdering some guy, and those who were well-versed in the nuances, the Burroughs angle included. For the most part the former group was composed of the youngest, poorest, and most disaffected of the city's inhabitants, the ones least likely to trust the police witnesses. They were potentially decent jurors for us except that Ashley was not one to evoke their sympathies.

Still, it was a group that we could mine for some good jurors.

The larger group was the mix. The common thread was at least a passing interest in current events, and the Ashley Bronson case was definitely au courant. There were far too many of them to dismiss so Warner ruled that bias was going to have to be clearly demonstrated to eliminate even the most well-versed among them. That was a big plus for our side because all the media speculation about Sherman Burroughs had "legitimized" our defense before the trial had even begun. Everyone who had followed the case wanted to know what he had to do with it, and if I did my job the answer would add up to reasonable doubt about Ashley's guilt.

None of this was lost on Rogavin. He worked hard to eliminate the so-called "Bronson buffs" from the jury panel but it was an uphill battle because the prospects didn't want to go, especially when they heard that they would only be needed for a week or so. Watching him wrestle with those he had marked for elimination had me laughing to myself, but I had my work cut out for me, too. That was apparent from our last strategy session when I asked who we should be afraid of. "Get rid of the women," urged Cory. "She's the prom queen that snagged your guy. They'll hate her."

"Get rid of the working men," said Andy. "She's rich."

"Watch out for the law-and-order types," warned Walter. "They're gonna vote guilty because they ain't lettin' anybody go."

The mission was straightforward: get rid of the men and women, then comb the rest for Rogavin's groupies. With the aid of that eminent psychologist, Dr. Feinberg, Ph.D., NYPD, I sifted the panel for self-described little guys, Clint Eastwood fans, and women with tiara-phobia, eliminating a few of each. Nobody gets a perfect jury. When the picking was done we were delighted with three, satisfied with four, nervous about three, and two had us scared shitless: all things considered, a pretty good start. We wanted an acquittal but any defense lawyer who said he wouldn't grab a hung jury in a murder case was a fool or a liar. I'd take a hung jury and run. The government wouldn't try her again unless it was at least a nine-to-three vote for conviction.

So, we were finally down to it: Thursday afternoon of the first week of trial, three and one-half days since Warner first rapped the gavel, and the government was outlining its case against Ashley Bronson.

"Ladies and gentlemen," Rogavin began, "Raymond Garvey is no more. His life, rich with achievement, is over. He has left his warm home for a cold grave just a few miles from where you sit. The evidence will show that the woman seated behind me, the one wearing the expensive black suit, murdered him." The jurors' gaze shifted momentarily to Ashley. The prosecutor began to pace, first to the left side of the jury box, then slowly along the rail, in sync with the unhurried rhythm of his speech. "Mr. Garvey's life ended on the chilly, rainy evening of November first. Shortly after ten o'clock he left his bedroom and went downstairs, walked along a hallway, entered his sitting room, and was killed by a bullet that entered his brain." Some jurors visibly recoiled; he paused to let them settle before adding, "We have the bullet. You will see it. There are marks on it, and experts can use those marks to match the bullet to a gun. We expect that it will be matched to Mr. Garvey's own gun, which he kept in a drawer in his sitting room."

He returned to his index card on the lectern and pretended to read as he added casually, "The gun has fingerprints on it. One set belongs to Ashley Bronson." He looked up. "Of course, hers were not the only ones. Others belonged to a friend and to a relative of Mr. Garvey, people who had no reason to wish him harm—certainly," he assured, "no reason to take the poor man's life." He approached the jury box and rested his palms on the rail; his tone became ominous. "But *someone* did. Indeed, shortly before Mr. Garvey died he was threatened with death—not a coincidence. That threat was overheard and the people who heard it are coming here to tell you the words and point at the person who said them." He left it to the jury to figure out who that might be.

Rogavin was indeed a pro. There were well over three hundred murders in the capital every year, and the story of another slaughtered citizen was a daily feature, like the weather or horoscope. As most residents, the jurors had become hardened to reality, if only to cope with their own fears as they ventured out to convenience stores, parking lots, and ATM machines. A savvy prosecutor had to cut through the callous to the nerve, to make them feel the loss and want justice for some guy they'd never met. By breaking the act of murder into its most elemental parts, by juxtaposing a warm home and a cold grave, Rogavin was reacquainting them with the tragedy of homicide.

He set the index card back on the lectern and began to pace once again. "While Raymond Garvey was descending the stairs to meet his fate, a man named Miles Kellogg was returning to his home from an evening at the movies. Like Raymond Garvey, Mr. Kellogg lived alone in a house in Georgetown. The men had never met but they had two other things in common. The first was a distinguished career in service to this nation. Raymond Garvey had risen to the position of Secretary of Commerce, appointed to that job by the President of the United States. Miles Kellogg had worked for U.S. intelligence and served this country in dangerous outposts all over the world.

"That night, as Mr. Kellogg crossed Q Street directly in front of Raymond Garvey's home, something caught his attention. Perhaps it was a sound or a movement, or maybe just the sixth sense developed from a lifetime of relying on instinct." He lowered his voice, as if the next part could only be shared with them. "He turned to his left." Rogavin turned, the jurors followed. "The lamp in front of a house was on, casting its light across the lawn, and there, not twenty feet away, standing quite still, was a figure, a woman." He pointed; they could see her. "The light shone full on her face. She didn't see Miles Kellogg but he saw her, and he stared a full moment before she hurried down the street." Rogavin waited as they watched her disappear. "Mr. Kellogg is coming to this courtroom to identify that woman, which brings me to the second thing he and Raymond Garvey had in common: the last person each saw that night was the same person"—he pointed his finger and declared—"the defendant, Ashley Bronson."

The jurors stared at Ashley again. He gave them plenty of time before he summed up in a voice that was matter-of-fact. "The evidence will show that on the evening of November first last year, in the District of Columbia, the defendant, Ashley Taylor Bronson, did, with malice aforethought and without justification, murder Raymond Bennett Garvey. And when all the evidence is presented, I will come before you again, and ask you to return a verdict of guilty of murder in the first degree. Thank you."

Rogavin returned to his chair, justifiably pleased with himself. The prosecutor's tale had definitely changed the mood. Some of the jurors peeked at Ashley while others counted the house; all looked somber. Ashley herself stared straight ahead, rigid. No amount of warning can prepare a defendant for the prosecution's opening statement. It doesn't matter that you know what you did: in your mind's eye, it's never as bad as the description.

"Mr. O'Connell," said Warner, "your opening statement."

I moved to the lectern and went right at it. "Well, Raymond Garvey is certainly dead. Shot in the head with a bullet from a gun that had Ashley Bronson's fingerprints on it. And if that was all the government had to prove we could all go home, because on that both sides agree." I left the lectern and approached the rail. "Let me tell you what else we agree on. Ashley and Raymond Garvey had an argument before he died. Not the moment before he died, mind you, or the hour, or the day, or even the week. In fact, they had a brief argument about two weeks before. Did she use the words, 'I'll kill you'? Yes, she did. The very same words so many of us have used in a moment of anger with a relative or someone we know very well."

I stopped moving. "And that's something that the government didn't tell you. Ashley knew Raymond Garvey *very* well, in fact, all her life; he was her father's closest friend and for all intents and purposes, her uncle. She was in his home, and he in hers, hundreds of times. Perhaps the government didn't tell you that because it doesn't know much about Mr. Garvey. But when a man is murdered in his own home you'd expect that there's a story to be told and there is, but the government can't tell you that story because it doesn't know it." I paused, then said, "*We* know it. We know it because *our* investigation didn't stop with the arrest of Ashley Bronson, who, by the way, was arrested because of the fingerprints and the argument, and *not* because she had been identified by Miles Kellogg. Why? Well, that's another thing the government didn't tell you. Mr. Kellogg didn't identify her until *after* her picture had been *on television* . . . and *everyone in Washington* knew she'd been arrested!"

Some of the jurors glanced at Rogavin.

"Would you like to know about the ring that Raymond Garvey joined just a few months before he died? The government doesn't know, but we do and we're going to tell you. Would you like to know about his secret meetings outside the city? Again, the government doesn't know, but we're going to tell you. Would you like to know about the large sums of money? The code names? Well, you won't learn about those things from the government because it doesn't *know*. Like you, it will learn the story behind Raymond Garvey's death when the defense puts on its case. Like you, it will have to wait until its own witnesses are through to find out what *really* happened. And when all the evidence is in, like you, it will know that it was wrong to prosecute

Ashley Bronson because she was *one* of several people to whom Raymond Garvey showed off his gun; because she had a silly argument with him long before he died; and because of an eyewitness identification made from a television screen. Like you, it will know the truth. Ashley Bronson isn't guilty."

I stepped toward my chair, then turned back. "Oh, I nearly forgot, there is one other thing that both sides agree on: Ashley's suit *is* expensive. But what does *that* have to do with who killed Raymond Garvey? Like the rest of the government's case: nothing at all."

Walter flashed a thumbs-up as I took my chair. Ashley squeezed my arm. At that moment I was no longer worried by the possibilities. Rogavin may have liked the competition but Noah was right: I lived for it. I needed the risk, and for the first time in years it was significant and personal. Ashley was out there in harm's way, and I was right there with her—loving it so much that I could hardly feel the guilt.

Warner said, "Counsel, approach," and Rogavin and I went to the side of the bench. He leaned over and said, "Since many of the facts are not in dispute, have you two talked about reaching some stipulations? We could dispense with the need for several witnesses."

"The government's willing to stipulate to as much as possible," replied Rogavin without hesitation.

Warner looked at me. "What about the defense?"

"We've stipulated to the testimony of a chain of custody witness who brought the bullet from the medical examiner to the police lab. We've also stipulated that the gun found at the murder scene is registered to Raymond Garvey."

"That's it? Nothing else?"

"No, Your Honor."

The judge looked unhappy. "You just told the jury that you don't dispute a lot of the facts. They're going to wonder why we have to go through all this. They could even hold the defense responsible," he added ominously.

I had known plenty of judges like Warner. Basically, he was a snob who would wink at those he regarded as his peers and crap on everyone else. Being deferential only encouraged him, but his kind could often be backed off by lawyers who fought back. "They don't even know that stipulations are an option," I said. "If it stays that way they won't hold the defense responsible for anything."

"Well, *I* would certainly appreciate expediency," he snapped. "This case has already taken up more of my time than it should." The ethics investigation was very much with us.

"I'm sorry to disappoint you, judge, but I have a client on trial for murder. Expediency is not my concern."

Warner's jaw was working. "Very well," he growled, and looked at Rogavin. "Call your first witness," he ordered.

The prosecution of Ashley Bronson began in orthodox fashion with the detective in charge of the case, Edward Mathis, one of the two who interviewed Miles Kellogg. Mathis informed the jury that on the morning of November second, a Saturday, he was summoned to the Garvey residence, which had been cordoned off in accordance with standard procedures. The officer on the scene led him to a room in the rear of the house where the body of Raymond Garvey was lying on the floor. They then covered the formalities:

"Mr. Garvey was dead?" asked Rogavin.

"Dead," agreed Mathis.

"How were you able to determine that?"

"I checked his pulse. He wasn't breathing."

"Anything else?"

"His pupils were fixed and his body was cold."

"Was there any indication of how he had died?"

"He had what looked like a bullet hole in the left side of his head, just above the temple." Rogavin showed him a close-up photograph which the detective authenticated as a fair and accurate depiction of the victim as he found him.

The picture was then passed around the jury box. The gasps and grimaces flowed down one row and up the other like some macabre version of "the wave." After the last gasp the questioning continued.

"Did you search the crime scene for clues?"

"We did. The forensic unit examined the scene for fibers, fingerprints, and other scientific evidence, and the medical examiner examined Mr. Garvey's body. Myself and the other detectives conducted our own search of the room and the rest of the house."

"What if anything did you find?"

"A thirty-eight caliber Smith and Wesson pistol was on the carpet, about eighteen feet from the body of Mr. Garvey." Again, a photograph was authenticated and distributed. It showed the gun, lying where Ashley had stood when she reenacted the scene for us.

"Detective, what happened to the gun shown in the photograph?"

"I placed it in an evidence bag, signed and dated the bag, and turned it over to Dennis Doyle of the Metropolitan Police Department for examination of the gun for fingerprints."

Rogavin tore open a manila envelope and removed a clear plastic envelope with a pistol inside. "I show you now Exhibit Four. Can you identify this gun?"

"Yes. This appears to be the gun I picked up off the carpet. The bag has the date and my signature, as I described."

"What else did you find?"

"The side doors leading from the room to a patio and the garden were unlocked. We searched the house and found the other doors locked and no signs of forced entry, indicating that those doors were probably the means of entry used by the killer."

"Were there any signs of a struggle?"

"No, sir."

That was it for the primary detective. Rogavin turned him over to me. I had modest objectives for cross-exam, having seen lots of defense counsel skewered by experienced cops.

"Detective Mathis, did I understand you to say that there was no forced entry into Mr. Garvey's home?"

Mathis was quick to retort. "That's *not* what I said, counselor. What I said was, there were *no signs* of forced entry."

"Meaning that a forced entry doesn't always leave signs?"

His jaw tightened at being maneuvered. "It's possible," he conceded.

"Does 'forced entry' include picking the lock?"

"I suppose it could. I don't include it."

"Was the lock on the side doors picked?"

"I don't know whether it was or not."

"So there could have been a forced entry that left no signs, or the lock could have been picked, is that right?"

"Yes."

"In your experience, are there professional criminals who know how to force an entry or pick a lock without leaving signs?"

"Sure."

"And of course, someone could have used a key?"

That surprised him. The key was Rogavin's theory; I was blunting the impact by going there first. "That's right," he answered.

"Looking at other possibilities consistent with what you found at the house, could Mr. Garvey have opened one of the doors to admit whoever killed him? Perhaps even the front door?"

"The hall lights were out."

"Couldn't the killer have turned them out?"

Mathis shrugged in response.

"You're going to have to speak your answer."

"Yes." He was looking more unhappy by the minute.

"Wouldn't it make sense for the killer to turn the lights out if he didn't want to draw attention to his departure?"

"I don't know what he—*or she*—might have been thinking."

"So, all things considered, the killer could have used a key, could have picked a lock, could have forced the entry, or could even have been admitted by Mr. Garvey himself, right?"

"You could say that."

"I just did. Would *you* say it?"

Mathis shifted in his seat. "Yes." He glanced at Rogavin to see if this was just chickenshit or if I was doing some damage. The prosecutor didn't look up from his pad.

"Well, which is it?"

There was silence in the courtroom while Mathis glared at me and I pretended not to notice. "Detective," I repeated, "which is it? Can you say?"

"No. It could have been any of 'em."

"And if the killer came in some way other than the side doors, then he might have unlocked the door on the way out, not the way in. Isn't that true?"

"You could . . . yes."

"Okay. Let's move on. You testified that there was no sign of struggle. Does that mean Mr. Garvey knew the person who killed him?"

"No."

"Does it mean that he *didn't* know the murderer?"

"It doesn't mean that he did and it doesn't mean that he didn't."

"I'm sorry. Then what is the jury supposed to conclude from that portion of your testimony?"

Mathis exhaled through his nose. "That there was no sign of struggle."

"So that fact doesn't point the finger at Ashley Bronson, does it?"

"Objection!" said Rogavin.

"Sustained," ruled Warner.

"Detective," I said, "does the fact that there was no sign of struggle indicate in any way who killed Raymond Garvey?"

"Like I said, it indicates that there was no struggle, that's all."

"Thank you. Your Honor, I have no further questions."

"Very well. Mr. Rogavin, any re-direct?"

"No, Your Honor."

Rogavin's next witness was the medical examiner, Dr. Harold Kranz, who had been summoned to the scene to examine the body. He opined that based on body temperature and lividity, Garvey had passed from this world some time between nine and eleven on the night in question. Kranz accompanied the corpse to the morgue, where an autopsy was conducted on a priority basis to assist the investigation. The examination confirmed that Garvey had died instantly of a single gunshot wound to the head that had penetrated the brain. The M.E. removed the bullet and placed it in an envelope which he signed and turned over to an FBI agent named Windemere. The bullet went into evidence along with some more grisly photos to inflame the jury. My cross-examination was two questions to reinforce the point that Garvey could have been murdered as early as nine o'clock, well before Kellogg saw Ashley.

After Kranz, Rogavin informed the jury that the prosecution and defense had stipulated that if Agent Windemere had appeared, he would have testified that he received the bullet in an evidence bag from Dr. Kranz, signed it, and carried it to Mark Rostrow at the police lab.

Rostrow was sworn in next. He was for all intents and purposes a professional witness, dividing his time between the police laboratory and the courtroom, where he'd testified hundreds of times. After Rogavin took him through his credentials in painstaking detail, he was admitted as an expert in the science of ballistics, and with a well-modulated voice and an engaging manner, gave our jury an introductory course in the science of matching bullets to guns. Progressing from theory to application, he offered his opinion, with "reasonable scientific certainty," that the bullet taken from

Garvey's brain was fired from the gun that was Exhibit 4. I passed on cross-examination, leaving the jury to ponder the irony of being murdered with a weapon bought for your own defense.

It was getting late in the afternoon when Rostrow stepped down and Warner declared a twenty-minute recess, releasing the pent-up energy of spectators and journalists. The hallway sounded like a train station by the time we reached the doors but every conversation stopped as Ashley passed by, creating a moving cone of silence around the defense team as we proceeded to our room. We all exhaled when Andy closed the door.

Ashley sank into a chair. "How are you doing?" I asked.

"The jury is watching me whenever someone isn't speaking," she said wearily. "I'm afraid that every time I move I'm confessing with body language."

"You're doing fine. You're used to people staring at you."

"Not like this. How are *we* doing?"

"So far it's going well, and what's more"—I looked at Walter—"it's going fast. Kellogg goes on tomorrow, maybe even in the morning."

"We're ready," he said. "I got everyone standin' by."

"What time did the spectators start lining up?"

"The first ones showed up around six. Anybody who came after eight and didn't have a media badge was shit outta luck. Tomorrow we'll have someone watchin' by five, and we'll make sure it goes smooth."

"All right," I said. "The next witness is their fingerprint man. When he's finished that'll be it for today. Afterward, we'll go back and finalize our plans."

Dennis Doyle was a twenty-four-year veteran of the Metropolitan Police Department laboratory. As with Rostrow, Rogavin laid it on thick. The jury heard about his education, the specialized courses he attended and the ones he taught, the gist of the articles he authored, the ten thousand fingerprint comparisons he'd done, and all the courts that had already accepted him as an expert—and we weren't even disputing his conclusion.

The examination of the gun received from Detective Mathis had revealed four complete fingerprints and one partial. Rogavin's team had been diligent, and working with a pieced-together list of friends, acquaintances, and neighbors, had managed to match people to all of them, which Doyle painstakingly demonstrated with blown-up photos of loops and whorls. One print belonged to Garvey himself, and one to Clark Benson, his cousin's husband. The partial print "probably" belonged to Robert McGuinn, a neighbor. We knew that according to their witness statements, Benson was going to testify that he was home in Orlando the night Garvey was murdered, and McGuinn was in Sibley Hospital recuperating from a gall bladder operation.

That left two prints, and despite my best efforts to defuse the issue, the pronouncement that they were the right forefinger and thumb of Ashley Bronson, delivered in Doyle's basso profundo, seemed to reverberate in the courtroom long after Rogavin retired to his chair. Certainly, the jurors looked more grim.

There's a saying that smart trial lawyers heed: "When you stand well, stand still." Nearing the end of the first, critical day, I thought we stood pretty well. Opening statements were at least a draw. Mathis's cross-exam had turned him into a plus for our side, and the rest of the witnesses had gone as expected. So far, no surprises and no blunders; all I wanted was to make a few points with Doyle and call it a day.

"Mr. Doyle, you say that fingerprint comparisons show that three people besides the deceased held the murder weapon?"

"That's correct."

"Who was last?"

"Pardon?"

"Which person held the gun last?"

"There is no way of knowing."

"Can you tell anything about the ages of the fingerprints?"

Doyle's brow furrowed. "No, counsel, no one can." He snorted and glanced at the jury with a bemused expression, as if they shared the joke.

"I take it then that you cannot tell the jury when Ashley Bronson held Mr. Garvey's gun?"

"That's correct."

"You cannot say that she held it the night Mr. Garvey was murdered?"

"That's what I just said. Her fingerprints are on the murder weapon, along with those of two other people and the deceased." He couldn't resist adding, "I think you'll be hearing from those other people."

"Are you referring to their whereabouts on the night Mr. Garvey was murdered?"

"I was, but that's for them to say."

"Of course. But if they *were* elsewhere that night, that would seem to leave Miss Bronson, wouldn't it?"

Doyle nodded. "You said it, counselor, not me."

"I did. And the person who murdered Mr. Garvey left his—or her—fingerprints on the gun, correct?"

"I think that's for the jury to decide."

"It certainly is, but I'm asking you as a fingerprint expert: based solely on your tests, did the person who murdered Mr. Garvey leave his fingerprints on the gun?"

"I don't know that for a fact."

"Why not?"

"Holding the weapon does not necessarily leave fingerprints. The check design on the grip does not produce a recoverable print, and the gun can be picked up and held in a way that doesn't leave any prints. And prints can be wiped off, although I don't think that happened here."

"Then there are gloves, right?"

"If gloves were worn," he conceded, "there would be no fingerprints."

"Did the murderer wear gloves or not?"

"I have no way of knowing."

"If that's true, then the killer could be anyone?"

"That's *not* the only evidence," he shot back.

"I understand that, but based on the fingerprint evidence, isn't it true that your conclusion in no way limits the possibilities, and that *anyone* could have killed Raymond Garvey?"

Doyle frowned. "All I've said is that Ashley Bronson's fingerprints are on the gun."

"Well, it's not unusual to find fingerprints at a crime scene that have an innocent explanation, right?"

Doyle stalled before answering, "That's true."

"Indeed, the fingerprints of Mr. Benson and Mr. McGuinn may be in that category, right?"

"I believe they *are* in that category."

"Mr. Doyle, did Ashley Bronson have an opportunity to be lawfully in the house and holding that gun, like Benson and McGuinn?"

"I don't know."

"Did you try to find out?"

"That's *not* my job," he replied, his cheeks coloring. "That's the job of the investigating detectives. I assume they did it."

"Well, we'll see. Thank you, Mr. Doyle. No further questions, Your Honor."

After Doyle left the stand, Warner addressed the jury. "Ladies and Gentlemen, we are going to adjourn for the day. I remind you that you are not to discuss this case with anyone, nor are you to read or listen to anything about it. That means no television news, no radio, and no newspapers. If you want to read the papers, have a family member or friend cut out any reference to the case before you do. Court will resume at nine-thirty tomorrow morning."

We all stood as the jury filed out. Warner pounded the gavel and the first day of *U.S. v. Bronson* was over. The prosecution team packed quickly, and as he led the way out, Rogavin stopped and leaned over our table. "Don't break your arm patting yourself on the back," he said, smirking. "Today was just the preliminaries. Let's see how you do tomorrow."

"Tomorrow? You're coming back for more?"

"You won't be making jokes when it's over."

"You know, for a guy who says he likes competition, you sure are touchy about a little ass-whipping." He glared at me for a second before he smiled and began nodding as if he had told himself a joke. Then he marched out with his team scurrying behind.

Ashley had been listening. "Usually, I like men fighting over me," she said. "Does it help to make him so angry?"

"Yeah. It helps *me* not to take his bullshit. Let's go."

With all our planning we forgot to have Harry and Dan meet us in the courtroom. Andy and Walter were lugging briefcases so I took Walter's baggage and told him, "I'll carry these, you make a path to the car. I don't want to stop moving until we're back in the office."

The media weren't allowed to question trial participants in the courthouse but a gauntlet of cameras and tape recorders awaited us on the sidewalk. After a full day as passive observers the press was ready for action, and they closed in as Walter and Andy barged toward the waiting sedan with Dan behind the wheel.

"Miss Bronson, how do you feel about today?"

"Ashley, are you going to testify?"

"Why are your fingerprints on the gun, Ashley?"

"Ashley, what is your relationship with Frank O'Connell?"

That one stopped her dead. She turned and looked at the questioner, obviously stunned. Walter and Andy, unaware of what was happening, kept forging ahead. Reporters poured into the gap and we were trapped.

"Do you have a comment on the story in the *Galaxy*?"

"Frank, why have you been spending nights at Miss Bronson's home?"

"Is your relationship more than attorney and client, Ashley?"

Anything less than "no" was "yes," but she could only turn from one questioner to the next, too dazed to respond. I wasn't much help; as replayed on TV all evening all I did was shake my head and search for Walter, who finally shouldered his way back to grab her hand. We started moving again, in the eye of a hurricane of swirling reporters, cameras, and microphones until we finally reached the car and tumbled into the backseat. One of the paparazzi stayed with us, leaning into the car so that we couldn't close the door. His lens remained fixed on Ashley's face until she covered it with both hands. I delivered a short jab to his groin and he stiffened before falling backward against the legs of the crowd behind him. Walter yanked the door shut and we started moving. No one spoke as we sped down Massachusetts Avenue. The only sounds were her muffled sobs.

\* \* \*

I returned to the office at seven to meet Walter and go over my outline for Kellogg one more time. Ashley was at home, encircled by reporters using the house for backdrop as they taped their own stories about the day's events. One of them had given me a copy of the *Galaxy*. The front page featured a surveillance-style photo of me leaving the house at sunrise. There were more of my comings and goings in the centerfold, as well as one of the two of us picking the Christmas tree. We got to see that one again on the six o'clock news.

Walter hadn't arrived yet. I swallowed four aspirins with a cold beer and surveyed my desk. My efficient secretary had sorted the reporters' messages into two piles marked "local" and "national." There was a third marked "other." The dreaded message light was on, too; the mechanical voice announced that there were thirty-two messages and my box was full.

I tried to focus on the implications of what had happened. First, there was the jury. If they followed Warner's instructions none of them would know about the story, but that was a big "if": there were usually one or two that couldn't resist newspaper or television stories about their case. I'd have to ask Warner to inquire.

Then there was our esteemed judge. After the Burroughs debacle and the way I had taken him on at sidebar, this could be the last straw. If he went off the deep end no one could help me, not even Pop. He could even declare a mistrial. It didn't take much analysis to realize that Ashley and I had no choice but to deny everything, and in the strongest possible terms.

When I was thinking that things couldn't get much worse, I thought of another implication. I drained the beer and dialed my former wife, praying that she'd gone on safari or an expedition to Everest. But when things go wrong they go wrong, and she answered on the first ring: "Yes?"

"It's me."

"I'm on the other line—don't hang up because I'll be *right* back." Her tone said it all. The phone suddenly felt very heavy; I rested it in the crook of my neck and closed my eyes.

"Frank?"

"I'm still here."

"I want to know if you're planning on seeing Brendan this weekend."

"What?"

"Brendan—your son, remember? You said you wanted to spend more time with him before we leave."

"Jesus, Moira. I'm kind of in the middle of something."

"So I've heard."

"I know. It's—"

"You know that saying, 'Every cloud has a silver lining'? Well, whoever calls to tell me the news, I just strike her name from my Christmas list. Next year I'm going to save a fortune on gifts."

"Honey, I'm sorry, but—"

"I am *not* your honey."

"So what the hell am I apologizing for?"

"Because you've got *a son!*" she yelled. "And he watches television!"

"Yeah, that's it. Look, if you want a piece of me you're at the end of a long line."

"Not anymore! Are you going to see him this weekend or not? I need to make plans."

"I've got a lot of problems to deal with right now, and I mean *this minute.* I'll call you as soon as this is over and we'll talk it out."

"I think you need to hear this now. Rob has said that we can go to California whenever I'm ready, and I've decided the sooner, the better."

I was out of the seat when I replied, "Did you decide this *today?*"

She ignored me. "I'm making arrangements to leave as soon as possible. You should probably adjust your schedule if you want to spend more time with him before we go."

I started to throw the phone but changed my mind and shouted into the mouthpiece, *"He's in the middle of his school year!"*

"It's only first grade," she replied, calm again. "I don't think this will affect his college plans."

"Moira, don't—"

"Good-bye, Frank."

"Goddammit! You—" I was still giving the dial tone a piece of my mind when I noticed Walter standing in the doorway.

"Sorry," he muttered. "I didn't realize who you was talkin' to until a second ago."

"Come on in and close the door. I've entertained the firm enough for today."

He took his spot on the couch and unbuttoned his shirt collar. "You seen any more TV?" he asked.

"No."

He shook his head. "Between the trial and the other stuff, I think we're the only thing that happened in America today."

"I'm sorry, Walter. You warned me and I fucked up."

He shrugged it off. "Ah, forget it. Anyways, my picture is *everywhere*. They said I was her bodyguard. Wait till Volvodick sees that." He laughed. "You can bet your ass I'm gonna be invited *next* Passover."

"Good. Take me along. I don't expect to have any family plans for the next few years."

"Was that the stuff about school?"

"They're going to California—'the sooner the better,' she said." I suddenly decided to kick my desk as hard as I could. It made a nice sound so I did it twice more.

"Maybe she'll cool down and change her mind."

"Sure. Have your guys cut off her electricity and telephone—and steal the newspapers while you're at it. In a couple of weeks she might forget why she's so pissed off."

"We had a good day in court today," he said, changing the subject.

"Everything ready for tomorrow?"

"Ready as we'll ever be. Are we definitely using Natalie?"

"I've been thinking about it. The way things are going, if we can damage Kellogg without using her I'd rather not risk it, because if it backfired . . ."

He finished the thought: "We lose."

The phone rang every few minutes while Walter catnapped and I shot crumbled phone messages at the wastebasket. Finally, with his eyes still shut, he asked, "What do you think is gonna happen tomorrow?"

"I think Warner is home sharpening his ax."

"Swell. What do *we* do?"

"We hang tough. That's all we can do."

# 17

The big day. Thanks to the *Galaxy*, I'd spent the night toss-ing and turning in my miserable little apartment. I picked up a *Post* on my way over to Dupont Circle for breakfast at six A.M. The front page took care of my appetite so I settled for a container of coffee and made my way to the office. Walter was already at the courthouse early to make sure everything was set up. At eight-thirty Andy and I were in front of the building waiting for the car when it pulled to the curb. Dan and Harry were in the front seat. Ashley looked as if she hadn't slept very well, either. We held hands while everyone else pretended not to notice.

The media were waiting where we left them. One entre-preneur had set up a stand selling T-shirts that said, LAWYERS DO IT IN THEIR BRIEFS. We made it inside relatively un-scathed: only one reporter asked if we would stay together if she was convicted.

By nine o'clock we were set up in the courtroom. Ro-gavin showed up with his entourage at nine-fifteen and took his chair across the aisle. He glanced at us and began doo-dling with just a trace of a smile on his puss. At nine-twenty one of Warner's clerks came out and announced that the judge wanted to see counsel in chambers. This time we were ushered into the inner office where Warner was waiting at his desk with a copy of the *Post*.

He began as soon as we were seated. "I've been a judge for eleven years," he declared, "and I've never had occasion to be involved in an ethics inquiry. Now, I'm heading for my second one this month, and Mr. O'Connell, they both pertain to you. How do you explain something like that?"

"I've done nothing unethical."

"Well, that remains to be seen, doesn't it?" He picked up the paper and shook his head. "Extraordinary," he muttered. "I suppose that we should discuss your relationship with your client."

"There's nothing to discuss."

He stared at me with his mouth open, wondering whether his hearing had deceived him. "That is the second time you've crossed the line with me, Mister, and that is two times too many. Choose your next words carefully, I warn you. *I* decide what will be discussed in connection with this case, not you."

"Judge, this is totally inappropriate. The only information you have is tabloid gossip—and about what? That I was an overnight guest at my client's home, that's all. That's no basis for an inquiry, and I'm not answering any questions about my relationship with my client."

Warner's face grew dark. "Perhaps," he sputtered, "the best course of action would be to declare a mistrial and let the Ethics Committee add this matter to its investigation of your misdeeds."

"Fine! Go ahead!" I shot back. "But I want to go outside and put a statement on the record objecting to any mistrial. When the Court of Appeals agrees that you were wrong and we were entitled to go forward, they will bar a new trial of my client on double jeopardy grounds. Ashley Bronson will never face a jury and you will be a national laughingstock!"

Warner recoiled. He looked from me to Rogavin and back to me, obviously unsettled. The truth was that I had no idea how the Court of Appeals would view this mess. Maybe we'd win, maybe we'd lose. The only thing I knew for sure was that if Ashley was tried again we'd never be in as good a position the second time around. I'd shown Rogavin some cards and next time he'd be prepared. But the bigger worry was Kellogg: we'd have to go at him again because our staged encounter would be too stale, and who could say what would happen?

Fortunately, I had an ally. Rogavin had made up his own mind. He knew that I might be right and he wasn't going to let her—us—get away. Combat had been joined and he wanted to see it through. "Judge," he said smoothly, "I think you'd be well within the law to declare a mistrial here but we could never be sure until the Court of Appeals ruled. Speaking for the government, I wouldn't like to see the accused murderer of an important citizen get off on a technicality."

"Are you suggesting that I ignore this?" asked Warner, tapping his copy of the *Post*. The words were more adamant than his tone.

"No, sir. I'm suggesting that you bring Miss Bronson in here and explain the situation. Once she understands the principles of the attorney-client relationship and that the court is trying to protect her welfare, she can ask Mr. O'-Connell to request a mistrial if she has any doubts about her own situation. But if she expresses no doubts, well, that should make it very difficult for her to claim ineffective assistance of counsel if she's convicted."

Convicted defendants sometimes won new trials by showing that their lawyers did a poor job, or didn't have their client's interest uppermost in mind. Rogavin was offering a way to limit the possibility of such a claim by having Ashley implicitly deny that anything had occurred between us. I had to hand it to him: he knew that we'd get the trial we both wanted.

By then Warner's primary concern was saving face. He latched on to Rogavin's idea with both hands. "Go out and get your client," he ordered.

The marshals had let the spectators in and the courtroom was full. The sketch artists were taking advantage of the delay to do more drawings of the woman whose celebrity grew with each passing day. I sat down and put my lips close to her ear. "Warner wants to see you in chambers," I whispered.

"Me? Why? What's happened?"

"He asked about our relationship and when I wouldn't discuss it, we banged heads and he threatened a mistrial."

I felt her stiffen. "No, we've got to finish this!"

"Hold on, hold on. There isn't going to be any mistrial. Our judge realizes the error of his ways. Rogavin doesn't want a mistrial either, and he threw him a lifeline. Warner's going to withdraw gracefully by giving you an opportunity to protect yourself from me."

"What does that mean?"

"He's going to advise you that if the attorney-client relationship has been compromised in any way, you might be better off with a new lawyer. He'll say that he's willing to declare a mistrial to allow you to get one."

"And all I have to do is tell him that I want to proceed?"

"That and be offended by the implications. But let me warn you, this guy is not Mr. Sensitivity. He may cross the line."

"It doesn't matter," she replied. "And it's too late to protect me from you."

Warner and Rogavin stood when we entered the office. A third chair had been added for her. The judge indicated that she should take the one in the middle, then cleared his throat and began.

"Miss Bronson, has your lawyer told you why I wanted to talk to you?"

"Yes, he has," she replied evenly.

"The attorney-client relationship is a fiduciary one, the highest known in the law," he intoned. "A lawyer is required to devote his skills solely for the benefit of the client, and to let nothing interfere with the professional objectivity that is crucial to the relationship."

"Of course."

Warner clasped his hands on the desk and adopted a paternal tone. "What I am trying to do here, Miss Bronson, is make sure that relationship has not been compromised in any way, and that you get the full benefit of the protection to which you are entitled." He waited a moment but Ashley remained silent, her eyes fixed on him. She wasn't nervous. In that room, stripped of all the trappings, Warner was another man with whom she had to deal, and she'd dealt with all kinds. The judge, however, seemed unsure where to go next. He shifted in his seat and let his gaze fall to the newspaper. "I take it you've seen the stories about, uh, you and Mr. O'-Connell?"

"Yes, I have. They say that he was an overnight guest at my home."

"Right," the judge said, nodding. "Well . . ."

"Do you want to know if it's true?" she asked.

"No!" exclaimed Warner, holding up a hand. "I don't want to know about *any* details. I'm merely—"

"I would have no difficulty answering that question," she said. "Is there some prohibition against a lawyer being a houseguest of a client?"

"Well, houseguest . . . no."

"Then I don't understand. Why would the attorney-client relationship be compromised if we'd done nothing wrong?"

The judge was beginning to fidget in his chair. "There has been *some* speculation by the media that the relationship is, um, *more* than hostess and houseguest."

"Am I required to defend myself from tabloid speculation?" She didn't take her eyes off Warner as she spoke. Having been in his place, I might have felt sorry for him if he hadn't asked for it.

Warner shook his head. "Of course not! It's only that . . . uh, as I said, we need to be sure that you get the full protection you're entitled to, that's all."

Ashley looked directly at me and said, "I'm very pleased with the protection I've received from Mr. O'Connell. I think he's always put my welfare first."

Warner realized that he had taken this as far as he could. "Well," he declared, resuming his judicial demeanor, "since the court has not been advised of anything to suggest that the sanctity of the lawyer-client relationship has been compromised, I believe that we should proceed with the trial." He glanced at Rogavin, who nodded approvingly. "We'll reconvene in ten minutes."

"One thing, Your Honor," I said.

"What is it?"

"I request that you poll the jury to see if they have followed your admonition about the newspapers and television."

"All right. We'll do that first."

We all stood up and returned to the courtroom. Walter looked at me questioningly and I gave him a nod. It was all systems go. Warner probed gingerly but none of the jurors would admit to violating his prohibition about reports on the case. Some of them were probably lying but we'd never prove it. I could only hope they were romantics.

The testimony of Benson and McGuinn went as expected. Each described his relationship to Garvey, the circumstances under which he got to hold the murder weapon, and his whereabouts on that fatal night. It wasn't very stimulating stuff but Rogavin added a little flourish when he finished each examination by asking, "Sir, did you murder Raymond Bennett Garvey?" Neither owned up to it, narrowing the field.

At late morning we got to the nitty-gritty with Edward Ward. He told the jury that he and his wife had worked for Garvey for seventeen years, she as a full-time cook and housekeeper, he as a part-time handyman, gardener, and helper. They found Raymond to be a "good employer," but didn't give the impression that they were deeply attached to their departed boss.

"Mr. Ward," asked Rogavin, "in the course of your duties did you have occasion to meet the defendant, Ashley Bronson?"

"Yes, sir. Many times. Since she was in high school."

"To your knowledge, was she related to Mr. Garvey?"

"No, sir. Miss Ashley's father, Henry Bronson, was a friend of Mr. Garvey's from before Miss Ashley was born."

"Did Miss Bronson continue to visit the house in recent years?"

"Yes, sir, she did, but not as often as before. It was usually as a guest when Mr. Garvey was entertaining. Sometimes, she might drop something off when Mr. Garvey was away and Mrs. Ward and I were off duty."

"On those occasions, how did she gain access to the house—if you know?"

"She had a key, sir. There was always a key kept over at the Bronson house." Several jurors' heads went down as they wrote on their pads.

"Do you know what locks that key fit, Mr. Ward?"

"All the doors on the first floor were opened by one key."

"Did that include the doors leading to the garden from the sitting room?"

"Yes, sir."

Rogavin approached the witness and stood alongside him, one arm resting on the witness box. "Mr. Ward," he said deliberately, "did you ever see or hear Miss Bronson and Mr. Garvey argue?"

Ward grimaced. Ashley had said that he and his wife were fond of her, and it was clear that this testimony did not come easy for the old man. "One time, sir," he said, his voice barely audible.

"And when was that?"

"In October of last year, sir. Mrs. Ward and I were cleaning the kitchen at the time—floors and cabinets."

"What did you hear?"

"We heard loud voices. They were coming from the front of the house. We didn't know if anything was wrong so we went down the hall toward the sound." Ward removed his handkerchief and blew his nose, glancing at Ashley before returning his attention to Rogavin.

"Were you able to make out any of the words?"

"Yes, sir. Miss Ashley came out of the parlor heading toward the front door. I heard Mr. Garvey call her and she turned back toward the parlor."

"What happened?"

Ward's hands were shaking. "Well, sir, she seemed very upset . . . and . . ." His voice faltered before he could finish.

"Take your time, sir," soothed Rogavin. "I know this is difficult."

Ward took a deep breath and exhaled his answer. "She screamed at him. She said, 'Stay away. If something happens, I'll kill you. I will.' And then she opened the front door and slammed it behind her."

"Did Mr. Garvey say anything?"

"No, sir. He came out of the parlor and saw us standing there in the hall, then just turned around and went back inside and closed the doors."

"How long after this was Mr. Garvey killed?"

"About two weeks, sir. Maybe a little less."

"Do you know what, if anything, Mr. Garvey did or threatened to do to provoke Miss Bronson?"

"No, sir."

"Thank you," said Rogavin. No further questions." Rogavin took his seat as several jurors finished making their notes.

"Mr. O'Connell, cross-exam?" said Warner.

"Mr. Ward," I began, "how long did you say you've known Ashley?"

"Seventeen years, sir, as long as I worked for Mr. Garvey."

"During all that time, did you ever see Ashley do anything to hurt Mr. Garvey?"

Ward shook his head. "No, sir. Nothing like that."

"Did you ever see her become violent in any way?"

"Miss Ashley?" He shook his head again. "No, sir, never."

Two jurors made notes. "Now, Mr. Ward, did you know that Mr. Garvey had bought a gun?"

"Yes, sir, I did. He bought it after there was a robbery on the street just a block from the house."

"Did you know he kept it in a drawer in the sitting room?"

"Yes, sir. In the cabinet, yes."

"Did he show it to you?"

"Yes, he did, sir. The day he bought it."

"Did you hold it?"

"Yes, sir."

"Did you ever see him show it to anyone else?"

"Yes, sir. Mr. Benson one time. And I believe he showed it to Mr. Glover when he was visiting."

"And who is Mr. Glover?"

"He is a business acquaintance of Mr. Garvey's. He was visiting from London at the time."

"Do you know why Mr. Garvey showed the gun to you and these other men?"

"Why?" Ward shrugged. "He just wanted to, I guess."

"You didn't have to ask him to show it to you?"

"No, sir."

"Can you think of any reason why he wouldn't show it to Miss Ashley as he did other people?"

"No, sir. None that I can think of."

I was watching the jury out of the corner of my eye. Several were writing; all seemed to be paying close attention. It was time to lay the foundation. "You said that you heard Miss Ashley shout at him about two weeks before Mr. Garvey was killed, is that right?"

"That's right, sir."

"Between that time and the time Mr. Garvey was killed, did you ever witness anyone else arguing with or shouting at Mr. Garvey?"

"Yes, sir, I did," replied Ward.

A few feet away, Rogavin's face froze. This was news,

and it was a safe bet that some poor detective was going to pay dearly for that.

I gestured toward the jury. "Mr. Ward, would you please tell the ladies and gentlemen of the jury what you witnessed?"

"Yes, sir." He looked over at the jurors, who had their pens poised. "On Wednesday, the day before Halloween, my wife and I were coming back from the supermarket. We always did the heavy shopping on Wednesday. We were two houses away when a man came out of Mr. Garvey's house. He stepped out on the stoop and turned back to the door. His head was moving and he was shaking his finger at someone inside that I couldn't see. He seemed angry."

"Objection!" said Rogavin quickly. "The witness is speculating."

"Sustained," ruled Warner.

"Mr. Ward," I said, "could you hear anything?"

"His voice carried to where we were but I couldn't understand the words; we were too far away."

"What happened next?"

"The man turned to go down the steps. There was a pumpkin on the stoop." Ward had naturally turned to face me to answer the additional questions, but he turned back to the jury to explain. "I always carve a pumpkin for Halloween, sort of fancy-like." By then everyone in the courtroom was hanging on his answer.

"Go on, sir. Tell the jury what happened."

"Well, this man pulls back his foot and kicks the pumpkin right off the step down to the sidewalk and into the street. It made a heck of a mess. Then he walks down the steps and gets into a yellow car, a Rolls-Royce. He drove away real fast."

"Did you notice anything unusual about the car?"

"Yes, sir. The steering wheel was on the other side."

"You mean what would usually be the passenger side?"

"Yes, sir. It was an English car. He drove right past us and I could look right at him."

All of the jurors were making notes, as was the press. Most of the people in the courtroom already knew who was driving the car, courtesy of the very same journalists who were making life miserable for Ashley and me.

"Had you ever seen this man before, Mr. Ward?" I asked.

"No, sir."

"Did you ever see him again?"

"Not in person. But I saw his picture in the newspapers and on television."

"Are you sure it's the same man?"

"Absolutely sure, sir."

"Did the newspaper and television stories state his name?"

"Sherman Burroughs, sir."

I ended there.

"Mr. Rogavin? Any re-direct?" asked Warner.

I didn't think Ward's story left much room; it was too simple and to the point. But Rogavin demonstrated how he had gotten his reputation. "Mr. Ward, you say you've never seen the man after that day on the steps, but you're sure that it was Sherman Burroughs?"

"Yes, sir. I am."

"You are positive about that?"

"Yes, sir. I'm positive."

"How far away from this man were you when you first saw him?"

Ward sat back and thought a moment before responding. "Well, first we were two houses apart. I'd say about a hundred feet or so. Then, when he drove away he passed by where we were standing on the sidewalk. I'd say we were about thirty feet apart, no more."

"And he was inside a car driving fast?"

"Yes, he was."

"So, how long did you get to see him at this thirty-foot distance, would you say?"

"Just a second or two, but long enough."

"Long enough to be sure when you saw his picture on television?"

"Yes."

Rogavin was nodding his head. I had to hand it to him: he had taken a hit but he was up off the canvas and fighting back. "So, Mr. Ward, if I understand your testimony, you can see a stranger for just a second or two at a distance of thirty feet, in a car driving fast, and then positively identify him *weeks* later from a picture on a television screen. Is that correct?"

Ward nodded solemnly. "Yes, sir. Absolutely. I am absolutely positive."

Rogavin smiled. "I'm sure you are. Thank you, sir. We *all* appreciate your testimony."

Ward was dismissed. There was a little bounce in Rogavin's step when he returned to his chair, and after conferring with his helpers, he asked for a sidebar. We huddled with Warner and Rogavin said that he wasn't going to call Mrs. Ward. Instead, his next witness was going to be Miles Kellogg. Warner supposed that the testimony would take some time and decided to recess for lunch. A few minutes later we were back in the defense room, passing around the sandwiches and drinks sent over from the office. Everyone was too tense to make small talk.

"Are we going to have any problem with seating after the lunch break?" I asked Walter.

"Nah," he said, chewing his chicken salad. "The numbers that were given out are good for the day. Anyway, no one's goin' anywhere. We're all set."

"Let's go over this one last time," I said, looking around the room. "If we go with the plan, act exactly the same. Don't show any expression and keep your eyes on the witness or on the table in front of you. Whatever you do, don't turn around toward the spectators at any time this afternoon."

Thirty more minutes. I was desperate to go out for a walk

but there were cameras all over the place. It would make a fine lead-in to that night's news: *Amid allegations that he and client Ashley Bronson have been having an affair, lawyer Frank O'Connell soloed around the courthouse during yesterday's recess.* That would be well received in Bethesda. I moved around to the seat next to Ashley. "How are you doing?" I asked.

"Ask me in a couple of hours," she said quietly. "I don't know how you do this—the thinking and planning and dueling out there. It seems so stressful."

"It's stressful for both of us. Try not to dwell on what's going on in there when you get a break."

"Okay, change of topic. Did the stories about us cause you any problems?"

"I'm not married anymore, remember?"

"That's not responsive."

"Not responsive? *I'm* the lawyer, remember?"

"Right. A fiduciary relationship. That means you have to be true to me, doesn't it? No lies, ever."

"For a fee."

"Oh, I've got to *pay* for the truth, is that it?"

"That's the lawyer's code. But go ahead, I'll give you a freebie. Ask me anything."

"I'll save it for later."

There was a knock on the door. Dan White came in and said to Walter, "We're ready."

# 18

"State your name for the record, please."

"Miles Patrick Kellogg." He looked at the court reporter and spelled, "K-e-l-l-o-g-g."

Rogavin's star witness might have come directly from the alumni section at the Yale-Harvard game: straight nose, strong chin, graying hair combed more back than to the side, with that innate, assured demeanor that could pull off a blazer and gray flannels in a courtroom full of suits.

"Mr. Kellogg, where do you reside?"

"Three-zero-eight-seven Avon Street, Northwest, Washington, District of Columbia."

They spent a few minutes on family and education before getting down to business. "Mr. Kellogg," Rogavin asked, "what is your occupation?"

"I am retired."

"What did you do before you retired?"

"I was in the employ of the Central Intelligence Agency," he replied.

In the employ? I glanced at the jury. None of them seemed put off, not even the younger ones who'd spent more time out of employ than in. If anything, they looked kind of impressed. I could feel the perspiration under my arms.

Rogavin looked impressed, too, although with him it was an act. "Sir," he asked, "can you tell us what you did in the CIA?"

"I'm afraid I cannot."

The prosecutor feigned surprise. "You cannot answer the question?"

Kellogg looked up at Warner. "I'm sorry, Your Honor, but I'm not at liberty to discuss any details of what I did."

Warner nodded appreciatively. "Can you say anything in the most general terms, sir?"

Kellogg pursed his lips, pondering the request, then offered, "I served in the field in various posts around the world. What I did is classified for national security reasons."

They were going to do the whole James Bond thing and we couldn't stop them. I looked back at Walter, who was making that up-and-down gesture with his fist again.

"Well," asked Rogavin, "can you tell us how many years of experience you had in the field?"

"About twenty-five years."

"Were you required to undergo certain training for your assignments overseas?"

"Yes."

"Can you tell us anything about your training?"

"Not really. It included a variety of things."

"Including skills for use in the field?"

"Yes." In the back row, one juror looked knowingly at another.

"How much training did you get?"

"Years of it. It never stops, actually."

"Are you required to use, shall we say, powers of observation in the field?"

"Yes. You're supposed to notice things as part of your job and for your own . . . protection."

Rogavin remained at attention in front of the lectern. He wanted all eyes on Kellogg. "Let me draw your attention to the evening of Friday, November first, last year. Do you recall where you were and what you did that evening?"

"Yes, I do. I had dinner at home and then went to the movies."

"Where?"

"The Biograph theater in Georgetown. The eight-fifteen show."

"Do you remember anything about the weather that night?"

"I remember it was raining and pretty cool. I know I wore my raincoat and carried my umbrella."

"What time did the show end?"

"It was about ten o'clock, I believe."

"What did you do after the show?"

"I walked home."

"In the rain?"

"Yes. I enjoy the rain, and I like to walk."

During lunch a screen had been placed next to the witness box. A projector was connected to a computer at the prosecution table. On cue, a blow-up of a street map of Georgetown appeared on the screen. Responding to questions and using a laser pointer like Rogavin's, Kellogg led the jury along his meandering route from the Biograph. As he spoke, dashed lines materialized on the map. When his narrative brought him to Garvey's street the image changed, zooming to a schematic of the street and its houses, with one in red. He led the jury down the street, stopping at a point across from the red house.

"Sir," asked Rogavin, "do you know what time you arrived at that location?"

"Between ten-fifteen and ten-twenty," replied Kellogg.

One of Rogavin's helpers tapped a few keys and the image zoomed in again. Now the screen was filled with the red house and the street immediately in front. The letter K marked the spot where Kellogg had left off.

"Would you describe to the jury what happened next?"

Kellogg stared at the screen, seeing it all in his mind's eye. On the side of the box farthest from the witness stand the jurors leaned toward him for fear of missing a word. "I crossed the street on a slight diagonal which brought me to the curb in front of the house here." His pointer traced his steps and a new K replaced the old one. "There was a lamp in front of the house that was on, right here." An L appeared on the diagram. "When I reached the curb something caught my attention. I looked to my left, and right . . . here"—he pointed at the spot and an X appeared—"I saw a woman standing on the lawn just off the sidewalk."

"How far apart were you?"

"No more than twenty feet away."

Rogavin moved from the lectern and positioned himself about twenty feet in front of Kellogg. "About this far?"

"No more."

"Can you describe this woman for the jury?"

Kellogg turned to face the jury box. "She appeared to be around thirty or so, taller than average, wearing a dark trench coat and a hat with a brim. I couldn't be sure because of the trench coat but she appeared to be slender, certainly not overweight."

"You could see her face?"

"Yes, very well. The light from the lamp shone on it. She was very attractive, a face you'd remember." The jurors reflexively looked at Ashley. There wasn't going to be any dispute about that.

"What happened next?"

"I watched her for a while. She was looking up and down the sidewalk but she didn't appear to see me, perhaps because I was standing between parked cars."

Rogavin held up a stop watch. "Mr. Kellogg, with the court's permission, I would like to demonstrate just how long you looked at the woman you saw that night. Beginning from the time I say 'start,' I'd like you to look at me as you looked at the woman. When you've looked for what you feel to be the same amount of time, just say 'stop.'"

Warner told him to proceed. Some of the jurors looked at their watches and I moved mine into my line of sight. Kellogg stared at Rogavin for what seemed like an eternity before he said, "Stop." The elapsed time was twenty-three seconds.

Rogavin returned to the lectern and turned a page. This time he really was using an outline, making sure to hit every point. "What happened next?"

"The woman stepped onto the sidewalk and walked away quickly to the west. I continued east toward my home." The screen went blank.

"At that time, sir, did you have any reason to believe that a crime had been committed inside the house?"

"No."

"When was the first time you learned about what had happened to Raymond Garvey?"

"Not until the following Tuesday." Kellogg told the jury the story about going to his cabin and being cut off from the outside world until his return to Washington, when he saw the news broadcast. "The television was on with the sound on low," he told them. "At eleven o'clock I went into the kitchen to get something to eat. A few minutes later I happened to pass the entrance to the living room. I glanced at the TV and the Channel Nine news was on. I couldn't hear what the news anchor was saying but there was a picture in the upper right of the screen. It was the same woman that I had seen in front of the house. The picture disappeared almost immediately but I caught the news on another channel and learned that the woman's name was Ashley Bronson."

Up until that point Kellogg hadn't looked toward our side of the courtroom. Rogavin showed him a still picture from the Channel 9 video, the news anchor with Ashley's picture behind him. Kellogg verified it and it was passed around to the jurors for comparison to the real article. The picture was a full face shot and good quality. There was no issue about resemblance.

Rogavin had reached the denouement. "Sir, putting the photograph aside, do you see the woman you saw in front of Mr. Garvey's house in the courtroom today?"

At once Kellogg looked over at the defense table and pointed. "Yes, she's sitting at that table in a blue suit. That's the woman I saw."

"Are you sure, sir?"

Kellogg looked at Rogavin for a moment, as if surprised by the question. Then he replied, "Sir, I have no doubt that the woman seated over there and the woman I saw are the same person. It was Ashley Bronson standing on the lawn that night."

"And what did you do then?"

"I called the police immediately."

Rogavin nodded solemnly. "Thank you, Mr. Kellogg. No further questions." Then he turned to me and said grandly, "Your witness, counsel."

I laid my notes on the lectern. Around me I could hear the sounds of spectators and jurors rearranging themselves after forty-five minutes of immobility. Suddenly, Andy was at my side. He laid a note in front of me written in Walter's scrawl: *"He wasn't there."* I looked over at Walter, who was nodding almost imperceptibly, and then back at the waiting Kellogg. The eyewitness wasn't. Whoever had seen Ashley commit murder was using a stand-in, but whatever it all meant, I wasn't going to figure it out at the lectern. My chest was pounding. I took a couple of breaths and tried to clear my mind. First things first.

"Mr. Kellogg, do I understand that you have received training in using your powers of observation?"

"Yes."

"I want to understand how it works. Has your eyesight been improved in some way through training?"

"No."

"Yes" and "no." Rogavin had him on a tight leash. "Do you have a greater ability to see in the dark than other people?"

"No."

"So as far as identifying someone you've seen on a dark street, you don't have any more ability than anyone else, is that true?"

He wasn't going to answer that one yes or no. "Being observant is not a matter of special eyesight," he explained, "but of effort—*application*, if you will. I was trained to observe. People often look but don't see because they are not applying themselves to the task."

"Do you turn this power of observation on and off, like a switch?"

He shook his head. "No. Once you're trained and you've practiced it becomes second nature. You pass someone on the street and you automatically think, 'Twenty-seven, five-foot-ten, one-hundred-sixty pounds, no facial hair.' As I said, application."

"Then if I understand what you're saying, your training is in mentally noting what you see, is that right?"

He nodded. "I suppose you could put it that way, yes."

"But as to the 'seeing' part, sir, isn't it a fact that even with *all* your years of training, you have no greater ability than anyone else"—I walked toward the jury—"than any of these jurors here, for example, to actually see and recognize the features of another person on a dark street?"

"I was trained to be a better observer."

"I don't understand your answer, sir. Are you admitting that your training gave you no greater ability than anyone else to actually see the features of another person on a dark street?"

"Yes," he said testily. But as we stared at one another he went from irritated to completely composed in a matter of seconds. The man's life was structured around overcoming setbacks to reach an objective. He wasn't going to be side-tracked into a test of wills.

"Mr. Kellogg, let's return to the night Raymond Garvey was murdered. It was raining heavily that evening?"

"That's correct."

"There was no moonlight or starlight to see by?"

"None."

"The street is tree-lined?"

"Yes."

"And in early November there were still leaves on those trees, yet another barrier to any light from above, correct?"

"That's true."

"Were you using an umbrella?"

"I was."

"There is no streetlight near the Garvey residence, is there?"

He looked toward the ceiling for a moment, thinking. "No, as I recall, the nearest streetlight is more than a hundred feet away."

"So that means that you had no moonlight, starlight, or even reflected light to aid your night vision, true?"

He shook his head. "I can't agree because I didn't need a flashlight to walk along. I could see the street and other features as I passed so I would say that there was some ambient . . . some background light there, maybe from the houses or the reflection off of low clouds. I can tell you that I wasn't walking into trees or signs and I didn't have a flashlight."

"Well, there was enough background light to walk, but not enough to make out someone's face at twenty feet, was there?"

"That's true," he agreed. "It was the lamp that made it possible to see her." He gestured toward Ashley when he said "her."

"Then let's talk about the lamp." I went to the defense table and retrieved a police report and a bag. "What kind of light source did the lamp have?"

"A single bulb, I believe."

I looked at the report and asked, "And if the police said that it was just a sixty-watt bulb, would you have any reason to disagree?"

"No, I would not."

I took the bag with me over to the jury box, removed a bulb from the bag, and held it up. The jurors stared at it as I made the introduction: "A sixty-watt bulb."

"Are you going to introduce that as an exhibit, Mr. O'-Connell?" asked Warner.

"Yes, Your Honor, I will." The bulb was marked with a label by the clerk and handed back to me. I made a show of proffering it to Rogavin for examination before placing it on the rail of the witness box so the jurors could look at it and Kellogg at the same time. "Mr. Kellogg, you said you were on your way home from the movies?"

"That's right."

"Do you go to the movies very often?"

"Fairly often. I like the old classics that they show at the Biograph."

"What did you see that night?"

"*Strangers on a Train*. It's a mystery directed by Alfred Hitchcock, made in nineteen fifty-one."

"I remember that one. It's a murder mystery, isn't it?"

"Yes, it is."

"You have to hang on to the end to learn how it turns out?"

"Mr. O'Connell," warned Warner.

"Sorry, Your Honor. Mr. Kellogg, are there any outdoor scenes in that movie, scenes shot in broad daylight?"

"Yes, of course. There are several."

"I want to ask you a question as someone who often goes to the movies. Would you agree that when one of those bright, outdoor scenes is being shown, there is a lot more light inside the theater than would come from that little sixty-watt bulb?"

"I'm not sure I understand. You mean light coming from the movie screen?"

"That's what I mean."

Kellogg wasn't sure where this was going. He wasn't there when Team Bronson grappled with an alternative to a risky on-site or courtroom demonstration with Ashley and the lamp. We needed a common experience, one where people had difficulty making identifications, and it was Ashley herself who came up with the movie theater scenario. I loved it because of the fit, but the best part was that the image people had of being inside a movie theater wasn't fine-tuned to the brightness of the screen. Movie theaters were dark places where you enjoyed yourself in anonymity, kissed your first date, or inched along searching for your seat.

Kellogg stared at the bulb, then glanced toward Rogavin before answering carefully. "I would agree that if there is a bright, outdoor scene being shown on the movie screen, the light coming from the screen is more than the amount of light that would come from a sixty-watt bulb, yes."

"You said that the woman you saw was about twenty feet away and wearing a trench coat and hat, correct?"

"That's right."

I went into the bag again and brought out a measuring tape. I measured twenty feet along the jury box, which was almost exactly one end to the other—eight seats wide. Rogavin, growing concerned, checked the tape before stipulating to the distance. "So," I continued, "if the jurors wanted to understand the kind of view you had, they could imagine themselves sitting in a movie theater looking at someone at the other end of the row who is wearing a hat. Is that true?"

"Well," replied Kellogg, sitting forward, "only if the screen was providing the light you mentioned before."

"Actually, sir, according to your testimony, if the screen was providing *that* much light, our juror would have a *better* view than you had that night, correct?"

He was liking my analogy less all the time. "I don't know," he replied.

"You don't know? Didn't you acknowledge a moment ago that there was more light coming off the screen than the bulb provided?"

Rogavin had had enough with my analogy. "Your Honor," he protested, "this movie theater silliness is simply too indefinite to mean anything. The witness said that there was enough light on the street to walk along even without the help of the lamp. Who can realistically compare the situation inside a movie theater to what Mr. Kellogg experienced that night, outdoors, with a lamp and other light assisting? It clearly calls for speculation. I move that the testimony be stricken and the jury be instructed to disregard it."

Warner looked at me for a reply. "There is no speculation involved at all, Your Honor. The jury was not there that night and we are merely trying to give them a benchmark to use to understand the testimony. The witness agreed that under the conditions described there is more light for viewing than was provided by the lamp. The defense believes that the jurors are perfectly capable of using the analogy properly in their deliberations."

Rogavin's objection was too little, too late. The jury wasn't going to forget what it heard. The judge knew it and he wasn't about to change course and maybe commit an error in the process. And Rogavin had made things worse by giving me a chance to position the defense as the side with faith in the jury's intelligence. "The objection is overruled," said Warner. "But we've heard enough about movie theaters. Move on."

"Mr. Kellogg, was the woman wearing lipstick?"

"I don't know."

"There wasn't enough light to tell?"

"I didn't see any lipstick. It could have been flesh-colored."

"What color was her raincoat?"

"It was dark."

"Was it black, blue, green, something else?"

"I don't know. I couldn't tell."

"So, it was so dark you couldn't make out colors, is that it?"

Kellogg shrugged. "I suppose so."

"And you saw a picture of the same woman on a television screen four days later, is that right?"

"That's correct. It was the same person."

"You didn't give this woman a moment's thought between Friday and Tuesday night, did you?"

"No, sir. I did." The first instinct of a hostile witness was to disagree.

"You did." I frowned. "Maybe once or twice in four days?"

"More than that, I assure you," he replied smoothly.

I waited. The vacuum of silence drew him out and he began to embellish: "The situation didn't seem right," he explained, looking at the jury. "A woman alone, in the rain and the dark . . . the way she was looking around and hurried away . . ." He shook his head. "I thought about her a good bit between Friday and Tuesday night."

"You *still* had the image of this woman on your mind when you returned to Washington?"

He was committed now and didn't hesitate. "Yes. I'd say that was true."

I picked up the exhibit from the clerk's desk and flashed it at him from a few feet away. "This picture shows Stuart Campbell, a local news anchor, looking at the camera with a picture of Ashley Bronson in the background, in the upper right hand corner of the screen, correct?"

He barely glanced at it before he replied, "That's what it shows."

"And this picture is the same size as your television screen?"

"Yes, it is."

"How far away from the screen were you when you saw this image?" I held it up again, just a few feet from his face.

"I believe it was measured by the police: sixteen feet."

I took out my tape measure and measured sixteen feet

from the witness box, which was right next to the lectern. I stood there and held the photograph up again. "Mr. Kellogg, when you glanced at the television that night, this woman was still on your mind, correct?"

He blinked. An alarm suddenly sounded within and he hesitated for just a second. "I don't know what was on my mind at that precise moment," he replied warily.

"Well, sir, the fact is that you were thinking about a woman's image for several days, and lo and behold"—I held up the exhibit again—"you glanced at the television and there's a picture of a woman on the evening news, right?"

"In a manner of speaking, yes."

"And you put two and two together and made an association between your mental image and the one on the screen."

Kellogg had begun shaking his head even before I finished. "No, that's not right."

"This isn't about powers of observation at all, is it?" I scoffed. "This is about jumping to conclusions!"

"No, sir!" Kellogg sat forward again. "That's *not* what happened."

"Mr. Kellogg, are we to understand that you saw a woman under conditions *darker* than we might experience in a movie theater, and then, *four days later*, from a *television screen sixteen feet away*, positively identified her as"—I held the exhibit toward him—"*this* woman?"

Kellogg pointed to the picture and said emphatically, "Sir, I'm telling you *that* woman is the woman I saw in front of the house!"

I took the picture to the clerk. "Your Honor, may we have this photograph marked as Defense Exhibit One?"

Rogavin stood up. "Judge, that's already marked as Government Exhibit Twenty-three."

"Not *this* picture," I replied.

The clerk put a sticker on the photograph, our re-touched version of the one that had been provided to the defense. I passed it to Rogavin, whose face reddened as he stared at it. He sprang to his feet. "Your Honor! I object to the admission of this exhibit!"

Warner called for a sidebar. The exhibit was passed up to him for examination while we champed at the bit to be heard. "This exhibit is a modified version of the government's exhibit?" he asked.

"That's correct, Your Honor."

Rogavin jumped in. "Your Honor, that picture was displayed to the witness before it was even marked for purposes of identification. That was totally improper!"

Warner made a face. "What about it, Mr. O'Connell?"

"Judge, this demonstration shows that Mr. Kellogg might have jumped to conclusions that night, and we couldn't have done it if we had to mark a new photograph for identification. It would have alerted the witness. What is important is that the photograph was not displayed to the jury before being received in evidence, and it *should* be received in evidence."

"This could all have been arranged before you began your cross-examination," Warner said. I would have instructed Mr. Rogavin to make no allusion to what was about to occur and we wouldn't be going through all this."

"Your Honor, I might have tried that but the court is well aware that Mr. Rogavin, or *any* trial counsel, knowing what was to occur, might have been objecting to every possible point as I lay the foundation, thereby destroying the very spontaneity that was crucial to the test. Judge, this is the government's eyewitness, the linchpin of its case against my client, and he just demonstrated his own fallibility in a legitimate test. The jury must know that!"

"Who is the woman in this photograph?" asked Warner.

"A model, judge. We replaced Ms. Bronson's picture with that of a woman with similar features."

"But if the witness acted in haste and really didn't look at the picture, what does that prove?"

"Precisely, judge," snapped Rogavin. "All this proves is

that if you get a witness angry enough, you can trick him. This isn't a trial, it's a magic show!"

I couldn't believe Warner was making an issue of this. "Judge," I said quietly, trying to keep the alarm out of my voice, "when I held up this photograph Mr. Kellogg had my client's image on his mind. He looked right at it and saw what he wanted to see. Now, the same thing could have happened the night he identified my client in his living room. That's one possibility. Another is that his eyesight is not up to distinguishing between similar-looking individuals under the conditions that he described. Whatever option you choose, this demonstration is important."

Warner rubbed his jaw. "You've put me in a pretty tough position, Mr. O'Connell. First there was that movie theater stuff, which I permitted, although I thought it was a bit of a reach. Now this. If you had come to me earlier I probably would have permitted this demonstration and told Mr. Rogavin here that there was to be no monkey business while you were asking your questions. The exhibit would have been marked and you would have had clear sailing." He sniffed and shook his head. "But you seem to have your own way of doing things."

It was payback time. He was clearly enjoying the prospect of placing a huge setback for the defense squarely on my shoulders. "I'm going to have to think this over," he said. "Do you have anything more for this witness?"

I felt hollow inside. Even though he was gunning for me I never figured Warner would take it this far. This was worse than form over substance but there was little chance an appeals court would call it reversible error. They'd buy his reasoning and nail me.

"Mr. O'Connell, I asked if you have anything more for this witness."

"Your Honor, when will you make your ruling?"

"Probably not until Monday. I want the time that you should have given me before you pulled your little stunt. In fact, if you've got some law favoring your position to cite to me"—he turned to Rogavin—"if *either* of you have any law to cite to me, you can give me a memo before then. Now, for the last time, do you have any more questions for this witness?"

With the possibility that the jury would never know about Kellogg's error, there was no choice to make. We had to go ahead with Natalie.

"Yes, judge, I have more questions."

"Then let's proceed. Step back, counsel."

I passed by the defense table on my way to the lectern. "We're going ahead," I whispered. "Remember what I said." My eyes met Walter's as I walked away. The body language at the sidebar had told him all he needed to know.

Rogavin was giving a thumbs-up kind of look to his witness as I returned to the lectern. Kellogg seemed reinvigorated and ready to do battle. I looked at his smug patrician features and made a vow: if Ashley went to prison I would do whatever it took to find out who put him up to lying and why, and there would be no court and no rules to protect him.

"Mr. Kellogg, that night in front of Mr. Garvey's home, I believe you stated that you were standing between parked cars when you observed the woman on the lawn, correct?"

"That's right."

"And what make of cars were they?"

Kellogg squinted at me. "What make?"

"The cars you were standing between. What were they? Ford? Chevrolet? Toyota?"

"I have no idea."

"Well, can you run the scene through your mind right now and tell us?"

Kellogg smiled and shook his head. "No. I didn't notice the make of the cars. I wasn't paying attention to the cars. I was paying attention to the person I saw standing in front of the house." He pointed at Ashley as he said it.

"All right. Let's talk about people you saw that night. Describe the person sitting to your right in the movie theater."

"I believe the seat to my right was empty."

"Was the entire row empty?"

"No, there were other people there."

"Okay. Describe the person closest to you, left or right."

"I can't do that."

"Was it too dark to see?"

Kellogg made a face. "I think we discussed that before," he answered.

"If it wasn't too dark, then why can't you describe the person sitting closest to you for—what—more than an hour and a half?"

"I wasn't observing that person. I was observing the movie."

"Did you observe anyone in the movie that night, say, before the lights went down or after they came up?"

"I saw people, yes."

"Describe one of them."

Kellogg looked around as if he expected someone to interrupt this foolishness. Rogavin, however, wasn't stirring. He knew Warner's tendencies and that the judge was soon going to be making a ruling that the government had to win. Our prosecutor wasn't about to spend any chips winning points that weren't critical, and as far as he was concerned the jury would never hold his witness accountable for not remembering faces in a theater two months before.

But Kellogg didn't know what Rogavin was thinking, and he wasn't going to roll over, not with his ego. If it was a description I wanted, it was a description I'd get. "Well," he began, "I recall that there was a man sitting in front of me and two seats over. I noticed him before the lights went down. I'd say he was, um, about fifty-five years old, balding, and pretty overweight. I can't tell you how tall he was because he was seated. I do recall that he was wearing a coat with a fur collar."

I didn't need Walter to tell me *that* was bullshit. Kellogg had carte blanche to elaborate without fear of contradiction and he was taking full advantage of the opportunity to dazzle the crowd. I asked, "Mr. Kellogg, do you see that gentleman in the courtroom today?"

"The man from the theater?"

"Yes, the one you just described."

He went through the motions of scanning the spectators before he replied, "No, I don't see him."

"After you left the theater, and before you reached Mr. Garvey's house, did you pass anyone on the street?"

"It was raining and most of the people I passed were using umbrellas. I don't recall looking at anyone's face."

"Well, how about the person at the box office that night who sold you the ticket? Can you describe him or her?"

"Well, I've been to that box office many times and they have a number of young men and women selling tickets. I can describe some of them but I really can't say which one was on duty that night. It may have been a young woman who's worked there for a few years."

"Describe her."

"About twenty-three years old, five-four, maybe one-hundred-forty pounds, a bit overweight for her size. Let me see . . . She's got reddish-brown hair and brown eyes, and is always chewing gum."

"This is a woman whom you've seen many times over the years?"

"Yes."

"Is she in the courtroom today?"

He looked around quickly and said, "No, she's not here."

"I'm more interested in people that you've seen once, like the woman on the lawn. Have you recently followed the route you took that night?"

"Not that particular route."

"Well, have you taken any walks through the neighborhood recently?"

"All the time."

"Okay. When was the last one?"

"The night before last."

"Did you pass anyone on the street?"

"I passed a few people, yes."

"Fine. Describe the last person you passed."

Rogavin finally had enough. "Your Honor, I'm going to object. The witness said repeatedly that the woman on the lawn grabbed his attention. That's very different from observing passersby on the street."

"Judge," I responded, "the witness also said that his powers of observation were not something he turned on and off when he wanted but were 'second nature'—I believe that's the phrase he used—and automatically engaged when he passed someone on the street. Now, I'm sure that I recall his testimony quite accurately, but if there is any doubt, I request that the court reporter retrieve it. If I'm right we're entitled to cross-examination on that point."

Rogavin raised his hand in a gesture of surrender. His instinct was still to let me have the little victories. "Your Honor, Mr. O'Connell's recollection is correct. I'll withdraw the objection."

"The witness will answer the question," ordered Warner.

Kellogg rubbed his chin for a moment. "That's a bit hard. It was a man. We passed in a mostly dark area and I couldn't see his face until he was very close to me, and then only for an instant. I'd say he was about my height, six feet, and slender. I can't be sure of his age because, again, there wasn't much light, but he looked about forty to forty-five. He was wearing an overcoat and a hat of some kind."

"Is he in the courtroom today?"

Kellogg looked around. "I don't see him but let me emphasize that I did not get a good look at this man. We passed quickly and didn't acknowledge one another."

"There was no wave or nodding?"

"None."

"And you didn't talk, even to say, 'Good evening' or 'Hi'?"

"No, nothing like that."

"Well, do you ever talk to people that you see on the street when you take your walks?"

"Sometimes."

"Have you met anyone recently that you looked at for more than a second or two, perhaps even spoke to?"

Kellogg looked at the ceiling, thinking, while we all waited. The only sound in the courtroom was the thump in my chest, which I was sure he could hear. After what seemed like an eternity, he nodded and grinned broadly. "Yes," he replied. "I had a conversation with a woman who was lost."

"Lost?"

"Sort of. She had been visiting someone in the neighborhood and couldn't remember where she'd parked. I helped her find her car."

"You mean you walked around the neighborhood looking for a car? Well, I'm actually more interested in—"

"No, no." He waved his hand. "I gave her directions when she described where she parked."

I kept my eyes fixed on the paper in front of me, scribbling loops like I was making notes. "Was this in the past two months?" I asked.

"Just last week, Christmas night."

"Was this in Georgetown?"

"Yes, it was on O Street, between"—he closed his eyes—"Thirtieth and Thirty-first Streets." He was clearly enjoying himself now.

"How long did you talk to this woman?"

"I'd say fifteen or twenty seconds, maybe a little more."

"How far apart were you?"

"Conversation distance, I'd say. Less than three feet."

"What were the lighting conditions like?"

"Pretty good. We were under a streetlight."

"Better than the lamp in front of Mr. Garvey's house?" I asked, sounding quite casual.

"No, I'd say the lighting was actually about the same. I could see her face pretty well, but I could see pretty well that night in November, too."

"What did this woman look like?"

"She was in her late twenties. Medium height, about five-six, and what I'd call a trim figure, not overweight, not thin. She was wearing a hat, a sort of beret. Her hair was not quite shoulder-length. And she was attractive."

I injected a hint of defeat in my voice when I asked, "Mr. Kellogg, do you really remember all this detail about a woman you met for twenty seconds last week?"

"Yes, sir, I do."

"Is she in the courtroom today?"

Once again, Kellogg looked past me toward the spectators. I resisted the urge to turn around to get his view of our handiwork. The objective had been to maximize our chances without being obvious. We initially decided on eight women of similar age and coloring to Natalie White, but finally concluded that the larger courtroom could hold fourteen without tipping our hand. The decoys were positioned so that there would be at least two in Kellogg's line of vision wherever he looked, and the one with the strongest resemblance was sitting in the section directly opposite the witness stand. Each was instructed to make direct eye contact.

Five seconds passed. My nervous system was in overload but somehow my pen kept making loops on its own. I could see the sweep hand of my watch going around. Ten seconds. The sonuvabitch was taking his time. Fifteen seconds. Did I tip it off? I began to feel discomfort in my chest and realized I was holding my breath.

With all the will I could muster I picked up my notes and turned the page. As I did, I looked up. "Mr. Kellogg?"

"I don't see her. . . ."

"You seem uncertain."

"No, no. I'm quite certain. She's not here."

"All right." I returned to the defense table and retrieved a manila envelope. Facing the jury, I made a show of tearing it open and removing the contents, two tape cassettes. I handed one to the clerk and asked to have it marked for identification. I gave the other to Rogavin. From a large litigation bag Andy removed one of those boomboxes with big speakers and enough power to fill the courtroom with sound. He carried it over and placed it on the lectern. His hands were shaking and the perspiration had soaked through the armpits of his suit. I took the tape from the clerk and held it up in front of Kellogg, who stared at it as if it were a snake.

It had finally registered with Rogavin. The color drained from his face and he bolted from his chair. "Your Honor!" he cried, but Warner was already waving us toward the bench. The prosecutor didn't wait for the stenographer to get within earshot before he attacked. "Judge, is this yet *another* stunt by the defense? First it was movie theaters, then improper exhibits, and now we've got some kind of tape that the government has been told nothing about!"

Warner was staring darts at me. "Has this witness been tape-recorded?" he asked.

"Yes, Judge, he has," I replied.

"What the—do you understand that interfering with a witness is a *felony*?"

"Nobody has interfered with Mr. Kellogg, Your Honor. We have as much right to speak to witnesses as the government, and if we can talk to Mr. Kellogg about the case to judge his ability to observe, we can certainly talk to him about other things for the same purpose. As you will hear, he was engaged in ordinary conversation on a public street, that's all. No one was interfered with or intimidated. Nothing inappropriate occurred."

"They taped him without his knowledge!" argued Rogavin.

I kept my eyes on Warner. "Your Honor, as you know, the District is a one-party consent jurisdiction. We didn't need his permission to tape the conversation."

Rogavin wouldn't quit. "Judge, we've been ambushed! This cross-examination should be adjourned until the government has had an opportunity to review the law and consider our position, at least overnight."

"I think that's what we should do," agreed Warner.

"That can't happen, Judge," I said. "Mr. Kellogg has testified about his observations in the courtroom, and the current array of spectators—who is here and where they're seated—is critical to the questions I'm about to ask him. If you adjourn this proceeding there's no way to re-create this moment, tomorrow or any other day. The surroundings will change and Mr. Kellogg will have ample opportunity to blunt the impact of what has occurred. This morning you were concerned about reversible error. If you adjourn and my client is convicted, not only will you be reversed but there's no way Ashley Bronson will ever have to stand trial again."

Warner didn't respond; he looked from me to Rogavin, then out at the spectators. The courtroom was stock-still. Everyone knew we'd come to the critical moment. Finally, he addressed Rogavin. "Can you give me a sound reason to rule this demonstration out-of-order? I mean, right now?"

The prosecutor stared at the judge's gavel, thinking hard, plumbing his creativity and years of experience before he finally shook his head. "Not right now," he conceded.

Warner grimaced. "Then I'm going to have to permit the defense to continue. You can go ahead, Mr. O'Connell, but know this: I don't like the tone of our conversations, and when this case is over there's going to be reckoning, you can count on it. Step back, gentlemen." We returned to our places and the judge told me to proceed.

"Mr. Kellogg, Defendant's Exhibit Two is a tape of a conversation. I'd like you to listen to it and tell us whether you can identify the participants and the circumstances." I put the tape in and hit the "play" button. After a few seconds passed the voices filled the courtroom:

*"Excuse me. I'm sorry, but I'm looking for my car and I got turned around. What street is this?"*

*"You're on O Street."*

*"Oh. I don't think this is where I parked."*

No one moved in the courtroom while the tape played on. Kellogg stared at the machine, absolutely rigid. Rogavin looked straight ahead while his foot tapped like a telegraph key. Warner had his head back and his eyes closed in concentration. Ashley was looking at me with the expression I'd seen a lifetime ago in a cellblock, when she decided that I was the one.

*"This is Natalie White. It is eleven forty-five P.M. on Wednesday, December twenty-fifth. I just had a conversation with a man whose photograph I have seen previously, and who was identified to me as Miles Kellogg."*

I walked over and turned off the tape. Warner's eyes opened and he looked at the witness. The jurors were all leaning forward, transfixed. "Mr. Kellogg," I said quietly, "is that tape a true and accurate recording of the conversation you described a few moments ago?"

Kellogg continued to stare at the machine.

"Mr. Kellogg?"

He raised his eyes to me. "That sounds like the conversation," he mumbled.

"Sir, I'll ask you again. Is the woman you spoke to that night in the courtroom?"

The witness, judge, and jury stared at the sea of faces behind the railing. Rogavin half turned in his chair, only mildly interested. The spectators looked at one another as if they might somehow pick her out. Another minute passed. Finally, Warner said, "Mr. Kellogg, can you answer the question? Is the woman in the courtroom?"

Kellogg extended his arm and said, "I believe that is the

woman over there. The one with the gray dress."

The young woman in the gray dress didn't react. "Your Honor," I said, "with the court's permission, can this woman be called forward to be sworn? I know that it is unusual but it would greatly facilitate matters to proceed this way."

Warner was as curious as everyone else. He called the woman forward and had the clerk administer the oath as she stood just inside the railing, between the defense and prosecution tables.

"Proceed, Mr. O'Connell," the judge said.

"State your name for the record, please."

"Cecilia Ennis."

"Ms. Ennis, where do you live?"

"In Arlington, Virginia."

"Ms. Ennis, is that your voice we heard on the tape?"

"No, it's not."

"Were you in Georgetown at or near the intersection of Thirty-first and O Streets on December twenty-fifth?"

"No."

"Have you ever met that gentleman sitting in the witness box?"

"I don't believe so."

I looked at Warner. "Your Honor, I have no further questions for Ms. Ennis."

"Any questions, Mr. Rogavin?"

Rogavin shook his head and Ms. Ennis was sent back to her seat. Warner told me to continue. "Mr. Kellogg, I ask you again. Is the woman in the courtroom?"

"I don't believe so," he mumbled.

"I'm sorry, sir, but you'll have to speak up."

"I don't believe so."

"You don't believe so? You're not sure?"

Kellogg had had enough. *"She's not here!"* he shouted. The jury recoiled in shock.

"Your Honor, with the court's permission, I'd like to call one of the spectators forward."

"Go ahead."

I turned around and nodded. Eight rows back, Natalie stood up and came forward through the gate to be sworn.

"State your name for the record, please."

"Natalie White."

"Ms. White, is that your voice on the tape?"

"Yes."

"You talked with the witness near Thirty-first and O Streets on the evening of December twenty-fifth?"

"Yes, I did."

I looked at my notes. "Are you in your late twenties, as Mr. Kellogg described?"

"I'm twenty-two."

"Are you about five-foot-six?"

"I am five-eight."

I pointed toward her hair, cropped in a boyish style. "Was your hair not quite shoulder-length when you met Mr. Kellogg?"

"No, it was the same length as now."

"Were you wearing a beret?"

"No, a hat with a brim."

"Aside from the 'attractive' and 'trim' parts," I said, grinning, "did Mr. Kellogg have anything right?"

"No."

"Thank you." I turned back to Warner. "Judge, with the court's permission, I'd like Ms. White to stand the same distance from Mr. Kellogg as she did that night while we play the tape again."

"Objection, Your Honor. What's the point?" Rogavin's mood was growing foul.

"What's the point, Mr. O'Connell?"

"On direct testimony Mr. Rogavin had the witness reenact staring at the woman on the lawn to demonstrate time and distance. The defense is entitled to do a similar demonstration."

Warner had no choice, and a chagrined Kellogg stepped

down to stand face-to-face with Natalie in a pantomime of their Georgetown encounter while the soundtrack again echoed through the courtroom. The conversation took a minute and ten seconds, a virtual eternity, and when it was through, so was the case against Ashley Bronson.

Warner thought it was over, too. He called a sidebar and seemed almost apologetic as he addressed the prosecutor. "Mr. Rogavin, I'll have to give strong consideration to the motion to dismiss that Mr. O'Connell will doubtless be making after you rest your case. In the interest of justice maybe the government should seek dismissal of its own case."

Rogavin nodded. "I understand the court's point, Your Honor. Certainly, Mr. Kellogg was not as strong a witness as we had hoped, but I was handed a memo during the last recess and I request a meeting in chambers."

"What about?" asked Warner.

"We have another witness." The judge's eyes widened, then he pointed at the door and told us to go directly to his chambers. We marched out. I could hear the recess being announced as the door closed behind us.

Rogavin avoided my gaze while we waited; he wasn't saying anything until Warner arrived. I was confused. If the real eyewitness was finally coming forward I didn't see how they were going to pull it off. If the government was keeping him in reserve—even for a single day—there was no way Warner would allow the testimony. The audacity of the attempt would end the case then and there. On the other hand, if the witness had just surfaced that day his testimony was worthless. As of opening statements, *the whole world* knew what Kellogg supposedly saw. They could bring in a carload of nuns to corroborate him and I'd let Andy do the cross-exam because it would be that easy.

None of that should have been lost on Rogavin. Had I overestimated him? It was at that moment when confusion gave way to worry. Almost twenty years in courtrooms had taught me that when words like *easy* and *overestimated* are running through your mind, you're probably missing something.

A bewildered judge entered five minutes later with his clerks in tow. He told them to wait outside and began venting as soon as they shut the door. "In all my years as a practitioner and judge I've never seen a case like this! I've never even *heard* of one! Go ahead, Mr. Rogavin, but this had better be good."

Rogavin held up a sheet of paper. "During recess I was handed a memo. It was from Dennis Yee, who I believe is known to the court. He's the deputy chief in the crime lab—"

"I know who Yee is," said Warner. "Get on with it."

"Mr. Yee says that last evening he re-ran some of the lab tests done during the investigation. I assure you, judge, this was not at my request or with my knowledge. He said he did it on his own and out of curiosity more than anything else. One of the tests was on a raincoat seized during a search of the defendant's home right after her arrest."

"So?"

"Well, he says that he found gunshot residue inside the right sleeve."

I felt dizzy.

Warner was shocked, too. "The first time they found nothing, and *now* he's found gunshot residue?"

"Yes, sir."

"And you want to put him on the stand *today*?"

"Not today, Your Honor. We would, of course, provide his report and an opportunity to examine the raincoat to the defense before calling Mr. Yee."

The judge rubbed his jaw. "And just when is that supposed to happen? We're in the middle of the trial."

That was my cue, and I managed to suck in enough air to speak. "Your Honor, the police laboratory has had ample time to test and re-test all it wanted long before now. As the court said, we're in the middle of trial, and I prepared our strategy and devoted our resources relying on what I was told about the government's case. If we go forward I have to do final preparation of several of our own witnesses, not to mention my closing argument. What am I supposed to do? Spend my time combing the country for a preeminent expert? Ignore everything else to prepare a competent cross-exam of Mr. Yee? Judge, I appeal to your sense of fairness. I don't know why Mr. Yee delayed until now to do his job but it isn't the defense that should have to bear the consequences!"

Rogavin jumped in again as soon as I paused for breath. "Judge, it's Friday afternoon. This jury isn't sequestered in a hotel so it isn't as if they would be inconvenienced if they had two additional days off. We could adjourn Monday and Tuesday, and that would give Mr. O'Connell four days to prepare. Some of the finest experts in forensic science live right in this area. I've handled gunshot residue evidence before and I know the court has seen it many times. It's just not that complicated."

Warner looked at me. "Have you ever dealt with that kind of evidence before?"

My heart sank. "Yes."

"You have? How many times?"

"Several. But it was many years ago, when I was a prosecutor. I didn't have to prepare to cross-examine a government witness. I was just putting on the witness to testify."

"But you had to educate yourself on the subject matter, didn't you?"

"Only in the most general sense. It would take me quite a while to be prepared to cross-examine Mr. Yee."

"I had a case involving gunshot residue last summer," Warner said. "The defendant's name was Anton Carter. Block prosecuted it."

"Warren Block," said Rogavin, helpfully.

"Warren Block," repeated Warner. "The defense expert was a retired FBI lab technician who lives in Alexandria, if I recall. I remember he didn't live far from me." He was going to buy it. All he needed was a little push and Rogavin was ready.

"Judge, Mr. O'Connell would have the assistance of an expert to prepare. I know that this is not the timing he would choose—neither would I if I were in his place. But the fact remains that we've just discovered very probative evidence in a murder trial that the jury ought to hear. Why not recess until Tuesday morning to see what Mr. O'Connell can accomplish? We're prepared to turn over Mr. Yee's report right away, and I'll make sure that the raincoat is available for examination any time, day or night."

Warner was nodding as Rogavin finished. "Mr. O'Connell, I've given the defense plenty of leeway since this case began and you've taken full advantage of it. I see no reason why I shouldn't grant the government the same consideration." He looked at Rogavin. "See that the raincoat is available," he said, "and get the name and phone number of the expert to Mr. O'Connell by six P.M. this evening."

"I'll get it as soon as we adjourn."

"Mr. O'Connell, you're free to choose whomever you want, of course," Warner said. "Anything else, gentlemen?"

I spoke up. "I want to place my objection on the record. I prepared and presented my defense based on the disclosures ordered by the court. This is trial by ambush and my client is being denied due process."

"You'll have your chance," Warner replied, standing up to indicate that we were through. "We'll have a hearing on Tuesday morning at ten A.M. to see how the defense is faring. Let's go back out. I'll tell the jury that they are off Monday and Tuesday and that they should check in by phone Tuesday night."

Rogavin and I got up to leave. "One more thing," Warner added. "Mr. Rogavin, I'd better not read about this witness until after he testifies—*if* he testifies. I don't have to tell you what will happen if I do."

Rogavin's head was bobbing like a cork. "I understand, Your Honor."

All of the spectators were in place when we returned to

the courtroom. Many probably thought the case was going to end. Walter took one look at me and frowned. I took my seat and Andy leaned over and whispered, "Is it over?" His face fell when I shook my head, but Warner entered before he could ask what had gone wrong.

"The court is going to be in recess until Wednesday morning," the judge announced. "The jurors are to call into the jury commissioner's office for any new instructions Tuesday evening, between five and six o'clock. I know that you all have the number." The jurors looked confused as they were led out. Warner pounded the gavel and behind us the buzzing started.

The reporters were caught by surprise by the sudden ending; they weren't going to have time to take up positions outside the courthouse. In the news business the choice between an angry judge and an angry editor was no choice at all. They started peppering us as we made our way out of the courtroom.

"Why the delay, Mr. Rogavin?"

"What happened in chambers?"

"Why hasn't the government rested its case?"

"Frank, is the defense still going to put on a case?"

The barrage continued into the elevator, which wouldn't move until a few reporters got bumped off. Ashley stood in the corner, hiding behind a glaring Walter while I muttered "No comment" into each tape recorder that got shoved under my nose. Somehow, Harry and Dan were waiting in the lobby to run interference to the car. We piled in and I told Dan to drive us to Ashley's. It was rush hour and we began a twenty-minute crawl up Massachusetts Avenue toward Georgetown. Everyone was on edge. We were in the car a full five minutes before Walter turned around and looked at me questioningly.

"They've got another witness," I told him.

Ashley had been staring out the window; she turned around, too.

"*Another* eyewitness?" he asked.

"No, a lab guy." I looked at Ashley and said, "They say they've just found gunshot residue inside the sleeve of your raincoat. That would be evidence that you fired a gun."

"They *can't* allow another witness now!" cried Andy. "It's unconstitutional! It's . . . not right!"

"Rogavin says the evidence was discovered last night. We argued about it in chambers but it looks like Warner's going to permit it. You heard him. There's no court Monday or Tuesday. We've got till Wednesday to prepare."

Ashley turned back to the window without saying a word. Out of the corner of my eye, I could see Andy wiping his eyes.

"It's not right," he mumbled.

# 19

The press had posted a rear guard. The short winter day was almost spent when we arrived in Georgetown but the house was illuminated by the klieg lights of TV cameras and surrounded by reporters determined to find out why the defense wasn't acting like winners, nor the prosecution like losers. There were cars and remote location trucks with their call letters and telescoping antennas parked up and down N Street. An enterprising coffee vendor had extended his business day to be where the action was and his van was doing a brisk business as the temperature plummeted.

The reporters were too cold and too frustrated to worry about private property: the walkway from the driveway to the house was blocked, so Harry let us out down the street. There were only the four of us to get her through but we were determined that there would be no repeat of the scene at the courthouse the day before. We formed a tight wedge with Dan White in front and moved as one. Like most cops, Dan had always treated reporters as the enemy and he wasn't making any friends as he plowed a path to the house.

Martha threw open the door as we reached the threshold and we piled in with the hounds on our heels. She took Ashley directly upstairs and the rest of us caught our breaths and assessed the damage. Dan had a button torn off the sleeve of his cherished Burberry trench coat and was still in the middle of a colorful stream of invective when the doorbell rang. The security camera showed the familiar face of a local TV reporter with a cameraman aiming over his shoulder.

"Let it be," I said. "He just wants some footage of us blowing him off." The bell rang again; we could hear him through the door talking with the cameraman about the light.

The bell rang a third time, then a fourth. "Asshole," grumbled Dan as he strode toward the door.

"Forget it," I said. "We don't want to be on the news."

"Trust me," he snarled. "We're not going to be on the news." He yanked open the door and smiled at the startled reporter. "Hey, how ya doin'?" he said in a friendly voice. "Ain't seen you in—what?—three, four years."

The reporter recovered instantly. "Yeah . . . at least," he said, grinning. "You're . . ."

"Dan White." Dan thrust out his hand.

The reporter switched the microphone to shake hands. "Sure, of course. How have *you* been?"

"Great, great. I retired," said Dan, still holding on.

"I'm jealous," said the reporter. "Listen, we'd like—"

"Hey!" Dan interrupted, pulling the reporter close and lowering his voice, "there wasn't any trouble about that night, was there?"

"Trouble?" the reporter replied. Some of the smile disappeared.

"Yeah. You remember—that reception at the Canadian Embassy. We were helpin' out on security and caught you in a limo gettin' a BJ. Your wife got real upset." The cameraman took his eye from the viewfinder to stare at the reporter.

"My wife?" Anxiety had erased the remnants of his smile.

Dan's smile was gone, too. "She *wasn't* your wife?" he said, eyes narrowing. "You know, we were wonderin' how you managed to get one half your age. Why don't you turn the camera on now, smartass?"

"Look, we'll just leave," stammered the reporter, trying to free his hand.

"Yeah, you do that," Dan spat as he let go. He shut the door muttering about "fuckin' parasites."

"They're all parasites!" cried Andy, "miserable, fucking parasites—worse than Rogavin!" The youngest member of the team was staring at the door with eyes blazing and hands balled into fists. Beyond him, frozen halfway down the stairs, was Martha, who recovered momentarily to offer coffee and pastry. As she led the way into the kitchen I promised myself that when this was all over my associate and I were going to have a long talk about his first case.

I checked in with my office and found out that Rogavin had already left the phone number of Arthur D. Bonner, our prospective expert. I called and reached Mrs. Bonner, who wanted to know if I was *the* Frank O'Connell, "the one involved with Ashley Bronson." She said that Arthur wouldn't be home before midnight and after apologizing for his thoughtlessness a dozen times, promised to have him call the moment he came through the door. I told her eight A.M. would do. Despite the urgency we all felt I knew enough about gunshot residue to understand that we weren't dealing with anything complicated. It was either there or it wasn't, and if it wasn't there before, it was now.

Barely thirty minutes after our arrival it was time to go. I went upstairs and found our client watching the siege from the bedroom window, still wearing her coat. I gave it my best shot: I told her it wasn't over; I told her she had to stay positive; I told her every cliché in the annals of locker room speeches, but her gaze never left the window. When I turned to go she touched my sleeve and we wound up clinging to each other, rocking back and forth, trying to awaken from a bad dream. I promised that I'd be back—fuck the *Galaxy* and the entire fourth estate.

\* \* \*

By six o'clock Team Bronson was assembled in the office to wrestle with the latest setback—in the sense that a mortal wound is a "setback." The mood was somber. Andy still hadn't recovered from the sudden reversal and Harry and Dan were grim. They didn't know the whole story but they figured that if a woman like our client actually murdered some guy, there had to be a little justification in there somewhere, and when you've spent a life stooping over convenience store clerks and drive-by victims, a little justification can go a long way.

Harry had brought refreshments and for several minutes the only sound in the room was popping tops. "Anybody got a great idea?" I asked, scanning the faces.

Everyone stared into their beers.

"I'll settle for a good one—shit, fellas, I'll take a bad one." No response.

"Dan, what about this guy, Yee?"

"He worked some of my cases. Seems like a straight arrow. I never heard anything otherwise."

"What about the other guy, the one who did the original test? Andy, what was his name?"

He already had the report on his lap. "Einbinder. He's a lab assistant." Dan didn't know him.

"For starters," I said, "we have to check out Yee. It'd be nice if he was a hopeless drunk."

"I think he's a teetotaler," said Dan. "Whenever I saw him with a glass, it was tonic water."

"Look, fellas, I'd love a picture of this guy comin' out of a motel room with a sheep, but if you can't get it just get me something to work with when he gets on the stand. Dan, speak to your old cronies."

"I'll try," he promised, "but you roughed up the department's image yesterday, bud, and cops stick together."

"Tell 'em it was nothing personal. Tell 'em I'll take fifty tickets to the next Policeman's Ball. Do whatever you have to do but find out how and when he's screwed up a case."

"What about the P.D.'s?" croaked Harry. The Federal Public Defender's Office would have encountered each of the MPD's lab technicians dozens of times.

"Good idea," I replied. "There's always a few of those guys working weekends. Go over there first thing in the morning, then call the rest of 'em at home. While you're at it, find out if somebody's pulled off any magic in a gunshot residue case. I'm not proud. If there's a clever trick out there let's steal it."

"Yeah," he said. "First thing."

"And don't mention who you're working for. If word of the GSR evidence gets out I want Warner to know who to blame. Just say that you're working for a big firm in town that would be very grateful if the P.D.'s could help out its investigator."

We spent the next three hours hashing it out but finally decided that unless there was a real contest about the presence of residue, there were only two theories to pursue: either it was planted or the raincoat had been accidentally contaminated since the first test. The more we talked about it, the more convinced I became that we'd have to claim a frame-up. We had three or four jurors who would be inclined to view an eleventh-hour discovery with a lot of suspicion. They were probably our last hope.

One way we could foster suspicion was by showing that a mistake by Einbinder was unlikely. Andy repeated that his review of the evidence showed the police and the laboratory had been painstaking. After going through all the reports and the physical evidence, the only error he'd found was a mix-up on some photographs; otherwise, the cops were perfect. We decided that we should confirm his findings but we only had duplicate reports. All the evidence was locked up at the MPD's property office.

"Can you get someone to let you look at the stuff again?" I asked Dan.

"Shouldn't be a problem."

"You're the logical guy to see if everyone followed procedures. If everything else was perfect it could make Einbinder's screwup look a little more suspicious."

"Sounds pretty thin," Harry muttered.

"It *is* pretty thin!" I barked. "It is pretty *goddamn* thin! But unless somebody here comes up with that sheep photo it may have to do!" It got real quiet in the room again. These veteran detectives had things figured long before the *Galaxy* pictures and they knew the kind of pressure I was under. When I regained my composure I added, "If they give you a hard time, Dan, let me know. At this moment Rogavin is dying to do me favors."

That was all we could think of to do right then. Andy was going to write a motion to exclude Yee's testimony. Walter told the detectives to stay in touch for new instructions.

\* \* \*

The short trip back to Georgetown was the first chance Walter and I had had to talk since the world spun off its axis six hours before. "Now that you know Kellogg's a liar," I said, "I thought maybe you'd like to tell me what the fuck this whole thing is about."

He shook his head with disgust. "I can't figure it," he grumbled. "I've been turnin' it over and over and it don't go nowhere." We rode a few moments in silence and then he began his analysis anew. "Start with what we know." He held up one finger. "Octagon squeezes the old man for his invention and he kills himself—okay, that makes sense. Two, Garvey, who was in on it, is shot dead—fine. Three, we got two stories about people leavin' the crime scene. On one hand, you got a former CIA agent who says the client left alone— he's a phony."

"You *are* sure about that, right?"

He glared at me. "Hey! I know what I know."

"All right, go ahead."

"On the other hand, this guy Bradmoor saw a woman leavin' who *wasn't* alone, and he's the only independent witness in the whole shebang."

"I'm getting nauseous," I said.

"Face it, kid. The joker in the deck is our client. If she's tellin' the truth, Kellogg is just standin' in for someone else, someone that can't—or won't—come forward. Why not? And does it have anything to do with Octagon and all that crap?" He looked over as if I might have some answers.

"Don't look at me. I can't get past number three."

"If she's lyin', then there's at least one other perp and she's covering for him."

"How did that happen?"

"She's the one that got caught. She doesn't want to go to jail, sure, but she's not going to drag anyone else into this mess, either. So, she takes her chances alone."

I lowered my window. "Then where does Kellogg fit in?"

"Maybe he's insurance for the others. If he doesn't surface then all the police got is Bradmoor, and then they start looking for who else was in the car." He glanced over and shrugged. "It ain't great, but it ain't impossible."

"I really don't want to ask this: between the two scenarios, which one makes the most sense?"

He sighed. "Remember our talk when we came back from Garvey's?"

"You mean about Raymond being dressed and her unusual marksmanship?"

"That's the one."

I stuck my face into the freezing air.

"What the hell are you doin'?" he asked.

"Just shoot me. Behind the ear."

He pulled to the curb at the end of her block and I stepped out into a biting wind that made it feel a lot colder than the twenty-two degrees flashing on the bank sign at Dupont Circle. A sliver of moon barely illuminated the landscape. The only sounds were the wind and the scraping of dead leaves cartwheeling down the street. Not a good night for voyeurs. I pulled up my scarf and set off down the block to check for any fanatics lurking in doorways or parked cars, trudging up one side and down the other before turning into her driveway.

It was Ashley, wearing a robe and slippers, who answered my soft knock. "Did you eat?" she asked as I hung my coat. I said no and she took me to the sitting room, where there was a single place setting on the coffee table, then went off to the kitchen. The warmth of the fire soaked into me, and with it fatigue that I could feel in my eyelids as I slid downward to rest my head. Except for the occasional rustling of pots in the kitchen, the house was dead quiet. It was gut-wrenching to think that but for one chemistry major with too much time on his hands, there might have been a celebration in the Bronson mansion that very night.

Ashley brought in a tray with a bowl of vegetable soup, a baguette, and two glasses of red wine. She opened my shirt collar and tucked in one corner of the napkin. "How did the meeting go?" she asked, massaging my neck.

I tried to keep the anxiety out of my voice. "We've got several things going on. This Arthur Bonner is supposed to be the mother of all experts and he'll be calling here first thing in the morning. We're checking out this guy Yee who supposedly re-examined your raincoat. And we're going over the procedures used during the investigation. If the police were as thorough as we think, maybe the jury will be suspicious about Yee's belated discovery."

"What do you think about it—the discovery?"

"I don't know if it was there or not."

"I mean, what effect do you think it will have?"

I didn't look up from my soup. "If the jury believes it they'll convict you."

"They'd pretty much have to, wouldn't they?"

"They'll only have one explanation for how it got there."

I ate my dinner while she sat in her robe, watching. We probably looked like a lot of married couples, although the wife doesn't usually go to prison if the husband has a bad day.

"You were magnificent today," she said, running her fingers through my hair. It sounded like the consolation prize.

"Was I?"

"The way you handled Kellogg."

"Kellogg was lying. He wasn't there."

"But . . . he told the truth."

"Did he?"

She stared at me. "What are you saying?"

I put down my spoon and took her hand from my hair. "We're out of moves," I told her. "Now, we're just going through the motions."

She lowered her eyes. "I understand," she said quietly.

"Maybe if I knew what this was all about, what really happened, there still might be a chance to keep you out of prison."

"What do you mean? I've told you everything—"

I held up my hand. "Don't. I'm too tired and I'm wound way too tight. You know, Warner was right today—what he said about professional objectivity. I'd lost mine, and I allowed myself to ignore too much evidence because of my feelings. I've let you down, Ashley. I let you deceive me."

She recoiled as if she'd been slapped. "Frank, I swear—"

"If you're taking oaths, tell me who else was in the house when Garvey was killed. Was it *Brown*?" Her eyes widened at the mention of his name. "I thought so. *Was* it you who shot Garvey, or were you just driving the car? And when you get through with that one, I'm totally confused about Kellogg—and whatever the hell you're involved in."

"You're wrong." Her eyes were tearing up now. "I haven't deceived you. . . . I love you."

"Yeah, well, let's stick with Brown."

She wiped her eyes and stared at the fire for what seemed like an eternity before she finally spoke. "He came to the house," she said quietly. "With Raymond. I didn't know his name until you described him."

I put down my spoon and shut my eyes. In my heart of

hearts, I'd still been hoping Walter was wrong. "When?"

"After my father's funeral I went to the cabin to get away for a few days. I took his journal with me and it was there that I read the last entry. After thinking about it and getting more and more upset, I flew back. Martha was off but Raymond had always had a key to the house. I found them in the library. There were papers scattered everywhere and they were taking books off the shelves and throwing them on the floor. I screamed at them to stop, but Raymond said that my father had some papers that belonged to him and he had to have them back right away. They wouldn't leave, even when I threatened to call the police, so I told him that I'd burned them."

"You *burned* them?"

She shook her head. "No, I just said I did. I had no idea what he was talking about."

"Jesus! What happened then?"

"Raymond didn't believe me. He told me to describe the papers. I said that there were some thick, sealed manila envelopes that my father asked me not to open, so I didn't. I must have sounded convincing because Raymond turned pale and collapsed on the couch."

"What did Brown say?"

"He asked me when I burned them and I said a few days before my father died. He just stared at me—he was so scary, Frank—and then he told Raymond that there was nothing more to be done."

"And that was it?"

"No. Raymond went crazy. He began screaming and cursing. He said that my father was a child that had to be led about by the hand, and if he hadn't inherited money he would have been nothing more than a contemptible little librarian—those were his words: 'contemptible little librarian.'" Her eyes were bright; just telling of the story had made her angry all over again, and I didn't need Walter to see that it was the truth. "I told him that my father was a thousand times the man he was, and he got this ghastly smile on his face and asked if I wanted to know the truth about my father, if I wanted to know Henry Bronson's little secret." She paused, struggling for control.

"Go ahead," I urged.

"Brown told him to shut up."

"And Raymond shut up?"

"Yes. He was afraid of him. Brown never raised his voice but he was still intimidating. You could tell he was capable of anything."

"What happened then?"

"They left. The library was a shambles. I sat there for hours getting more and more upset about what they had done."

The next part was easy to guess. "And then you went to Raymond's house?"

She nodded.

"Why didn't you tell me this before?"

"Because I didn't want to know about my father!" she cried. "He was dead and buried. *Why* did I have to know what Raymond meant? What the journal entry meant? I told you what I did and why and I thought that's all that mattered. But I knew that if I told you about Brown, somehow you'd end up searching for him to find out why Henry Bronson killed himself. So, I didn't."

"That's the whole story? You *were* alone when you shot Garvey?"

"I'm telling you the truth, Frank. Now, it's your turn."

"What do you mean?"

"You've been holding back. You know, don't you? You figured it all out."

"I know," I admitted.

"Now I want to know, too."

"You do? Why the change of heart?"

"Because not knowing is *worse*. This whole thing is like a fog that enshrouds all my memories of my father, and I need them now—more than ever. Frank, I don't know what you've learned, but Henry Bronson was a good man and whatever he did, I'll deal with it. I'll put it in its proper place and then I'll have my memories again."

Maybe if I wasn't so tired I would have dug in. But my resolve was gone, and she had a point.

"Do you remember the photograph I showed you? It was taken in California, near a place called the Lawrence Livermore Laboratory, a secret installation where they worked on atomic bomb design. Your father worked there. The man sitting next to him on the bench is Herbert Epstein."

She looked at me, puzzled. "Atomic bombs. Is that what you've—"

"There's more. The third man in the photograph was a Russian spy. Herbert and your father passed him secrets."

"My father?" She shook her head, dazed. "Did Herbert tell you my father was a spy?"

"Yeah. And he confirmed other evidence."

She covered her face and whispered, "Oh, my God!"

"Ashley, that's what Raymond was using against him."

"But why?"

"Your father designed a trigger device for a bomb. It was simple, and the design is worth a fortune today to anyone who has the other components to make one. Raymond's friends do, and with your father's design they could offer one-stop shopping to any terrorist group that could pay. They gave him a choice: turn over the plans or be exposed. So—"

The first sob escaped her, and then it all came out, her anguish over her father, the trial, and her future, everything she'd been holding in for weeks. I took her into my arms and began to rock her gently. "I'm sorry, Ashley. There's one more thing you should know. Herbert said that your father believed that sharing atomic secrets was the only way to make the world a stable place. He did what he thought best for humanity. Anyway, none of it matters now. It's a story that will never be told."

"Let's go upstairs," she pleaded. "I want you to hold me. I want this day to end."

So that's what we did.

\* \* \*

I dreamt that we lost. The jury shouted "guilty" and the bailiff moved between us and began to lead her away, and I tried to stop him but my legs were heavy and there was something wrong with my shoes, and then I had to go around Rogavin, which delayed me even more, and when I reached the holding cell the door was shut and she was gone, so I started pounding on the door.

When I opened my eyes I was looking at the ceiling through the lace canopy over her bed. The dream was gone but the pounding continued, only not quite so loud. It went away and came back again, and when my head cleared I realized that someone was tapping lightly on the door. I rolled out of bed and opened it a crack to Martha, who whispered that there was a Mr. Bonner on the line. I slipped on my pants and shirt, then tiptoed downstairs to the library and picked up the phone. The voice on the other end was awake and crisp.

"Is this Mr. O'Connell?"

"It is. I called you on behalf of Ashley Bronson."

"I figured that. The woman who answered said it was the Bronson residence."

"Yes, uh, we've been having a breakfast meeting."

"I've been following the case. I guess everyone has."

"Let me ask you something, Mr. Bonner, before I begin. Do you have any conflicts or any other reasons that would prevent you from doing some work on this case?"

"None. If I turned this down my wife would kill me."

"Well, what I'm about to tell you is very confidential."

"You have nothing to worry about. I won't kid you, we talk about my work, but we've been married almost forty years and she's never said a word to anyone about my cases, and we've been through some pretty big ones."

"Okay, you're hired. Are you ready to go to work?"

"Dressed, fed, and ready."

"The deputy director of the police laboratory did a gunshot residue examination on a raincoat that belongs to my client, and claims to have found some on the inside of the sleeve. This just happened yesterday. The raincoat was examined in early October by a lab assistant and nothing turned up. They will claim that the first examiner missed it."

"Pretty sloppy."

We agreed that Bonner would examine the raincoat that morning to find out what he could. He warned me that it was unlikely that he'd find some source of contamination, and essentially all he could do was determine whether the residue was there or not. How it got there was anybody's guess.

# 20

It was late Saturday morning, D day plus one, and I had nothing to do. It was often like that in trial preparation: you fight for as much time as you can get; then you figure out what you need. Sometimes it's very little, as when you're trapped and have no moves left. Bonner was arriving at the lab just about then, perhaps even running his first test. Andy was writing the brief, Dan was checking out Yee, and Harry Lerner was trying to make himself understood over at the Public Defender's office. I was twiddling my thumbs because a few hours' sleep and a lot of pondering hadn't produced any new ideas. By eleven o'clock I decided to get out of there so Ashley wouldn't see me moping around. I told her that I had work to do at the office and headed off to twiddle someplace else. A brisk walk to Dupont Circle provided no stimulation, and I was still facing the prospect of nothing to do when I entered my office and found Walter lying on the couch.

"Did you spend the night here?"

"I'm still thinkin' about Kellogg."

"And?"

"And nothin'. I'm drivin' myself crazy."

"Then allow me to provide some more fuel. We guessed right about everything else. Garvey, Sherry, and Mr. Brown were in it together and they were after some papers they thought Henry Bronson had. The plans for the firing mechanism is still a guess, but a good one."

He looked at me. "Where's this comin' from?"

"Raymond and Mr. Brown showed up uninvited and ran-sacked the old man's library. She came home and they had it out. Raymond said Henry had some papers that belonged to him and they were going to search the place. In a moment of inspiration she said that she'd burned them."

*"No shit?"*

"And she was convincing. Mr. Brown decided that it was all over. Raymond went ballistic and got very nasty about her father before they left."

"And then she paid him a visit."

"After a few hours to get in the mood."

Walter sat up and reached for a coffee container on the floor. He sipped thoughtfully as he collated this new input. "So, she was holdin' back on us."

"Yes, but that's all." He looked at me. "I'm sure of it. She went there alone and shot Raymond. And she left alone."

"Then unless we're missing somethin', Kellogg is a stand-in, which raises all them questions: why can't the real witness come forward, and does it have anything to do with Octagon?"

The phone rang. I hit the speaker phone button and Dan White's voice filled the room. "Frank?"

"It's me and Walter. What's up?"

"I've been through the stuff. I suppose it's good news be-cause everything's in order. It was a textbook investigation."

"By the lab, too?"

"Yup. If it helps, there wasn't even a mix-up with the photographs. The MPD had all its crime scene shots in one envelope. The other photographs weren't included because they weren't taken by the MPD. It was just some stuff that the forensic unit picked up at the scene, but I could see how the kid would think it was a screw-up."

"Why?"

"They look like police photos, too."

"Maybe they are."

He snickered. "Listen, kid, I spent twenty-three years on homicide, remember? The police department don't spring for no Polaroids."

Walter was standing up, leaning over the speaker; his face was flushed. "Dan, tell me about the Polaroids."

"There's three of them," came the reply. "One is of a desktop. The other two look like the insides of drawers. Looks like somebody was practicing or something."

"Listen, Dan," he said urgently, "is there anyone around? Anyone watching you?"

"Nah. The property sergeant led me back here and wished me luck."

"Take the photographs and bring them back here."

There was a moment's hesitation on the other end. "Jeez, Walter, they're evidence in an open case."

Walter was unmoved. "Listen, we gotta have the originals, understand? Stick 'em in your shirt and get back here as fast as you can."

"You're the boss. I hope the client can afford to pick up my pension."

"She can," he replied, and hung up. He retreated to the couch and began rubbing his chin, muttering to himself. I'd never seen him that agitated. "Nineteen seventy-two," he said finally, and fell silent again. Several minutes passed.

"Nineteen seventy-two," I prodded.

He nodded and repeated, "Nineteen-seventy-two."

"Right," I said. "Nineteen seventy-two. Nixon won the election, Miami won the Super Bowl, and somebody won the goddamn World Series. That's it. I'm out of guesses and *this close* to strangling you."

"Remember them people Bradmoor saw?"

"What about them?"

"I think they left their calling card. Wait till Dan gets here. I wanna be sure and I got some thinking to do."

Dan showed up fifteen minutes later, perspiring heavily

despite the cold. He had the Polaroids under his shirt. "As ordered," he said, handing them to Walter. "I hope this is worth my ass."

Dan didn't even want to be in the same room as the contraband; he left to continue his investigation of Yee.

Walter shuffled through the photos and began shaking his head. "It's gonna be *somebody's* ass," he said, grinning broadly.

He got up off the couch and took the chair next to the desk. "Nineteen-seventy-two," he said.

"We're back there again?"

"We're on a burglary stakeout on the Upper West Side and nothin's goin' on. Dead. We're about to call it a night when we catch a call. Some old biddy is seein' flashin' lights in an office buildin' across the alley from her apartment house. We know the buildin', right? You can get on the roof from the one that backs up to it, so we park on the next street, go up to the roof and make our way across and down the staircase real quiet-like. We listen at the door and—sure as shit—there's a burglary goin' down, but it don't make no sense because the office belongs to one of them wacky newspapers that was always callin' for Nixon's impeachment and the arrest of the Pentagon. What the freak they got that anybody wants to heist, right?"

"Just tell me this has something to do with the case."

He held up a palm. "So we go in with guns drawn and hit the lights. The next thing you know, *everybody's* got a gun, right? We're yellin' 'Police,' they're yellin' 'FBI,' and we're *all* yellin' 'drop the gun.' It was the goddamndest thing you ever saw. There were a lot of red faces that freakin' night. We had to get a lieutenant down there to try to straighten things out. While we're waitin' I take a look around. They were tossin' the place, see? All around is Polaroid pictures taped to desks, drawers, filing cabinets—everything, even the wastebaskets. And they was all numbered with a marking pen—just like these." He held up the Polaroids. Each had a number written with a black marker in the top right corner: eighteen, nineteen, and twenty-three.

"What for?"

He ignored me. "The lieutenant shows up and some phone calls get made, and both sides decide to retreat."

"I don't get it. The FBI was executing a search warrant?"

He shook his head emphatically. "Search warrant, my ass!" he spat. "They were doin' a bag job." I looked at him blankly. "A black bag job," he elaborated. "That was their name for one of those kind of searches."

"How do you know about this?"

He snickered. "Later on there had to be an official explanation, see?—'cause the citizen call and the radio call were recorded. In them Hoover days the relationship between the NYPD and the Bureau was shit at the top levels, so I get sent to a liaison meeting with the guy who was the ranking Fibbie on the scene that night. Well, the guy turns out to be a freakin' Irishman from Fordham and we grew up in the same parish. Anyway, we put a cover story together over a few beers that turn into a lot of beers, and before the night's over I got the whole history of the Bureau and black bag jobs."

"And now you're going to tell it to me."

"Yeah, you need to know. It started back in the forties when they was chasin' Nazis around New York. They were goin' in and out of office buildings all the time lookin' for your sympathizers, spies, and sabotage guys. It was considered national security stuff durin' the war and nobody was botherin' with the legalities, although Roosevelt was supposed to know. Anyway, they kept it up during the fifties when McCarthy was doin' his thing, only they were checkin' out Commies and all them Fifth Columnists. Hoover supposedly put an end to it in the sixties, but it didn't take."

"Why not?"

"The New Left. The SDS, the Weathermen, and all them antiwar groups that popped up at the colleges. Nobody gave a shit till the bombs started goin' off all over Washington, and then the Fibbies were under a lot of pressure to find the perps. Bingo! The black bag guys are back in business."

"No warrants?"

"How the freak could they get a warrant? They didn't have probable cause to believe shit. Half the time they couldn't tie anyone to a crime."

Then it rang a bell. "Wait a minute. I remember. There was a prosecution of some Bureau officials over that— what—fifteen years ago? Twenty? I can remember some big debates about it in the D.A.'s office over whether those searches were reasonable even if they didn't have a warrant. They were convicted and the president pardoned them after he got elected."

"That's right. They were goin' into the homes of relatives, friends, and sympathizers lookin' for leads to the bombers. It was your basic fugitive hunt taken up a coupla notches, and a lot of people thought it was okay."

"So the guys in the newspaper office were looking for leads on the whereabouts of bombers?"

"You betcha. The underground was always in contact with the newspapers to publish their manifestos and shit."

"All right. Black bag jobs. Nazis, Commies, and the New Left. Are you telling me that the FBI did a black bag job at Garvey's house?"

"You win the prize," he said, smiling. He fished around in his breast pocket and produced a toothpick wrapped in white paper. It was one of the mint-flavored kind that he usually saved for after a meal, much as a cigar aficionado would harbor a good Cuban. Apparently, this was some kind of occasion.

"The Polaroids tell you it was the FBI—like the newspaper office?"

He nodded. "A bag job ain't your regular burglary. They're not there to take anything. They're there to get information and get the hell out without leavin' a trace. If you don't want

to leave any signs you've been there, you got to put everything—and I mean *everything*—back where it belongs."

"So you take Polaroid photographs."

"Nothin' gets touched until the area's been photographed.
The guys with the cameras go into the room and snap everything. If there's a desk with papers on top, they shoot it. If
they're goin' through drawers, they shoot 'em. If they got to
go through a bookshelf, they shoot it. And they tape the photographs to the desk, drawer, shelf, whatever. Before they
leave the place, the area has to match the photograph again."

"Why do they number them?"

"To be sure they take 'em all when they go. If they took
twenty-four shots, then they should have Polaroids numbered one through twenty-four when they leave. No traces
left behind."

"But they left three behind at Garvey's house."

"That's right."

"Why?"

"Can only be one reason. They left in a big hurry."

"So Garvey came home?"

He snorted. "No way! The timin' is all wrong. Bradmoor
saw them scramblin' out of there around ten-forty-five. Garvey died between nine and eleven."

"That still leaves a few minutes."

"Look, they're way too careful to get caught by the
homeowner. All the known occupants are under surveillance
while the bag job's goin' on. Garvey goes to a restaurant,
they got a Fibbie watchin' the entrance, maybe even eatin' at
the next table. He calls for the check, the guys doin' his
house know before he pulls out his credit card. They'd *never*
be caught by the owner of the house."

"But someone surprised them."

"Yeah. *Someone*." His eyes remained leveled at mine.

It was my turn to shake my head. "No. *No . . . fucking . . .
way!*" He didn't respond, but waited for me to catch up. I
went to the window, running the scene through my head as

she demonstrated. *Ashley approaches the property in the dark, goes to the garden patio, and lets herself in. The FBI is inside the house. And then what?*

And then my stomach goes through the floor. I wheeled around and gasped, "You've got to be shitting me! Walter, goddammit, you tell me right now that you don't think she killed an FBI agent!"

"I don't think she killed an FBI agent," he said calmly.

"Thank God!"

"I think she shot an FBI agent. She probably didn't kill him."

I staggered back to the chair and collapsed. Walter was no longer looking at me; he was thinking and nodding to himself as he put the finishing touches on this absurd scenario that he had constructed from a few Polaroid pictures.

"Okay," he said, "here's how it plays, maybe not a hundred percent, but probably pretty close. Let's start with what we already figured. It's the nineteen-fifties and the old man is passin' secrets to the Russians and they knew about his design for the trigger. Octagon has been around a long time, probably part of the network handlin' the material. Almost fifty years later you got a country fallin' apart and Herbert says that people are peddlin' plutonium to the highest bidder. The hard part is comin' by the trigger, and the old man's design is now worth a bundle. Somebody remembers it and whaddya know?—the old man's still alive. All they gotta do is get him to part with it. Sherry puts them onto Raymond and they approach him to be the middleman."

"Now we pick up from there. The FBI was onto them?"

"Sure. Herbert said the black-market for bomb stuff is full of intelligence agents posing as buyers. And the Bureau had already been onto their network for years."

"Right. Your silent FBI friend in New York."

"With Raymond as the contact they start to apply pressure. The whole thing goes wrong when the old man does himself, which causes a big panic."

"That's when Mr. Brown left the message for Sherry," I said.

"Yeah. And you just filled in the next part. Raymond and Mr. Brown decide to take things into their own hands and go to the house to find the design. She shows up and tells 'em that they're too late, and it's bye-bye, Raymond."

*"Bye-bye, Raymond?"*

"These guys didn't stay in business fifty years by leavin' a lot of loose ends layin' around. Raymond had already come close to spillin' the beans when he got all upset at the client's house, and he made the mistake of doin' it right in front of Brown."

He'd sucked me in. "And with no chance to get the plans, Raymond became a loose end. He and Brown were in Ashley's house sometime in the afternoon. A few hours later, he's dead."

"He probably got killed closer to nine, 'cause sure as shit is brown and night follows day, Raymond is dead when she enters the house."

"You said the FBI wouldn't take any chances with a bag job. If Raymond's in the house and they went in there, they must've known he was dead."

"Yeah. The best bet is that they had the house wired, and if they had it wired, they heard Raymond get popped."

"Raymond is dead and they come running—is that it?"

"Has to be. They got plenty of reasons. The jig is up and maybe they catch Brown still in the house with the body. The murder rap is the best leverage they could get for whatever they want from him. If they miss him, it's still their last, best chance to search Raymond's house. And don't forget—they got some microphones to retrieve before the MPD gets there. The Fibbies had plenty to do and not much time to do it."

"So nobody's watching the door."

"They got no reason—who's comin'? It's a stormy night and they're inside doin' their thing when she comes waltzin' in the side door with a key."

"And an agent walks into the room and—bang!—all hell breaks loose. Why don't they grab her?"

"Look at it from their side. They're not supposed to be in there, right? They got a guy down, they got microphones all over the house, and for all they know, the police are on the way. What are they gonna do—arrest her? That commits them to a shitload of explanation. Look, I know these Fibbies. Nobody who's so low on the totem pole that he has to risk his ass on a bag job is gonna make a decision that can compromise the Bureau. He's gonna maintain the status quo until the top floor makes a call. That means somebody follows her home and I.D.s her in case the bosses want to do somethin' about her later."

"You know, you can see the logic of it from their side. Once they realized that it was Ashley who shot their guy and that she didn't run to the police, they figured she intended to commit murder, and there was no way they were going to let her get away with it. They couldn't arrest her for what she did, so they did the next best thing: arrest her for what she intended to do."

Walter wasn't sympathetic. "Unless I'm wrong, it wasn't no fair exchange. They moved her up from attempted murder to murder one."

"Which explains another thing that was curious about this case: the generous deal that Rogavin was instructed to offer. If we had accepted and she pled guilty to manslaughter, she would have gotten no more time than the standard sentence for attempted murder. In fact, she would have gotten *less*. Think about it. She's sentenced for the crime she intended, and gets less punishment than she actually deserves. If you're determined to punish the guilty and save the Bureau from being torn apart, it's the perfectly logical solution. All they needed to do was figure a way to put on the case."

"Enter Kellogg," he said.

"Right. Enter Kellogg. The intelligence community pulls together and comes up with a witness, someone with a plausible explanation for being on Garvey's street late at night."

"That's how it figures," he agreed. "They had to be burnin' the midnight oil at the Hoover building 'cause they had him on his way to West Virginia before dawn. And they kept him on ice until they were sure they needed him. If she confesses or they come up with other evidence, he ain't necessary. But if they don't, he's gotta surface, and with a goddamn good reason why he didn't call the cops before."

"And they created other evidence," I said. "The bullet from Garvey's brain matches the gun. That only works if Brown used Garvey's gun, which is possible, or somebody does a switch, and a switch offers a hell of a lot better explanation than Rogavin's for why an FBI agent wound up ferrying the bullet from the morgue to the laboratory."

"And why he didn't want to testify," added Walter.

"Yeah, the Bureau has its integrity. They frame Ashley and then get queasy over a little perjury by one of their boys. Now tell me this. You said that she probably didn't kill the agent, only wounded him. Why?"

He smiled. "Black bag jobs ain't suicide missions. They don't have to find agents with no families who'll never be missed. The men—and women—who went in that house probably live around here and have families. If one of 'em gets killed they can't hardly sweep it under the rug. They're gonna have to make it public and come up with a cover story, and they got to have one of them big funerals where the Attorney General makes a speech about all them Fibbies who got killed to save America. I don't remember any story about one gettin' killed."

"Maybe she missed him altogether," I said hopefully.

"Her killing Garvey at that distance always bothered me," he said. "When I went back to the house that night I searched the study. There were no bullet holes in the walls or the furniture, and no fresh paint or impressions in the rug to show that anything was missing or moved. Besides, there was only fifteen minutes max between the time she fired the shot and the Fibbies went scramblin' out of the house—no time to do any repairs. For my money, a woman agent went for the car while the wounded guy was helped out of the house."

There is this thing called "the scientific method." It's used to figure things out. You start with a theory about something you're curious about, say, the structure of the atom, or what really happened the night Raymond Garvey died. Then you test it against the known facts. As long as it holds up you hang on to your theory; when it doesn't, you discard it for a new one. So far, Walter's theory about the FBI, crazy as it was, had passed all the tests.

"Okay," I declared, "I'm on board. Our client is being tried for a crime she didn't commit, and there are people in the government who know it. Now there's the small matter of getting her off the hook."

# 21

"It works."

Thus spoke the Horse. Walter had just finished relating our theory of what happened and why. He'd included all the essential details, save three: how Henry Bronson died, what Garvey and his co-conspirators were actually after, and what they had on Henry for leverage. Nobody groused when he explained that certain details were need-to-know.

More importantly, neither Dan nor Andy disagreed with Harry's verdict, which was pretty remarkable given that barely thirty minutes earlier they were all wondering if I'd lost my mind when I announced that Ashley Bronson was innocent and we were taking a new approach. No one got up and walked out but there was a lot of head-shaking as Walter's tale unfolded, and when he got to the part about her shooting an FBI agent, even Harry—a guy who knew a thing or two about shooting people—raised an eyebrow. Nevertheless, our detectives had made lives of following wherever experience and deduction might lead, occasionally to surprising conclusions. As each piece fell into place, astonishment gave way to conviction, and when we examined the Polaroids, the congregation was converted.

"It's one hell of a story," said Dan, "but where do we go from here? We've always had the evidence to prove that Garvey and his pals were up to something that was going sour, but how do you prove that Brown was the doer? The government is sittin' on that gem, and if we find Brown, he isn't likely to confess."

"Maybe we can persuade him," offered Harry.

"We'd have to find him first," said Dan. He looked at me. "You think he's still around somewhere?"

"I doubt it. He's probably not even in the country. We could stake out Octagon's front up in New York but Walter tried that once with no luck. There's no telling when—or if—he'd show."

"The other guy's around," said Harry. "Maybe we could talk to him."

"I can tell you from experience," I said, "that Burroughs will just hide behind his lawyers. And why not? Even if he knew how Garvey died, we have nothing to use on him to get a confession."

Dan said, "If we prove that they were trying to extort something from her father when he died, and what happened in the library between Raymond and Mr. Brown, the jury can see that Raymond became expendable."

"You'll have to take my word for it. We're not in a position to prove what they wanted from Henry Bronson or what they had on him. Even if we were, she's the only one who knows what happened in the library and she's not taking the stand to tell her story. If the jury didn't believe the Bureau was in Raymond's house, then her testimony would be tantamount to a confession."

Andy summed it up: "So we've got a story that makes sense if you accept a lot of stuff we can't really prove."

"That's about it," I agreed. "We'll never prove that Brown killed Garvey. The only way this jury will come back with 'not guilty' is if Bonner testifies that Yee is full of shit, and I don't think that's going to happen."

"Then what's our move?" asked Harry.

"The key for us is not proving what she didn't do. It's what she *did* do that matters. The FBI was nearly torn apart by the scandals created by black bag jobs in the seventies. If the government thought it was going to go through all that again, it would horsetrade with us and drop the case, no doubt about it."

"I'm lost," said Dan. "If we can't prove what these guys were up to with the client's father, then we can't prove why the Bureau would be interested in Garvey's house in the first place. And let's not forget that the absent chain-of-custody agent and Rogavin's generous plea offer are only suspicious if you know the rest of the story. That means the only way you have to tie the Bureau to this thing is the Polaroids, and they don't prove anything by themselves."

"You're right," I told him. "We need something to go with the Polaroids, something to give them provenance."

Harry squinted at me. "Give 'em what?"

"Authenticity," Andy explained. "Something to prove that they are really connected with the Bureau."

Walter smiled. "Like a Fibbie with a bullet hole."

"Exactly," I said. "If an agent showed up wounded at some hospital that night with a story about shooting himself—"

"Or herself," added Dan.

"Or herself," I agreed, "while cleaning a gun, that would be one hell of a coincidence, wouldn't you say?"

"So let's go visit some hospitals," said Harry.

"How far they woulda carted him depends on how bad he was hurt," said Walter. "We'll start in D.C. and then out to the suburbs. If that doesn't do it we're gonna have to get real smart real quick."

"What about police reports?" asked Andy. "The hospital would have to report a gunshot wound."

Dan shook his head. "Maybe not. If the guy was a federal agent brought in by other agents with a good story, the doctor may not have bothered. But those reports go to the district in which the hospital is located, and I'll see what I can do."

"How are we going to get the hospitals to open their

admissions records if we're not the police?"

"Well, we're all *ex*-law enforcement," said Walter.

Andy looked confused. "Sometimes," I told him, "a little imprecision can save a world of explanation."

"I got a question, too—for our counselor here," said Harry. "Let's say you go walkin' into the U.S. Attorney's Office with some pictures and some hospital records, threatenin' to bring down the FBI, maybe the whole f-in' government." He shrugged. "Hey! I don't know how it works down here, but in New York, half the people got the goods on the other half, but it don't mean shit unless you got the juice. I don't mean no offense—you're one hell of a mouthpiece, kid, and if I had you a few years back I mighta saved myself some grief, okay?—but lemme ask ya this. You got the kind of juice that can put a scare into the Fibbies? If not, we're just jackin' off here, right?"

"Don't worry about it," I said. "If it comes down to juice, I've got something better."

"Which is?"

"I know Mr. Tropicana himself."

\*   \*   \*

The phone was answered on the first ring. "Brennan residence."

"Bridey, it's me."

"Francis! Love of God!" she cried. "We've been watching the news and saying our prayers, me and Joseph." Joseph was Pop's factotum: manservant, chauffeur, yeoman, and trusted messenger. He carried the messages that could never be put in writing, so he, too, was a blood relation, the son of first cousins from County Clare. Together, he and Maggie Mac could write the mother of all tell-all books, but they never would.

"Thank you, Bridey."

"They ought to be ashamed, printing such filth about you

and that poor girl. Mr. Brennan says they're jackals, the lot of 'em."

"Yes, well . . . is he around?"

"Francis, Moira was here last night, without the little darling. She and Mr. Brennan had a long talk."

"Uh-huh."

"And, well . . . now, Francis, I know it isn't my place . . ."

"What is it, Bridey?"

"Joseph was saying this morning that he hasn't seen him like this since you and Moira had your troubles. He hasn't come downstairs and he didn't want breakfast or lunch. I couldn't even bring him tea. He's just sitting up there in the study and he won't even take phone calls."

"I'll be there in thirty minutes," I said, and hung up.

Pop had to be wondering how it had all gone so wrong. On those evenings we sat in his office he'd often talked about the retirement he planned for himself, a gradual withdrawal, easing me into the relationships from which the power and prosperity of the firm was derived. He dismissed my doubts about filling his shoes, insisting that I was the right man for my times, as he was right for his, and that the firm would be more prosperous than ever. He planned on spending a lot of time with his grandson, "seeing the world through a child's eyes once more," and perhaps even writing his memoirs—for posthumous publication. "My penance," he called it. Now, he had no successor, and he was facing the winter of his days without family close at hand. It seemed an incongruous end for a life so well lived.

The Brennan residence was the venue for the small and large gatherings that were intrinsic to Pop's position in the city's aristocracy, and it was up to the purpose: a large colonial just a block off Chevy Chase Circle that occupied two acres, including a garden that was a replica of the one at Bantry House in County Cork. When Moira and I were first married it seemed that we spent more time there than in our new home. If we weren't there to eat—Pop hated dining alone as much as Bridey hated cooking for one—then it was for business meetings to integrate me into the firm's practice, or to plan one of the frequent parties or fund-raisers at which Moira would act as hostess.

Bridey was at the door waiting when I parked by the side entrance usually used by family. "He's still up there," she said nervously, taking my coat. I followed her upstairs to Pop's study, feeling nervous myself, and when there was no response to her light knock I stepped past her and opened the door.

He was in his corner chair by the window, barely visible in the winter twilight, with a shawl around his shoulders and his chin on his chest. For a moment my heart froze. It didn't begin beating again until I got close enough to see his still-broad chest rising and falling in the cadence of sleep. I touched his arm and said gently, "Pop?"

He opened his eyes. "Francis?" he said wearily.

"It's me. How are you feeling?"

"Just a little tired," he said, putting his hand over mine. He noticed Bridey standing in the doorway. "I'm all right," he said, grumbling. "You can stop your carrying on." He waited until she shut the door, then said, "I guess you heard about her visit?"

"Only that she was here," I lied.

He nodded and continued to rub my hand. "It's bad news."

"What is it?" I said quickly, alarmed.

"She's marrying that fella," he replied, the anguish plain in his voice, "and she's taking my grandson to California." He looked at me and detected the relief on my face: it was bad, but it wasn't news. "You knew about this?" he asked.

"Yes, Pop, I did."

"I'm sorry to hear it. I was going to ask if you could talk to her, lad, for both your sakes—and for the boy's."

He was the father I never had, the man who had done

more for me than I could repay in two lifetimes, and his thanks was the loss of what he cherished most. And I didn't think I could hurt him more than I already had. "Pop, if there was anything that I could do . . ." It sounded so lame I couldn't finish. "I'm sorry, Pop," was all I could mumble.

It grew dark as we sat there, him in his chair, me on the ottoman with my face buried in my hands. "There's a bottle and glasses over there," he said finally. "I think we both could use a stiff one." I went over to the sideboard and poured a double measure of malt whiskey in two crystal tumblers from a set bearing the presidential seal. He drank half his glass, then looked at me and asked, "What's on your mind?"

After all I'd done I wasn't about to ask him to face down the U.S. government to rescue me and the woman I was sleeping with. "Nothing, Pop," I replied. "I just called to say hello and Bridey was a little concerned about you, so I thought I'd come by."

He snorted. "That woman was born concerned. You wouldn't believe how she's been wringing her hands over you. I had to put one of those damn little TVs in the kitchen so she could watch the latest reports on the trial, and with all that tabloid crap it's all she can do to let go of her rosary beads long enough to cook."

"I guess that story's another thing I've got to apologize for."

He waved it off. "Lad, I don't put any stock in those rags. Twenty-five years ago they had me climbin' into bed with every woman on Capitol Hill. Anyway, the latest doings have pushed all that stuff off the front pages, that's for sure. I thought you had 'em on the run but they're speculating that something's gone wrong for your side."

"They've come up with more evidence. We'll have to cope with it but I think we'll find a way."

He smiled. "I always knew you'd find your way, lad, and not just in this trial. I have faith in you."

"Jesus, I don't know why, Pop. I've never done anything but let you down."

He shook his head. "You know what I'd like to see happen, but in the end, you can't live your life for me—or even for her. If you're not true to yourself you won't be much of a husband or a father. The misery will just rub off on everyone you care about. It's just hard for me because I'm a selfish old bastard used to getting his own way, and because *this*"—he touched his heart—"tells me that the two of you have never stopped loving each other."

"That was always the easy part," I said.

He asked me to stay for dinner but I begged off due to pressing matters, not the least of which was a client who was still under the illusion that she was a murderer. I entered Chevy Chase Circle intending to drive south down Connecticut Avenue to Dupont Circle, but at the last second turned off toward Bethesda. Halfway to the house I thought better of showing up unannounced and stopped to call. Brendan answered.

"Hi, Dad!" he cried. "I saw you on television! You were carrying your briefcase."

"That was me, buddy."

"I'm going to a birthday party, Dad. It's a skating party."

"Wonderful! Whose party?"

"Ricky Foster. He's in my school. He's got glasses." He filled me in on the highlights of Ricky's life before turning me over to his mother.

Moira was cordial, as she always was whenever Brendan was within earshot. "Hi. He's off to a party. He's getting picked up in ten minutes."

"Oh. I was over at Pop's so I thought I'd come by to see him."

She was instantly wary. "Did Pop call you?"

"No, no, I called him. Bridey was acting concerned because he hadn't come downstairs and wouldn't eat, so I took a ride up there. He's okay, Moira."

"No, he's not. We have to talk, Frank. I know you love him so let's put aside everything else and deal with this."

"I'm by the Safeway."

"If you come right over you can catch him before he goes to the party."

I arrived just a moment before Brendan was picked up by Jim Castleman, who was ferrying a van-load of boys to the skating party. The Castlemans had a son Brendan's age and we'd met them in the boys' first year of nursery school. Jim was in research at the National Institutes of Health, a congenial guy who came home five o'clock each day and reminded you of Henry Fonda. He was the Cub Scout den leader and was always pitching in when it came to transporting kids to and from the never-ending activities that define modern childhood. Jim waved from the van when he saw me come out with Brendan. "Frank!" he cried. "Get your skates! I need help!"

"It'd take more than the two of us to deal with those marauders."

"I've got reinforcements waiting at the rink but I think the Fosters invited about twenty kids. Who has twenty kids to a seven-year-old's birthday party? We're calling it 'horror show on ice.' Anyway, I've got a minute, so grant a condemned man's last wish and tell me everything about Ashley Bronson: measurements, perfume, turn-ons, turn-offs, did she kill Garvey, what the heck's going on in that trial, and whether you're gonna win."

"What'll we talk about for the rest of the time?"

He laughed. "Seriously, Jan and I are pulling for you, Frank. And we miss you."

"Thanks. Tell her I miss you guys, too. And the answers to the last three questions are no, nothing we can't handle, and yes."

"I knew it! Listen, if you get in a tough spot"—he pointed

a thumb at the mob behind him, at that moment laughing hysterically over the word "butt"—"just remember, you could be taking *this* crew to an evening on ice skates. How would you like to be doing *that* tonight?" He waved at Moira and pulled away.

I followed her into the house to our regular meeting place at the kitchen table. "Do you want something?" she asked.

"Can I have coffee?"

"Coffee, we've got." She went into the refrigerator where she kept the whole beans that she ground each morning. Moira took her coffee seriously. "Did Pop tell you that we spoke?" she said, her head in the refrigerator.

"Yes."

"And he didn't ask you to talk me out of it?"

"He could see that I already knew, and he figured that it was no use."

She glanced at me over her shoulder before ducking back in to retrieve table cream and something wrapped in foil. "I've got half a sandwich here from Sutton Gourmet," she said. "Lean pastrami and corned beef combination."

"I haven't had pastrami or corned beef in years."

"Let me warm it a little." She put the sandwich in the microwave and punched several buttons to unleash a nuclear bombardment. "I need you to stay close to Pop," she said, leaning against the kitchen island. "Closer than you've been for the past few years. He thinks of you as his own son, Frank, and with Brendan and me so far away . . ." She bit her lip. "You know him. He needs to have family around. I'm not saying every week, but if you would go over and have dinner and maybe do some things together, that would mean a lot."

"You don't have to worry. I intend to act like a son from now on. I'll stay close." She turned back to stare at the microwave but I could see her hand brush across her eyes.

"Why did you call him?" she asked, her back still turned

to me. "From the news, I thought you'd be pretty occupied right now."

"Actually, I called him for help."

She turned around. "Help? For the case?"

"There's been some developments."

"Apparently. They said your side left the courthouse looking pretty grim."

"These developments have nothing to do with what went on in court."

She brought over the food and sat down. "Well, I've heard most of it, a pastrami and corned beef combo ought to be worth the rest."

Even lawyers with high regard for the attorney-client privilege share information with their spouses, if only to have a sounding board for their ideas and strategies. Moira had always filled that role for me when we were married, but with an added bonus: when it came to figuring things out she had few peers. I always said that she would have been in Walter's league as a detective. If there was a downside to her talent, it was that I knew the end of every movie before I finished my popcorn.

Our theory had already passed muster but I wanted to tell her anyway, mostly for the opportunity to spend some time dealing with something other than the fallout of our divorce. "I'll tell you the story," I said, "but you're going to find it pretty hard to believe." I started from the photographs, filling in all the parts that she hadn't heard before and explaining our theory; unlike the office presentation, no details were held back. She was transfixed, shaking her head in wonder as I told her about Henry's design, and her eyes widened when I revealed his spying and how an old network reached out fifty years later for the key to riches. But when I got to my re-creation of what occurred in Garvey's study the night he died, and our theory about Kellogg and the bullet, she was visibly shaken.

"Are you in any danger?"

"Danger? From whom?"

"From *whom*?" she cried. "Well, for starters, there's a spy ring that traffics in nuclear weapons and kills people who know about its existence. And then there's the FBI that you want to expose for illegal searches and suborning Kellogg's perjury. Apparently, they're not beyond framing innocent people."

"I'm not in any danger. Killing me doesn't accomplish anything. There are too many people who know the information that the defense was prepared to introduce at trial about Octagon, including what Brown looks like and the checks to Garvey. Besides, unless I'm wrong, the FBI is already chasing these guys and they're unlikely to hang around. As for the FBI itself, they knew Ashley was guilty of attempted murder and they weren't about to let her walk. I think that's as far as those folks are going to go in terms of framing anybody. Now, tell me, what do you think of the story?"

"It's incredible, but I believe it—it fits together too well to be coincidence. But where does the evidence come from? You need witnesses to prove all that stuff about the Russians and plutonium and nuclear triggers, and about the FBI and black bag jobs. How are you going to do it with the time you have left?"

"We're not going to try."

"Oh. Well, in that case," she replied, smiling, "you've got no problem."

"What we want is to scare them into dropping the case to avoid the kind of scandal that would tear the Bureau and the Justice Department to pieces. We can make a hell of a convincing case in a forum where the rules of evidence don't apply."

"Like a congressional hearing?"

"Exactly. And don't forget the Bureau's investigative files. If they were on to Octagon there's a lot of corroborating information just waiting to be subpoenaed."

"Files can be destroyed."

"This is the age of the whistleblower. Too many agents and administrative staffers know those files exist. They'd be scared to death of a leak."

"So you went to Pop," she said. "You think that with him on your side the threat of hearings carries a lot more weight."

"That's right, but I changed my mind."

"Why?"

"Because the FBI's got a lot of friends in this town, and Pop didn't become who he is by making a hundred enemies to help one client."

"You knew that before you drove up there and you went anyway."

"I didn't ask him. Let's leave it at that."

"Do you really think you can scare them into dropping the case?"

"It depends on whether we can find that wounded agent, and we don't have much time." I started to get up.

"That was only a half-sandwich," she said, nodding toward my plate. "Would you like something else?"

"I've got to go. Aside from Walter and me, you're the only one who knows the whole story. Now I've got to tell her."

"Will she make you dinner?"

"What?"

"Never mind," she muttered, reaching for my plate, "that just slipped out."

* * *

"I don't believe it. I can't."

We were in the sitting room. I'd rehearsed it ten different ways during the drive down from Bethesda but finally decided to just tell it without a big preamble. She didn't know what was coming until the punch line, and predictably, it had taken a few moments for it to sink in.

"Ashley, if anyone knows what you've been through, especially the last couple of days, it's me. I wouldn't be telling you this unless we were reasonably sure."

"I'm afraid I'm dreaming."

"It isn't a dream, it's the end of a nightmare. You didn't murder anyone. Now, it's like I said. We're looking for more proof, but even if we don't find it we'll try to back them off. I can't promise anything, but if there's a God in heaven we're going to bring you out of this okay. The only thing you need to do is what you've been doing all along. Pray for the best, but be prepared for the worst."

She put her arms around my neck. "There must be a God in heaven," she declared, "because he sent you to me."

"Not me, Saint Walter."

"I'd ask him to marry me but I think Martha's got the inside track."

"Good. The way she feeds him, he's not going anywhere."

She got up and went to the portrait of her mother. Herbert was right: Audrey Taylor Bronson was not a raving beauty, but the artist had captured the tungsten eyes and the smile. You could imagine her listening attentively, lovingly, as her awkward Henry, the poor little rich boy who became a spy to save humanity, shared all the treasures he'd mined in his precious library. Did he tell her about his adventure in the real world that frightened him into one of his own making? I searched her face for a clue and decided he hadn't: he'd buried that secret deep, where it lay entombed until that day Raymond came calling.

"My mother died when I was seven," she said, touching the picture frame. "She was a year younger than I am now. Near the end, my father brought her home from the hospital, and I remember lying on her bed while she brushed my hair and told me not to be afraid. She said that life was a precious gift that could be taken away at any time, and made me promise to live with that truth in mind." She turned and said, "If I get a second chance I want to honor that promise. Just pack the bags and go—no plans, no itinerary, just go."

"Any place in particular?"

"Anywhere and everywhere. I feel like I've been under lock and key and I want to escape! The Amalfi coast. Zurich. Athens."

"That's a lot in eight days."

"I'm taking all the time in the world. Then, someplace else, maybe South America. Have you ever been to Rio?"

"Once."

"Did you love it?"

"Yes, I did." I could remember a hotel suite. It was early evening and a light mist was falling, just enough to dim the traffic sounds below. The stereo was playing a piano solo of "Stardust"—it might have been Hoagy Carmichael himself. It seemed to fit the mood so perfectly that I wondered if he had ever been there, in that suite, at dusk, with a light mist falling and Moira on the terrace.

"I would love going back with you," she said. "We'd go everywhere we wanted, the two of us."

"Would we come back?"

"Sometime. But I want to be free again, Frank. I want to be able to pick up and go whenever and wherever I want."

"I know."

"And I don't want to go alone."

"Criminal lawyers don't usually hear from clients after the case is over. We're a reminder of something they'd rather forget."

"Did those clients love their lawyers?"

"I suppose, some of them, in a manner of speaking."

"In the manner that we have?"

"No, I'd say we've broken new ground."

"Well, I'm going to be in love with you long after the case is over. Next week, next month, next year, and"—she kissed me—"all the years after that."

"And I'll be in love with you. Always."

\* \* \*

Walter checked in at ten o'clock. It was a slow process. Hospitals were busy places, even after normal business hours, and notwithstanding the "official" nature of the request, getting someone to research admissions records took time. They had managed to cover all of D.C.'s hospitals and were now working the immediate surrounding counties. So far they had found two cases of gunshot wounds treated that night. One was a would-be holdup man in Prince Georges County who ran into a Korean liquor store owner with a .44 magnum; the other was a seventeen-year-old shot in a drug altercation in Anacostia. They were going to go all night. "What about Dan?" I asked.

"The only thing the MPD had was the Anacostia shooting," he said.

"Do you think they took him to some kind of private clinic?"

"It's possible," he acknowledged, "but if they did, no one's gonna show records to some guy off the street. We may have to do some bag jobs of our own. Did you talk to the old man yet?"

I sighed. "That's a problem."

"He turned you down?"

"No, I didn't ask. It's hard to explain." That was met by silence; he probably thought he had the hard part. "I'll explain when I see you," I added.

"I'll call in the mornin', 'less I got news. How's she holdin' up?"

"Fine. She wants to marry you."

"Yeah." He grunted. "They all do."

\* \* \*

Sunday morning started badly. There was no call from Walter during the night, but when I heard the phone ring downstairs at seven-thirty it was still early enough to mean good news. I sprang out of bed and was in the hallway in my pants and shirt to meet Martha coming up the stairs. The call was from Arthur Bonner. The report was short and sweet: there was gunshot residue inside the sleeve, no question about it. He and Yee would be in agreement.

Walter didn't call until nine-thirty. They had covered Alexandria, Arlington, Fairfax, Montgomery, and Prince Georges Counties, and had found one more gunshot wound, a nineteen-year-old woman shot in the buttocks during a domestic dispute. "Where do we go from here?" I asked.

"As we go out the circle gets a hell of a lot bigger," he complained. "We got more territory, more hospitals, and a lot more drive time in between. What if they ferried him somewhere in a helicopter? The NYPD has got a lot of 'em. The Fibbies could have a freakin' air force around here."

"Then we'll hire helicopters. That way we can cover more ground. Where are you?"

"Upper Marlboro. Listen, it's too much ground and too many hospitals. And you can't land a helicopter on any rooftop you want, so you got to have ground transportation when you land. You start talkin' helicopter rides, you're talkin' Greater Baltimore and even Richmond. Them two cities alone would take us an entire day. This ain't workin', kid. We got to get smarter."

There was no arguing with him; it was becoming a needle-in-the-haystack exercise, and for all we knew, the agents might even have prevailed on the hospital to seal the record or throw it in the trash can in the name of national security. "When can you get everyone back to the office?" I asked.

"Give 'em time to shower and change their underwear. Eleven o'clock."

"Round 'em up. I'll see you at eleven."

Ashley had come downstairs in her robe. "Nothing yet," I told her. "Walter is bringing everyone in for a meeting."

"I heard. I want you to tell them something for me. No matter what happens from now on, I woke up this morning knowing that I wasn't a murderer. My gratitude is more than I can express right now but I'll find a proper way when this is all over."

I got to the office at ten-thirty. The coffee was on in the kitchen, indicating that someone besides me was working Sunday morning. As I passed the entrance to the library I saw the top of Andy's head in one of the carrels and knocked on the doorjamb. He looked up, bleary-eyed. "When did you get here?" I asked.

"Never left." He yawned, stretching. "I think I've read every case on or near point. Letting in new evidence is almost always a judgment call for the trial judge. The only reason an appeals court would reverse Warner is if he abused his discretion, and I only found three cases where that happened. It's going to be tough to make them fit here."

"Well, do the best you can. We've got to take a shot at it."

"What's going on with you guys?"

"Everyone's coming in for a meeting. They've checked all the hospitals in the city and the surrounding counties. If we go out any farther it becomes overwhelming."

Andy nodded, making a face. "Did they check the FBI hospital?"

"The what?"

"The FBI hospital. I had a friend at Columbia who decided to join the FBI instead of practicing law. He got this weird virus while he was in training and wound up in a hospital ward for like, nine weeks or something, and I think there was mostly FBI people there. Why are you slapping your forehead?"

I rushed to my office and called Walter's cell phone. I reached him on the Baltimore-Washington Parkway. "Does the name 'Quantico' ring a familiar note?" I asked.

A string of curses mixed with the static. "Jesus H. Christ!" he squawked. "Three freakin' detectives in a room and we don't come up with the Fibbies' own training academy! There was a clunk as he banged the phone against the steering wheel. "They make it an accident on the shootin' range and there's no doctor to report nothin'!"

"They probably put him on a helicopter over by the Pentagon and had him down there in ten minutes."

"Yeah, it's Quantico—got to be," he shouted. "You win the blue ribbon." Walter didn't completely trust wireless technology, and felt he had to yell to assist anything that was battery-powered.

"It wasn't me. It was our young associate."

"Andrew? Ain't that a kick in the balls?" He laughed. "Outta the mouths of babes . . ."

"Okay. What now? Are you going to drive down there?"

"What for? They ain't gonna pull out no records for the cops," he yelled. "I'm comin' in. *You're* the one who got to sleep last night. It's your turn to have one of them inspirations."

\* \* \*

Everyone was assembled by eleven and brought up to speed. Andy was in awe of the detectives, especially Walter, and when I explained that he came up with the Quantico angle the murmurs of approval—including a wink from Harry— made his eyes shine. As for the detectives, if there was some chagrin over the fact that the puzzle had probably been solved by the team mascot, they were too tired to show it. The predominant feeling in the room was one of relief and anticipation: we were closing in on our provenance, and if our success happened to come at the expense of the FBI, so much the sweeter.

"Walter says that hospital isn't going to open its records for anyone with a cop's badge," I informed them. "Does anybody disagree?" No one did. "I don't, either, so if we're going to get those records we're going to have to come up with something more clever than what's been working at the civilian hospitals. What do you guys think of a pretext call?"

"What's the pretext?" asked Dan.

"Well, who would be interested in the admissions record of an agent who'd been shot?"

"Maybe Fibbie headquarters in Washington," said Dan. "We could say that we're processing some paperwork for the guy."

"No good," said Walter. "You could wind up talkin' to someone who works for the Bureau, maybe someone who deals with headquarters all the time on shit like this. If you can't speak the language and you don't know the players, you're gonna get tripped up. We only got one shot at them records, so it's got to be good."

"Who else would care about them records?" Harry asked. "An insurance company? Some kind of health insurance deal?"

"Maybe," I said. "But we don't know how their insurance works and we could still wind up with someone who's talking a language we don't understand. If we're an organization that they're not used to dealing with all the time, the person we talk to won't understand our agency's procedures, and our agency's person would plausibly be unfamiliar with the Bureau's procedures."

"Which agency?" asked Andy.

"How about the Office of Personnel Management? That's the agency that oversees civil service issues government-wide. Maybe it's doing a report of some kind, like . . ."

"Disabling injuries!" cried Andy. "They're compiling a report and need to get the admissions record."

"That could work," said Walter. "But we have to cover the fact that we don't know the guy's name, and we have to be definite enough to get them to pull one record, not to begin some goddamn study or somethin'. And when is this going to happen? The hearing with the judge is Tuesday."

"Let's try this," I said. "We've got an employee of OPM working Sunday to prepare an overdue report. She's got to have a replacement for this illegible record, blah, blah, blah. Since we're calling on Sunday we've got a decent chance to get someone who's not usually dealing with the records."

"I like it," said Dan. He suggested that Andy make the call because he sounded more like a young bureaucrat than any of the detectives.

"I'll tell ya something about pretext calls," said Harry. "I knew a guy who used to be on the bunco squad, bustin' up these con games they use to snatch your life savings or get your credit card number. He told me that when these guys set up a boiler room, guess who they line up to work the phones? Old ladies. He said there's nothin' like a call from an old biddy that sounds like your grandma to get people to drop their guard."

"Makes sense," said Dan. "Who could we get?"

\* \* \*

Martha was nervous. We'd gone over it with her a couple of dozen times but she flunked every rehearsal. Having all of us around wringing our hands wasn't helping, so we sent everybody else to lunch. I was getting antsy but Walter was unruffled: he'd spent thousands of hours smoothing the feathers of very nervous people to get them to do his bidding. What finally got her ready was writing out her spiel and responses to all the questions she might be asked. The three-by-five cards were all laid out in front of her when she dialed the number of the hospital at Quantico with Walter and me listening in on the speaker.

The phone was answered on the first ring. An enthusiastic male voice said, "Base hospital, Corporal Dearman."

I nodded at Martha, pointing to the card. "Good morning," she said. "This is Mrs. Wilson at the Office of Personnel Management in Washington. Could I speak to the admissions office, please?"

"One moment, ma'am."

There were several clicks and the phone was ringing again. It rang for almost a minute. I was about to tell her to hang up to call the main number again when someone picked up the receiver. For a moment there was no response, but we could hear a woman's voice in the background. She seemed to be holding the phone and speaking to someone nearby; her voice increased in volume as she brought the phone closer to her mouth. "Admissions," she said.

Martha read from the card. "Good afternoon, this is Mrs. Wilson at the Office of Personnel Management in Washington. Who am I speaking to please?"

"This is Jane Needham."

"Hi. I guess we're both working Sunday. I don't usually have to work on a weekend."

The woman didn't warm up. "What can I do for you, Mrs. Wilson?"

"I'm preparing a report on productivity losses due to work-related injury for the Federal Bureau of Investigation. It's for the calendar year just ended, and it's supposed to be up at the Government Affairs Committee on the Hill tomorrow. The problem is that I've got an illegible record here for an FBI agent who was admitted there last November first or second. I was wondering if you could fax me a better copy."

"The people who work in records are off today. They come in at eight tomorrow morning. Okay?" The woman seemed about to hang up; Walter tapped on another index card.

Martha looked at the card and read. "Oh, dear," she said. "I have to have this report done today. I was supposed to have it done by Friday but my grandson had a bone marrow transplant on Wednesday and I couldn't leave the church, I just couldn't. I told my supervisor I was sick and I feel so terrible about lying." She sniffed. "I promised I would have the report at the Committee first thing in the morning."

A sigh came through the speaker. "November first or second? What's the name?"

"Oh, bless you," Martha said. "I can't read the name. It looks like the admission time was . . . this could be an eleven or twelve something, and there's a box here that says 'GSW,' whatever that means."

"Gunshot wound," replied Needham. "That shouldn't be too hard to pick out. Hold on while I boot up the computer."

"Thank you, Miss Needham. You're so kind to do this for me."

"No problem. Just hang on." She laid the phone down on the desk and the sounds of office activity in the background blended with the louder noises nearby. We heard the gong and whirring sound as the computer booted up, then the clicking of the keyboard. Needham was a fast typist; I hoped it was indicative of her familiarity with the records. I listened to the machine react to her tapping with more whirring of the hard drive. Once I heard that distinct beep that usually indicated that you'd done something the program didn't like, and I heard Needham grunt. She hit several keys and it beeped again. My heart sank a little with each beep.

Three minutes passed like three years. Walter stared at the speaker; only the frequency of his toothpick vibration indicated his anxiety. Martha's eyes were closed and her lips were moving in silent prayer. It was a fitting moment for a case that from the very start seemed to be a test of every fiber of my being, and if it wasn't so macabre I would have laughed out loud.

"All right," said Needham, "I got it. SA David Conroy admitted eleven-fifty P.M., November first. Gunshot wound in the right leg, some kind of training accident."

"Oh, wonderful," said Martha. "That must be it, I can see part of the 'Conroy' on my copy."

"I'll print it. What's your fax number?"

"Hold on," said Martha, "There's a machine down the

hall. I'll put you on hold a second and get the number."

"Okay, go ahead. It'll take a minute to print."

Martha hit the hold button and we all exhaled. "Okay," I told her, "we are one step away and you're doing great. We'll give it two minutes."

We waited while I kept an eye on my watch. Walter wrote down the information that Needham had read off the record, just in case. "Are you ready?" I asked, as the last seconds ticked away.

"Let's do it," she said, smiling. Walter pushed the next index card in front of her and she punched the button again and assumed a frazzled voice. "Miss Needham? I'm sorry, but I can't get into that office. I called my daughter-in-law. She lives up at Cleveland Park, just ten minutes from here, and she has a fax machine. She said my son would drive down here with the fax."

Needham laughed. "You're going to go through all this and I'll bet that report never gets read by the bigwigs up there."

"You're probably right. I'll bet your job is a lot more interesting, working in a hospital."

"It has its moments. What's the number?" Martha read her my fax number. "Here it comes," she said. "If you don't get it, call me right back. I'll only be here for another thirty minutes."

"Thank you so much, Miss Needham. You are a lifesaver."

"I hope everything turns out okay for your grandson. They're having a lot of success with those procedures these days. Bye-bye."

I walked over and stood by the fax machine; Walter and Martha followed. Two minutes later our provenance eked out of the fax printer. Walter picked it up, scanned it, and handed it to me. "Here's the ball, kid," he said, grinning. "All ya gotta do is lug it across the goal line."

I went to the phone and dialed Rogavin's office. I didn't

figure him to be taking any time off before it was over, and he didn't disappoint. "Kyle Rogavin."

"It's Frank O'Connell. I thought there was a chance you'd be at the office."

"I like to enjoy my weekends," he said. "And I just couldn't think of anything I'd rather do than work on our case. Have you employed Bonner?"

"He's already been over to the lab to look at the raincoat."

"And?"

"And he finds it hard to believe anyone could be so sloppy as to miss that residue the first time around."

"Which means that he doesn't dispute its presence."

"It's there *now*," I conceded.

"Tsk, tsk. We *are* suspicious, aren't we? In the interest of fair play, I'm putting you on notice that Mr. Einbinder will take one for the team and say that he didn't test inside the sleeve. Then I've got Mr. Yee batting cleanup. As a matter of fact, I'm just doing a little buffing of his direct examination as we speak. What do you think sounds better: 'beyond a shadow of a doubt' or 'beyond peradventure'?"

"We'd like to have a meeting to discuss disposing of the case."

"What's this? *A plea bargain?*" he cooed. "Hmm. I'm afraid that train's left the station."

"I'd like to hear that from the U.S. Attorney himself."

He laughed. "I think you've got an exaggerated sense of your client's influence. She had an opportunity—two of them in fact—but her lawyer booted them."

"Tell the U.S. Attorney we want to meet at nine o'clock tomorrow at his office, and I'd like a representative of the FBI to be there, someone in upper management."

"The FBI? This is an MPD case."

"Mathis should be there, too. Just let the Bureau know that I've got information it will find intriguing and that we're prepared to deal."

"You know," he said, snickering, "I think you've lost your mind. It's the stress, isn't it? Defending your woman and all that. It's too bad, really, because I'd be the first to admit that you put up a pretty good fight."

"Listen closely to what I'm going to tell you. We have a mutual dislike, but as long as we're making admissions, you're not a bad trial lawyer, either, and I think we respect each other in the way adversaries do. I'll tell you lawyer to lawyer that if it should come to light that we had this conversation and you *didn't* pass along my request, then even I won't enjoy what'll happen to you next. Now, the really good trial lawyers can tell when they're being bullshitted, so let me ask you this. Does it sound like I'm bullshitting?"

The idea that there might be aspects of his case that he wasn't privy to upset him, as did the fact that I was going over his head. In his place I would've felt the same way. "What the hell is this all about?" he snapped.

"You'll find out tomorrow. If I didn't make it clear, you're invited to the meeting, too." He slammed the phone down without a good-bye, just like old times.

I called Ashley. "We found him," I said. "They took him to a hospital at the FBI Academy down in Virginia, and we've got the proof. I've set up a meeting with Rogavin's bosses for tomorrow morning."

"I'm afraid to breathe," she said, "so I'm just going to hold my breath until whatever happens, happens. When will I see you?"

"Not tonight. I've got a lot of thinking to do before tomorrow, and I do it best when I'm walking."

"Maybe this will be the last night you'll ever spend on patrol."

"We'll see."

"I know. You're superstitious, but I'm a big believer in the power of positive thinking, so I'm going to pass the time thinking of us breakfasting in bed in every five-star hotel in the world, one hotel at a time."

"We'll see."

"Okay, okay. I don't want to jinx us. Good luck. I love you."

Before I left the office I called Moira and told her about finding Conroy. She dropped into her best imitation of her father and said, "Lad, you know what you do when you're in the driver's seat, don't you?"

"What?" I asked.

"You drive."

# 22

I probably shouldn't have been surprised when I entered the office of U.S. Attorney Gordon Sims and saw who was representing the FBI. Assistant Director James Lloyd was the head of the Criminal Division and essentially the number three man in the Bureau; his presence was a form of provenance in itself. Sims and Rogavin may have been duped, but Lloyd would have known all about Octagon and was probably one of the people summoned to headquarters to clean up the mess in Georgetown.

It was Sims's office so he rated the head of the table, although Lloyd was the bigger player in federal law enforcement. Rogavin was sitting to Sims's right, and next to him was the rumpled Mathis, plainly unhappy to be rubbing elbows with lawyers and feds. Next to Mathis was Lloyd's deputy, Oscar Wallace, doodling on a legal pad with a huge Mont Blanc fountain pen that was being eyed suspiciously by Mathis, a ballpoint kind of guy. Lloyd was ensconced at the foot of the table, resplendent in a charcoal suit with pinstripes a shade wider than Rogavin's.

Walter and I took the seats to Sims's left, opposite the prosecution. "Thanks for having us," I said after introductions.

Sims cleared his throat. "Let's agree that this is a conference regarding a possible disposition of the case, and that nothing said here can be used by either side in a court of law."

"Fine," I replied.

"Furthermore," he continued, "since we are all aware of the intensity of the public interest in this case, let's also agree that what is said here is confidential, and that no one is going out to hold a press conference after this meeting."

"Agreed."

The U.S. Attorney was sensing capitulation, and after the soundness of the government's case had been openly questioned by some commentators, was obviously feeling expansive. "You put up a hell of a fight, Mr. O'Connell," he said genially. "Gave our ace here a run for the money." Rogavin blinked but said nothing.

"Thanks. It's been a battle, in and out of court."

"Well," he said, "the press's job is to sell papers, I guess. I'll tell you in all honesty, if she were *my* client, I'd hold a press conference and say it was all true. I'd be the most envied guy in Washington." No one laughed; he became serious. "It's your party," he said, "but before we begin there's something you ought to know about the policy of this office on plea bargaining. Once the trial began and we devoted our resources, all offers were off the table. We won't discuss anything as favorable again."

"I'm not here to ask for the same deal."

"That's good. Maybe we can reach an agreement. What did you have in mind?"

"That you dismiss the case and walk away."

Sims looked around the table for a sign that his hearing had deceived him. "Why in the hell would we do that?" he growled.

"Because it will spare some people in this room the loss of their reputations—or possible prosecution."

The U.S. Attorney turned crimson. Rogavin just shook his head, doubtless convinced that I'd lost my grip. Mathis was staring at something over my shoulder; only the vigor of his gum-chewing indicated the cauldron bubbling inside. At the other end of the table, Lloyd was expressionless as he glanced at a note scribbled by his deputy. "This meeting is over," said Sims, sputtering. He stood up and pointed at Rogavin. "Go in there tomorrow and finish this goddamn thing."

"Prosecution for what?" asked Lloyd evenly.

"For framing Ashley Bronson for a murder she didn't commit. We know what happened the night of November first, Mr. Lloyd, the entire story." He looked at me with a deadpan expression, waiting for more.

Sims slowly sank back into his chair, his eyes riveted on me. "I've seen some reckless bullshit in my career," he snarled, "desperate lawyers out to save a client or make a reputation and a fast buck, but never anything approaching this. You're finished, Mister, absolutely . . . professionally . . . finished. You won't be going back to the cellblocks when this case is over because no judge in this city will have anything to do with you. You think you can come in here—"

"Is the meeting over, Mr. Lloyd?" I said, ignoring Sims.

Lloyd looked at Sims before replying. "Well," he said, "I'm here at the request of the United States Attorney, but I'll admit you've certainly piqued my curiosity, probably because I know the least about this case. For that matter, I don't even know why I'm here." He looked at Wallace, who seconded with a nod.

Walter turned to me and said, "He's lyin'." Lloyd just glared at him in response.

I said, "Mr. Feinberg here is a former homicide detective with the New York Police Department. His powers of deduction are the stuff of legend up there, but his real gift is knowing when someone is lying. He's sort of a walking polygraph machine, only more accurate. They used to bring him into interview rooms just to listen to people tell their stories."

"Very impressive," said Lloyd.

"You have no idea," I replied. "For example, he knew immediately that Miles Kellogg was lying and that he was nowhere near Mr. Garvey's home the night he died. I looked at Rogavin and explained, "Kellogg was a stand-in; the real witness couldn't come forward."

"*Real* witness?" Rogavin scoffed. "You want to hear from a real witness? Yee says that your client fired a gun."

I shrugged. "Since we're operating under Mr. Sims's ground rules, why don't we say for the purposes of this meeting that Ashley Bronson entered Raymond Garvey's house on the night of November first at around ten-fifteen P.M., took his gun from a drawer, and fired it."

"That makes her a murderer," declared Mathis. "We got the bullet, and it came out of Garvey's head."

"You've got the bullet," I agreed, "but it didn't come out of Garvey's head."

"Of course it did," said Sims. "If it didn't come out of Garvey, where did it come from?"

"Out of him," I said, tossing several copies of the hospital report on the table. They sat there in front of Mathis, who seemed determined to ignore them, until Rogavin casually reached over and picked one up. As he read he began to uncoil from his slouch, his eyes darting back and forth across the boxes in the report. Watching, Sims could no longer contain himself: he stood up and snatched one. Lloyd held out his hand and Wallace passed one to him before taking one for himself. Mathis turned a copy toward him so he could read it without leaving fingerprints.

A secretary knocked on the door and entered. She placed a pink message form face down in front of Sims, who ignored it while he perused the report.

I was watching Lloyd as his eyes flicked across the form. The vein in his neck began to twitch, and when he finished he just stared straight ahead, his jaw tight.

"What is this supposed to mean?" asked Sims. "That she shot an FBI agent?"

"That's right."

Mathis had heard enough. *"Bullshit!"* he shouted, slapping the table. "We got the gun and the box of ammo he bought with it. There was one spent and five live rounds in the gun, and there were forty-four rounds in the box. That's fifty, the whole box! The bullet went right from Garvey to the ballistics test and it matched the gun!"

"No, it didn't," I said.

*"We got a chain of custody!"* Mathis bellowed.

"That much is true," I replied. "On one end you've got the medical examiner, and on the other, the ballistics expert. But who's in the middle?"

Mathis thought for a second and said, "The FBI guy."

"That's right. Tell me, detective, in all your years of experience, how many chains of custody can you recall that had an FBI agent as one of the links?"

Wallace interrupted. "Agent Windemere went over to the morgue as a matter of routine. The deceased was a former high-ranking federal official, and if he was murdered because of something he did or didn't do within the scope of his government position, it could be a federal offense."

"Right," I said. "Raymond Garvey served in the Carter administration. Who would have killed him—Rip van Winkle?"

Mathis was hostile but he was still a detective, subject to the same code as Walter: you go where logic and your gut take you. He cocked his head toward the hospital report and said, "Your sayin' that Windemere switched bullets?"

"That's right."

"Then who killed Garvey, and what was this Conroy doin' in the house?"

I glanced over at Lloyd. "Jump in anytime," I said.

He frowned and said, "No thanks, I'm not playing," then looked at Sims. "Is the U.S. Attorney's Office going to trash an airtight murder case because of a firing range accident at Quantico?"

"We are *not* going to dump this case," declared Sims. "Not on the basis of a coincidence."

"Coincidence, my ass," said Walter. He spoke directly to

Mathis, cop to cop. "Look, you got her goin' in around ten-fifteen and you got this guy showin' up at the hospital at eleven-fifty. Who the hell's on the firin' range that late? They got to clean up their mess, line up a helicopter, drive him to a pick-up, and fly him to Quantico. The timin' fits too good. Then you got your chain of custody. If the guy wants a take on why Garvey got killed, where does he go? To the freakin' morgue? What are *they* gonna tell him? He went there for the bullet and he got it. Where I come from that ain't no co-incidence, it's probable cause."

"Then answer the questions," said Mathis.

Rogavin hadn't said a word since he'd read the hospital report, but he was paying attention and he was watching Lloyd. I pushed our next documents across to him and said, "We planned to put these in evidence. They're copies of two checks deposited into Garvey's account totaling one hundred thousand dollars, drawn on something called Octagon Associates. If you investigate all you're going to find is that it's a New York corporation with a Manhattan law firm for an address. There's nothing else to indicate that it's doing business, even though it's been around for over fifty years. You'll also find that Octagon bailed out Sherman Burroughs with his creditors. You already know that something was going on between Burroughs and Garvey, and Burroughs wasn't too pleased. What you don't know is that there was a third man, and we have two witnesses who met him: Burroughs's former housekeeper and his chauffeur. The man was European and he used the name Brown."

"That doesn't answer either question," said Sims.

"I'm getting to it," I replied. "Octagon wanted something from Henry Bronson, and it was using his friend Raymond as the contact man. That's how Raymond earned his money. But Henry wasn't cooperative, so Sherry was pressing Raymond, and Raymond was pressing Henry."

"The Wards heard her tellin' Garvey to stay away," said Mathis. "You're sayin' that was about layin' off the father?"

"That's why," I agreed. "And while this was going on, Mr. Lloyd's people were watching all of them. The FBI was on to Octagon. For all we know the Bureau's file goes back a long way, maybe the whole fifty years."

"So, what did they want from Bronson?" asked Mathis.

"We have a good hunch," I replied, "but I'm not at liberty to answer that."

"Hunch?" said Lloyd. "'For all we know'? 'Not at liberty to answer'? This whole thing is pure conjecture. You've no proof that we were investigating this Octagon organization, and you're speculating that it was Octagon that brought Burroughs and Garvey together."

"Yeah, that must be another coincidence," said Walter.

When I continued the story I spoke directly to Rogavin. "The day Henry Bronson's death became public, Brown called Burroughs's house sounding very agitated. This time he used the name Mr. Clay and it was probably a code. The housekeeper took the call. She recognized the voice and is prepared to testify. A few days later Garvey and Brown showed up at Henry Bronson's library and began to ransack the place. They told my client that they were looking for documents that belonged to Garvey. She didn't know what they were talking about, but to get rid of them she said that she burned the documents on her father's instructions. She was convincing. Brown believed her and that made Garvey a loose end."

Mathis made a face. "You're sayin' that *Brown* killed Garvey?"

"That's the way it figures, and we believe that the FBI had listening devices in Garvey's house. When he was murdered they came running, and they were in the house when my client fired the gun."

Lloyd slowly clapped his hands in mock applause. "Congratulations, it would make a good movie," he said, smirking. "I really hate to spoil it with the facts." He looked up the table at Sims. "Our involvement in this case was limited to a visit to the morgue and doing a favor for the medical examiner—that's it. Garvey may not have been in government for years, but he was once in the Cabinet. You know how it is, Gordon. When the story gets printed, it's 'Former Secretary Murdered,' and everybody calls the FBI for a comment. This Director is no different than his predecessors. He likes to have answers, and he doesn't care whether it's a matter within our jurisdiction or not because the public doesn't understand our limits, and for that matter, neither does three-quarters of the Congress. They just ask questions, and if we have to say, 'We don't know,' it doesn't inspire the confidence of the people who approve our budget. The rule over at the Hoover Building is simple. If we're likely to get asked about it, get the facts. Windemere was told to check it out. It was too late to go to the crime scene so he went to get a look at the body and find out what the M.E. could tell him. As for what happened at Quantico, there were several witnesses and there's a careless agent named Harvester who's currently on administrative leave pending disciplinary action. That's it. That's your big conspiracy."

"That makes sense to me," said Sims. He looked at me and said, "On the other hand, your story makes no sense. If you were to be believed, then FBI officials plotted to frame your client for a murder she didn't commit. It's so preposterous that I shudder to ask why they would do such a thing."

"It was the obvious choice," I replied. "No doubt they felt the wounding of Agent Conroy was a crime that shouldn't go unpunished. And they were under the impression that Ashley Bronson went to Garvey's house to commit murder, so they would only be framing her for the crime she intended, which I suppose made it more palatable.

"Are you sayin' she *didn't* go there to kill Garvey?" asked Mathis.

"I think you're overlooking another possibility. She went to Garvey's house to confront him and after entering with a key that he gave her, stumbled into a burglary in progress."

"That's ridiculous!" barked Sims.

"I don't think it is. In the eyes of the law Conroy *was* a burglar. On the other hand, Ashley Bronson had lawful access to the premises. Shooting him was no crime."

Lloyd chuckled and shook his head. "I've got to hand it to you. You're living up to your billing as one very creative lawyer. So, we mistakenly believed that your client was guilty of a crime, and rather than see her go free we framed her for a more serious one. Pretty sinister, I'd say."

"Believing that she was guilty wasn't your motive. It was the rationale for doing what you wanted to do—actually, *needed* to do."

"Really? So tell us: what *was* our motive?"

"Saving your collective ass. If you didn't hand the MPD an open-and-shut case, there would have been an investigation and a lot of resources devoted to finding out who killed Raymond Garvey. It would've only been a question of time before the police came up with the Garvey-Burroughs connection, then Octagon, and eventually, Mr. Brown. That would have meant they were messing around in what the FBI regards as a very sensitive case involving national security."

"How's that protecting themselves?" asked Mathis.

"It isn't, but if there *was* an investigation then you'd be paying closer attention to the evidence you found at Garvey's." I took the Polaroids out of the envelope and pushed them across to Mathis. "Remember these?" I asked. He spread them out and scanned them one at a time. When he finished he slid them over to Rogavin.

"Yeah," said Mathis. "They were picked up by the forensic unit in the sitting room. These are the originals. How did *you* get 'em?"

I ignored the question. "What did you make of them?" I asked.

"We didn't. We figured someone was practicing with a camera."

"Did you find a Polaroid camera in the house?"

"No."

"Do you know what a black bag job is?"

"A black bag job? No."

I turned it over to Walter and he repeated the lecture on the history of the Bureau and black bag jobs, then explained that the photographs were left behind in the scramble to get Conroy and the microphones out of the house. When he finished, I said, "Some of you besides Messrs. Lloyd and Wallace here may remember what happened the last time the Bureau was exposed for this kind of thing. Congressional committees tore it apart, and two of its highest-ranking people were prosecuted and convicted. The simple fact was they were afraid of being put through the wringer again. The Garvey case needed to be closed."

Rogavin had been silent a long time, fingering the Phi Beta Kappa key that hung from the chain on his vest. "When it comes to sentencing time," he said quietly, "it's a big step from attempted murder to murder."

"Not if we'd accepted your generous offer," I replied.

"May I see those pictures?" said Lloyd. Mathis pushed them down the table. Lloyd glanced at them and shook his head. "I've been in the Bureau twenty-two years," he declared, "and lived all through those prosecutions and investigations that Mr. O'Connell mentioned, but I've never heard of this Polaroid business. Have you, Oscar?"

"Never," answered Wallace.

Lloyd pushed the pictures back to the center of the table. "Gordon, they want you to tuck your tail between your legs and dump the most highly publicized case this office has had in years. It was solid *before* you turned up the gunshot residue and they're not disputing it's genuine. If you dismiss you're going to have to answer a lot of questions. What are you going to say, that you were flummoxed by smoke and mirrors? You've got half the criminal law professors in the country looking over your shoulder from TV studios, and you can bet your career that they're going to want to know what *proof* caused you to walk away from a compelling murder case. Now, think about everything you've heard from the defense side and separate the conjecture from the evidence. What do they have that they're prepared to introduce tomorrow?" Lloyd looked at me and said, "Unless I've missed something, you've got witnesses to prove that Garvey, Burroughs, and this man Brown were involved in some deal. You may even imply that Brown was shady. But where do you go from there? Unless your client testifies you can't prove that they were pressing her father, and you can't prove that they wanted something from his library."

"What about it?" asked Sims. "Is your client going to testify?"

"We have no plan to put her on the stand," I conceded.

"That's only the beginning," continued Lloyd. "You can't prove that Octagon is some illicit organization, you can't prove this silly bullet-switch theory, and you can't prove there is or was an FBI investigation going on—which, by the way, we adamantly deny. So, what have you got? A hospital report that you can't connect to your case without speculating. The prosecution, however, has several agents who can testify to what happened to Conroy. On that record Warner won't even allow it into evidence. And as far as these photographs go, I don't think the jury is going to put a lot of stock in what the defendant's paid investigator says, so unless you've got something more the Polaroids aren't going into evidence, either." He looked at Sims. "Gordon, I'm not a lawyer, so if you think I'm off base here please say so."

"You're not," replied Sims, "and I am *not* going to allow this office to become a laughingstock. O'Connell, you really don't expect us to dismiss the case based on a story spun out of whole cloth, do you? The rules of evidence govern our decisions in these matters."

I shrugged. "The rules of evidence won't matter on Capitol Hill. There's plenty here for a Congressional committee to get its teeth into, and once it gets started it will be Mr.

Lloyd's story that won't hold up. There are too many people who know the truth about the Octagon investigation—not just agents, but clerks and typists, too. The same people know where Conroy was assigned and that there was no range accident on the night of November first. It will leak—you can count on it—and when it does it will be like a neutron bomb went off here and at Bureau headquarters because the buildings and furnishings will be standing, but the people will be gone." I leaned toward Sims. "Do you really think we're going to rest one minute while Ashley Bronson sits in prison for a murder she didn't commit? The Bronson family has immense resources, and they will be devoted to seeing that everyone at this table gets his due."

Sims stood up, trembling with anger. "You son of a bitch!" he snarled. "You are so goddamn far over your head. . . . You've got no idea who you're screwing with—none! Do you know how you're going to be received on Capitol Hill? As the desperate lawyer for a convicted murderer, a shyster who just narrowly escaped being sanctioned for making reckless allegations against a reputable man and for shacking up with his own client! They're going to laugh at this pile of crap you've been shoveling here, your bullshit conspiracies and second bullet theories, and you can bet your ass there won't be any goddamn hearings, not on *your* say-so! And when you're all through we'll be there to sweep up the pieces of your license to practice law. Now, Rogavin here has a case to prepare. This meeting's over so get the hell out!"

Walter and I looked at each other: there was nothing else to be said. I reached down for my briefcase, determined not to let them see the despair that was welling up inside. "Think it over," I said to Sims as I closed my case. "You're being used."

"Good-bye, Mr. O'Connell," he spat. "And don't forget your papers." He pushed his copy of the hospital report toward me, and noticing the pink form for the first time, swiped it up and read the message. His eyes widened, then he seized the phone behind him and punched a button. His urgent tone caught everyone's attention when he said, "He's outside? What did he say?" and then visibly sagged at the reply. "Show him in," he muttered, then hung up the phone and looked at me. "Your co-counsel is here," he said.

I didn't answer, too puzzled over what Andy could have done to get that kind of reaction. The door opened behind me and I heard the voice before I turned around: "Sorry I'm late, lads, but I've been waiting outside for almost thirty minutes. I was beginning to feel a little unwanted."

"I'm sorry, Mr. Brennan," stammered Sims, plainly contrite. "My secretary put the message down without saying anything. I didn't realize you were out there."

"Well, no harm done, Gordon." Pop smiled. "We had a pleasant little chat, she and I." He looked around the room and nodded to the assemblage. "And good morning to all of you gentlemen." By that time everyone in the room was standing, each of them smiling in the way you do in the presence of important people. Pop moved around and shook hands with them all, needlessly repeating his name once or twice. He spent an extra moment exchanging pleasantries with Lloyd, having already identified him as the principal adversary in the room. Walter moved over to give Pop the center seat on our side of the table. He clapped me on the shoulder as he sat and said, "Sorry, I'm late, lad. You've acquainted these gentlemen with the facts of the matter, have you?"

"I have," I answered.

"Well, gentlemen," he said, "you can see we have an interesting case for your consideration."

"I didn't know you practiced criminal law, Mr. Brennan," said Lloyd.

"Well, I don't," said Pop. "When it comes to the criminal law I know just enough to know when to leave a meeting." Lloyd laughed and Wallace and Sims followed suit. Mathis and Rogavin were poker-faced. "Anyway," he continued, "I wasn't hired to be a criminal lawyer. I leave all that to Francis here." He looked at Rogavin. "I understand that you're a pretty fair criminal lawyer, too, sir," he said. "I'm sure you must be to rate such an assignment."

"Thank you," said Rogavin.

"What *were* you hired for?" asked Wallace, drawing a glare from Lloyd.

Pop directed his response to the entire table. "Well, Miss Bronson seems to think I can be of some help on the . . . uh . . . *political* aspects of her case, you might say."

"Political aspects?" mumbled Sims.

"Yes, Gordon, political." He turned to Lloyd and said, "You know, it's a funny thing how history repeats. The last time this happened your Director asked for my assistance on behalf of the two gentlemen who'd been convicted. Your agency had just been through some very rough treatment by Congress, and it was feared that their punishment would paralyze the Bureau for years." Pop looked around the table for any dissent before continuing. "Well, as luck would have it, a new president had just been elected and I was one of those privileged to be asked to provide some assistance during the transition. I told the Director that I'd be glad to do what I could, and with the considerable efforts of others more talented and capable than myself, the president was persuaded to grant them a pardon."

"That was a totally different situation," insisted Wallace. "We deny that any FBI agent broke the law, and we deny each and every allegation that has been made here today."

Lloyd laid a hand on Wallace's arm to indicate that he would do the talking. "We've heard Mr. O'Connell's and Mr. Feinberg's theories," he said, "and we've offered some facts of our own to show that they are way off base. With the exception of one agent on a short fact-gathering mission, we've had no involvement in this matter at all."

Pop stared at Wallace for a long moment. Slowly, almost

imperceptibly, his genial demeanor evaporated and the room itself seemed to cool. "Do you take me for a fool, Mr. Lloyd?" he said quietly.

For the first time Lloyd looked unsettled. Wallace was watching his boss, grateful that he'd been sidelined. "Of course not, Mr. Brennan," Lloyd replied, raising his hands in a no-offense gesture.

Pop spoke directly to his deputy. "You're right, Mr. Wallace, this *is* different. It won't be just the liberals calling for your heads this time. After the mess in Waco and Ruby Ridge, you'll have the heartland conservatives to deal with, too. When the truth comes to light—and it will—there'll be no mercy shown, and sure as hell, no pardons."

"Mr. Sims doesn't think Congress will be interested," I said.

Pop dismissed that with a wave of his hand. "We'll begin with the *Post* and the *Times*," he said. "The public interest in the case will mean front page coverage and it won't be a one-day or one-week story, you can be sure. The reporters will be working it like nothing since Watergate itself. And the morning the story breaks I'll be breakfasting with the chairmen of the oversight committees."

"We're not without resources," countered Lloyd. "There are plenty of senators and congressmen who don't want to see the Bureau subjected to groundless attacks."

"Be my guest," said Pop. "Go up there and round up your allies, then we'll get to counting heads. I've played this game with the best, including a few presidents, and I never threaten what I can't deliver." He looked over at Sims, whose collar was now damp with sweat. "Gordon, I don't believe you had a part in this, not intentionally. When you were being considered for nomination to this job, I was pleased to make some introductions and smooth your way. I believed then and I believe now that you want to do the right thing. Have I ever steered you wrong?"

Sims shook his head vigorously. "No, Mr. Brennan. It's

just . . . I'm trying to make sense of this thing, that's all."

"They're desperate, lad, and they're playing a dangerous game. But when this is over even pure motives won't matter, and that's a fact."

It was quiet in the room again while each of the men facing us digested Pop's warning. Mathis was absolutely rigid, his eyes still fixed on the Polaroids. Finally, Rogavin stirred. "Gordon," he said quietly, "the deal we offered, whose idea was it?"

Sims ignored him. "Look, Mr. Brennan, I've got people to answer to no matter what we decide. We're going to need some time on this."

"I'm afraid there's precious little left," Pop replied. "Let me give you one last word of advice. If you decide to go ahead with this travesty then I must be sure that the president isn't blindsided by what's going to happen. I'll be seeing him tomorrow night for dinner. It would be better for you if you told him first."

"I wasn't aware there was a White House function tomorrow night," said Lloyd, "and we keep track of those things."

"There isn't," said Pop. "The dinner is at my home." With that, he got to his feet; Walter and I followed. "Good day, gentlemen," he said. "For the sake of all concerned I hope we can conclude this business today."

We followed him out of the office and into the hallway. I could barely contain myself, but before I could say anything, Rogavin came out behind us. "O'Connell, can we talk a minute?" he asked. Pop and Walter continued down the hall while we followed at a distance. "Look," he said, "I'm not sure who's telling the truth in this deal, but I hope to hell to have a better idea by tonight. If it turns out that you're right I want you to know that I had nothing to do with it."

"I never thought you did. Can I make a suggestion?"

"Go ahead."

"They're buttoned up tight on this over at the Hoover Building. Your best bet may be Kellogg. I'd grab Mathis and get to him before they do. Tell him that it's all come apart and he's got one chance to save his own ass. You can add that you already know he rented *Strangers on a Train* from a video store in Georgetown as soon as he got back from West Virginia."

Rogavin stopped and exhaled. "I may do just that. One way or another, you'll be hearing from me tonight."

"If I'm not at my office I'll be waiting with my client." I gave him the number.

When I got outside Joseph was just shutting the rear door of the limousine. I hurried down to the curb and Pop lowered the window. "Can I drop you, lad?" he asked.

"Walter's got his car," I said.

"What did our young prosecutor have to say?"

"I think he believes us, but he's going to have to save Sims from himself. He's got his work cut out for him."

"Well, let's hope Gordon sees the light."

"Pop?"

"Yes, lad?"

"How did she do it?"

He laughed and shook his head. "Well, she made it very simple. She asked me when I would like to see my grandson again—this weekend or, say, his college graduation."

"Christ! That *is* hardball."

"My own daughter! And I was bouncing the tyke on my knee at the time!" He grinned in admiration. "Where did she learn to squeeze 'em like that, I ask you? Her dear mother was a proper lady."

"I can't imagine. Listen, Pop, you've worked your share of miracles and done more for me than I could ever repay even *before* today, but Jesus, if you go to the Hill on this they'll make you spend every chip you've got, and the president won't be coming to dinner again anytime soon."

"My words to her exactly. 'And will you bring the boy to see me in the poorhouse?' says I. No effect. Her own father."

"Pop, I don't—"

"Not to worry." He laughed. "Listen, lad, I've played this game a long time, but I'm not too corrupt to care about the fate of an innocent young woman, and after you're the biggest lawyer in the city you can send me all the business I'll need to get back on my feet."

"We need to talk, Pop. There's a lot of things—"

He held up a hand. "Save it for tomorrow. With a little luck we'll be raising a glass or two."

"I've got to go see her."

"Wait till we talk first. Can you do that for me, now?"

"Anything. Anything you ask." The words no sooner left my mouth when I remembered Saturday night in his study and how I'd let him down. He read my mind.

"Don't worry, boyo," he said softly. "Things have a way of working out for the best. Call me as soon as there's news."

I reached in and we clasped hands. As they pulled away Walter stuck a toothpick in his mouth and winked. "Ya know," he said, grinning, "he oughtta leave a silver bullet or somethin'."

# 23

The night of the big day. I was sitting in my office with the lights off, not thinking about the defense of Ashley Bronson. I was thinking about me, and for the first time in several years, embracing the possibility of possibilities. It made for an interesting several hours. At life's critical junctures making choices is less about reasoning than discovery. You discover what you want, and in the process, who you are.

The phone rang. I willed it to be Rogavin.

"O'Connell?"

"Yeah."

"We're dismissing tomorrow morning."

It didn't register immediately; it was too much news in too few words.

"Are you still there?"

"Yes. Yes, I'm here."

"Congratulations."

"Thanks." As oxygen again began to reach my brain, shock gave way to curiosity. "Did you see Kellogg?"

"No. We went across the street instead. Sims decided to dump it in the Attorney General's lap."

"Wow. Maybe not a great career move."

"Tell me about it. 'What if the story's true?' I said. In this town deniability is everything, and he wants to play Typhoid Mary."

"What happened?"

Rogavin sighed. "This is between us, right?"

"You've got my word."

"When the A.G. hears what it's about he sends his assistants out of the room and it's just the three of us at the big table. Gordon describes the meeting, every goddamn detail. He goes on for thirty minutes and the A.G. never says a word—no questions, no comments. He doesn't even grunt."

"Jesus, you'd think he'd bust a blood vessel or something."

"He just sucked on his pipe through the whole thing. I wouldn't want that guy in a poker game."

"Pretty strange."

"No, strange comes later. When Gordon finishes he asks us to wait and goes into his inner office. He's gone for over an hour while I contemplate the end of government service."

"Maybe he called the Director. The Bureau is part of the Justice Department, right?"

"Yeah—on paper. Anyway, he finally comes out, sits down, and asks if we know much about the law concerning warrantless searches. Gordon tells him that we often deal with those issues in motions to suppress evidence, but the A.G. says that he's talking about something different: the power of the Executive Branch to do what's necessary to protect the country from external threats."

"External threats? You mean like foreign powers?"

"That's it. Then he lights his pipe, leans back in his chair, and launches into this lecture on constitutional law like he was back on the faculty at Harvard. What it comes down to is that there are different schools of thought about whether the Executive needs to go to court to get search warrants when dealing with external threats to national security."

"Like Octagon," I said.

"Well, you'd know more about that than me. By the way, I don't suppose you want to tell me what they were after."

"I can't, but if you look up 'external threat' in the law dictionary there's a picture of those guys right there."

"Well, then it fits."

"No search warrants, huh? That doesn't mean that the Bureau can act on its own hook, does it?"

"When we got back to the office I did some quick research. If—and I do mean *if*—the Executive has this special power, it probably could only be exercised by the president or the attorney general, and then only on a case-by-case basis."

"You think one of them sent those guys in there?"

"Nah, it was the Bureau all the way. I think the A.G.'s point was that the law in this area is vague. If judges and law professors can argue about it, who wants to explain it to the tabloids? It'd be Watergate without the charm."

"There's nothing vague about framing someone for murder. How can he rationalize letting them walk on that one?"

"He didn't. Actually, he handled it pretty cleverly. He said he'd break this thing wide open if we were *absolutely certain* that your client was framed. But if there was any possibility that she was guilty—he repeated, '*any* possibility' three times—then as far as he was concerned, it was more important that the FBI regain the public trust after all these recent debacles."

"He wasn't subtle, was he?"

"Since we were stupid enough to walk in there he probably thought he had to tattoo it on our foreheads. He asked us what we thought these militia guys would do with stories about the feds breaking into homes and framing innocent women. He said we'd have to triple the protection of every federal building in the country."

"Did he happen to mention that there were a few careers at stake, too?"

"You mean other than ours? He didn't have to, he's a major league politician. The circles he moves in care a lot more about careers than a few buildings. My guess is that they've decided that this thing is radioactive: open the box and everybody dies. Those at a distance will just kick and scream a little longer."

"So that left the middle ground."

"When he finished the lecture he asked us if we might

find a way to prevent a possible injustice to Miss Bronson, avoid further harm to the Bureau, and not make the Justice Department look foolish in the process. He didn't have to spell it out."

"How will you explain it?"

"It won't be hard. After the grueling cross-examination of our eyewitness by the brilliant defense counsel, the prosecutors, acting in the interest of justice, concluded that there was indeed reasonable doubt."

"Pretty noble."

"Thanks."

"You're forgetting Yee. It will leak."

"Yee is a team player. He just discovered a source of contamination that cast doubt on his findings."

"I hear there's a lot of that going around."

"Yeah. I suppose we can all use a shower after this one."

"Listen, I'd like not to bring her down tomorrow. It'll be a circus."

"We'll waive her appearance. Tell her she can sleep in, my treat."

"Thanks. So, that's it?"

"That's it. You win on a technicality. But I've got a feeling we'll be seeing more of each other."

"Maybe we will. See you in court, counselor."

"Yeah. In court."

* * *

Bad news, they say, travels fast. In the nation's capital all news is bad; it is also good. If it's bad for the Republicans, it's good for the Democrats. If it's bad for Smith's career then it's good for Jones's. It's a zero-sum game, complicated by the fact that the same news can be good or bad for the same person, depending on who gets to put the spin on it. The abrupt end to the Ashley Bronson murder case was news badly in need of spin, so much so that passing it on to her lawyer was not the priority. It's hard to say how many people knew before I got the call from Rogavin, but I like to think I was in the first hundred, which didn't bother me as much as not being the one who got to tell my client. That pleasure fell to the friend who told her to turn on the television, any channel.

Martha seized me when she opened the door. "It's wonderful!" she cried, and we hugged while she murmured her thanks to the Almighty and invoked His blessings upon Walter and me. When I finally recovered I reminded her that it was she who had gotten the key piece of evidence that saved the day, and she began to sob uncontrollably, using my shirt for a tissue. Eventually, she regained her composure and pushed me toward the library.

The only light in the vast room came from the fireplace and a television in the corner. A reporter was explaining that according to a source close to the prosecution, the decision to dismiss was made after U.S. Attorney Gordon Sims expressed concern about the testimony of Miles Kellogg, and questioned whether the interests of justice would be served by the continued prosecution.

I moved behind her. "Congratulations," I said.

"It's true?" she asked, still looking at the set.

"It's over."

She pointed the remote at the television and the room went quiet. "I can't feel anything," she said woodenly. "I should feel elated, but I can't. I'm . . . empty."

I led her to the couch. "It's the shock," I offered. "By tomorrow morning you'll be walking on air."

"I found them," she said hoarsely.

"Found?"

She looked upward toward one corner of the room. Protruding from the topmost shelf, barely visible in the firelight, was another false front of books, wider than the one that had concealed the journals. It was tipped forward with the "bindings" facing downward. "It wasn't hard," she explained, "when you know what to look for. I just kept tapping until I struck wood. They're over there."

A bundle of documents tied with a black ribbon was sitting on the ormolu desk. I unrolled them, pinning the edges with makeshift paperweights. There were nine sheets of blueprints rolled around seven letter-size pages in Henry's handwriting. The block capital letters at the top of the first page said, DESIGN FOR TRIGGER FOR FISSION REACTION. There was a description of the device and how it worked.

Ashley had moved behind me. "You were right," she said dully. "Part of me didn't believe it. I had to know for sure."

"Herbert said that your father never gave them these plans. Whatever he may have done, he made the right decision in the end and it couldn't have been easy. He must have been torn between his patriotism and his fears for humanity."

She ran her fingertips over the handwriting, as if the sensation might offer some clue to his torment. "What do we do now?" she asked.

"What should have been done a long time ago." I rolled up the drawings again. "Do you want me to do it?"

She stared at the bundle, then shook her head. We went back to the fireplace and I placed her father's creation in her hands. Her jaw trembling, she clutched it to her, as if it were their last real link. "Daddy," she whispered, then placed it in the fire.

We watched it start to burn. "I need to leave," she said quietly. "As soon as possible."

"You can start packing now. You don't even have to go to court tomorrow. They're waiving your appearance."

"I don't have to go back?"

"No, just the lawyers. It'll be crazy. Think about whether there's something you'd like me to say; otherwise I'll just tell them that you're gratified and you never lost faith in the system."

She put her arms around my neck. "My faith was in *you*. Did you persuade them, or were they just scared?"

"They were persuaded they should be scared, but not by me, by Edward Brennan."

Her brow wrinkled. "Your father-in-law?"

"Himself."

"Why?"

"We needed someone big enough to scare the whole government. That's a pretty short list."

"But they'll get even. They'll ruin him!"

"The way things have turned out there won't be any problems. The people who know what happened have every incentive to bury this thing as deep as possible. Taking on Ed Brennan would be suicide. Besides, he's an Irishman. He relishes a good fight."

"He did it for *you*," she insisted, resting her head on my shoulder. "And you asked him for *me*. Do you love me that much?"

"I love you."

"After you called this afternoon, when I was thinking that this nightmare might nearly be over, I got scared."

"Of course."

She squeezed more tightly. "No, scared that I might lose you. I kept thinking about the look on your face the other night when I talked about us going away. I wasn't sure what you were feeling."

Neither was I. It was only a few hours before, in my office, when I'd figured it out.

She waited for the reassurance while I groped for the words, then looked into my eyes. Sometimes it helps to be transparent. "You're not coming with me, are you?" she said.

"I can't."

She let go and sank onto the couch. "I knew it all along. I just didn't want to face it."

"Ashley, when I married Moira I had everything a man could want handed to me on a platter. Eventually, it made me miserable, and soon I made her miserable, too. And that was with me working hard. How long do you think we'd last traveling the world on your credit cards? Besides, I don't think you'd really want a man like that—not for long."

"But I can't stay here!" she cried. "Some people will always believe that I killed Raymond, and the rest will just wonder. Everywhere I'd go they'd be whispering and pointing, and the reporters who were camped outside aren't going away!" She shook her head emphatically. "I couldn't face it, Frank. Maybe later, but not now."

"I know. And you've still got that promise to keep. If you didn't, you'd regret it. Loving someone doesn't compensate. I've learned that lesson."

"And you *still* love her." It wasn't a question. She read my expression and explained, "That night you'd been drinking."

"Ashley, Moira's about to get married, and she's taking our son to California to start a new life. If I stay I stand some chance of not losing him completely, but if I get on a plane with you, that would be the end. I couldn't do it."

"Then it isn't just the money," she said.

"No, my life is here."

She wiped her eyes. We watched the fire a moment before she spoke in a barely audible voice. "The moment we met I knew I'd love you. And after I did, I knew we'd never end up together." She looked at me and smiled. "You know, I think it was just too romantic. I could never picture us without the uncertainty, without . . ."

"Without the risk?"

"I suppose. I never thought of it that way, but the fact that we were surrounded, that our romance was—what? forbidden?—I think it brought us closer together." She shook her head. "In the movies they fade out after the heroine is rescued. They never show you what happens afterward." She reached for my hand and we faced the fire, watching the last of Henry's drawings curl up and brown in the flames. "So," she said softly, "the heroine is rescued and it's almost afterward. What will you think when you think of me?"

"That we rescued each other. I was drowning and you threw me a lifeline. And later, when I started to slip, you wouldn't let me go. You had everything to lose and nothing to go on but your heart and your intuition, but you did it anyway. As much as anyone, it was you who saved us both."

"We rescued each other," she agreed. The tears flowing down her cheeks reflected the firelight. "Remember when you asked me to kiss you like I never kissed a man before?"

"And you did."

"Do you think you could do the same for me?"

"Yeah. I could." I took her into my arms.

"Make it like in the movies," she whispered. "The one where they fade out."

\* \* \*

They were replaying my press conference when Maggie Mac showed me into Pop's office. He was sitting in his chair, smiling and nodding at the screen. "The prodigal son returns," she announced. Pop sprung up and spread his arms wide.

"Well, Margaret," he declared as we embraced, "we're in the presence of the town's newest star, that's what they're sayin'. This is the fella they'll all be wantin' to hire."

"Well," she said as she closed the door, "I hope he remembers all the little people when they're pinnin' on the ribbons."

Pop went to the bar and opened his ceremonial single malt. "I'll bet Miss Bronson is celebrating right now!" he said, grinning.

"Actually, she's packing. She's going overseas."

"Well, she'll be needing some time to get over the ordeal." He handed me my glass. "A vacation will do her good."

"It's more than a vacation, Pop. I don't think she'll be back for a very long time."

He regarded me thoughtfully. "And you, you're . . ."

"She's a very special woman, but we've said our good-byes."

"I see." He raised his glass and smiled. "Well, lad, congratulations. You set out to make your mark and now you've done it."

"With a lot of help."

He shrugged. "It usually happens that way, doesn't it?"

"I know that now. I'm just sorry it took so long. I might have saved us all a lot of heartache."

"All in the past, all in the past. So, what's next? I suppose Birch and Hayes would be delighted to have a new partner."

"Maybe, but I was thinking of something smaller."

"Too much bureaucracy for you, eh?" He laughed. "I don't blame you. Never could see the attraction myself. Anyway, there's a lot of good, small firms around, that's for sure."

"Well, I had something pretty specific in mind. I was looking for a small firm with solid business connections that could use a courtroom hand."

He lowered his drink and frowned. "Francis, lad, you don't have any obligations here. What I did, I did out of love. You do what's best for you."

"This isn't about obligation, Pop. I was never as happy as I was in this office with you."

"But that changed."

"Yes, it did. Maybe things were too comfortable. Maybe I thought I had to do it all on my own. Whatever the reason, I've done what I needed to do, and even learned a few things along the way. You're right, Pop. We don't get anywhere in this world alone. We're always standing on someone's shoulders, aren't we? The trick is to be deserving and to be a shoulder when you get the chance. I'd like to come back. This is where I belong."

In combat I saw men age ten years in a matter of moments, but I never saw a man shed ten before. "More whiskey?" he asked, heading for the bar.

"No, thanks."

"Suit yourself." He poured another and went over to his chair by the fireplace; I took the one that had been mine. He sipped from his glass, eyeing me as he did. "Contracts are a two-way street," he mused.

"That's true."

"There's something I'll be wanting in return."

"Anything. Just name it."

"Tell me how you feel about Moira—the truth."

I should have seen it coming. "Pop, what's the point? I know what you want but it's time to let go."

"I'll have my answer," he insisted. "I'm entitled."

The truth? Easy to know, hard to admit; harder still to voice. "Pop, last night I told Ashley Bronson that I loved her, and I was sincere. I did, and do. But I'll never feel about another woman the way I do about Moira. I wanted to marry her the moment we met, and the day I looked down the aisle and saw you bringing her toward me, I was sure it was a dream."

He sighed. "I remember that moment, too."

"Then Brendan came along. Sometimes, when I'd see the two of them together, when I'd see the gift she'd given me, I'd . . ."

I couldn't say any more.

Pop leaned over and put a hand on my knee. "If that's the way you feel, then there's something else I want."

"What?"

"Tell her."

"I can't."

"Yes, you can. If you won't do it for yourself, then you'll do it for me!"

"Pop, think about what you're asking! It's not her lot in life to sit around and wait for me to grow up. She's getting married—to a pretty decent guy as near as I can tell. What I've got to do is be as supportive as I can—for her and for Brendan. I've got a lot of making up to do."

"I asked that jackass Lloyd," he said, "and I'll ask you, Francis: am I a fool?"

"No."

"Do you think I don't know my own flesh and blood?"

"I didn't say that—"

He held up his hand. "You fought body and soul to save Miss Bronson. Does your family deserve any less?"

"That's not fair, Pop. I'd do *anything* if I thought it would get them back."

"Then do this. *Trust me.* Have I ever let you down? Ever given you cause to doubt my judgment?"

"No, Pop, you never have."

"Well, then, it's settled, isn't it?"

\* \* \*

It felt like snow when I entered the street. The clouds were gray and dense, hovering just above the oaks that lined both sides, and the air seemed almost mild, the way it can before the flakes begin to fall. As the house came into view I saw Moira walk down the driveway and turn into the street, heading away. She was wearing a scarf and a heavy wool sweater over her jeans and boots. I pulled alongside and lowered the window.

"Hey!" she called, leaning in. "I thought you'd be making the tour of the TV studios."

"I've tired of fame. I'm retiring to the country to lead the simple life, commune with nature and cleanse my soul. Where are you going?"

"Just getting some exercise. Park the car and we'll commune together." I pulled into the driveway and a few moments later we were strolling through the neighborhood.

"I'm taping the local news station for Brendan," she said.

"You figured out the VCR?"

"One of us had to."

"Thanks. My ego was on a roll."

"Actually, Rob showed me."

"Maybe I'll just lie down in front of the next car."

"You'll change your mind when you see the tape. I've got your news conference, and there's an interview with a criminal lawyer from Los Angeles who thinks you're brilliant."

"You know, they're very perceptive out there."

"I've heard that."

"Around here, some might think I just had the right people in my corner."

She shrugged. "Maybe both."

"Would you care to tell me why you did it?"

She dug her hands into her pockets. "I thought . . . I thought that if you won this case, you'd . . ." Her voice broke and she turned away.

I put my arm through hers and drew her close to me. "Tell me, please. I'd what?"

She inhaled deeply. "You'd discover what you've been looking for since you left."

"I see. . . . You were right."

"Oh. It didn't take long," she said quietly.

"I'm sure, though."

She nodded vaguely. "She's a very accomplished woman, Frank. My friends who know her say nice things, and you don't often hear women talk that way about another woman who's rich *and* beautiful."

"They talk that way about you."

She managed a smile. "Thanks. Anyway, you found what you wanted. I'm glad for you."

"Moira, Ashley Bronson is a special woman, but we don't belong together. She's leaving the country this evening and won't be back for a long time. We've said our good-byes."

She didn't say anything. We entered the grounds of Landon School, a private school for boys, and walked across the wide expanse of lawn that served as practice fields. I watched her closely, trying to divine the effect of my news, but she managed to avoid eye contact. "I saw Pop," I said. "I left his office just an hour ago."

"He must've been popping his buttons. He's so proud of you."

"I asked him if I could come back."

She stopped dead in her tracks. "*Back? As his partner?*"

I laughed. "Unless he wants me to start over again as an associate."

"What's this about, Frank? I know I asked you to look after him, but that doesn't—"

"Wait! This is what *I* want. I mean it. There isn't anything in Washington that even comes close." She looked dubious. "I swear to you, Moira, it has nothing to do with your going to California."

She sighed and said, "He's a cagey old bastard."

"Why?"

"Because I'm not going."

"*You're not?*" My obvious joy startled her; I tried to recover. "I mean . . . it's a surprise, that's all. I thought you were about to go, and now . . . you'll, uh, be around. What happened?"

"Your concern is touching. I moved the date up to spite *you*, and don't be smug because it was obvious." She shot me a look and I raised my hands in surrender. "Anyway, Rob deserves better than that, so we changed our plans."

"Are you still going out there in June?"

"Pop sent you out here, didn't he?"

"Not exactly."

"Not exactly," she repeated.

"He set what lawyers call a 'condition of employment.' I had to answer one question truthfully."

"Go on."

"I had to tell him how I felt about you—about us."

"Then what happened?"

"There was a second condition."

"Of course."

"He said I had to come out and tell you. And here I am."

She shook her head. "He really *is* a cagey bastard. He did the same thing to me."

"He did?"

"I went over to the house Saturday night and told him what you were up against. I figured that was all I needed to do, but he's one for the surprises. He said that it would be like extorting the president himself to threaten a scandal of those proportions, and he wouldn't have a friend left in the city."

"He said you used Brendan on him."

"I lost my temper. Then he asked me why he should risk everything he's worked for to help a woman he barely knew. I said that it wasn't for her, it was for you. He said he wasn't prepared to go that far, but he might do it for me if I told him what he wanted to know."

She stopped there. We walked past the tennis courts and around the Administration Building, but she wasn't talking. My mouth was so dry I could barely get the words out when I finally asked, "What did he want to know?"

"You're the hotshot lawyer. Can't you figure it out?"

My knees were getting weak. "Can we sit down?"

"Fine," she said, and walked over to a bench. There was room for me but somehow I wound up kneeling in front of her. I took her hands in my own, wanting to say something original, worthy of the occasion, more than just, "I love you." Nothing would come, and then she was wiping my face with a tissue.

"I'm supposed to be good with words," I mumbled.

"That's what everyone is saying."

"I was scared, Moira. I never had much, and then one day

I had everything: you, Brendan, a partnership with Pop, and a big house filled with expensive things. I couldn't accept that life could be that easy. I mean, Pop started with nothing and he got on a ship, crossed an ocean, and made a life. It seemed like cheating to have him entrust everything to me, including *you*, and I was afraid that somehow it would all be taken away because I hadn't *earned* it. What made it worse was that I knew that I could, just like Pop. Noah says I like taking chances, so maybe that was what it was all about, I'm not sure. What I *do* know is this. I've done what I needed to do. I don't know why or even how, and God knows I didn't do it alone, but I'm ready to make up for all the lost time if you just let me. And there's one thing I know most of all. I couldn't possibly love you more."

"That was pretty good," she said softly, "for a lawyer."

"It was my closing argument. I'm pleading my case for a second chance to make you happy." She freed a hand and wiped her own eyes. A moment passed. My legs were shaking. "Has the jury reached a verdict?" I stammered.

She nodded. "It has." She took my face in her hands and bent toward me.

"Hold still," she whispered. "We're about to get engaged."

\* \* \*

## HENRY BRONSON'S JOURNAL

*August 31, 1994. As a young scientist in the thrall of the great minds of my generation, I knew that professional achievement was the means to fulfillment and the measure of one's worth. The consequences were thus: wasted years cursing the fate that brought politics and science to calamitous intersection at the moment of my opportunity. But later I had a wife, then a child, and for a few precious years, both. And I know now, as sure as any immutable law of nature, that the value of our existence can only be computed in the hearts of those we love, and who love us in return.*

*In the end, my family was my greatest joy.*